Rita Bradshaw was born in Northamptonshire, where she still lives today with her husband, their children and two dogs.

When she was approaching forty, Rita decided to fulfil two long-cherished ambitions – to write a novel and to learn to drive. She says, 'The former was pure joy and the latter pure misery,' but the novel was accepted for publication and she passed her driving test. She went on to write many successful novels under a pseudonym before writing for Headline using her own name.

As a committed Christian and fervent animal-lover, Rita has a full and busy life, but she relishes her writing – a job that's all pleasure – and loves to read, walk her dogs, eat out and visit the cinema in any precious spare moments.

Rita Bradshaw's earlier sagas, ALONE BENEATH THE HEAVEN, REACH FOR TOMORROW, RAGAMUFFIN ANGEL and THE STONY PATH, are also available from Headline.

The Urchin's Song

Rita Bradshaw

headline

First published in 2002
by HEADLINE BOOK PUBLISHING

First published in paperback in 2002
by HEADLINE BOOK PUBLISHING

10 9 8 7 6 5 4 3 2 1

ISBN 0 7472 6708 1

Typeset in Times by Palimpsest Book Production Limited,
Polmont, Stirlingshire
Printed and bound in Great Britain by
Mackays of Chatham plc, Chatham, Kent

HEADLINE BOOK PUBLISHING
A division of Hodder Headline PLC
338 Euston Road
LONDON NW1 3BH

www.headline.co.uk
www.hodderheadline.com

For our first grandchild, Samuel Benjamin Thompson, born 18th October, 2001 – the most gorgeous, beautiful and precious little baby in the world. Thank you, Cara and Ian, for letting us share the day of his birth so generously. We love you all so much.

Acknowledgements

As always, thanks to all the staff in the many wonderful libraries and museums authors rely on for research material, but especially Sunderland's City Library and Arts Centre's great Local Studies department; Sunderland Museum and Winter Gardens' Archive department; the Beamish Museum; and Phil Atkins, librarian, at the National Railway Museum, York. Lastly, a sad farewell to The Big Bookshop in Sunderland – thanks, Steve, for all the great research material your books have provided through the years.

It would be impossible to list all the resources and books I've called on for the history of the music hall in Britain, but the following were particularly useful: *The Northern Music Hall* by G.J. Mellor; *British Music Hall – An Illustrated Who's Who from 1850 to the Present Day* by Roy Busby; *Music Hall in Britain* by D.F. Cheshire; *The Last Empires – A Music Hall Companion* by Benny Green; *A Hard Act to Follow* by Peter Leslie.

A special thank you to my lovely husband, Clive, who somehow manages to track down the most obscure facts and dates for me, and who will never accept defeat!

The Urchin's Song

Give me a song that touches the soul
From a heart that is tender and true,
A song that transcends this dark mortal vale
And reaches to heights unseen.
A song of beauty and sweetness and light
With words yet only dimly perceived,
And I'll give you a song from the heart of a child
That makes kings and queens of us all.

Anon

Prologue

1890

The night was bitterly cold, but the big blowsy woman who was just about to enter the Mariners' Arms on Custom House Quay was well padded against the icy mist rising off the river. Not so the two little girls huddled in front of the wooden barrels standing on the filthy, muck-strewn cobbles.

In spite of the raw winter chill, they wore only dirty ragged dresses, with tattered strips of sacking round their thin shoulders passing as shawls. Their legs and feet were bare and they wore no underclothes, but the eldest one, a little scrap of nothing who looked to be about five or six, managed to speak despite her wildly chattering teeth. 'Spare a farthin', missus?' Her tone wasn't hopeful. She knew from experience the regulars of the riverside pubs were more generous when they left, normally heavily intoxicated and merry and therefore inclined to throw the odd coin or two her way.

'Ee, this is no night for bairns to be out.' The child sank back against the questionable protection of the barrels; she recognised a refusal when she heard one. But then, instead of the 'You get yerself home now, lass,' she saw the plump face peer closer, and the voice was softer when it said,

'You're one of Shirl's bairns, aren't you? Shirley Burns? I grew up next door to your mam in James Williams Street, although she was Shirl Pearson then. Good friends at one time, me an' your mam were.'

The woman smiled, but when there was no answering smile on the child's face and the little tot just put a skinny arm round her sister, drawing the smaller child in to her, the stout figure straightened. 'Worst thing Shirl ever did, marryin' Bart Burns,' the woman muttered to herself, before she said, her voice louder, 'You waitin' for your da, hinny? He inside then?'

The child shook her golden-brown curls, limp with months of grease and dirt and clearly harbouring vermin, and now her great brown eyes with their thick lashes looked down at the black slimy cobbles as she whispered, 'Me da . . . me da'll skin us alive if we go home. We've not got enough yet.'

'Enough?' And then as the small girl raised her gaze again the woman understood. 'By . . .' It was said on a long, slow exhalation of breath.

Vera Briggs was a hard-headed, pragmatic woman and not given to sentiment, but the plight of these two small infants who dared not return home until they had begged enough pennies to satisfy their drunken thug of a father couldn't be ignored.

Of course bairns like these ones were ten a penny in Sunderland's notoriously squalid East End, where the rank odours of excrement and slow decay were rife summer and winter amid such diseases as consumption, dropsy, rickets and a hundred and one other culling devices that took the weakest – but these were Shirl's little lassies, Vera reminded herself, as she stood on the greasy step of the pub hesitating.

The beginning of icy drops of sad winter rain drumming

on the barrels made up her mind. 'You hungry, hinny?'
The dark eyes were answer enough. 'Look, lass, our
Horace is meetin' me here in a minute or two an' he's
bringin' a bite with him. You an' your sister come with me
an' at least you'll go home with full bellies the night.'

Vera's magnanimity did not run to putting any of her
hard-earned wages from the corn mill into Bart Burns's
pocket, but at least this way she could do something for a
couple of poor Shirl's bairns. She held out an encouraging
hand to the children, and when an icy little paw answered
the gesture, Vera's big full mouth tightened. Ee, he wanted
shooting, that Bart Burns. If ever there was an out-and-out
wicked so-and-so on God's earth, it was that man.

As Vera opened the door of the pub, her hand still
clasping that of the child, who had the smaller tot hanging
on to her skirt, the smell and noise were overpowering. The
air was thick with Shag tobacco smoke from myriad pipes,
and the filthy sawdust on the floor was congealed with
black globs of spittle, dried urine from the skinny little
mongrel dogs that accompanied their masters, and bits of
this and that which had been carried in on boots from the
quayside.

Vera's narrowed gaze under her faded black bonnet
swept over the cauldron of humanity, and her popularity
was evident by the number of voices which greeted her.
She replied to one or two as she made her way to the far
corner of the crowded room, and on reaching a wooden
bench set against the wall, pushed at one of the occupants,
saying, 'Move over, Ray, an' let us have a seat, man. Me
legs are killin' us the day. An' get us a gin, an' a couple
of squibs for the bairns. Horace'll make it right with you
when he comes.'

'Aye, all right, lass.' The man was short and thickset,
with a droopy moustache stained orangey-yellow at the

3

edges from the regular soaking it got in Burton's bass, but his tone was not unkind as he nodded at the children pressed against Vera's legs. 'Who're they then? One of your brothers' bairns?'

'You think any of my flesh an' blood would let their bairns out on a night like this, clothed in rags an' lousy?'

Vera's voice had been sharp and Ray scuttled off to the bar without further pleasantries. Vera was a grand lass, none better, but she had a tongue on her that'd cut steel, he told himself, allowing a full minute to elapse in the hope that she would have cooled down before he asked the landlord for the measure of gin, along with two tiny glasses of the same spirit known as squibs sold specially for young children.

'There you go, lass.' He handed Vera her glass and then brought his tubby frame bending towards her, saying in an undertone as if conveying a secret, 'An' here's the squibs for the bairns.'

'Ta, thanks, man.' Vera's tone was conciliatory, and reassured, Ray said, 'You lookin' after 'em or summat?' nodding at the two little girls as Vera placed the miniature glasses in their hands.

Vera swallowed half the contents of her glass in one gulp before shaking her head, saying briefly, 'I used to know their mam years ago, an' they were beggin' outside.' And then they both laughed as the eldest child, having taken a tentative sip of her drink, coughed and spluttered until her eyes streamed.

'You get it down you, hinny, her an' all. It'll put fire in your belly an' keep the cold out, an' there's not many as needs it as much as you. Eh, Ray?'

'Oh aye, Vera, aye. You're right there, lass.' Ray nodded his head, his grimy cap sitting like a pancake on top of his wiry hair. 'Poor little blighters.' But it was said without any real feeling. For every bairn that reached five, one or two died, that was the way of things and nowt'd change it. Why on earth Vera had taken it upon herself to waste good money on these 'uns who looked to be on their last legs, he didn't know. Barmy, he called it.

However, when Horace – a tall, thin man who was the very antithesis of his plump wife – appeared, and on Vera's instructions handed over a hot meat pie to each child, even Ray was moved at the children's stunned bewilderment and delight. They ate so quickly that Vera was compelled to reach out a restraining hand, saying, 'Slowly, hinnies, slowly does it. You'll be makin' yerselves sick now,' as she glanced at the two men and shook her head.

Replete for the first time they could remember in their short lives, the two small girls sat docile and quiet in the sawdust at Vera's feet. They had licked their grubby fingers clean of every little morsel and taste of food; the younger one falling immediately to sleep as she sat propped against the security of her sister's bony shoulder. Not so the elder; her huge brown eyes were wide open as she stared at the scene in front of her, which grew louder and more bawdy as the night progressed.

It was a good two hours later when, after 'The Rocky Road to Dublin' had been sung enthusiastically at least five or six times to the accompaniment of a merry fiddle, Vera seemed to suddenly remember her old friend's offspring. She bent down to the eldest child who had twisted round to face her. 'They're well oiled the night, hinny,' she said softly, her voice full of meaning. And when the child didn't answer her but continued to stare steadily into her eyes, Vera said, 'You know any songs, lass? You sing 'em a tune an' you'll soon get a few pennies to take home to your da, the mood they're in.'

A number of seconds elapsed before the whisper came.

'Me sisters, our Dora an' Ada, sing sometimes if me da's not in.'

'An' can you remember what they sing, hinny? The words an' all?' Vera's mouth had tightened briefly. From what some of her former neighbours in James Williams Street had told her, this one's older sisters didn't have much to sing about. If what she'd heard was true – and she'd bet her eye-teeth it was – Bart had put the two lassies on the game when they were nowt but nine or ten. Evil swine.

'I know "Father, Come Home" an' "The Boy I Love is Up in the Gallery".'

'You do? That's a canny lass.' Vera stared into the little face for a moment. 'Father, Come Home' was a good one. Vesta Tilley had been about this one's age when she'd entreated a drunken father to come back to his wife and reduced her half-boozed audiences to maudlin tears. Aye, that should do very well. If this didn't get the bairn enough to avert a good hiding she'd eat her hat. 'Look, hinny, Horace'll set it up for you an' you don't be shy, eh? Don't matter if you can keep a tune or not, you just belt it out an' they'll love it. All right? An' have another sup to warm you up a bit. What's your name, lass?'

'Josie.'

'Josie Burns. Well, Josie, you heed what I say an' you'll do just fine.'

By the time Horace beckoned the child over to where the fiddler was standing, the little body was trembling, and when Vera's husband reached down and lifted her on to a battered table, Josie gave a partly smothered squeal of alarm that made those nearest guffaw into their glasses.

But within a few moments they weren't laughing any longer. Emboldened by Vera's confidence that she could earn some pennies, and aided by the food she had eaten and not least the fortifying effects of the gin, Josie closed her eyes to shut out all the slack-mouthed, grinning faces and began to sing. Note after crystal clear note silenced the pub and brought even the most inebriated revellers upright in their seats, aware that they were privileged to hear something rare.

Those who were still sober enough to be able to think sensibly might have expressed amazement that such a voice could spring from this tiny, undernourished frame, but for once the Mariners' Arms, one of Sunderland's most ribald dockside pubs, was so silent you could have heard a pin drop.

The absolute stillness continued for a moment after the child had finished singing, and when Josie opened her eyes she gazed around bewilderedly, frightened she had done something wrong and disturbed by the staring faces. From her vantage point on top of the roughly hewn table she searched out Vera's face. Her mother's old playmate was weeping unashamedly, but had time to give the child a reassuring nod and smile and thumbs-up before the place erupted in a roar of clapping and whooping and cheering.

Three songs later Josie had made more money in half an hour than she had been able to collect in whole days spent begging. At just seven years of age, she had taken the first steps to grasping control of her life.

Part 1
Breaking Away
1895

Chapter One

It seemed like weeks and weeks since the sun had shone. Josie adjusted the collar of her old blue serge coat more securely round her neck, wrinkling her face against the whirling snow as she slipped and slid on the packed ice beneath her boots. Only November and already everything was frozen up; it was going to be a long, hard winter. They'd had to push pieces of burning paper up the tap in the yard to get a trickle of water for days now.

And then she thought of the big pile of scrag ends and six pigs' trotters rolled up in newspaper in her shopping bag, and smiled to herself. Mr Duckworth was nice, oh he was, saving them for her, and she'd managed to get three penn'orth of pot stuff for a penny just because the cabbages were browning and the taties and onions had gone over. They'd be fine in a stew though.

She passed another butcher's shop, gas flares burning amid the joints of meat, but, owing to Mr Duckworth's generosity, she didn't stop to look in. She needed the rest of her money for flour, yeast and fat anyway. They had no bread at home.

The pavements were crowded and it was hard going, but it was always the same late at night when the market stalls began to pack away. Bruised fruit and spotted vegetables could be picked up cheaper then, and for some families it meant the difference between eating and going hungry.

Every evening saw raggedy little urchins fighting and rolling about under the stalls for a half-rotten apple or squashed orange or two, kicking and biting until they drew blood.

Public penury and private ostentation meant conditions were grim in Sunderland's wretched East End. Back-to-back tenements, noxious chemical works, breweries, brickworks, foul-smelling abattoirs and the like, all co-existed in rabbit warrens of filth and human misery. Homes which had originally been built for prosperous merchants were now notoriously overcrowded, with whole families living in one or two rooms, and the area was a breeding ground for all manner of unsavoury activities and crime.

And still, in the midst of it all, good, decent folk struggled to bring up their children the best they could. The desperately respectable housewife and mother, working eighteen-hour days taking in washing or carding linen buttons and sewing endless hooks and eyes by the dim light of a tallow candle, and all the time trying to ignore the goings-on in the brothel across the way.

And fathers, enduring gruelling ten-hour shifts unloading iron-ore boats at the dockside, trousers wet and cold up to the thighs and every day an accident of some kind, whilst men they had grown up with – sometimes brothers or friends – stole and murdered for their living and taught their children to do the same.

One such individual, a crony of Josie's father, now lurched out of a gin shop a few yards in front of her and stood swaying slightly as he surveyed the passers-by with bleary eyes. Josie's stomach tightened, but she forced herself to continue without checking her stride. For a moment she thought he was too drunk to recognise her, but then a bony hand reached out and fastened on her coat-sleeve. ''Tis the bonny Josie.' The stink of his breath almost knocked her backwards. 'An' how're you, me little lassie?'

'Fine, thank you, Mr Duffy.' She was staring into the mean sallow face without blinking and her voice was flat. She didn't like any of her father's associates but this one, a small wiry Irishman with hard black eyes and a vicious temper, was a particularly nasty piece of work. She would rather have died than let him see it but this one frightened her.

'That's right.' His eyes crawled over her and she wanted to rub where they had touched. 'You bin doin' a bit of shoppin' for your ma? That's a good lass.'

She continued to stare at him but she said nothing, her face blank. He always wanted to touch her, this man. Whenever he called for her father at the house he would find some excuse to pat her arm or brush against her, and the smell of him – a mixture of acrid body odour and stale alcohol – was as repugnant as the man himself. That he had some hold over her father she didn't doubt. Bart Burns's normal bullying ways were replaced by a sickening obsequiousness in Patrick Duffy's presence.

'Your da tells me you're doin' well for yerself at nights then, in the pubs? I said to him, "There's no flies on your Josie. Knows how to give 'em what they want," eh, darlin'?'

In spite of her determination to show no emotion Josie drew back, her face expressing her distaste. Her work in the rough riverside pubs for the last five years had brought her into contact with all sorts, and she couldn't have failed to pick up the hidden meaning in the last words, even if he hadn't emphasised the smutty innuendo by winking at her.

'I just sing, Mr Duffy, that's all,' she said bluntly, and pulled her arm free. He was horrible, he was, and she didn't care if her da said they'd all got to be nice to Mr Duffy or he'd knock them into next weekend. She was tired of smiling and pretending not to mind when he touched her, or said what a big girl she was growing into with his eyes on her chest, like he'd done the other day.

She saw the ferret face straighten as he blinked rapidly, obviously surprised at her temerity, but in spite of the way her stomach had turned over, she schooled her face to show no fear when she said, 'Me mam's waiting for the shopping so I've got to go. Goodbye, Mr Duffy,' as she backed away from him.

Patrick Duffy made no attempt to return the salutation, but his eyes were gimlet hard as he watched the small upright figure with the enormous cloth bag walk on. He saw her pause in front of an open fish shop, where flickering candles enclosed in greasy paper lanterns cast their dim and tallowy light over wooden tables slimy with the remains of the day's cheap fish, but then she was bobbing in and out of the crowd on the cobbled pavement again and was lost to view.

He swore, softly and obscenely, under his breath, before moving his thin lips one over the other for a moment or two. Right, so that's how it was, eh? By, if ever there was an upstart in the making, she was one. Not that she had anything to hold her head up about. He'd seen the muck-hole she was born into; rats lived better than Bart's bairns had. True enough, the girl had cleaned it up a bit in the last few years since she'd started this singing lark, but Long Bank was rough, even by East End standards.

He allowed his mind to picture Bart's dwelling the first time he had seen it some eight years ago. Two rooms, with six inmates, the walls, ceiling and furniture filthy. The floor had been bare and the walls covered with blood marks and splotches that spoke of the vermin which had been swarming about. Dirty flock bedding had occupied all of one room, and a rickety table and two chairs, along with a couple of orange boxes and the remains of a dresser, the other. There had been no fire in the range and the rooms had been as cold as ice, and if he remembered rightly, Bart's missus had been about to deliver another of the brats he planted in her every nine months. He couldn't remember if that one had been stillborn; quite a few had since he'd got to know Bart.

Duffy drew the air in between his teeth in a slow hiss as his thoughts returned to the child who had just affronted him. Her sisters had been a couple of years younger than her when he'd first had them, aye, and paid Bart proud for the privilege. First Ada and then Dora when she'd turned ten or thereabouts, and he'd put Bart on to the right connections for them to continue to earn for their da after he'd deflowered them. No one could say he hadn't played fair. It hadn't even crossed his mind it'd be any different with Josie, and if he'd had to choose any one of them it would be her, damn it. She was a beauty, was Josie, even now at twelve years old.

His thoughts intensified the feeling he'd been cheated out of what was rightfully his. Bart should have told the chit what was what, like he had with the other two, but the trouble was that Josie earned more with her caterwauling than the other two ever had on their backs. And since Dora and Ada had skedaddled to pastures new just after that one had started singing, Bart wasn't about to upset the applecart of his main provider. The bit his lads brought in with their thieving could be something or nothing depending on their luck, and the other one – Josie's sister Gertie – was ailing more than she was out begging.

The thought of Gertie Burns made his cruel little eyes narrow still more. Patrick Duffy liked them young, the younger the better, and the life of villainy he had chosen meant he could afford to pay well. Every so often a man like Bart would come his way and he'd make the most of the opportunity . . .

The sister was a scrawny little piece but it had been some months since he'd tasted something fresh and unspoilt. Slowly now, he turned and began to make his way along the frozen pavement, his gait unsteady, not least because of the swollen member between his legs which his thoughts had made rock hard. He'd set things up with Bart over the next day or two, and he hadn't given up on the other one either. There were more ways to kill a cat than drowning it. The alleys and back lanes were chancy places come nightfall, and he knew the haunts Josie frequented and the routes she took. 'Course, nine times out of ten she had her sister with her, but if he had a word in Bart's ear likely Gertie would be despatched same as Ada and Dora once he'd broken her in, which would leave the upstart to walk alone.

He smiled to himself, bringing a yellow, furry-coated tongue over his lips before he caught a drip from the end of his nose on his coat-sleeve. He'd see his day with that one all right, by, he would, and it would be all the sweeter for the wait.

By the time Josie had reached Walton Lane and then turned right into New Grey Street, she had forgotten all about Patrick Duffy, her mind full of the groceries she had yet to buy. The meat and vegetables would keep them going for a couple of days, but she still needed a quarter stone of flour and that would be fivepence even for seconds, and then there was the fat. She'd have to buy the lamp oil today too, they were completely out, and the cheapest she'd get would be thruppence a quart. Thank goodness she'd got a sack of coal in yesterday, and although there was quite a bit of slack in it, the majority of it was roundies. Eked out with the sack of cinders she'd made Jimmy and Hubert collect from the tip, it would see them through to the end of the week if they were careful. That's if her da didn't stoke up the range until it was a furnace when she was out, like he'd done last night.

The thought of her father caused Josie's soft full mouth to tighten and her nostrils to flare. She knew why he'd done it. Oh aye, she knew all right. She'd given him the beer, baccy and betting money he'd demanded at the end of the week – precious shillings they could ill afford but without which she knew her da would certainly beat the living daylights out of them all at the slightest provocation – and then he'd wanted more yesterday for one of his 'certs' on the horses. She knew how that would turn out – more often than not he lost the lot but on the rare occasions the horse came in he'd drunk his winnings the same night, treating all and sundry in the pubs as though he was Lord Muck.

So she'd stood up to him and received a swipe round the lug for her refusal to hand over the rent money which he'd taken anyway. She paused, her hand unconsciously touching her bruised cheek. She hated him. She couldn't remember a time when she hadn't hated him, but she hadn't realised her mam felt the same way until an incident which had occurred just after she'd started the singing some five years ago.

The Council had been digging out the foundations for the new Town Hall in Fawcett Street – right bonny it was now with its lovely clock-tower – and her da hadn't been home for a couple of nights. One of their neighbours had been funning with her mam and had joked that her husband might have fallen in the hole, and her mam had smiled and that, but . . . Josie started walking again, her breath mingling with the starry flakes of snow. She'd seen the look in her mam's eyes and she'd known. She had known her mam wished her da dead.

She reached the little shop where she intended to buy the flour and, pushing open the door, stepped inside the dim, dusty interior. She always bought her flour here for two reasons. One, it was cheaper than most places and although there was a lot of chaff in it and what her mam called boxings, it made as much bread as the nice white flour and moreover it was filling. Secondly, the man who owned the shop – a big jolly Scot called Mr McKenzie – frequented one of the pubs in which she sang, and he always gave her a little extra flour for her money. His brother had a smallholding on the outskirts of Bishopwearmouth and Mr McKenzie often had some pig's fat at the right price for his favourite customers, of whom she was one.

'Hello, lass.' Mr McKenzie was busy weighing out bags of flour from an enormous hessian sack in the far corner of the shop, and he continued with his task as he said, 'Is it flour you're wanting?'

'Aye, yes please.'

She waited quietly until he had finished what he was doing and then smiled as he straightened his massive frame and walked over to her. 'Don't tell me – a stone, is it? Or maybe two the day?' It was their little joke. Josie never varied in her order. And then his face lost its smile when he said, 'You walked into another door, lass?'

Josie was looking straight into Mr McKenzie's eyes and she made no reply to the remark. The door excuse was her stock explanation when her father's fists left visible marks. It didn't happen so often now, not since she had started singing and her da had realised she needed to look presentable to woo the punters, but occasionally his temper got the better of him, especially if she defied him. And she was doing that more and more lately; she just couldn't help herself somehow.

'I'd like to take that door into a back alley and give it a hammering it wouldn't forget in a hurry.' Mr McKenzie knew Bart Burns and it was a constant source of amazement to the big Scot that Josie came from such a family. 'Rose on a dungheap' was how he described it to his wife. He looked at the slender young girl in front of him, her poor clothes and ugly black boots unable to hide her natural grace and poise, and great velvet-brown eyes under dark curving brows stared back at him. Her skin was like rose-tinted cream, her features delicate, and he knew – although her felt hat was sitting low on her forehead – that beneath it there was an abundance of thick, wavy, golden-brown hair.

By, if she was his daughter he'd dress her like a little princess. There was his Beatty and him, been married twenty odd years now and still no sign of a bairn, and yet worthless so-an'-sos like Bart and his missus churned them out as easy as blinking. There was no justice in the world. But likely this little lass knew far more than him on that subject.

When Josie staggered out of the shop a few minutes later the quarter stone was approaching half, and Mr McKenzie had refused to take any money for the large portion of pig fat.

She had to stop every few yards now, the weight of the bag pulling her arms out of their sockets, but once she had purchased the lamp oil and she knew she could go home it didn't seem so bad.

The lamplighter had long since finished his round of igniting the gas lamps with his long poke in the main thoroughfares, but the side streets and back lanes and alleys were as black as pitch where there were no shops to provide a little light. The darkness didn't bother Josie unduly, but she knew better than to risk venturing into certain alleys and short cuts; the painted dock dollies regularly used them for their furtive business.

Once in High Street East, she walked as quickly as the heavy bag allowed. She passed one of the entrances to the market, the others being in Coronation Street and James Williams Street, but most of the stalls had packed up, it being after ten by now. Her da wouldn't like it that she hadn't gone to work tonight, he'd have her performing every night if he had his way, but the last couple of years she had determined that every Monday she'd clean their two rooms from top to bottom and then go shopping once it was late and bargains could be had. She could make a penny stretch to thruppence that way.

By the time Josie reached Long Bank she was puffing fit to burst and – despite the raw night – sweating profusely. Long Bank joined High Street and Low Street, and the pungent smell of fish was always heavy in the air from the kipper-curing house, but Josie didn't mind this. There were worse smells than fish.

A flat cart trundled by her, its presence made visible by a swinging lamp near the driver behind the plodding horse, and when a voice said, 'What now, Josie lass. How y'doin'?' she recognised it as Archibald Clark's, the lad who delivered the wet fish to various shops and some of the big houses in the better part of town.

'I'm all right, Archie, but it's a cold one.'

'Aye, you're right there, lass.'

Josie stood for a moment watching the glow of the swinging lantern grow fainter before she opened the door of the house and lugged the bag inside. The hall was in total darkness but she knew the narrow steep stairs were straight in front of her. These led to the two rooms at the top of the house which were occupied by Maud and Enoch Tollett, an elderly couple whose eleven children had all long since flown the cramped nest.

Josie liked the two tough old northerners. She could remember times before she had started her singing when, once the pair upstairs were sure her father was out, they had appeared with a pot of broth and a loaf of bread, or a plate of chitterlings and pig's pudding for her mam. They had all known they had to eat the food quick and get the pots back to Maud before Bart returned. Enoch had still been working at the Sunderland Brewery on Wylam Wharf then, but since he had seized up with arthritis his children had managed to pay the old couple's rent of one and ninepence a week between their eleven families, and provide the basic essentials to keep their parents alive. Essentials, in their book, however, didn't run to baccy for Enoch or half a bottle of gin for their mam, and no one but Josie and the old couple knew how often she secreted little packages up the narrow stairs.

By memory rather than sight, Josie now moved along the passageway and fumbled for the door handle on her left. Her fingers having found their objective she opened the door quickly, heaving the bag half across the threshold as the door swung open, and then she stood for a moment surveying the room immediately in front of her. As always, a faint glow of pleasure flushed her checks as she contemplated the changes she'd been able to make. Hard-won changes they were, too, because she had had to fight her father every inch of the way to keep back some of the money she earned.

The floor in front of her, like the one in the kitchen which was just visible through the interconnecting door – left open during the daytime – was covered in large flagstones Josie had scoured with soda that very day. Two raised wooden platforms which acted as settees during the day and beds at night – one housing her parents and the other her brothers – stood either side of the small iron grate in which a good fire was burning, a bright clippy mat in front of it and another lying lengthways in front of each of the platforms. In the far corner of the room next to the interconnecting door, a table and four hardbacked chairs were squeezed against the wall, an oilcloth covering the battered wood on which reposed Josie's most recent gift to her mother and one which had aroused her father's fury at such useless extravagance – a red earthenware pot of pure white hyacinths.

Either side of the window, which again was clean and sporting bright yellow curtains of thin cotton, were two orange boxes covered with the same material as the curtains and housing one spare set of darned clean bedding, one folded white tablecloth and the few extra items of clothing the family owned between them.

Above the grate on the thin flat piece of wood which didn't deserve the grand name of a mantelshelf were two brass candlesticks complete with flickering candles, and in the centre of these stood an empty oil lamp. And it was to this item Josie now directed her gaze as she said, 'I've got the oil, Mam, and the flour and everything. Mr McKenzie gave me the pig's fat free an' all.'

'He did?' Shirley Burns was lying on one of the wooden platforms, a faded patchwork quilt pulled up to her chest; so slight was her thin body she barely caused a rise in the covers. Numerous miscarriages and stillbirths – the last being two years ago at which point both the doctor and the parson had warned Bart that the next pregnancy would take his wife's life – had stripped her of her health and her looks, and she appeared twenty years older than her forty years.

Shirley's voice was soft when she said, 'That bag's too heavy for you, lass. I've told you afore: you should get one of the lads to help you of a Monday night.'

Josie smiled at her mother but said nothing as she lugged the bag through the doorway, shutting the door behind her before she walked through to the other room. They both knew the furore that would erupt should she ask for help from one of her brothers. She didn't like to think what Jimmy and Hubert were about most nights, but knowing her father was at the bottom of it, it was bound to be sailing close to the wind, if not downright illegal.

Like the first room, the kitchen was a different place from the filthy hole it had been five years before. The shining, blackleaded range had another clippy mat – larger than the ones in the living room – lying in front of it, and the brass-tailed fender reflected its colours in a rainbow haze. A large wooden table to one side of the range held a tin bath, a smaller tin bowl and assorted cooking utensils, along with plates, mugs and cutlery, all clean and scrubbed.

Along one wall was the desk-bed where Josie and her sister slept. The bed was made from wooden lathes and they had to lift the chiffonier storing their meagre food supplies to get the bed out each night, whereupon the hard lumpy flock mattress was revealed in all its glory.

Her mother had suggested the lads sleep on the desk bed when Josie had first purchased it some three years before, but Josie would have put up with far more than the stiff limbs and aching muscles the mattress caused, for the joy of sleeping in a separate room to the others with just Gertie snuggled beside her.

A smaller and very battered table used for preparing food, with a wooden box slotted beneath which did as a seat, made up the sum total of furniture in the kitchen.

Another door led out into the end of the hall. Beyond this, the back door of the house led into a communal yard shared by the inhabitants of seven houses. The privy – a square box with a wooden seat extending right across the breadth of the lavatory and filling half its depth – could be a stinking place both winter and summer, depending on the cleanliness of its last occupant. Josie had got into the habit of leaving a full bucket of fresh ashes, along with squares of trimmed newspaper, by the kitchen door at all times. Although there was a daily rota which accounted for each household taking its turn in cleaning the privy, there was rarely a day that one or two buckets from the kitchen didn't find their way down the round hole in the middle of the seat.

Along with the privy there was a communal washhouse and tap in the yard, with several lines of string hung up at one end for drying bedding and clothing, should the weather permit.

After placing the shopping bag on the smaller table Josie now picked up the big black kettle at the side of the range which, as normal, was empty. The lads were supposed to keep the kettle full, along with the bucket used for fetching water from the yard, but they were experts at remembering to forget this particular chore. Sighing, Josie went out into the cold again with the bucket and was relieved to find the tap hadn't frozen up again, although the trickle of water was painfully slow.

Once back in the warmth of the kitchen she stoked up the fire in the range and put the kettle on to boil. That done, she fetched the lamp from the other room, and once she had trimmed, filled and lit it, carried it in to her mother, bringing the candles back into the kitchen once she'd blown them out. The light from the living room along with the glow from the range was just adequate in the kitchen, and at fourpence a pound, candles couldn't be wasted. Especially with the rent money gone again.

After scooping the drips of tallow from the candlesticks Josie put them into the small iron pan containing other remnants, along with the small ends of used candles, to be melted down for further use when there was sufficient. The candles dealt with, she put the shopping away before making a pot of tea, and it was only whilst it was mashing that she finally slipped out of her coat and hat.

She poured two cups of black tea and took them through to the living room, handing one to her mother who had been lying motionless with her eyes closed but who now pulled herself into a sitting position as Josie said softly, 'Here, Mam. Have a sup tea.'

'Thanks, lass.' Shirley's tired eyes looked at her precious bairn, and as always she found herself wondering, much as Mr McKenzie had earlier, how on earth she and Bart could have brought forth such a child. Twenty endless years she'd been married, and knocked from pillar to post for the first eighteen of them, until the dire outcome of the last pregnancy and the constant bleeding that had resulted since had caused her to become a semi-invalid. But it had all been worth it – aye, and she didn't say it lightly – for the joy of having this one special bairn.

Josie sat down by her mother, taking a sip of tea before she said, 'Gertie should be back soon.'

'Aye.' Shirley's voice was low when she continued, 'I dunno how long it can go on, lass, without him findin' out. He's as cute as a cartload o' monkeys, your da. Always has bin.'

'Vera wouldn't say anything.'

'Oh aye, I know that, hinny. She's a grand lass, Vera.'

The two of them stared at each other for a moment, and when Josie rose jerkily and walked over to stand in front of the fire there was an aggressive quality to her words as she said, 'There's no way he's sending her out to beg in this weather, Mam, whatever happens. She's not strong like the lads, you know she's not. It'd be the death of her. If he's so desperate for the bit she brings in he can go out and get work himself.'

Shirley didn't reply to this and Josie didn't expect her to. Her father had never done a real day's work in his life and he'd see them all in the workhouse before he lifted a finger. Anything he came by as a result of his criminal activities never saw its way into the house. But he wasn't going to kill Gertie with his laziness.

'How much did you slip her to bring back this time?' Shirley asked after a minute or two, with a sidelong glance at her daughter.

'A few pennies, all in farthings and ha'pennies. He couldn't expect more. And one thruppenny bit. I told her to tell him a tale about a toff coming out of the Villiers and giving her that. And Vera was going to leave Gertie's coat out in her back yard for a bit before she sent her home. He noticed last time that she wasn't very wet, and it was only Gertie thinking quick and saying she'd been standing under an awning most of the night on Mackie's corner that saved us.' Josie's eyes met her mother's.

'Oh, lass, lass.' Shirley knew what would happen if her husband discovered his youngest daughter was sitting in Vera's kitchen on the nights he sent her out begging. There'd be hell to pay. From the very first night Vera and her husband had brought the two bairns home five years ago, Vera had made it plain exactly what she thought of Bart and he, in his turn, fully reciprocated the feeling. Not that it bothered Vera. By, she was a lass if ever there was one. Shirley allowed her mind to dwell on her garrulous old friend for a moment, and in spite of her anxiety, her spirits lifted fractionally. She thanked God most days that Vera had come back into her life again, and this bairn had been the means by which that had happened, along with everything else that was good.

And as though to emphasise that thought she now became aware of a small brown-paper bag being thrust into her hands. 'Here, Mam,' Josie said. 'Eat 'em now before *he* gets home.'

Shirley again said, 'Oh, lass,' but this time with a little catch in her voice as she gazed at the quarter of marzipan tea cakes. Every week her lass bought her something, like the pot of hyacinths that had lit up the room with their beauty the last few days. She hadn't been a good mother; God Himself knew how weak and wicked – aye, wicked she'd been in never standing up to Bart, not even when he'd made Ada and then Dora . . . She shut her eyes tight and then opened them again as Josie, now in the kitchen, called, 'I'm just going to soak the oats and them stale crusts for a boiley tomorrow, Mam, and then I'll get you another sup. All right?'

'Aye, all reet, pet.'

Josie was humming to herself as she mixed equal parts of milk and water with the oats and bread, ready for the currants and sugar to be added the next morning before the whole was browned off in the oven. It was lovely being able to give her mam the odd little present; no one had ever really been kind to her mam. According to Vera, her mam's da – who had died along with his wife of the fever the year Ada was born – had been as bad as her own da for using his fists on his family. Mind, Vera had said, Josie's grandfather *had* been respectable. Josie wrinkled her nose against this. Vera had said it as though it excused her mother's da somehow, but a good hiding hurt as much either way, didn't it?

The sound of the living-room door opening cut off her thoughts and brought Josie's head turning, but instead of the small figure of Gertie she'd hoped to see, her father walked in followed by Hubert, her youngest brother who was seven years old. Josie's stomach tightened. It wasn't unusual for the lads to return home any time up to midnight or even later, depending on what they had been about and whether they'd spent the evening in their father's company, but Bart never got home before the pubs closed at the earliest. And the types of pub her father frequented took no account of normal hours.

Josie found she had to swallow deeply before she could say, her glance directed at her brother, 'Where's Jimmy?'

'What's it to you?' It was her father who answered.

Bart Burns was a big man, tall and thickset with dark bushy brows over cold, strikingly blue eyes and a full head of springy brown hair. His ruddy complexion and permanently red, bulbous nose spoke of his addiction to the drink, but it was his weakness for the dogs and horses that was his main obsession. The fact that his dead cert had run like the ragman's old nag and finished last, thereby proving Josie right, was galling. His eyes focused on the young girl; his temper all the more bitter for not having release.

Josie was aware of his ill-humour and she guessed immediately what had caused it. She also knew that her father would seize on the faintest excuse to vent his spleen, but that – although his anger was directed mainly at her – it would be one of the others that he punished. Therefore she kept her voice quiet and flat when she said, 'I only wondered, that's all. The two of them are always together.' She didn't look at him as she spoke.

'Aye. Well, Jimmy's doin' a little job for me. All reet? A little job that should've bin done a while back if I'd had me wits about me.'

There was a definite threat in his tone, and out of the corner of her eye Josie saw her mother squirm anxiously. Immediately she wanted to say, 'Don't worry, Mam, and don't say anything. That's what he wants. Don't you see?' But as that was impossible what she did say was, and coolly despite her churning stomach, 'There's some tea in the pot, and a bit of brawn and cold pease pudding but I've no bread to go with it until I bake tomorrow.'

'I want nowt.'

'Can I have some bra—' Hubert's voice was silenced by a vicious cuff round the ear which sent the small boy reeling against the table in the corner of the room, but still Josie didn't respond. This was a lead-up to something, she recognised the signs, and she had a horrible feeling her father had somehow been made aware of the subterfuge concerning Gertie.

Into the silence broken only by Hubert's whimpering they all heard the front door open, and now Josie was praying soundlessly whilst pretending to concentrate on the task in hand. She placed the jug containing the remainder of the milk for morning on the tiled kitchen windowsill where it would stay cool, and turned back just as Gertie stepped into the living room.

It was obvious the small girl, who looked much younger than her ten years, sensed the charged atmosphere, for her brown eyes darted from one face to another as she remained frozen just inside the door. And then, as her father said very softly, 'You got anythin' for me, lass?' Gertie fumbled in the pocket of her thin coat and brought out a handful of coins, which she held out to the big man in front of her.

'There . . . there's a thruppence, Da.' Her voice was trembling.

'Oh aye?'

'One of the toffs in a top hat comin' out of the Villiers give me it.'

Just then, the front door opened again, a gust of icy wind blew into the room through the open dining-room door, and when Josie saw the expression on Jimmy's face she knew it was all over, even before her brother said, 'I waited, Da, an' she come out of that old bitch's house sure enough. Smilin' an' wavin' halfway down the street, she was.' She had never fully realised it before but their Jimmy was the spitting image of how their da must have been at nine years old, in nature as well as looks. Josie cast Jimmy a glance of deep loathing and nerved herself for her father's reaction.

In the same moment that her father's hand came down and swiped the coins out of Gertie's outstretched hand, Josie took several rapid steps forward, crying, 'You leave her be, Da! I mean it! If she's called in to see Vera for a bit warm-up before she came home, that's no crime.'

'A bit warm-up afore she came home?' Her father's big bulk swung back from the cowering Gertie to fully face her, and he swore, obscenely, before he hissed, 'You think I'm half sharp, lass — is that it? I'll flay the pair o' you, you see if I don't.'

'She hasn't done anything!'

'Jimmy, what time did you start watchin' the house?'

'When you left me there, Da.' Jimmy could neither read nor write, and telling the time would have been beyond him even if there had been a clock handy in Northumberland Place where Vera lived.

'Which was early on, reet?' his father ground out slowly.

'Aye, Da. She must've bin there afore I got outside.'

'So how come this bit warm-up was all night, eh? An' where did this lot come from? Or are you after tellin' me it was Vera who gave her the night's takin's out of the goodness of her heart?'

'Bart—'

'Not a word, *not a word* from you, mind. I'll get round to you later.' Bart swung to face his wife for a moment, his expression murderous, and Shirley sank back into the quilt, her hand plucking at her scrawny throat.

'You touch her or me, or any of us, and I'm out of here, I mean it. There's plenty'd take me in and you know it. I've had offers from them touts who're on the lookout for talent to play the halls. I'd do just fine.' Josie's voice was low and quivering with hate, and the fact that she was speaking the absolute truth lent a weight to her words that was undeniable. It wasn't the voice or manner of a twelve-year-old child, but there were many in Sunderland's East End who knew that age was relative. Childhood was short in Long Bank.

Bart was dumbfounded but he recovered almost immediately, and as the meaty hands went to the belt of his trousers, Josie knew a moment of searing panic before she warned herself not to lose control. 'If you want me money then think on,' she said in a voice that was not shrill and high as might have been expected, but almost guttural. 'You do all right now but if I go you'd soon feel the pinch.'

'You wouldn't leave her.' He gestured with his thumb over his shoulder at his wife without taking his eyes off Josie's white face. 'Soft as clarts, the pair o' you.'

Josie stiffened, her spirit rising up against the arrogant self-assurance that he had them all where he wanted them. 'You would be surprised at what I am capable of, Father.'

Quite unconsciously she had spoken in what she termed her 'night' voice, a voice she had purposely cultivated to enable her to deal with any difficult or over-familiar individuals in the pubs. The words of the songs she needed for her nocturnal activities came easy to her – she only had to hear something once and it was locked in her memory – but the way they were pronounced, the right way of speaking so that the song wasn't distorted by her broad northern accent, had taken some time to learn. However, once she had mastered the knack for her singing, she'd found that if she used what Vera called her 'iron knickers' voice, adopting the confident, cool manner which seemed naturally to accompany it, even the worst drunk or ruffian was put in his place. 'Twelve goin' on thirty' was another of Vera's maxims, but always said with an approving wink or nod. Josie didn't tell Vera she didn't feel thirty inside, that half the time she was scared out of her wits when she pretended to be this other person, this other Josie Burns. And that had never been so true as right at this minute.

Bart stared into the defiant, uplifted face of his daughter, and they could all hear his strong discoloured teeth grinding over each other. That she had surprised him for the second time in as many minutes was clear, but none of them were sure what he would do next. Bart himself wasn't sure. What he would *like* to do was to flay her alive, and if any of the others, including that useless bit of scum behind him – here he turned and glared at his wife for a second – had said half as much, he'd have marked them for life. But Josie was different.

He couldn't bring himself to admit that he was being held over a barrel by a mere lass; rather that this one had never responded to a leathering like the others. 'I'll do what I want in me own house, an' don't you forget it.' But his hands had moved from his belt. 'An' you – you're still sayin' you got that afore you went to Vera's?' He was speaking to Gertie, and when the little girl nodded and said,

'Aye, aye I did, Da. Honest,' he let the pause stretch and grow as Gertie, sensing the time was right, went down on her hands and knees scrabbling about the floor collecting the coins her father had knocked from her hand. 'I won't go again, Da,' she said, offering them up to him.

He took them from her, slipping them into the pocket of his old faded trousers as he said, 'You do an' it'll be the last time your skin'll cover your bones – an' that's a promise. You bin there afore?'

'No, Da.' The lie was immediate and instinctive.

'She has, Da. I told you—'

Jimmy's voice was cut off by his father making a downward motion with his hand, but even as her father was saying, 'Let tonight be a warnin' to you,' Josie was thinking what a nasty bit of work their Jimmy was. She could just imagine him sniffing about and then running to tell tales to their da.

However, as she busied herself banking down the fire in the living room with damp tea leaves and slack, Josie's thoughts were not with her brother. Now the crisis had passed she couldn't believe her own temerity, nor that her father had backed down from the confrontation without using his belt. And he'd known, he'd *known* Gertie was lying, that they both were, and he'd just pretended to believe them to save face in the end. The knowledge was a revelation and suddenly, miraculously, his power wasn't absolute and Bart Burns had become a mere mortal, like the rest of them.

Chapter Two

After the events of the previous evening, Patrick Duffy's offer to buy Gertie's innocence fell on receptive ears, especially as Josie had further angered her father that morning by making sure Jimmy and Hubert attended the Board school in James Williams Street along with their youngest sister.

For the last fifteen years the education in the Board schools had been free, unlike the church schools which charged a small fee of a penny or two a week. Since elementary education had become compulsory four years before, Josie had attended school whenever she could, until she had left at the official age of eleven, and she encouraged her sister and two brothers to do the same.

It had been an uphill battle in the lads' case, not least because Bart often made use of them during the day when more youngsters were about and their pickpocketing activities were likely to be less noticeable. It didn't help that the boys themselves couldn't see any point in learning to read and write, a point of view shared by Gertie, who nevertheless was more amenable than her brothers due to her desire to please her big sister whenever she could.

'So, same deal as afore then?'

'Aye.' Bart inclined his head, glancing round the smoky interior of the noisy public house. The Masons' Arms in Dunning Street, off High Street West, was Bart's favourite haunt, being a hotbed of illegal bookmaking. 'An' what about after?' he said, his voice low. 'You got anybody lined up to take her on?'

'What do you think?' The Irishman grinned. 'You can trust Patrick Duffy to take care of everythin'. You know that.'

Aye, he knew that sure enough. Bart smiled back into the sallow face, but weakly. He had never made the mistake of underestimating the power of the insignificant-looking little man in front of him, but he knew of those who had and who had lived to regret it. There was an innate viciousness about Patrick Duffy that was at odds with his undersized body.

'Later tonight then.' Patrick slid a small cloth pouch bulging with coins across the greasy table and Bart quickly pocketed it. 'I'll be waitin' at the back of the Trafalgar Square almshouses near the graveyard round eightish, an' make sure your missus keeps her mouth shut when the little 'un don't come back for a day or two. Give it till the weekend an' I'll bring her back here with her handler – and you'd better make sure this 'un don't skedaddle like the other two. Less than best pleased was old Douglas about that.'

'It weren't my fault.' There was a slight whine to Bart's voice. 'I lost out same as him, don't forget.'

'That's as maybe. Just make sure this 'un stays put.'

'It might be better . . .' Bart's voice dwindled away. With Ada and Dora it had been easy to keep them living at home and working the streets at night. It had meant he'd had all their earnings after the cut to their whoremaster. But Josie had been nowt but a bit bairn of five or six when he'd put her older sisters on the game; she was twelve now and she thought the world of Gertie.

'It might be better if Douglas keeps her in one of his

houses,' Bart said reluctantly. 'Easier on her mam, see? Out of sight, out of mind.' He couldn't bring himself to admit to Patrick that it was his other daughter's wrath he was wary of, should she find out the truth. Or rather the very real possibility that Josie would remove herself from the family home, taking a valuable source of income with her.

Patrick's brows lifted but he merely shrugged his shoulders before saying, 'You know your own business best, but Doug'll take a hefty slice of her earnings that way.'

'Aye, I know, but it can't be helped.' Bart swallowed the last of the whisky Patrick had bought him and stood to his feet before saying, his voice louder now, 'See you.' He didn't wait for a response, turning and passing through the press of bodies and out into the street.

A weak winter sun had been shining earlier in the day but now, at just gone six in the evening, the air was bitterly cold and here and there a snowflake drifted aimlessly in the darkness. Bart pulled his cap further over his forehead and adjusted the muffler tucked in his cloth jacket before thrusting his hands deep into the pockets of his trousers. His fingers closed over the small bag and he gave a grunt of satisfaction as he began to walk home. Strange how Patrick liked them young, but then it took all sorts, and with Gertie being none too bright and sickly into the bargain, this was the best thing all round. She was little use to him, like her mother. All them bairns he'd given Shirl and only six had lived, and four of 'em lasses at that. Mind, he had no complaints with what Josie brought in, and just by opening her gob. Who'd have thought it?

When he opened the door of the house some minutes later he could hear Josie singing. The sound irritated him, it always had, although he hadn't got it in him to analyse why. If someone had told him it was because the sound epitomised his daughter's refusal to be brutalised by her life and her surroundings, he wouldn't have acknowledged the truth of it anyway.

The table was set for four when he stepped into the living room. Jimmy and Hubert normally ate their meal sitting on their bed due to lack of space at the table. The smell of stew from the big kale-pot on the stove was heavy in the air. A full loaf of bread was sliced ready in the centre of the table, and Josie and Gertie were busy in the kitchen, his wife and the lads sitting in front of the glowing fire.

Shirley raised her head at his entrance but said nothing; they had all learned the hard way it was better to remain mute until Bart's mood had been gauged. Once he had seated himself at the table she too rose, making her way to her chair slowly, like a very old woman. Gertie now scuttled in with a pint mug of black tea which she placed in front of her father, returning a moment later with one for her mother, whereupon she received a quiet, 'Ta, me bairn.'

Josie brought her father's plate to the table first. It was twice the size of the rest, being a deep tin one with high edges, and it was full to the brim with thick meaty stew, several dumplings reposing in the middle. Bart reached for a shive of the bread Josie had made earlier which was neither white nor brown but a mixture of both, owing to the quality of Mr McKenzie's flour, and without acknowledging his daughter began to eat. This released the others to take some bread, the boys sidling up to the table and securing a piece before they returned to their seat quickly, mindful of the fact their father had been in a foul temper that morning.

Gertie brought her mother's plate next and then one each for her brothers, Josie carrying her sister's and her own. All this was accomplished without a word, although the two rooms had been merry before Bart had arrived home. Josie had been teaching Gertie the first verse and chorus of Lottie Collins's song, 'Ta-ra-ra-boom-de-ay!', purposely hamming it up in order to make her mother laugh. She loved it if she could make her mam smile. And the lads, entering into the spirit of the thing for once despite their earlier sulkiness at being dragged to school, had chimed in too.

Starting on a demure note for:

> 'A smart and stylish girl you see,
> The Belle of good society.
> Fond of fun as fond could be,
> When it's on the strict QT . . .'

Josie had then struck a pose for her mother's benefit, her hand on her hip and wiggling her bottom as the lads and Gertie had joined in the singing amid shrieks of laughter:

> 'I'm not too young, not too old,
> Not too timid, not too bold,
> But just the very thing I'm told,
> That in your arms you'd like to hold.
> Ta-ra-ra-boom-de-ay, ta-ra-ra-boom-de-ay . . .'

They had carried on like this until tears of laughter had run down their mother's thin cheeks, but there was no jollity when Bart Burns was around. Josie sat down at the table, her thoughts making her face straight. She couldn't ever remember their da smiling or even talking softly to them. Why had her mam married him? The only good thing was that no sooner was he home than he was off out again.

And as though her thoughts had prompted him, Bart

now raised his head, looking at Gertie as he said, 'You, you're comin' with me tonight,' before turning to Jimmy and Hubert and adding, 'An' you two are stayin' put.'

As her father reached for another shive of bread and dunked it into the rich gravy on his plate, Josie and Gertie looked at each other in surprise. Of them all, her father had the least time for Gertie, his only communication with his youngest daughter usually consisting of a clip round the ear. Gertie felt herself beginning to tremble; she didn't want to go anywhere with her da. Whatever he'd got in mind for her to do, it would only end with a beating because she hadn't been quick enough or bright enough.

But it was Shirley who brought Josie's eyes opening wide as she said, her voice a whimper, 'No, Bart, no. Not again.'

'Shut your mouth, woman, or I'll shut it for you.'

'You . . . you're not goin' to make her—'

'I said shut your mouth!'

As her father's hand rose, Josie cried shrilly, 'Leave her be, Da! She hasn't done anything!' There was an edge of bewilderment to her words. Her mam never talked back to their da or questioned him about anything. There had been times – lots of times – when her da had taken every last penny they had and left them without coal or oil and not a bite to eat, and their mam hadn't said a word. Not a word.

'You can't, Bart, not now. Not with Gertie. We don't need the money like we did with Ada an' Dora—'

As the flat of her father's big hand across his wife's face sent the sick woman rocking backwards on her chair, Josie jumped to her feet, her chair skidding into the wall behind her. Without pausing to think she threw her plate of stew straight into her father's angry face. Bart was stunned into immobility for a moment, more by the shock of one

40

of his own daring to commit such a crime than by the liquid running down his face in rivulets. In those couple of seconds' grace, Josie had sprung round the table to her mother's side.

The stew had been hot but not scalding, but by the torrent of abuse which now began to pour out of Bart's mouth, one could have been forgiven for thinking he had been branded.

In the same moment that Bart lunged forwards, Josie bent and whipped up the heavy black poker standing to one side of the small grate, and now she was screaming at the top of her voice, 'You dare! You dare touch me and I'll kill you! I will, I'll kill you!'

It was Bart's misfortune that he chose to ignore her. As he made another stab for her, Josie brought the poker whacking down on his right forearm with all the force her slight, twelve-year-old body could muster, and they all heard the bone snap.

His scream ascended into the two rooms upstairs, bringing Maud and Enoch bolt upright on the hard wood settle in front of their small fire, and then he was on his knees holding his dangling arm and his curses filled the house.

Josie was shaking uncontrollably as she remained standing close to her mother, but she kept the poker raised in front of her, not at all sure whether her father would try to attack her again. And then, as Gertie edged behind her and Jimmy, who now cautiously approached his father, said, 'Da? You want me to get someone, Da?' her brain whirred into action.

'Leave him.' It was a curt snap, and such was Jimmy's surprise that he did exactly that, backing away from the kneeling figure of his father as though Josie was going to wield the poker at him next.

Josie couldn't have said exactly when in the last few seconds her father's intentions had become plain to her, only that it was as if a fog had cleared somewhere in her memory. Now she recalled Ada, and then some many months later Dora, leaving the house with her father, and her mother spending hours crying into her apron. And when her sisters had returned they had been different somehow, quite different, barely speaking to her mam any more and only really having time for each other.

It had been Vera who had told her, quietly and gently one night not so very many months ago when someone in one of the pubs had sniggered on hearing Josie's surname and made a comment she hadn't understood, the rumours about how her estranged sisters had earned their living before they had left Sunderland. All her mother had ever said was that Ada and Dora had run away to parts unknown to escape their father; something Josie had been able to accept quite readily. But she'd assumed, naively she now realised, that her sisters had chosen their path in life themselves.

'You did it, didn't you?' She advanced on her father, hearing her mother's, 'Lass, lass. No, lass,' through the swirling horror in her head. 'You made Ada and Dora do that.'

Her father made no response beyond more muttered curses, his face as white as a sheet as he sank back against one of the table legs, leaning against it for support as he held his broken arm to him, clearly on the verge of passing out.

'And you'd have done the same to Gertie tonight.' She was speaking the words out loud, but even now she could hardly believe them. She knew her father was harsh and unfeeling, a bully and the type of man who had little conscience, but this . . . She fought the tide of nausea rising in her throat. This was something so unnatural, so *wicked*. Oh, Gertie, Gertie. She turned, staring into her sister's small bewildered face, her plain, snub-nosed, *dear* little face, and the urge to bring the poker down again, this time on her father's head, was so strong it frightened her.

Gertie stared back at her big sister. She'd gleaned enough to know that whatever her da had had in mind, Josie wasn't having any of it, and as Josie was the one person in all the world she trusted implicitly, that was good enough for her. Her mam was scared rigid of her da, they all were – except Josie. Even their Jimmy wet his pants if he thought he was going to get wrong by their da.

Josie turned from her sister to where her mother was watching her. 'You knew? All the time you knew about Ada and Dora, that it was me da who'd made 'em do that?' Josie asked heavily.

'Aye, I did. I did, me bairn, an' may God forgive me 'cos I can't forgive meself.'

'Oh, Mam.' Josie had been standing very straight, her face grim, but now she visibly deflated and what she said was, 'I can't leave you here with him, Mam. You must come with us, and the lads too.'

'I ain't goin' nowhere.' It was Jimmy who spoke and in spite of his nine years, his voice was adamant. 'Neither's he.' He pointed to Hubert who was cowering against the edge of his platform, clearly overwhelmed by the amazing turn of events.

'Lass . . .' Shirley hesitated, and then, as the man on the floor tried to move and, swearing profoundly, fell back again against the table and into silence, she continued, 'He's passed out. You go, eh? These won't go' – she indicated her two sons with a sharp movement of her hand – 'an' I can't, lass. For better or worse me place is here, but you're young. You've got the rest of your life

43

in front of you, an' you've got to get Gertie out of it. If you don't, he won't rest until she's gone the same way as Ada an' Dora.' She didn't add that with all that had transpired this night, the fragile protection Josie's singing had given her – or more to the point the income it had brought in – would be no defence now. Bart would kill the bairn.

Josie said again, 'Oh, Mam,' but in answer to the unvoiced plea, Shirley said, 'I can't, lass, an' that's that. An' you have to. There's an end to it. I'll be all right. Old Maud an' Enoch are good, an' many's the afternoon we spend together. They'll not see me in a fix. I know I can always go upstairs. You both get off quick now, afore he's on his feet.' Shirley turned and clasped the sobbing Gertie to her, and then pushed the child towards her sister. 'Get your coats an' skedaddle,' she said urgently. 'An' not a word as to where, mind. Little cuddy lugs are twitchin'.'

Josie glanced towards her brothers and met two pairs of wary, watchful eyes. For a moment the dire urgency of the situation was overshadowed by the bitter knowledge that Jimmy and Hubert would have no compunction in betraying their sisters' whereabouts to the man who was intent on harming them. But then they'd been brought up knowing their best chance of survival was to side with the strongest camp. It wasn't really their fault.

A dazed groan from the man on the floor brought her reaching for her sister's hand. She edged them both carefully round her father's sprawled legs and then hurried Gertie through to the kitchen. Once the door was shut behind them, Gertie clutched hold of her, saying nervously, 'Josie, where are we goin'? Where was Da goin' to take me?'

Josie looked down into the little girl's face. Gertie gave the appearance of being no more than six or seven – which had been to her advantage when her father had sent her out to beg – and she wasn't smart like their Jimmy. He might not be able to read or write but he was cuter than a cartload of monkeys, and intuitive too. She didn't doubt Jimmy had got a fair idea of the fate which had been about to befall Gertie. But she had to make Gertie understand the danger she was in for her own protection, although she worried what effect the knowledge might have on her sister.

She explained as gently as she could, her arm round the skinny shoulders, and at the end of it Gertie's brown eyes with their short stubby lashes were glittering with tears and her voice was quivering when she said, 'I hate me da. I really hate him.'

That made two of them. Josie now chivvied Gertie into her coat and hat before donning her own, her ears cocked for any sound from the room next door. Their few items of spare clothing were in one of the orange boxes in the living room; they'd have to leave with nothing, not that that mattered. She had to get Gertie out of here. She picked up the poker again, holding it tightly.

As her sister managed a wobbly smile, Josie's shoulders straightened. Gertie was such a tiny little scrap of a thing, and her own father had been going to give her to people who would make her do *that*. Until the conversation with Vera concerning the shadow over her name, Josie hadn't fully understood what *that* entailed, in spite of having slept in the same room as her parents until she had bought the desk-bed for herself and Gertie. Vera's brief but explicit explanation as to what her older sisters' occupation actually meant had led on to an equally frank exposition of the facts of life, for which Josie had been thankful. She knew her mother would never have talked of such things but she hadn't felt embarrassed with Vera; you just couldn't somehow, Vera wasn't like that. Perhaps it was because Vera had never had any children of her own, but Josie had always felt that the woman was part second mother, part sister, part best friend . . . oh, a whole host of things. Josie made a decision there and then. Vera would help them; she had never been afraid of their da like most folk.

'Come on.' Josie opened the door leading into the hall and, after ascertaining that the living-room door was still closed, she led Gertie into the darkness where, surprisingly, a candle was flickering.

'Josie, lass? Is that you?' Maud and Enoch were sitting on the top tread of the stairs, Enoch clutching a tin candlestick holder. 'What's bin happenin', lass?' Maud enquired in a stage whisper. 'Sounded like someone'd bin murdered.'

'You wait there.' Josie pushed Gertie to the front door before giving the old couple a rapid explanation.

'Couldn't have happened to a nicer bloke.' This was from Enoch, who had never had any time for Bart. 'Good on you, lass, he's had that comin' for a long time to my way of thinkin'. An' don't you worry about your mam neither; me an' Maud'll look out for her right enough an' spit in his eye in the bargain.'

'Thank you, Mr Tollett.' The kindness was weakening, and now Josie turned to Gertie again, her voice thick and verging on harshness as she said, 'Stay there, mind,' before she walked from the stairs to the living-room door, thrusting it open and standing in the aperture as she surveyed the scene within.

Her father was sitting slumped on one of the hardbacked chairs and he was cradling the arm she had struck with the poker; it was all bloody. Jimmy and Hubert were standing either side of Bart, and one of Hubert's hands was resting on his father's knee.

It struck Josie that their pose was that of a picture she had seen in a storybook one of her old schoolfriends had brought in one day. In the book, the father was about to kiss his sons good night before their pretty mother took them up to bed. Bart had clearly been speaking before she had opened the door but now he was silent, his eyes like two chips of blue glass as they fastened on her white face.

It was her mother, still sitting where Josie had left her, who broke the silence, saying, 'Lass. Oh, lass.'

'We're going, Mam.'

'The hell you are.' Her father had jerked in the chair as he'd spoken, the movement taking all the colour out of his face and causing the spate of cursing that followed.

'We are and you can't stop us.' Josie now looked straight at Jimmy and she made her voice sound like it needed to sound. 'And if he's told you to try and follow us, you or Hubert, I'll use this poker again, I swear it.'

She saw Hubert's eyes widen, and Jimmy turn to their father, saying, 'Da?' and knew instantly that her hunch had been right.

'I'll see me day with you, girl. You'll live to regret this night.'

Josie held her father's malevolent gaze as she replied, her voice shaking slightly in spite of all her efforts to control it, 'I won't regret it, not ever. You're bad – evil, you are. I know what you made Ada and Dora do, and you're not making Gertie do that. I'll . . . I'll tell the constable about you, I will, if you come after us.'

Bart's eyes sprang wide, his good hand rising from where it had been nursing his broken arm to form itself into a fist, but Josie didn't wait to see if he tried to get up. She banged the door shut, hurrying along the hall to where Gertie was waiting. She was aware of Maud and Enoch calling goodbye, but she didn't answer them, using her breath to say to Gertie, 'Get out, quick.'

It was bitterly cold outside, the sort of piercing cold which penetrates any amount of clothing and chills the flesh and bones beneath, and the ground under their boots was a sheet of black ice.

Holding the poker in one hand and Gertie's arm in the other, Josie whisked her sister along the street as fast as she could. Once they had turned the corner into High Street East, however, she paused, drawing Gertie in to the side of her as she pressed against the brick wall of the public house on the corner.

The freezing night had made sure that there were fewer folk about than normal, but it was a full minute before Josie moved again. It was a quarter of a mile to Northumberland Place where Vera lived, but Josie stopped twice more on the way, once after she and Gertie had turned into Hartley Street and again at the corner of Lucknow Street, but there were no furtive shadows dodging into dark corners as far as she could see.

Reaction was beginning to set in by the time they reached the pitch-dark back street where Vera lived, and although the cold was enough to take your breath away it didn't quite manage to neutralise the stench coming from one or two of the privies at the end of the small yards. It was obviously time for the scavengers to call with their long shovels.

Would Vera mind them turning up like this? For a moment after she had knocked on the door Josie experienced the sickening churning of self-doubt. Her da was a nasty customer at the best of times; perhaps it wasn't fair to involve Vera and Horace in their problems. But where else could they go?

And then Vera opened the door, and as Gertie burst into noisy tears and Josie said quietly, 'I'm sorry, Vera, but we had to come. I couldn't think of anywhere else,' the older woman was drawing them into the warmth of the bright, cheerful little house that was representative of its occupants, and Josie knew they were safe.

For the moment.

Chapter Three

'You'll have to get right away come mornin'. This is the first place he'll have watched, lass.'

It was now past midnight and Gertie was fast asleep on a shake-down at the end of Vera and Horace's enormous double brass bed. Josie, Vera and Horace were sitting at the kitchen table in front of the glowing range, and Josie was full to bursting, having recently shared Vera and Horace's supper of panackelty. Vera's answer to any problem was food and she was a wonderful cook. The panackelty had been just as Josie liked it; slowly cooked for hours in the old coal oven so that the potatoes had absorbed all the flavour of the corned beef and stock, the onions almost caramelised and the whole lot deliciously crusty at the edges. In spite of the direness of their situation it didn't seem so bad with a plateful of Vera's panackelty inside her.

'But where to, Vera? You know how Gertie is; she's not strong enough to put up with living rough even for a night or two until I find work.'

'Oh aye, I know that, hinny. No, our Bett'll put you up as long as you don't mind bein' a bit cramped like. It's a cryin' shame when me an' Horace have got all this room, but your da's not daft. We've got to go to work an' you'll be on your own then. I wouldn't put anythin' past Bart Burns.'

Neither would she, but like Vera had said, it was a

51

shame. She would have loved to live in this little house for a while. It had an upstairs and a downstairs, and apart from the second bedroom which was rented out to one of Vera's fellow workers at the corn mill, the couple had it all to themselves. It seemed like unimaginable luxury to Josie. Vera had kitted out the front room just grand, with a stiff horsehair suite, a little glass-fronted cabinet with nice bits of china and knick-knacks inside, and a highly polished piano and upholstered stool. It even had a square of carpet and a rug – not a clippy mat but a proper, shop-bought rug – standing in front of the small ornate fireplace.

Josie had stood in awe when Vera had opened the front-room door and shown her the room, but she hadn't dared venture inside for fear of spoiling such perfection. As far as she knew, Vera and Horace never went inside either, and the slightly musty, cold air which wafted out into the hall suggested the grate – hidden behind an embroidered fire-screen of neat uniformed roses enclosing a verse of scripture promising severe retribution for the unholy in the hereafter – rarely saw a fire.

The kitchen – the other room downstairs in the two-up, two-down dwelling – was a lovely, warm place, however, with the biggest clippy mat Josie had ever seen covering a good part of the stone-flagged floor. Horace had built cupboards from floor to ceiling all down one side, and in front of the table and four chairs were two lovely big rocking chairs with fitted feather cushions, positioned so they got most of the warmth emanating from the blackleaded range. A large hardwood settle with several plump flock-stuffed cushions completed the rest of the furniture, and Vera had already made it up into a bed for Josie with several thick blankets.

'Thank you for letting us stay tonight.' Josie put her

hand on the older woman's arm. 'I didn't know where else to go.'

'Lass, if you hadn't come here I'd have wanted to know why.' Vera's voice was uncharacteristically tender as she stared into the lovely face in front of her. Until she had met Josie that night in the Mariners' Arms just over five years ago, Vera had always prided herself on being a sensible, unemotional woman who had a reputation as being something of a tartar. The eldest in a family of eight children, she had virtually brought up her six brothers and one sister when her mother had died giving birth to the last child when Vera was just thirteen. By the time she met Horace at the age of twenty-five, she had resigned herself to spinsterhood, something – in view of the dribble-nosed toddlers, endless washing and ironing and constant rounds of meals over the last twelve years – that wasn't altogether unwelcome. When Horace had shyly confessed in their third month of courting that he was unable to father children due to an unfortunate accident in his youth, he'd been surprised and pleased at Vera's response, and they had married before the year was out.

She had never regretted the decision, not once. Her quiet, orderly house, with Horace for companionship and her job at the corn mill during the day had met all her needs, but then a thin little waif with velvet-brown eyes and the voice of an angel had come into her life, and all her hitherto non-existent maternal feelings had flooded in with a vengeance. She had had no real interest in renewing her acquaintance with Shirley beyond the fact that her old friend was Josie's mother, but in the event she had found the two of them had got on as well as ever. She always made sure her visits coincided with a time she knew Bart would be out, which wasn't difficult as he was rarely in.

Josie had brought a dimension to her life that Vera would

have found impossible to put into words, but which, having once experienced it, she couldn't do without. Shirley's child was the daughter she would never have and had never desired, and Vera loved her with a deep, compelling love that was as pure and sacrificial as that of the noblest of natural mothers.

'Ee, you're dead on your feet, lass.' Vera stood up, her voice brisk now. 'You get yourself to bed an' in the mornin' I'll ask Ruby to tell 'em at the mill I'm middlin'. She's a good lass, she won't let on. The sooner you're both away to our Bett's, the sooner me mind'll be at peace. Even if your da gets wind of where you've gone it'll be like lookin' for a needle in a haystack in Newcastle.'

'Newcastle?' Stupid, but she'd forgotten Vera's sister had married one of the miners from Gallowgate Pit. 'But we can't go to Newcastle, Vera.'

'Why not?'

Josie didn't answer for a moment but swallowed hard, her throat suddenly dry. Newcastle was a place she'd heard talk of but which was miles and miles away, another world. She'd never even passed over Wearmouth Bridge into Monkwearmouth; how on earth could she take Gertie as far away as Newcastle? What about their mam? 'There's Gertie,' she said slowly. 'She's always ailing, and Mam. When would we be able to see Mam?'

'Our Bett'd look after Gertie when you were workin'.' Vera hesitated, and then said frankly, 'Look, you've got to get used to the idea you won't be seein' your mam for a time, hinny, not if you want to watch over that little lassie upstairs. Your mam'd be the first to understand that.'

Suddenly, and with a speed that was making Josie's head spin, everything had changed.

'It's for the best, lass.' Vera patted the girl's arm awkwardly. 'An' Newcastle isn't so far away – just twelve miles or thereabouts, with a few stops on the way. When me an' Horace go to see our Bett we get the early train at five to five an' we're in Newcastle Central by quarter to six. Course, any one of me brothers'd have the pair of you if I asked 'em, but they're all local an' you don't want that. No, Bett's is safer. Mind, we won't catch the four fifty-five. Dit early for man an' beast that, eh?' She made a little moue with her mouth.

Josie gave no answering smile in return. 'How much will it cost on the train?' she asked quietly.

'Ee, now don't you go worryin' your head about that.'

'How much, Vera?'

'Just a bob, lass, that's all, third class, unless you fancy goin' first class an' swankin' a bit?'

Josie looked into the rough plump face in front of her, and her voice was soft when she said, 'That's two shillings with me and Gertie, and I'll pay you back, Vera, I promise. And I'll pay Betty if she can put us up for a bit. Make sure she understands that, won't you? I intend to pay our way.'

'Now look you here, lass.' All the laughter gone from her face, Vera reached out and gripped Josie's hands across the table. 'Me an' Horace do all right with just ourselves to look after, an' with rentin' the room out upstairs an' all. We don't want for nothin', thank God, but if we was down to our last penny it'd still be a privilege to give it to you. I don't want no more talk about payin' us back. Am I right, Horace?'

She turned and looked over her shoulder at her husband, who nodded, before winking at Josie as he said, 'Be more than me life's worth to disagree, eh, Josie lass? It takes a brave man to disagree with Vera.'

'Oh you.' Vera leaned back in her chair, flapping her hand but smiling. 'Daft as a brush without its bristles, as me old da used to say.'

The lighter mood continued until Vera and Horace went to bed, but after Josie had settled herself – fully dressed apart from her stockings and garters – on the settle, she lay thinking about what she was going to do as the banked-down fire in the range cast a soft comforting glow into the darkness.

She could see the sense in going to Newcastle, oh aye, she could, and if she thought about it now she'd always known, deep inside herself but barely acknowledged, that one day it would come to this, her leaving home and probably taking Gertie with her. The lads would be all right; Jimmy was so like their da already she knew he'd always land on his feet, and it was as if Hubert was connected to Jimmy by a piece of string, so close were they. And if there was one person Jimmy was fond of it was his brother; it'd always been that way. No, it was just her mam she was worried about, but with things as they were she had to put Gertie first.

She twisted on the hard flock cushions but her discomfort was from within rather than without, and despite the late hour she was wide awake. She sat up eventually, clasping her knees over the coarse thick blankets and staring into the faintly flickering shadows.

And now she found herself feeling a slight thread of excitement. She shouldn't be looking forward to tomorrow and she wasn't, not really, at least not about leaving her mam, but – and here she put her hand to her heart as it began to thump in her chest – this was her chance to make something happen for *herself*. Perhaps her only chance.

Twice she'd been approached in the last year, and a couple of times before that too, by touts who'd assured her they could get her a slot in one of the local music halls. One had been really persistent, coming back night after night and claiming he knew the proprietor of the Wear

Music Hall and saying that she was just the sort of new act he was looking for. But Josie knew that to get anywhere in the halls you had to be prepared to travel and move around. You needed nice clothes and fancy costumes too, and all her money went the minute she had it in her hand, what with paying the rent and feeding and clothing them all. And she couldn't have left Gertie at the mercy of their father, not the way he knocked her about. That had always been at the back of her mind too. But now . . .

She hugged her knees hard. She'd find some work in the day; she didn't care what it was. A laundry, a factory, a shop, anything, and then at night she'd sing. She could ask around a bit, find out the best places for someone to notice her. Perhaps Vera's sister would know? She slid down under the blankets again, willing her mind to stop its racing. She had to go to sleep; tomorrow was going to be a full day.

She must have fallen asleep eventually because early in the morning she awoke to the double chime of a tugboat sounding on the still frozen air outside. The sound was a familiar one; many a time in the kitchen at home she and Gertie had fallen asleep listening to the tugboats on the river and, on a very quiet night, the rhythmic churning of the big paddles.

For a moment she remained still, the events of the previous day crowding into her mind, and then she roused herself, throwing back the blankets and reaching for her stockings and garters. Once her boots were on she busied herself stoking up the fire in the range and putting some more coal on, after which she lifted the kettle – already full with water – on to boil. The kettle, like everything else in Vera's kitchen, was beautifully clean, and unlike their range at home which had one oven with a circular door, this one had two ovens, one for baking and one for roasting. It was a canny kitchen. She glanced round the room which was still in deep shadows, the small patch of sky outside the narrow window charcoal grey with only the hint of daybreak.

She would have a kitchen like this one day, and her own house with an upstairs and a downstairs that she shared with no one but her family. And a garden. Not a back yard, not even one like Vera's that boasted its own privy and washhouse, but a real garden with grass and trees and high walls so no one could see inside. One of the girls she had gone to school with had got set on as a kitchen maid at one of the big houses near Mowbray Park, and she'd been full of what she had seen when she'd had her interview with the housekeeper. But of all Miriam had said – and she had said plenty – it was her description of the Havelocks' garden that had captured Josie's imagination. She would have a garden like that one day. Somewhere where the air was filled with the soft scent of flowers and where she could hear the birds sing. She loved birds. One of the best compliments she'd ever been given was when a woman in one of the pubs had said she thought she sang as sweetly as a bird.

'Ee, lass! You're up bright an' early, an' I see you've got the kettle on for a brew. I could do with keepin' you on; always fancied meself with a parlour maid.'

Vera's voice was overbright and Josie knew why. Vera was worried her da was going to arrive on the doorstep before they could get away, or that he'd got the lads watching the house. And he might, he might. But something strange had happened when she had brought that poker down on the arm of the man she had hated and feared all her life. It hadn't just broken the bones in his arm; it had broken something in her, something that had been afraid and cowed under the threat of the physical pain he inflicted with so little conscience. She meant what she had said to Jimmy the night before: she would use the poker again if she had to. Not on her brother, not that, but if her da tried to stop Gertie leaving . . . The poker was going to accompany them to Newcastle anyway. She glanced at it, propped against the range. It was better than a big burly docker for protection, her poker

'What?' She must have smiled because Vera's voice was surprised and curious, and when she told the older woman the nature of her thoughts, Vera laughed out loud. 'Well, it don't eat so much, that's for sure, an' I dare say it's cleaner in its habits an' all, lass.'

Once Horace and Ruby had departed for work, Josie and Vera took stock. The fact that the two girls had escaped the house the night before with just the clothes they stood up in presented an immediate problem, and one which Vera was determined to assist with, despite Josie's protestations that they would manage until she could get work and buy more. It was only when Vera put her hand on Josie's arm and said, her voice soft, 'Please, lass. Please let me help you in this,' that the girl became silent. 'We'll call in the Old Market an' pick up a few things. Stamp's stall is a good one, he don't have so much rubbish as some, an' once you've washed 'em through at our Bett's they'll come up as good as new.'

Josie glanced at Gertie, whose eyes were bright with anticipation at the thought of new clothes. Never mind they were second- even probably third-hand; they weren't her big sister's outgrown things and were therefore possessed of their own magic. 'Thank you, Vera.' She spoke with deep gratitude as she pressed the hand on her arm, knowing she would miss Vera's solid presence in her life more than any other apart from her mam.

Josie always thought the Old Market had a smell unlike anything else. It came from the second-hand clothes stalls, the bacon and meat stalls, the fruit, confectionery, fish, tripe, grocery, and numerous other stalls jostling together under the high roof. There was no one particular odour which was predominant, but as she stepped through the entrance in Coronation Street the smell assailed her nostrils – neither pleasant nor unpleasant, just the unmistakable aura of the market.

The building was a beacon to many folk looking to make a subsistence income stretch a little further, and it wasn't unusual to see harassed pitmen's wives wheeling pillow cases or sacks containing two or three stones of flour from the market, along with bundles of second-hand clothes and all manner of goods. These would be transported to the station, or to a horse and cart waiting in a side street, and taken back to the pit villages. It was safe to say that there was nothing you couldn't buy from some stall or other within the Aladdin's cave that was the Old Market.

Vera now made her way to Stamp's stall down the aisle left clear in the middle of the stone-flagged floor, nodding to Joe the Bacon Man – as he was generally known – who had the reputation of being something of a character among folk who were all characters in their own way. Stamp was another one. ''Tis the fair Vera.' Cyril Stamp was a little roly-poly figure of a man, his shape made the more incongruous by the ancient swallow-tail coat and pork-pie hat he wore on all occasions. 'Never mind the bitter chill of an unkind winter outside, it is summer in me heart now I've set eyes on the fair Vera.'

'Oh, stop your blatherin'.' Vera sniffed loudly, but Josie knew her friend was trying to keep a straight face. 'I'm lookin' for a few things for these two.' She indicated Josie and a wide-eyed Gertie. 'An' none of your rubbish mind, I want decent stuff.'

'Vera, Vera, Vera.' The little man put his hand to his heart, his expression pained. 'You cut me to the quick, lass. Aye, you do. Have you ever known me sell rubbish in me life?'

'Aye, I have, to them as are daft enough,' Vera returned smartly as she began to rootle amongst the heaped clothing after motioning with her hand for Josie to do the same.

'Do good to them as despitefully use you, as the Good Book says.' Cyril wasn't about to let Vera have the last word, winking at Gertie as he spoke and making the child giggle. 'Here, cast your lovely eyes, eyes that would make a man leave hearth an' home for sure, on this little lot.' From beneath the stall he drew out an orange box. 'Come from a nice place near West Park, an' if I remember rightly, the bonny wife had a couple of bairns about these ones' ages.'

He did remember rightly, and Josie had to stifle a gasp of delight as numerous items of underwear – all seemingly as new – and several plain but good frocks were revealed, along with a thick coat in a dove-grey tweedy material that looked to be her size and was just beautiful.

'Hmm.' Vera flicked at the items with a critical finger. 'Not bad, but a bit shabby round the edges.' She was playing the game, and Josie, Cyril and Vera were all aware of it, but protocol had to be maintained before serious haggling commenced. 'Is that the best you can do, then?'

'The best?' Cyril raised his eyes heavenwards, apparently wounded beyond words, and then he smiled as Gertie, shyly stroking one of the dresses with the tip of her finger, said, 'I think they're bonny.'

'A lady after me own heart. Here, hinny' – he drew a

small slab of hard toffee out of his pocket – 'I was just wonderin' what to do with this stickjaw afore you come.'

Ten minutes later Josie and Gertie were the possessors of vests, drawers, petticoats and two dresses each, along with the grey coat for Josie and a smart hat to match it. The whole lot had come to twelve shillings, which seemed an inordinate amount to Josie, but which meant – Cyril had mournfully assured them – he wouldn't be eating all week, the great loss he'd had to incur.

'They're good stuff, really good stuff, lass,' Vera had murmured once they were making their way into High Street East, for the walk to Central Station further along in High Street West. 'An' kept real nice. You want to give the right idea when you're lookin' for work, now then, an' these are a cut above.'

Josie nodded, her arms tight round the brown-paper package containing the clothes. She would pay Vera back every penny but she knew better than to mention it now.

Although the beautiful clock-tower and brick façade of the station on the High Street side was familiar to Josie, she had never ventured inside, and now, as she accompanied Vera and Gertie into the building, her first impression was of the height of the arched ceiling. It seemed to rise up and up, and it was when she was turning round in a circle to admire it fully that she became aware of a small figure darting out of view outside.

Jimmy. She glanced at Vera who was pointing out the weighing machine to an entranced Gertie, and the other machine which apparently enabled the user to punch out their name and other details on to a tin strip. She had been keeping an eye open from the moment they had left Northumberland Place, but he must have been trailing them all along. Was her da with him?

'Here.' She handed the parcel of clothes to a taken-aback

Vera, securing the poker from her friend who had been holding the instrument of protection since the market. 'If you want to get the tickets I'll be back in a minute. I'm just going to have a word with Jimmy.'

'He's here?'

'Outside.' Josie flicked her head towards the entrance.

'Alone, lass?'

There was a grim warning in Vera's tone, but although Josie knew what she meant, she said quietly, 'Stay with Gertie, Vera. Nothing can happen, even if he's not alone.'

Jimmy wasn't alone. When she emerged from the entrance to the station she saw them immediately, the small boy and the big man standing on the pavement opposite. Her father had his arm in a sling but the sight aroused no emotion in Josie except to make her grip the poker more firmly. Nevertheless her stomach was trembling as she approached them, their faces reflecting a surliness which made them even more alike. Her father spoke before she reached them. 'What the hell do y'think you're doin' gallivantin' about?' he growled. 'Get your backside home where it belongs.'

She did not answer him for a moment, and then she said in a voice even she recognised did not sound like her own, 'We're not coming back.' And then, more loudly, 'We're not coming back ever.'

'My belt says different.'

Again she didn't answer immediately, but as her hand instinctively flexed on the handle of the poker she saw his eyes flicker to it. 'You won't ever use your belt on me again, nor your fists either. And you're not coming within six feet of Gertie. I meant what I said last night; if I have to I'll go to the police and tell them everything.'

'Everythin'?' Her father gave a hic of a laugh, his eyes fixed hard on her pale face. It had started to snow again in the last minute or two, small light flakes that were without substance. 'An' what's that – that me eldest two trollops took themselves off whorin'? "So what?" they'll say. "Plenty do." An' you'll report that I wanted to take me bairn for a walk one night, eh? They'll think you're doolally, lass. Ripe for the asylum.'

'I'll take my chance on that.' Her head was up and her shoulders were back, and then as Jimmy chimed in with, 'Da's done nowt,' she snapped back fiercely, 'Oh, he's done nothing, all right. He never does anything except sponge on the rest of us. He's never done a day's work in his life. No, *he's* done nothing – but what he's made Ada and Dora do is not going to happen to Gertie. *No matter what* – you hear me, our Jimmy?'

'You've got it all wrong, lass.' There was a faint wheedling note in Bart's voice now; he could see his living slipping away from him in front of his eyes. And Patrick – he'd given the little Irishman his word and taken money on the deal. He felt fear tighten his stomach; he'd seen what Patrick arranged for folk who double-crossed him. He never dirtied his own hands, oh no, he was too wily a customer for that. Patrick always had a crowd of alibis when the deed was done. He'd already be more than a bit put out that Bart hadn't shown last night with the bairn. 'Look, I swear to you, on me own life, right?' he said persuasively. 'I had nowt to do with Ada an' Dora goin' down that road.'

'You can swear all you like but it won't make any difference.'

'You're upset, you're not thinkin' straight, lass, an' that's understandable after last night. But I don't hold you no grudge for me arm. It was a misunderstandin', that's all.'

She stared at him, wondering if he knew how much she

hated him. She hated him so much it had swallowed all the fear and panic.

'An' there's no need for you to be walkin' about with that thing neither.' He nodded at the poker. 'What'll people think?'

'That I'll use it if I have to.' It was flat, but something in her manner must have conveyed he wasn't going to manage to sweettalk her.

His attitude changing, he snarled, 'You're a bit bairn an' you'll do what you're told if I have to skin you alive.'

'I'm not a bairn.' Her voice was low and very bitter. 'I've never been a bairn, none of us have, you've made sure of that, but I tell you one thing – me and Gertie are going and you can't do anything about it.' As she saw his hand rise as of old, hers holding the poker jerked aloft, and for a moment they stared at each other through the snowflakes which were now whirling more thickly. Whatever he read in her face made her father's hand fall limply to his side, but now their mutual hate snaked between them like a live thing, and it was only a man who had been passing by, saying, 'Here, what's goin' on? You all right, lass?' as he paused at the side of them, that broke the contact.

Josie didn't answer. Her legs felt funny, weak, but she turned and walked quickly across the road and into the station without looking back. This was the end, really the end, but when would she ever see her mam again now? But she couldn't think like that; she'd sort out something, she would. She had to see her mam. Oh, Mam, Mam. And then Gertie and Vera were there in front of her and it was all she could do to stop herself bursting into tears.

Vera stared into the drawn little white face in front of her. Bart had been out there sure enough, it was written all over the lass's face, but she wasn't going to waste time asking her about it now. Once they were on the train to Newcastle she'd breathe a mite easier.

The iron-framed glass roof covering the platforms gave a spacious, airy feeling in summer, but with thick snow blanketing out the light, the station was gloomy and grey. The 9.54 a.m. was steaming away and ready to leave as they boarded, but although Gertie was vocal in her excitement the final confrontation with her father had knocked all the stuffing out of Josie. It wasn't until after they had stopped at Monkwearmouth, East Boldon and the following two stations that the colour came back to Josie's cheeks, and Vera felt she could ask her what had happened.

Josie briefly explained, finishing with a shrug of her shoulders and a glance at Gertie, who was oblivious to them both, her nose pressed up against the window and her eyes popping out of her head at the changing scene outside the train, which was occasionally shrouded in deep billows of smoke from the engine.

'I'll look out for your mam, hinny, you know that. There'll always be room for her with us, young Hubert an' all, if need be.'

Josie smiled and nodded but said no more. She couldn't explain to Vera that she felt the weight of her mother – and Hubert, to a lesser extent, and even their Jimmy, bad as he was – like a lead brick crushing down on her heart. Vera would brush such sentiment aside, saying Josie was doing the only thing she could in getting Gertie out of harm's way. And Vera was right, she knew she was right, but . . . It didn't make it any easier.

The train chugged its way into Felling Station, and then Gateshead East, and by the time it stopped at Newcastle Central in a great exhalation of steam and puffs, it was exactly ten thirty-two.

Nothing had prepared Josie for the size of the Newcastle station or, as they left by the main entrance in Neville Street, the different smell and feel of the town. The smell was due, in part, to the sheep- and pig-market and beyond that the huge cattle-market to the left of the station, which had the Royal Infirmary squeezed between them, but as they crossed over the road, Josie clutching the parcel containing their clothes and Gertie now in charge of the poker, everything seemed so much bigger and noisier than in Sunderland.

Still a little dazed by the train journey and the fact that it had taken such a short time to be transported into this strange world, the girls followed Vera past a cathedral on their left and into a wider street which seemed full of inns and hotels. After crossing what seemed like hundreds of different streets but in reality was only three or four, Vera said, 'This is the bottom of Bath Lane. Remember that if you get lost any time. An' you keep followin' it until you turn left into Seaham Street an' then Spring Garden Lane off Pitt Street. There's a fine big park, Leazes Park, in Castle Leazes just over the way from our Bett's, an' it's right bonny, with a bandstand an' fountain an' all sorts. You'll like that, won't you, hinny?'

This last was directed at Gertie, who was looking petrified at the mere thought of going astray in this massive, confusing labyrinth that was to be their new home.

'Bett says the old castle's down by the waterfront still,' Vera went on, undeterred by Gertie's silence. 'Fancy that, eh? A castle in the middle of town. Mind, accordin' to Prudence, our Bett's stepdaughter who reads a bit, Newcastle has grown up around the castle. A wooden one, first of all apparently, an' built by the son of William the Conqueror. An' then, when it'd become an important port an' trading centre, they built a wall right round the town an' kept it all squashed up. It's only been in the last hundred years or so that folk have moved outside the original walls, an' Prudence would tell you that's a good thing. Great one for change, is Prudence.'

Vera gave a loud sniff at this point and Josie shot a quick glance at the older woman. She got the impression Vera wasn't too keen on her sister's stepdaughter.

''Course, all the new houses an' such meant more jobs,' Vera continued as, having turned into Seaham Street, she had to raise her voice above the noise from the colliery to their left. 'You ask Frank, Bett's husband, to tell you about the time his old grandda helped build Grey Street. Two hundred an' fifty thousand cartloads of dirt it took to fill in the burn that ran through the town, an' Frank's grandda always maintained it was a cryin' shame. Sweet as a nut, that water was, an' now some streets don't have no more than a couple of taps atween 'em. Now, where's the sense in that, I ask you?'

Josie and Gertie didn't know where the sense was; they were both feeling they had little enough left of their own. But at least the gridwork of mean streets they were now walking in bore some resemblance to home and the familiarity was comforting.

It was half a mile from the station to Spring Garden Lane, and it was beginning to snow heavily by the time the trio reached Vera's sister's two-up, two-down terraced house. It was identical to hundreds in the tight network of streets stretching west from the Gallowgate colliery, but vastly superior to the grotesque squalor of the slums down by the waterfront. In Sandhill, and Pipewellgate – situated on the other side of the gorge – it was not unusual for as many as ten families to live in one house, Vera informed the girls with a shake of her head, and the proximity of the slaughterhouses meant folk died like flies in hot weather.

Betty's house was towards the middle of the street, and on seeing it, Josie knew immediately Vera's sister was not out of the same mould as her friend. The outside of the windows was filthy, the paintwork was flaking and dirty, and the step hadn't seen a bath brick for years. She and Gertie glanced at each other but Vera had already opened the door, calling, 'Yoo-hoo, Bett! It's me, Vera,' as she entered, gesturing for the girls to follow her into the house.

'Ee, our Vera, as I live an' die.' A small and enormously fat woman appeared at the end of the hall, wiping her hands on the none-too-clean apron straining across her vast stomach. 'What's brought you, the day? Nowt wrong with Horace, is there?'

'No, no, lass, nothin' like that.' Vera turned sideways in the narrow passageway, nodding towards her two charges as she said, 'I've brought these two lassies, Bett. They're in trouble an' it's bad. I was wonderin' if you could put 'em up for a while?'

'Here?' And then as a small child clothed only in a grubby top and with a bare backside crawled round her feet, the little woman said, 'Come here, you; where do you think you're goin'? Need eyes in the back of your head with this one. Come away in, the lot of you, an' have a sup tea.'

Josie and Gertie followed Vera into a kitchen which was as far removed from Vera's bright shining room as it was possible to be, but which nevertheless exuded warmth from the huge fire blazing in the range. Besides the toddler who was now sitting on a thick clippy mat there were two more small children in the room, along with a baby in a rough wooden crib to one side of the tall cupboards that flanked the fireplace. The two children, a boy and a girl, were eating a slice of bread and jam, their faces smeared with a mixture of dirt and jam and their feet bare, but they looked plump and happy, as did Betty herself.

'Here, lass, sit yourself down.' Betty stretched out a hand and cleared the seat of a large wooden settle by the simple expedient of pushing all its contents on to the stone-flagged floor. 'You too, hinnies. We'll have a nice sup tea an' I've some sly cake just cooked an' coolin'. You like sly cake, hinny?' she asked Gertie who was half hiding behind Josie, overcome with shyness.

An hour later, Betty having been fully acquainted with the reason for their hasty departure from Sunderland, and her visitors stuffed full of tea and sly cake, the atmosphere in the kitchen was relaxed and even merry. Betty's children were sitting in a huddle in front of the fire finishing off the remains of the pastry crammed with currants, sugar and butter, which they were picking off the old, thick dinner plates it had been cooked on, and Betty's youngest was at one of her enormous breasts, feeding lustily.

Josie had learned that besides these four younger children Betty had two more who were presently at school, along with five stepchildren from her husband's first marriage, his wife having died in childbirth. Apparently only the two youngest of these – a boy and a girl – lived with Betty and Frank now, the others having married, and of these two the boy was due to be married within weeks.

'Barney goin''ll make more room but there's plenty anyway.' Betty paused for a moment to bawl a warning at the three on the clippy mat who were arguing over a nice morsel, the baby at her breast continuing to feed serenely in spite of the sudden thunder above its downy head. 'Me an' Frank sleep yonder,' she flapped her hand towards the front room, 'an' the lassies have one room upstairs an' the lads t'other. We were thinkin' about takin' in a lodger once Barney goes an' there'll only be Frank an'

Prudence's wages comin' in, but it'd have meant the lads sleepin' down here an' gettin' a desk-bed or summat. No, it'd work out fine you comin', lass.'

She smiled at Josie who smiled back. There was something immensely comforting about Betty.

'An' Prudence might be able to get you in at the laundry off New Bridge Street where she works an' all. I'll put it to her, lass. But if not that, then you'll pick up summat.'

'Thanks, Bett.' It was Vera who spoke. 'It'll put me mind at rest, knowin' they're with you. He's a nasty bit of work, Bart Burns.'

'Aye.' Betty nodded. 'I know the type all right. All wind an' water but a big man with his fists when it comes to bit bairns an' women. My Frank don't hold with nowt like that; he'd knock him into next weekend an' the week after, given half a chance. Mind, I'd have a go at him meself if it come to it. Aye, I would. I might look as if a breath of wind 'ud blow me away, but I can pack a wallop, lass.'

She roared with laughter at her little joke, and the others grinned. Betty had the sort of meaty forearms a ten-ton wrestler would be proud of. It would be a brave soul, be they male or female, who would dare to take her on.

It was gone four o'clock by the time Vera made a move to leave, and Betty's two oldest children, twin boys, had been home from school for half an hour or more. By now Josie had the strangest feeling that she had been part of this family all her life, but nevertheless, she found she had a lump in her throat as she, along with Betty, stood on the doorstep and watched Vera pick her way carefully down the icy street. The recent fall of snow had coated the already lethal black ice covering the pavements with an innocent veil of white, and it was treacherous underfoot.

'She should've gone earlier.' Betty's gaze lifted from the bulky figure of her sister to the swiftly darkening sky as she spoke. 'There's more snow comin', you can smell it in the wind. By, it's goin' to be a bad winter, this one. Still, we won't let it bother us, eh, me bairn? Snug as bugs in a rug, we'll be.'

Vera having paused they both waved their goodbye, and then she had disappeared round the corner and Betty was saying, 'Come away in, lass. It's enough to cut you in two out here.'

The warm confines of the kitchen were redolent with the smell of the pot pie which had been steaming away for the last two hours, and as Josie and Gertie left the womb-like cavern a minute or two later, armed with a tallow candle and a bundle of bedding to make up the spare pallet in the lassies' bedroom, the icy chill hit them like a physical blow. The bed was organised in double-quick time and they scuttled downstairs again. Two minutes later, Betty's husband Frank arrived home. He'd stayed after his shift on union business, according to Betty, who now busied herself filling the tin bath in the tiny scullery off the kitchen with hot water for her husband's stripdown wash to remove the black grime of the pit.

Frank's greeting was cursory initially, but once he'd had his bath and was dressed in the clean clothes which Betty had taken through to the scullery before beating his pit clothes free of dust in the tiny back yard, he came and sat in the big, flock-stuffed leather armchair to one side of the range. He was as short and thickset as his dumpy wife, with a voice that could shatter a crate of milk, but by the way his three youngest children immediately clambered up on to his lap Josie assumed, rightly, that the gruff exterior harboured a heart of gold.

She looked into the heavily jowled face, topped by short grey hair that had a little tuft sticking straight out from his forehead like a compass pointer, as Frank said, his voice loud but kind, 'So, lass, you an' the little 'un are goin' to lodge with us for the time bein' then?'

'If that's all right, Mr Robson?'

'Oh aye, lass, it is. It is that. An'' – and now he leaned forward, almost dislodging the youngest of the three on his lap – 'if you catch sight of hide or hair of your da, you tell me, eh? Aye, you tell me.' He puffed ferociously at his clay pipe, tamping dark brown rough tobacco with the juice still in it, before he repeated, 'Aye, you tell me an' we'll see what's what, right enough.'

At a few minutes to six the kitchen table was set, the settle having been pulled close to it one side with six straight-backed chairs on the other. Barney and Prudence were due home any moment. Apparently Barney was employed at the concrete works in the centre of the town, a short walk from the laundry where Prudence worked, and the two normally walked home together.

'He's a good lad, is Barney.' Betty was bustling about, lifting the sizzling dish of sliced potatoes, onions and turnips, the accompaniment to the pot pie, out of the cavernous oven as she spoke, and it wasn't until much later that Josie registered that she hadn't mentioned Prudence in the acclamation.

'Not a miner mind, like his da an' three brothers, but he's followed his own road an' that's no bad thing. Couldn't handle bein' underground, you see. He was all right when he was doin' the screens, the conveyor belts up top where the coal gets sorted, but once he went down . . .' Betty shook her head, making her thick bun of coarse brown hair wobble. 'It's not for everyone, workin' in the bowels of the earth, an' I don't hold with the idea you're born to it meself.'

She cast a sidelong glance at her husband as she finished speaking, and Frank stared stolidly back at her as he puffed on his pipe. Although nothing had been said directly, Josie got the feeling this was something which had been discussed between husband and wife before, and moreover that they saw it quite differently.

Josie had ushered the children through to the scullery to wash their hands before the meal – a suggestion which had been greeted with some surprise when she had first voiced it – when Barney and Prudence arrived home. The twins, Martin and Kenneth, having sidled back into the kitchen as soon as they could, she and Gertie were occupied in dealing with the three youngest children, Robert who was four, Freda aged three and little Clara, and therefore they heard Betty's two stepchildren before they saw them.

There had been a high voice and a deep one at first, then silence except for Betty as she had given the bare bones of an explanation, and then the high voice had said, 'Here? Stay here, you mean?' and it was expressing disapproval.

Josie hotched Clara further up in her arms as she glanced at Gertie over the child's head, but there was no time to speak before a small, darkly clothed figure appeared in the doorway. It was the same female voice which said, but flatly now, 'So you are Aunt Vera's waifs and strays; Josie and Gertie, isn't it? Which is which?'

Josie found herself staring, and it was a moment or two before she responded, saying in as flat a tone as the young woman had used, 'I'm Josie, and this is Gertie.' Clara was wriggling in her arms, and in reaching for the rough piece of towelling to one side of the tin bowl, Josie broke the hold of the green eyes looking at her with such hostility, occupying herself with drying the infant's small, dimpled hands.

It would be kind to say Prudence Robson was plain; the truth of the matter was that she was ugly, and no one was more aware of this than Prudence herself. Her face was long and thin, her nose and mouth equally so, which made her small squat body all the more incongruous, but it was the overall colourless quality of her eyes, skin and hair which emphasised her severe features. Her eyes were green but a muddy, indistinct shade, and this same dingy, turbid trait was reflected in her skin and the mousey brown of her hair. In comparison, her four brothers had all taken after their mother who had been a good-looking woman, and there was barely a day that went by that Prudence didn't reflect on the unfairness of this.

She knew she was an impassioned person, the feelings which racked her made all the more intense because they could have no outlet. Pretty girls were allowed to be frivolous and bright and sparkling, even catty or inconstant on occasion, but an ugly one had to be quiet and self-effacing, never putting herself forward or assuming anything, and it was a pose Prudence Robson had adopted from infancy when she was outside the home, even though she knew she was ten times more intelligent than those about her.

There were only two people she liked in all the world – her youngest brother, Barney, and the girl he was soon to marry. Pearl had been her friend since childhood – her only friend – and Prudence rarely allowed herself to dwell on what she secretly knew to be true, that the other girl's friendship had been motivated by the fact that Prudence had four handsome older brothers, and that Pearl was well aware she appeared all the more comely and appealing beside the ugly duckling. Prudence needed the support and security of Pearl's friendship too much to delve into things better left buried.

By the time Josie raised her head there was a tall man standing just behind the unfriendly young woman. His shock of dark brown hair, liberally coated with a dusting of white powder, first drew her eyes, and then, as she lowered them to the smiling face, also smeared with concrete dust, she met a pair of the most startlingly green eyes she had ever seen.

'You've got your work cut out trying to clean up this crew.' His smile widened and Josie smiled back shyly, even as she was thinking, So this is Barney, Betty's youngest stepson. But I never expected him to be so . . . so . . . But she couldn't find words to describe the way she was feeling because she had never felt like it in her life before.

Chapter Four

As November turned into December, the severe snow storms sweeping the North of England were making life harder than ever for poor families like the Robsons. Despite the recent development of an electricity supply on Tyneside, the powers that be had not yet converted the horse-drawn tramway system to electric traction and, in any case, half of the workers in Newcastle's mines and factories often walked miles in freezing conditions to save the cost of the fare. Despite the steadily increasing prosperity of the area as world demand grew for its products – ships, engineering, coal, chemicals – workers like Frank did not feel the benefit.

There was many a heated discussion in Betty's kitchen between Frank on the one hand, and Barney and Prudence on the other, as to how far the unions – who were just tentatively beginning to flex their muscles – should go.

'Aa've said it afore an' Aa'll say it agen – you have to tread careful, man. There's always some so-an'-so ready to step into your boots given half a chance.' Frank was a great one for eying his two irate children over the top of his pipe as he delivered such statements.

'It's just that sort of sentiment that the owners and managers promote.' Barney and Prudence would always be beside themselves by the end of the discussion whereas their father would still be sitting puffing away contentedly.

'Don't you realise the wealth of industry that exists here, *has* existed here for the last century? Look what Richard Heslop wrote fifty years ago, and nothing's changed, Da:

'There's chemicals, copper, coal, clarts, coke an' stone
Iron ships, wooden tugs, salt, an' sawdust, an' bone
Manure, an' steam ingins, bar iron, an' vitrol,
Grunstans, an' puddlers (Aa like to be litt'ral).'

This last quote and others like it would invariably come from Prudence, who spent any spare money she had on books and was always popping into the free library near the laundry.

'What're you sayin', lass?'

Josie suspected Frank's manner with his daughter was distinctly tongue in cheek most of the time, but with the mental and physical torture Prudence put her through at the laundry, Josie couldn't help deriving a certain measure of satisfaction as she watched the older girl being wound up by her father until she was ready to explode.

'I'm *saying* working men and women have got the upper hand if only they had the sense to realise it! There's thousands of us and a few of them, and if we all stood together – which is what the unions advocate, after all – things would change.'

'Aa dunno aboot that, lass.'

Josie also noticed that Frank's northern accent was particularly predominant at such times, and when he smiled and winked at her and Gertie after Prudence had flounced out of the room – a common occurrence – she'd smile back. It was about the only time she did smile these days, she thought sombrely one evening in the first week of December when she was sitting on the settle in the kitchen, too tired to move. Nothing had gone the way she'd dreamed

78

that day on the train when she had left Sunderland. She didn't regret leaving – she'd do the same thing again, she reassured herself firmly, but nevertheless . . .

She flexed her toes in her hard black boots, every muscle and joint aching, and then picked up the shirt she had offered to darn. There was always a stack of mending to do in Betty's household, and Prudence would come up with every excuse under the sun before she would help. It had taken Josie no time at all to realise there was little love lost between Betty and her stepdaughter. In fact, there was little love lost between Prudence and anyone else in the household – other than Barney – if she thought about it.

In her capacity of assistant head laundress at the laundry in Higham Place off New Bridge Street, Prudence had secured an interview for Josie the very next day after she had arrived in Newcastle, with the result that the young girl had started work immediately.

The post was described as laundry checker and sorter, and it was at the very bottom of the ladder. Checking in the dirty washing and entering each receipt of an article into a ledger was the worst bit. Josie hated handling the soiled linen, and somehow it seemed as if the vilest items came her way when Prudence was around. Invariably the other girl on duty with Josie would be given the task of checking and booking out the clean laundry. The heaviest baskets, the most disgusting and smelliest clothes and bedding were piled high at her station of work, and always – *always* – Prudence would be constantly deriding her for being too slow, too stupid, and a hundred other things besides.

The baskets which transported the linen to the washing bays ran on little wheels, and oft times the ones which Prudence put Josie's way were so heavy it took every ounce of her strength to even move them a few yards.

Every evening she walked home with Prudence and Barney in an exhausted daze, and it was only Barney drawing her out that broke through the stupor.

Josie was well aware that the attention she received from Prudence's brother during these walks was another nail in her coffin as far as the other girl was concerned. The next day, Prudence would make her pay dearly for every smile, every thought she shared with Barney, but Josie didn't care. It was worth it. Prudence's veiled glares made it clear she bitterly resented Barney bothering to talk to her at all, and the fact that they got on extremely well into the bargain was salt in Prudence's wound.

But Barney was so *nice*. And funny. Definitely funny. Sometimes Josie thought he must have made up some of the stories he told about the happenings of his day – just to make them laugh – but whether he did or not she always entered the house in Spring Garden Lane feeling as though the world was a good place. And she liked to listen to him too, when he talked about the unions and politics and things like that. She even liked to listen to Prudence because Barney's sister was interesting in her own way, besides which Josie found herself silently agreeing with Prudence's sentiments regarding the downtrodden working class and a whole host of things. She had tried to tell Prudence this more than once, but had always got her head bitten off for her efforts. All in all, Josie enjoyed the walk home at nights, even if she was so tired at times she wondered how she was managing to put one foot in front of the other.

Once in the house though, after she had had a couple of cups of the strong black tea Betty seemed to drink all day, she found what her mam would have termed her 'second wind'. She usually helped Betty dish up the evening meal and would feed the youngest Robsons their portion before she ate her own, but she rarely managed more than an hour or so of darning and mending before she collapsed into the hard pallet bed she and Gertie shared in the room where Prudence also slept, comfortable in a single bed with a thick mattress, and little Freda and Clara, who shared a bed identical to the one Josie and Gertie slept in.

Gertie, too, had her share of problems. Unlike the teacher at the Board school in Sunderland's East End, the one in the school in Douglas Terrace just a short walk away was a stern disciplinarian.

Gertie was not a bright child and was easily reduced to tears, and besides the cane applied at frequent intervals she'd had to endure sitting in a corner with her face to the wall and a paper hat on her head. One day she had arrived home hysterical after the teacher had shackled her to the desk all afternoon until she could repeat a verse of scripture to the woman's satisfaction. When Josie had got in from the laundry over two hours later, Gertie's thin little wrist had been chafed raw from the harsh rope used to secure her.

The fact that such practices seemed quite normal and acceptable to Betty and Frank had not reassured Josie in the least, and she had made her feelings known. Prudence had laughed at them both and sneered at Josie's concern for her sister down her long nose, and Betty and Frank, kind though they were, had been quite unable to understand her concern. It was only Barney who had taken Josie's distress and Gertie's terror seriously.

'Do you want me to go and have a word with Mrs McArthur?' he'd asked Josie quietly the next morning on the way to work.

'Have a word?' Prudence had snorted on Barney's other side. 'What good would that do? You and I have both survived under Mrs McArthur and are none the worse for it. The girl needs to toughen up, that's all. Besides, you know what Mrs McArthur's like. If you go and see her she could well take it out on Gertie. She's like that. Spiteful.'

The pot calling the kettle black.

Josie's thoughts must have been written all over her face because Prudence had glared at her in the next instant, and that morning the baskets had been so heavy and so disgusting Josie had been quite unable to stomach any lunch. However, after she'd considered Barney's offer in her mind Josie had to admit she thought Prudence was probably right. Barney complaining would not endear Gertie to the teacher, and with the absolute power the woman had over her pupils she could make Gertie's life even more miserable. But it had been grand of him to offer. The thought warmed Josie for the rest of the day. When she thanked him that night on the way home for his suggestion and explained her reasons for refusing, he took her hand in his for a brief moment, squeezed it and told her she must tell him if she changed her mind, and she felt a warm glow right down to her toes.

However, Gertie continued to weigh heavily on her mind. The child had complained of stomach-ache for the last few days and stayed off school – encouraged by Betty who made good use of her – but a visit by the School board man the day before, followed by a stern admonition that he expected her to attend school for the next nine months until she was eleven, had put paid to that ruse.

Josie thought it ironic that in all the time they had lived in Sunderland, and with her brothers attending school just an odd day here and there more often than not, they had never once had a visit by the School board man. But things were different in Newcastle. As she was finding out more and more.

'Well, lass, how do I look? Good enough to pass with

Lord an' Lady Muck?' Betty stood in front of her, clad in her Sunday best.

Betty had long since christened Barney's prospective in-laws with the title, something which made Prudence tight-lipped but only made Barney laugh. Pearl Harper was an only child and her parents ran a substantial inn at the end of Pitt Street; they had made it quite clear in the past that they considered their daughter a mite above a miner's son. Nevertheless, in much the same way they had conceded to Pearl's friendship with Prudence, they allowed their headstrong daughter her way with regard to Barney. Betty had often longed to point out that it was Pearl who had done all the running. 'Set her cap at him from when she was nowt but a bairn,' Betty had confided in Josie one night when Gertie and the children were in bed and the others were out; she and Josie were sitting in front of the fire with a basket of mending between them. 'Shameless at times, she was, but he couldn't see it. Men can be right fools when it comes to a certain type of lass. Still, it's done now.'

Josie was reminded of this conversation in the next moment when Frank ambled through from the front room attired in his Sunday suit, his neck straining awkwardly out of his stiff white collar and his face as black as thunder. His wife glanced at him before saying, 'It's no use lookin' like that. The weddin's only two weeks away an' there's things to be sorted, you know that as well as I do, an' I'm not havin' them lookin' down their noses at us. We can show 'em we're just as well set up as them, leastways.'

'Don't talk daft, woman.'

'Well, we can offer to pay a bit towards the jollifications, can't we, an' I can do a bit of bakin'.'

'An' I had to be wearin' me suit for you to say that?'

'Aye, you did.' It was sharp and pointed. 'An' don't you

have more than a pint or two, should they offer.' Betty now turned to Josie, and her tone was warm and soft when she said, 'You'll be all right, hinny? There's a pap bottle on the side should you need it, but she'll likely sleep till I'm back after screamin' all day, poor little blighter.'

Barney and Prudence had already left for Barney's future in-laws', and Josie was in charge of the house and the children, including three-month-old Millie, who had been suffering from a bout of diarrhoea. 'I'll be fine.' Josie smiled at Betty but didn't add, as would be customary in the circumstances, 'Enjoy yourself,' because she knew that was the last thing Betty was concerned with. She hadn't been looking forward to this evening and had approached it like a necessary military procedure, instructing Frank on what he could and couldn't say until the two had finished up having the mother and father of a row the night before.

Josie followed Frank and Betty to the front door, waving them down the street before reseating herself on the settle. She didn't take the more comfortable armchair that was Frank's in spite of the fact she was now effectively alone downstairs, apart from little Millie asleep in her crib. No one in the household, not even Prudence, would have dreamed of sitting in the large, high-backed seat which dominated the kitchen and was set at an angle to the range.

Josie gathered up Frank's spare working shirt again and commenced her task of attempting to draw the frayed pieces of cloth together. The shirt had been washed and darned so many times it was threadbare. The monotony of the job allowed her mind to wander to thoughts of her mother, something it did frequently. Although Vera had called the weekend before and told the two girls that their mother was fine, worry was an ever-present spectre sitting on Josie's shoulder, restricting her appetite and causing her to imagine all sorts of things. After a while her fingers became slower, the warmth of the fire and the steady ticking from the wooden clock on the mantelpiece above the range bathing her in exhaustion. Within moments she was fast asleep.

Prudence sat watching her father and his fat waddling piece of lard – as she termed Betty in her mind – attempting to make small talk with Pearl's parents, and it was all she could do not to let her contempt show on her face. Ignorant halfwits, the pair of them. Him, with his narrow bigoted way of looking at things, and Betty laughing her way through life like an idiot. How they irritated her! They all irritated her – her brothers, and her half-brothers and half-sisters. All except Barney, of course. He was different from the others, you could hold an intelligent conversation with him, and he was the only one of her brothers with the gumption not to blindly follow their da down the pit.

Prudence became aware of Pearl looking at her, her friend's finely arched brows raised in amused understanding. Pearl was well acquainted with Prudence's views on her family; moreover she shared them with regard to Betty and Frank although she'd always been very careful not to express her disdain in front of Barney.

Prudence straightened her scowling face quickly; there'd been a warning in Pearl's eyes too. Don't rock the boat, it had said. Keep everything sweet and hunky-dory tonight. They might be senseless clods but we know what we're doing, you and I. And what they were doing was removing Barney from her da's and Betty's influence. Pearl would make something of Barney; she'd always wanted him and had played him like a violin for years. This thought carried mixed emotions. Reluctant admiration that her friend could keep up the pretence of being all sweetness and light when Prudence was well aware there was another side to Pearl, and faint guilt regarding her brother. But Pearl would make sure Barney got on, Prudence comforted herself quickly. He'd soon be living in the smart little house in St James Street which overlooked the park, and which Pearl's mam and da had insisted on doing up and furnishing throughout as their wedding present. And that was just the first step as far as Pearl was concerned. She wouldn't rest until Barney left the concrete works and joined her uncle who managed Ginnett's Amphitheatre in Northumberland Road. Big business, the halls.

'So, Frank . . .' Prudence was brought back to the conversation in front of her by Pearl's father's heavy patronising tones. 'We will have a little do back here then after the church, and provide a bite and such. Can't have folk saying me only daughter had a dry wedding, now can we?' He gave a hearty smile. 'But me and Marjorie'll stand it – you and Betty have got enough to do with your brood.' He made it sound as though they were animals in a farmyard.

'Me an' Frank'd like to do our bit, Stan.' This was from Betty and her voice was politely aggressive. 'I've already iced the weddin' cake like I've told Marj an' I've a mind for plenty more bakin'.'

'You don't have to, Betty. Really.' Marjorie Harper was a small, neatly dressed woman who always spoke in what she fondly imagined was a refined voice but in reality was merely annoyingly quiet and stilted. 'We can lay on whatever is necessary. Pearl is our only one, after all.'

'Mouldy bun? What's a mouldy bun got to do with anythin'?' Frank was somewhat deaf due to a fire-damp explosion at the pit in his youth which had taken his best friend and three brothers, and consequently found what he termed 'that blasted woman's whisperin'' intensely aggravating. 'We're discussin' a weddin' here, aren't we?'

Prudence closed her eyes for a moment as her face flamed with embarrassment. Her da! She wished – oh, *how* she wished – it was her leaving the menagerie in Spring Garden Lane in a few days' time. How would she stand it after Barney was married? Still, Pearl had consoled her by telling her she'd be welcome to call at any time, and she'd do just that. Anything to escape home. And one day she would escape for good. That was what all the careful saving of the last years was looking towards.

Seven years she had been working at the laundry, ever since she'd left school, and she'd had three rises since then but she still paid Betty the same as when she'd first started. Even when her da had been laid off for eight weeks a couple of winters ago, she had offered no more and waited to see what Betty would do. But she was as soft as clarts, Betty. After her stepmother had mentioned she'd be grateful for a bit more to tide them over the bad spell, she hadn't mentioned the matter again. And why should *she* stump up extra to feed and clothe the brats Betty turned out like clockwork?

Prudence opened her eyes, remembering how Barney had doubled his board to Betty. She'd warned her brother he was stupid and that he'd be expected to keep it up once their da was in work again, but that was Barney all over. Governed by his heart and not his head, and always a sucker for a sob story. You got nowhere in life like that.

She glanced round the expensively furnished private sitting room, frowning slightly. It might take years but one day she'd buy her very own place. You had to make things happen in this life and the end always justified the means – and there was one thing she meant to bring about in the very near future. She didn't intend to share her room any longer with that little baggage her Aunt Vera had foisted on them.

Prudence didn't include Gertie in the thought; the younger child's presence had barely impinged on her consciousness, but from the second she had set eyes on Josie's fresh glowing face, framed by its mass of wavy golden-brown hair, she'd felt immediate antipathy.

But for Vera's interference Betty would have been looking to offer the lads' room to a lodger once Barney was gone; that had been the original plan, Prudence told herself bitterly. The twins and Robert would have managed perfectly well on a desk-bed in the kitchen, and apart from Freda and Clara on their little pallet, she would have had the room to herself. As it was, you couldn't move for bodies at night. It wasn't to be borne.

Prudence moved irritably on the stiff horsehair sofa she was sharing with her brother, screwing her fleshy buttocks into the seat, and in doing so caught Pearl's eye once more. Her friend's pretty, slightly babyish face again signalled caution, but this time the emotion it brought forth from Prudence was one of testiness.

With her pale blue eyes and curly chestnut-brown hair, Pearl had been spoilt by her doting parents from the day she was born. What did Pearl know of being forced to share a bedroom with virtual strangers, or existing day after day in a household of morons? Prudence became aware her hands were clasped together so tightly her knuckles were shining white, and forced herself to relax her fingers one by one until they were loose in her lap. She felt she would go mad at times, stark staring mad, and since that mealy-mouthed little madam of Vera's had arrived, the feeling had increased tenfold. Wheedling her way in with Betty, offering to do this and that, and simpering at her da until she'd got him eating out of her hand. She thought she was so clever, Josie Burns, but she'd got a shock coming.

Prudence now sat very still as she allowed herself to reflect on the journey she had taken the previous weekend, and the satisfactory outcome which had ensued. It had been sweet, very sweet to find out she had been right all along – that what she'd suspected from the first day the baggage had arrived was true.

Her Aunt Vera was a fool, they all were – even Barney because he wouldn't hear a word against Josie – but she had seen straight through the little strumpet. All that talk about her da and Gertie, what did Josie take them for? Well, the others might not have the sense they were born with, but she was on to Josie's little game. The chit had got tired of looking after her mam and running the household in Sunderland. She'd decided to get away and, knowing Vera had a sister in Newcastle, had told a pack of lies and duped them all. All except herself, Prudence Robson. Her lips formed in a mirthless smile. Young Josie was going to find out very soon that Prudence Robson wasn't as daft as she looked . . .

At first Josie thought it was the dream she had been having which had woken her. It wasn't the first time she had had it; it had been the same for years now. Sometimes whole months would go by and she would think it had finally gone, and then night after night, sometimes for a week at a time, she'd awake hot and desperate and gasping for air.

It had begun not long after she had met Vera, and the night after her mam had been ill all the previous day. Her mam had been crying and moaning on and off with the belly-ache for hours, and Maud from upstairs had been sitting with her for a long time before she'd shooed them all into the kitchen. Hubert had only been a little baby then;

she remembered that because he'd only just learned to sit up and he'd been screaming all day, even when she'd tried to feed him his pap bottle.

After a while her mam had stopped making a noise and then Maud had come out with the chamber pot which she'd been going to take out into the backyard. Then Gertie had fallen over and cracked her head on the fender and Maud had put the pot down quickly just outside the kitchen in the hall, by the back door. Gertie had been bleeding everywhere, and Jimmy had been bawling and Hubert had made himself sick and then filled his napkin, and in the ensuing pandemonium Maud had forgotten about the chamber pot. And then she, Josie, had been going out into the yard to swill Hubert's bit of rag through, and she had seen – *she had seen what was in it*. It had been tiny, the babby, so tiny, but with little arms and legs, and she had wanted to reach down and lift it out of the chamber pot which her da used most nights when he'd been drinking. She hadn't wanted it to be in there.

And then in the midst of it all her da had come home. There was a gap in her memory here because the next thing she could recollect was her and her da in the yard, and she'd been hanging on his arm because she knew what he was going to do. But she hadn't been able to stop him and he had leathered her after with his belt; she still had the scars from his buckle on her back. But she hadn't cared about that, not even when the blood had caused all her clothes to stick to her for days afterwards and her skin had felt as though it was on fire. All she'd been able to think about was the minute baby lying amongst all the filth and excrement in the privy and being scraped out by the scavengers' long shovels and tossed in their stinking cart.

It was from that day she had really hated her father and that night that the nightmare had come. It was always the same. It would be all right at first. All of them, her mam and her three sisters and Jimmy and Hubert would be sitting in a boat on the sea, but a funny sea – black and dark. And then the dreadful fear would fill her and a sense of horror that was paralysing. The sea would begin to lap over the side of the boat but it was thick, like mud, and her da was suddenly there, shouting they were all too heavy. One by one he would push the others out, and she could see their desperate eyes and hear their screams but she was unable to move, held down by some invisible force. And the black sea would suck them under but slowly, horribly slowly, and then she would know it was her turn . . . But she always woke up in the moment that her father's hands reached out for her.

Why had she dreamed the dream now? It hadn't come once since she had been in Newcastle and – foolishly per-haps, she acknowledged as she rubbed her damp palms on her skirt – she had told herself the break from Sunderland had set her free from it.

And then the knock came at the door again, and she real-ised someone was outside. Whether it was the inexplicable feeling of dread the dream always left in its wake, or a primeval sixth sense, or just the fact that Josie suddenly became very aware she was all alone in the house apart from the baby, and Gertie and the children upstairs, she didn't know, but the hairs on the back of her neck were pricking. In the warmth emanating from the range she shivered.

'Don't be so daft.' She spoke out loud as she rose from the settle, dropping the shirt on to the dingy cushions and reaching for the oil lamp in the middle of the kitchen table. Someone was outside, a friend of Betty and Frank's maybe, or perhaps one of Frank's pit cronies. It wouldn't be any of

Frank's married children or their wives, they would have come straight in without due ceremony.

She made her way slowly along the hall, but when she reached the front door and the knock came again, she found herself sliding the bolt instead of opening it, much to her surprise. She frowned, holding her free hand to her heart as it thudded into her throat. What was the matter with her? She was going doolally. Nevertheless, and in spite of now feeling slightly ridiculous, she called, 'Who is it? Who's there?'

There was silence for some ten seconds, and then the knock came a third time. She stared at the battered front door and then stooped down, placing the oil lamp on the floor before opening the door into Frank and Betty's front room. Before the arrival of Frank's second family this room had been used rarely; it had held a green plush suite and a highly polished oval table and six upholstered chairs. The suite remained, but now a double brass bed stood in the alcove which had housed the table and chairs, with a space at the side of it where the crib – containing the youngest Robson – stood at night. Along with this was a huge wooden airer constantly filled with damp and drying clothes and a rickety wardrobe, which meant careful negotiation when edging to the bed. But it was to the window that Josie made her way, carefully folding the moth-eaten velvet curtains back a fraction as she peered out into the dark street.

But she hadn't been careful enough. As the big broad man outside turned and stared straight at her, Josie felt a scream which was never voiced spiral in her head, and then she heard the front door being rattled as her father realised he had been tumbled. She let the curtain fall back into place and now she stood in the darkness, no semblance of colour left in her face and her hands gripping the bodice of her dress as her eyes stared wildly about her.

He was here. Her da had found them. But how? How had he found out where they were living? She stumbled back into the hall, entangling herself in the airer on the way and causing it to fall backwards into the wardrobe. If it had fallen the other way the clothes would have landed on top of the glowing fire in the grate, kept burning day and night courtesy of the free coal the miners received, but such was Josie's state of mind she wouldn't have known.

'Josie? It's me. Da.' His voice now came clearly. 'Open the door, lass.'

He was speaking in the wheedling tone he had used once before outside Central Station, as though he was a normal father dealing with a recalcitrant child who needed careful handling. And she answered him as she had then, her voice flat and controlled. 'Leave us alone,' she said.

'Come on, lass, open the door. I only want to talk to you an' see how things are. Your mam's bin half mad with worry.'

That was a lie if ever she heard one because Vera had told her that Shirley was pleased they were out of harm's way. And when had her da ever bothered about how her mam was feeling anyway? He must think she was daft to swallow that one. Josie took a long shuddering pull of air and said once more, 'Leave us alone. We're not coming back.' She was leaning against the cold wall for support but then, as the door was rattled violently on its hinges again, she sprang forwards and banged on it herself, hissing, 'You leave us be or else I'll call Barney and Mr Robson. They know all about you.'

'Oh aye? An' they're sittin' by the fireside, are they? Best place, lass, on a night like this. Well, you call 'em an' we'll all have a crack together, eh? Mind, I might be inclined to say what I think about folk who take a pair of bit bairns away from their rightful mam an' da.'

She stared at the door, biting the end of her thumb. And then his voice came again saying, 'Well? I'm waitin', lass. Or could it be they're oilin' their wigs some place? A little bird told me there's the comin' nuptials to get sorted.'

He had known. He had known all along that the house was empty except for her and the bairns. As the thought hit home she knew in the same instant her father had been keeping her talking deliberately, but then a hard hand was slid across her mouth as she was grabbed from behind and held close to a body which she recognised from its smell. 'Now you just keep nice an' quiet like a good little lassie an' no one'll get hurt.' Patrick Duffy was holding her fast despite her struggling, and Josie would never have believed his strength if she hadn't felt it. 'Y'know, you've put me to a fair bit of trouble, me darlin', an' I'm not too happy about that.'

His hand was so tight across her nose and mouth that Josie couldn't breathe, but still she continued to struggle and kick as Patrick forced her towards the front door. She could hear him cursing, and in the moment he removed his hand from her mouth she sucked in a pull of air intending to scream, only to receive a blow across the side of her face that made her neck crack as her head bounced on her shoulders.

The shock of it stunned her for a second, but as Patrick Duffy slid the bolt and his hand went back to cover her mouth, she twisted her head and bit down on his flesh with all the power in her jaw. Again the hall became full of softly hissed profanities, but this time it was her father's fist that sent Josie whirling into darkness, although as she lost consciousness she thought for a moment she heard Barney's voice and it was yelling . . .

Chapter Five

If he was honest, Barney had been glad of the excuse to nip home and check on Millie when Betty had asked him. He could take Pearl's mam and da in small doses, he admitted wryly to himself as he stepped out of the front entrance of the inn and began walking along Pitt Street, but lately, what with the wedding and all, he'd seen a mite too much of them for comfort. Still, he wasn't marrying Stanley and Marjorie, was he.

The moon was casting a cold white brilliance on the icy street and pavements, the already heavy frost coating the layers of ice and snow with a film of sparkling silver. Barney stood for a moment, his head uplifted to the night sky in which the stars stood out like twinkling lights, and he breathed deeply, taking the clean crisp air hard into his lungs.

By, it was good to be alive on a night like this. If he had his way he'd walk for miles now, not thinking, just drawing the essence of the night into him until he had a surfeit to carry him through the next days and weeks. And then he shook his head at himself, smiling self-consciously as though someone had told him he was being fanciful and womanish. It was funny, the way he needed to see the sky and wide open spaces; his da, and their Amos, Reg and Neville didn't. His mouth straightened. The united attitude of his father and brothers when he had told them he couldn't follow them down the pit had hurt him with its lack of understanding and barely concealed recrimination. But Betty had been for him. She was a canny little body, Betty.

He took another great breath of frost-flavoured air into his lungs, savouring its sharp cleanness after the cloying dust of the concrete works in which he laboured six days a week.

Aye, he and Betty got on all right, and if Prudence had given their stepmother half a chance it would have been a happier household the last few years. Nevertheless his thoughts were tinged with pity when they touched on his sister. It must be doubly hard for a woman to look like she did when she was a thinker, and Prudence was a thinker all right. If there was one thing he would miss when he got married it would be the talks – arguments sometimes – that they'd shared, because Pearl wasn't made that way. Social reform, the fight the unions were engaging in, the burgeoning Suffragette Movement were all beyond Pearl. Not that he minded that, he quickly reassured himself. Pearl was soft and sweet and docile, everything a woman should be. Aye, he was lucky she'd looked the side he was on. He *was* lucky. He didn't question why he had to emphasise this in his mind.

He passed the junction with Wellington Street and continued on along Pitt Street, knowing he had to be quick to avoid suffering one of Pearl's wounded silences when he got back. They were killers, those silences of hers, when she'd look at him with big hurt eyes and quivering lips if he stepped out of line in some way. He perhaps should have told Pearl he was cutting along home for a minute or two when he'd made the excuse he needed the privy, but he'd known Betty wanted it kept just between them two, to avoid Prudence and his da dismissing her anxiety about Millie. And he could be home and back in minutes.

His hobnail boots were loud on the icy ground as he turned right into Spring Garden Lane, and then he paused. For a minute there he'd thought someone had just gone into their house, but it must have been next door's. Who'd be calling round at this time of night?

Nevertheless his steps quickened, and as he reached the open door and his brain registered the struggling girl and the big man's fist slamming into her face, his yell was purely instinctive as he launched himself forward, kicking over the oil lamp which was still on the floor as he did so.

Bart, already hampered by his broken arm in its sling, was caught off-balance and knocked halfway down the hall with the force of Barney's body, but it was Patrick's scream as the oil lamp smashed over his boots and trousers that brought Josie back to consciousness. She wasn't aware that the bottom of her own skirt was on fire until Barney was kneeling beside her, smothering the flames with his coat as he dragged her out into the street, but the main contents of the lamp had gone all over the little Irishman as the cries and shouts from within the house professed.

However, between them Bart and Patrick must have managed to put the flames out, because by the time Barney was able to leave Josie sitting against the wall of the house and re-enter the hall, the two had vanished the way Patrick had come in – through the back yard – and only smoking floorboards remained.

By now Gertie and the children were all awake and streaming downstairs and little Millie was yelling her head off in her crib in the kitchen, but all Barney was concerned with was the slight figure propped against the wall outside.

The neighbours came out in force, and after a brief and blunt explanation Mr Stefford next door was off at a run to the inn in Pitt Street, and Mrs Stefford was dealing with a weeping Gertie and the other children. Mr Middleton, on the Robsons' other side, was dispatched for the doctor, and his wife – a stout and very capable midwife – helped Barney settle Josie in the big armchair in the kitchen before she picked up the screaming baby and, together with Mrs Stefford, took all the children back into her house.

Josie was only dimly aware of all this. The pain in her head was excruciating, and combined with the accompanying swirling and dizziness, kept her swimming in and out of consciousness. But she knew she was holding on to Barney's hand, and she kept holding on even when the others arrived home and the doctor came and their hushed voices hovered about her.

'. . . concussion after blow on the head like that. Man ought to be strung up by his thumbs.' She didn't recognise this voice and assumed it must be the doctor, but was too sick and disorientated to open her eyes. '. . . take it further. It had to be her da, who else would have attacked a little lassie?' This was from Frank, and such was the distress in his voice Josie would have liked to be able to reassure him she was all right, but she must have lost consciousness again, because when she next came to she was being carried before being placed on something very soft.

At this juncture she was longing for the blackness to take her over again because the pain in her head was unbearable, and when oblivion came she sank into it gratefully, even as she thought, I must let go of Barney's hand, he can't stay here with me. But perversely her fingers tightened and as she went down and down into the waves of darkness, his voice was saying, 'Go to sleep, lass – aye, that's right. You'll feel better come morning.'

*   *   *

'You told me you'd set it all up.' Patrick Duffy was speaking through gritted teeth as he hobbled through the back streets, the burned flesh on his legs making every step agony.

'I did, man, I did. Look, I told you—'

'Oh aye, you told me all right.' There followed a spate of cursing that brought white flecks of spittle to the corners of Patrick's mouth, and only ceased when they came to the horse and cart they had left tied up in the back yard of an inn some streets away.

'You take the reins.'

Bart did as he was told; Patrick's hands were blistered and the blackened skin was hanging in strips in some places where he'd tried to beat out his burning trousers in the first panic-filled moments before Bart had been able to get to him and smother the flames with his coat. Bart was terrified. Duffy was not known for his magnanimity at the best of times, and this definitely was *not* the best of times.

'Patrick, man, I'll sort it—'

'*Shut your gob.*'

Bart glanced at the small man hunched on the hard wooden seat beside him. His thin sour face was grey with pain, and even in the darkness the enmity shooting from the two black jets that were his eyes was chilling. Bart knew he had to make this right somehow. By all that was holy he had to make this right, but how? He sucked in a lungful of icy cold air, sweat born of terror making his armpits damp beneath his layers of clothing.

As the old nag clip-clopped on towards Gateshead the silence was only broken now and again by a groan from Patrick as the pot-holes in the rough roads caused the cart to bounce and rock, and with each exclamation Bart's dread increased.

Bart took the same road on which they had travelled into Newcastle, a route which skirted the main town of Gateshead. The road was dark and lonely at times, the heaped snow either side of the banks and hedgerows and the ice beneath the horse's hooves making the going laborious. The plan had been to tie the children up with the rope they'd brought and gag them, hiding them under the old coal sacks in the back of the cart. This route had been ideal for its isolation. Now Bart wasn't so sure. He was well aware of the fisherman's gutting knife Patrick carried with him at all times, and having seen its sharp, vicious blade his flesh was twitching.

To his knowledge no one had ever dared lay a finger on Patrick, and he'd unwittingly been the means of something much worse. His own heartbeat was thumping in his ears and his throat was dry with terror. By, this damn ride seemed endless . . .

'You let on to that little baggage back there about me an' Doug in that do afore she skedaddled? Mentioned names, did ye?' Patrick's voice was oddly quiet, and Bart's terror increased.

'No, man, no, I swear it. You know me better'n that. If Shirl hadn't opened her big mouth 'bout Ada an' Dora the lass'd be none the wiser the day, an' I denied everythin' anyway.'

Patrick didn't speak for some seconds, and then he said with a change of voice, for his words now came almost friendly-sounding, 'An' you've never told Shirl anythin'?'

'I've told her nowt. What she thinks she knows hasn't come from me, an' Ada an' Dora knew better than to blab. I dare say Shirl put two an' two together, but she'd never let on.'

'She told that 'un back there.'

'*No*. I've told you – it wasn't like that!'

'So you say.'

They had passed Gateshead when Patrick spoke next, still in the friendly voice. 'Keep on this road instead of turnin' off. I've a bit of business to do in Washington afore we go back. Cut across the moor an' go on past Brandy Row an' Old Washington, all right?'

'Aye, just as you say, man.' Bart darted a quick glance at the little man but Patrick was staring straight ahead into the dark night. Bart had accompanied Patrick to the village of New Washington – half a mile north of Old Washington – once in the past, when the Irishman had had some business there. Bart had known better than to ask what had been afoot and Patrick hadn't told him, but the straggling village built for the colliery workers and holding rows of terraced houses, a few good shops, a Methodist chapel and the Bath Brick Works hadn't impressed him. However, Washington itself – where they were now headed – was larger than New Washington and Old Washington, and he'd feel a mite more comfortable there than on this lonely road. He'd buy Patrick a few drinks and perhaps they could get his burns seen to before they carried on to Sunderland? Whatever he had to do to make this right he would.

Nothing more was said until they had ridden right into the town, past the school and then the rectory, until they reached the Cross Keys public house opposite the smithy. Then Patrick said, 'Wait here a minute.'

'Why don't I come inside with you?' Bart had jumped down from the cart in order to assist Patrick to dismount, but the other man ignored his outstretched hand. Bart heard him gasp as he lowered himself to the ground. Patrick was in a lot of pain, that much was obvious, and the knowledge was turning Bart's bowels to water.

Patrick looked at him for a moment and his face was grim, but when he spoke he merely repeated his previous words. 'Wait here a minute.'

Bart waited. Indeed, he did not dare move from his place at the horse's side, but now his flesh was beginning to creep. He wished he was home. By, he wished he was home all right. The feeling he had on him took him back to the times when, as a bairn, he was waiting for his da to get back from the docks. Six foot, his da had been, big and burly and an out-and-out swine. The big man's favourite trick had been locking him in the large oak chest down in the cellar of the riverside house they'd rented. It had flooded regularly, that cellar, and apart from the terror of being buried alive, Bart had always been petrified he'd be forgotten down there and the flood waters would come before anyone remembered him. But it had been the waiting *before* the event that had regularly made him mess his trousers.

By the time Patrick re-emerged with two other men, a full half an hour had passed. Patrick smelled of whisky but the alcohol obviously hadn't dulled the effects of the flames as the small Irishman was moving with painful stiffness. 'This is Wilf an' Lenny.' Patrick gestured at the small, gnome-like person with shifty eyes and a lump on the side of his neck like a bunion, and the other man who had a big scar down one side of his face. Bart nodded at them but they just stared back. 'I've some stuff to pick up while I'm here so we'll go down yonder' – Patrick indicated the road which led past the smithy and the graveyard of Holy Trinity Church – 'an' there should be some bits 'n' pieces waitin' in a spot by the old gravel pit. Wilf an' Lenny here'll load it on the wagon.'

Bart wanted to say that Wilf and Lenny weren't needed; that he could do any humping that was required, but with his broken arm it wasn't true and besides, he didn't dare. Instead he forced himself to speak in as natural a tone as he could manage as he asked, 'Where you takin' the stuff?'

'Not far.' Patrick looked at him with his soulless eyes. 'We'll walk; you lead the horse an' keep it quiet – there's the polis house over the way.'

Bart glanced at the police station which was situated next to the Cross Keys public house. For the first time in his life the law represented safety, but there was no way he could break away from the three men and reach the small brick house without being overpowered. Dear God, dear God. He repeated the blasphemy over and over in his mind as he led the way past the newly extended church with its recently raised roof on his right and what looked to be a sandpit on his left, whereupon the road narrowed into a thin dark lane with buildings belonging to the gravel pit some way in front of them. Once they were past the pumping station it was very dark and very quiet, the only sound coming from the horse's hooves as it clip-clopped along the side of the old gravel pit, a row of trees on the right of the road standing stark and bare against the harsh night sky.

'Where . . . where do you want me to . . . to stop?' Bart was stammering but he couldn't help it. Patrick might be a skinny little runt of a man but that knife made two of him, and although Wilf was small the other one, Lenny, was built like a bull. He should've followed Patrick into the pub and stayed there, or even nipped across to the police house. But he couldn't have done that, he argued with himself as he led the horse and cart along the frozen track leading off the lane, after Patrick called for him to turn left. Now there were windswept white fields on the one side and the black cavernous hole of the pit on the other. No, he couldn't have done that. What could he have said?

And maybe he was imagining things here. Was afeared over nothing.

'Round here's about right.'

As Patrick's voice brought everyone to a halt Bart turned, saying nervously, 'You want me to help 'em load, Patrick? Where's the stuff hidden?' He faced the three men standing looking at him from a distance of a few feet away.

Patrick did not answer this, but what he did say was, and quietly, 'How long have you known me, Bart?'

'How long?' He had to wet his lips before he could say, 'Nigh on eight or nine years, maybe longer.'

Patrick nodded. Producing a small leather whisky flask from his pocket and taking several gulps he replaced the stopper and shoved it back inside his coat. 'An' would you say I'm a stupid man, Bart, or careless? Eh? Would you say that?'

The big fellow, Lenny, had moved round the far side of the horse and cart while Patrick had been speaking, and now Bart was effectively closed in by Lenny, the horse and cart, and Patrick and Wilf on the one side, and the abyss which was the gravel pit on the other. 'Patrick, man . . .' It was a whimper. 'Look, I said I'd make it right. Anythin' you want, anythin'.'

'You've put me to a lot of trouble, Bart. You've taken my money an' not delivered, an' as for tonight . . .'

'I'll pay you back, man, you know that, *an'* I'll get the bairns, both of 'em – all reet?'

'That 'un back there'll open her gob after tonight, you know that, don't you? You'll have a visit from the law come mornin', sure as eggs are eggs, an' what are you goin' to say when they ask you about me, eh?'

'Nowt, I swear it.'

'Nowt.' Patrick turned to the little fellow with the lump

104

as he repeated again, 'Nowt. Now from his own mouth the lass an' her mam know nothin' concrete about me, Wilf. Nothin' they can prove, leastways.' He laughed out loud, along with Wilf, and Bart forced a weak smile. 'As I see it,' Patrick went on, 'the only one who does is our Bart here. An' folk get jittery in a cell in the polis house. You ever noticed that, Wilf?'

'Oh aye.' Wilf was still grinning widely, clearly enjoying himself. 'Many's the time I've seen it. Aye, I'll grant ye that all reet, Patrick, man. I divvent know many as don't. What say you, Lenny?'

There was just a grunt from the big figure behind Bart, but Patrick obviously took it for agreement, saying, 'So we all see eye to eye. A feller's entitled to protect his best interests, eh, Bart? I'd be daft to do different, an' we've already agreed I'm not daft. An', of course, there's the little matter of this.' He held up his hands, the palms and fingers raw and blistered and bleeding in places, for Bart's eyes to inspect. 'It'll be a while afore these an' me legs let me forget this night's happenin's. Yes, I deserve payment for this.'

Patrick made a sharp movement with his head, and before Bart could react he was grabbed from behind by a pair of massive meaty hands which pinned his arms to his sides as he was lifted right off the ground and held close to Lenny's huge torso.

The same blind terror which had gripped the boy Bart now caused the man to lose control of his bladder. He tried to wrap his flailing legs round a stunted tree at the side of the cliff-like wall of the gravel pit but to no avail, and then Patrick and the little man were standing close.

'Scared, Bart?' Patrick gave a quiet, mirthless laugh. 'You should be. These two know how to make it last a long, long time, an' I'm goin' to let them have their fun tonight, the way me body's painin' me.' He took out his knife, and again he made the mirthless sound before he said, his voice even quieter but his words terrible-sounding to the petrified man, 'You'll be beggin' me to finish you off with this afore they're done, I promise you. An' don't worry about what you owe me, Bart. Those two lads of yours are brighter than you'll ever be, an' slippery into the bargain. I shall take them under me wing when you go missin', out of the goodness of me heart like. They'll train up right dandy, they will.

'Gag him.' This was to Wilf who promptly obeyed, stuffing a filthy neckerchief in Bart's mouth before tying it in place with his muffler. 'An' move him over there a bit.' He gestured a few yards ahead. 'We don't want to frighten the horse, now do we?'

Chapter Six

'But someone must know *something*!'

A week and a half had elapsed since the attack on Josie. Barney's wedding was only three days away, but the main subject of conversation in the house in Spring Garden Lane was the same as it had been for the last eleven days – the disappearance of Josie's father.

Barney, in particular, was tireless in his desire to bring about Bart's arrest, and had travelled down to Sunderland three times in the days since that fateful night, harassing the police both in Sunderland and Newcastle and making a general nuisance of himself to those in authority.

Pearl had let it be known she was feeling distinctly neglected; Betty had taken it upon herself not to let Josie or Gertie out of her sight; Frank had begun to bolt both the front and back door every night – an unheard of occurrence – and Prudence had moved into lodgings the day after the attack when her part in the incident had come to light. She hadn't tried to deny her involvement when Frank and Barney had put two and two together. She admitted that she had purposely made contact with Bart Burns, but maintained he had tricked her by telling her a pack of lies. Prudence's absolute refusal to accept any blame for the subsequent events had made Barney see red, and the two of them had had a row which had rocked the house.

Prudence had left the next morning, white-faced but

dry-eyed, and with not a word to anyone as she carried her bags out of the house. Betty had since heard from Mrs Middleton – whose work as a midwife took her far and wide – that the girl was lodging in a house in Oxford Street which was just a stone's throw from the laundry.

Josie herself had felt considerably better about everything once she had emerged from the disturbing half-world into which the concussion had plunged her.

It had taken a few days for the effects of her harsh treatment at the hands of her father and Patrick Duffy to diminish, but even then she was still black and blue all over from her father's fist in her face and her fall when she had been flung aside at Barney's dramatic entrance into the hall. However, once her mind was her own again, Josie found she could cope with her physical state quite easily. Part of this was due to the overwhelming sense of relief she felt when a family conference a week after the attack decided her life at the laundry, should she return, wouldn't be worth living with Prudence now estranged from them all. Josie didn't let on to them that it hadn't been too good before.

According to what Pearl had relayed to Barney, Prudence was effectively blaming Josie for most of what had transpired and was wallowing in self-pity. At least, that was the way Barney had interpreted whatever Pearl had said to him, hence the family conference. 'You know Prudence has got a tongue on her at the best of times.' Barney's face had been grim. 'And Josie's been through enough lately. She's not going back to the laundry for Prudence to make her life hell. And my dear sister is quite capable of doing that, as you well know.' No one had argued with him and so that had been that.

Josie had made it plain she would look for work elsewhere as soon as she was fit, but for the moment the doctor had been quite explicit in his stipulation that his young patient must rest until he saw her again, which would be the Monday after Barney's wedding. As Betty was determined to follow the doctor's decree to the letter, there was nothing Josie could do but accept her enforced inactivity with good grace.

'Most people'd be glad of the chance to sit with their feet up and be waited on,' Barney had teased her on the night of the family conference once Frank and Betty had gone to bed, Frank being on the early shift at the pit. They were sitting by the kitchen range and Josie was warming her toes on the brass fender, having slipped off her heavy black boots. Barney had just made a pot of tea and with all the rest of the household in bed and only the light from a small flickering oil lamp and the rosy glow from the range to light the room, the effect was cosy. 'But Betty tells me you've been trying to do this and that all day. Ants in her pants, Betty described it.'

Josie had pulled a wry face. For the first time in her life she had time on her hands and she had found she didn't like the experience one bit. If Betty had let her help with the bairns or even do a bit of washing or cleaning it would have been different, but just to sit around all day . . . She couldn't bear it. From being so tired she was asleep as soon as her head touched the pillow, she was now lying awake most of the night, listening to the others breathing! 'I shall be glad when I've seen the doctor on Monday and can go back to normal,' she admitted quietly.

'Bored?'

'Oh aye.' It was said with feeling.

'Not ready for bed?'

'No.'

'Fancy a chat?'

They had talked till gone one in the morning and when

they'd realised what the time was, neither of them had been able to believe it was so late. Josie had found herself telling Barney all sorts of things she'd never revealed to anyone else; the misery and shame of her beginnings when she'd been forced to beg just to survive; her father's brutality to them all and the times she could recall her mother being black and blue after one of his drunken bouts; her worry about the lads and the road her father was setting them on . . . And he, in his turn, had spoken of the horror which had gripped him the first time he had gone underground, the feeling that he was buried alive and the silent screaming in his head which had filled his ears with a deafening sound until he hadn't known who he was or how to breathe.

It had been good that night, very good, Josie reflected now as she watched Barney frowning at the constable who had called to tell them the latest progress in the case. With her father apparently having vanished from the face of the earth, and Jimmy and Hubert following in his footsteps two days after the attack on Josie – something which made Josie and her mother, along with Vera and others in the know confident that Bart had spirited the lads away to quieter shores until the furore had died down – Vera had insisted that Shirley move into the house in Northumberland Place for the time being, and had arranged for the family's meagre collection of furniture to be stored with a friend of hers.

Consequently, and for the first time since arriving in Newcastle, Josie's mind was at peace about her mother's well-being, and this had affected her whole attitude towards the attack.

Not so Barney. And it was Barney who now repeated, his voice urgent as he stared into the patient face of the middle-aged policeman, 'Surely *someone* knows something? I just don't believe two men and two lads can disappear so completely without someone seeing them or knowing where they are hiding. Josie's father is well known in the East End, like this Duffy bloke. It's one thing for Josie's brothers to drop out of sight – one bairn is much like another – but not so the two men. Not from what Josie's told me about them, anyway. And don't forget I was here that night they had a go at the lass, and nasty isn't the word for 'em. They can't be allowed to get away with it. Someone knows where they are; I'd bet my life on it.'

'If they do, they're not saying, lad.' The constable forbore to mention that with Patrick Duffy's name featuring in this incident, he hadn't expected anything else, from what his colleagues in Sunderland had known about the Irishman in question. Big fish in a little pond, had been the general comment, but a fish with sharp teeth and a long memory. True, the lass had never actually seen Duffy's face – only her da's – but she'd been adamant the other man involved in the skirmish had been Patrick Duffy. That being the case, all tracks would have been well and truly covered, and although the mention of that particular name had taken the incident beyond one of a normal domestic fracas, it had also immediately presented a new set of problems.

'I don't believe this.' Barney sat back in his chair, his good-looking face set in a scowl of frustration. 'Her da tried to kidnap her, for cryin' out loud, and the man's violent as well as everything else! You know what he did to her sisters.'

'We know what Miss Burns *told* us he did to her sisters,' the constable corrected gently, and as Barney reared up in his seat and opened his mouth, the policeman continued, 'And I'm not saying we don't believe this young lady, far from it, but believing is no good without proof, Mr Robson. Even the young lady's mother hasn't got that.

And as for this other . . . gentleman, Mr Duffy, being involved, there are any number of folk who can confirm that he spent all that night in a certain public house in the East End of Sunderland, before retiring with a Mr and Mrs Gibson to their house in Bishopwearmouth, the latter being his sister, apparently.'

'It was Patrick Duffy who helped my father, Constable Skelton.' Josie spoke from her seat on the settle which had been pulled close to the glowing fire. 'I didn't have to see him to know that. The smell of him, his voice . . .' She shuddered. 'It was him all right, and you've Barney's description to go on too.'

'It was dark in the hallway and the lamp had been kicked over, Miss Burns,' the constable said quietly, his voice reflecting his dislike of what he had to point out. 'Mr Robson said the gentleman in question was of a small build and wiry, from the glimpse he had of him once he had dealt with your father. Half the men of Newcastle meet that description, I'm afraid. Mr and Mrs Gibson and several other folk insist Mr Duffy was with them all evening. According to Mrs Gibson, the next morning her brother left for urgent business Hartlepool way, but she has no specific address we can contact him at.'

'How convenient.' This was from Barney and it was bitter. 'And I suppose Josie's father accompanied him on this "business"?'

'Not to our knowledge, but that could well be the case.'

Barney now closed his eyes and bowed his head, shaking it slowly from side to side three or four times before he said, 'And I thought the law was supposed to protect the innocent! Well, you live an' learn as they say.' He raised his head and looked into the policeman's stolid face. 'The pair of 'em will get away with this, that's what you're

112

saying at heart, isn't it? Well, all I can say is that if Bart Burns or this other feller are found in a dark alley one night with bootmarks all over them, don't be surprised.'

'I'll pretend I didn't hear that, Mr Robson.' The policeman's face had lost its understanding look and had become stiff. He now rose to his feet, nodding at Betty who was sitting next to Josie on the settle. 'Thank you for the tea, Mrs Robson,' and to Frank in his armchair, 'Good night, Mr Robson,' and then, his gaze mellowing, he bent down to Josie and said quietly, 'Don't you worry now, lass. They won't try this again, not now they know we're on to 'em. You'll be quite safe.'

Josie smiled at the policeman but said nothing. He meant well, but she had lived in the East End for twelve years and was well aware there were two worlds outside the four walls of this house. One was the normal, day-to-day existence that Betty and Frank and people like them enjoyed, and the other was the subterranean world of the likes of Duffy and her da. That world lived by its own rules. She agreed with Barney on this; her da and Patrick Duffy would get away with trying to snatch Gertie and herself because they were more cunning than this kind-faced man in front of her and others like him.

But she'd been warned now, and she would be on her guard. She'd already got Betty to make her up a little bag of pepper that she intended to carry with her everywhere. One or two of the painted dock dollies who had frequented the pubs she'd sung in in Sunderland had used pepper thrown in a violent customer's face for protection and it was lethal stuff. And she would keep the poker close to hand too when she could. Gertie was being taken to and from school by an ever-vigilant Betty, and Frank was forgoing his usual pint with his cronies in the Singing Fox and not budging from the house once he was home from the pit. And Barney . . . Barney was just kindness itself.

As Betty showed the policeman out, Josie let her mind wander. Barney had arrived home the night before with a magazine called *The People's Friend* for her and a bag of whipped cream bon-bons. It wasn't the first time since the attack he'd done something similar. They'd talked till way into the night again – they'd had some right good cracks over the last ten days when it was just the two of them. She had known Barney was nice before, and he had always made her laugh on the journey to and from the laundry, but Prudence had been with them then. Somehow, over the last little while, she felt she'd seen a side to him no one else had. But then she was probably just being silly, she warned herself quickly. He'd be the same with Pearl, of course he would – caring, kind, funny and warm. It was just because of the attack that he was being extra nice now; sitting up late with her when he knew she wasn't tired enough to go to bed.

Anyway, there was nothing in his manner to suggest he saw her as anything but a bairn, even if they had become such good friends recently. And come Saturday he would be Pearl's . . . Josie's large, heavily lashed eyes darkened and she watched Barney's face as he talked with his father. He'd be Pearl's; they'd be man and wife and committed to spending the rest of their lives together.

Pearl had come to visit her when she'd still been confined to bed and Josie had to admit she'd found the visit a strain. The other girl had been effusive in her condolences, and she'd brought a bottle of her mother's special cherry-flavoured tonic – 'to build you up, you poor little thing' – but the smile on the bow-shaped mouth hadn't reached the pale-blue eyes. And she didn't know if she was imagining it, Josie reflected, but there had been a couple of things Pearl had said, or perhaps it wasn't the words she'd used exactly but a certain inflexion in her voice, that had suggested Pearl considered she ought to be up and about and back to normal.

But Pearl was bonny. Oh aye, she was bonny all right, and she'd been beautifully dressed, right down to her brown kid boots which had been of fine quality. Finer than any Josie had seen before anyway.

Perhaps Pearl disliked her because Barney had been so involved in trying to find Patrick Duffy and her da in the lead-up to the wedding? Or maybe it was because Pearl thought Josie was the cause of Prudence leaving the household? She understood from Betty that the two girls had been close friends since they were bairns. Josie suddenly realised where her thoughts were taking her. She'd had the feeling that Barney's fiancée didn't like her, but now she allowed the thought free rein she knew it was true.

All the time Pearl had been in the house in Spring Garden Lane she had acted as though she was a cut above the rest of them; Josie had understood why Betty's private nickname for her stepson's future wife was 'Duchess' once she'd met Pearl. And Pearl's parents had really gone to town with the wedding; closing the pub for the night and hiring fiddlers and a melodeon player and all sorts. It would be a grand do.

Josie shrugged off the mood of depression which had accompanied these thoughts, irritated with herself for feeling that way. She glanced across again at Barney and his father, her eyes resting on the younger man's strong, springy brown hair and wholesome young face, and then, as Betty bustled back into the kitchen bewailing the fact that it was snowing again, Josie picked up the darning she had been attending to when the policeman had called.

*　　*　　*

He was wed.

As Josie entered the warmth of the inn which was redolent with rich smells from the kitchen, her head was high and she was holding on tight to the twins' hands. Martin and Kenneth had already disgraced themselves that day by putting a frog down little Freda's neck halfway through the church service. The resulting pandemonium had caused Mrs Harper to ask for smelling salts and Pearl to look as though she'd like to do murder. But all Josie could think of was that now Barney and Pearl were wed. And Pearl looked bonny, so bonny in the white satin dress and lacy veil, the tight-laced waist showing off her full breasts beneath their glossy covering. Josie looked down at her own small burgeoning breasts which didn't even swell the material of her smart coat, and her mouth drooped, only to lift almost instantly as she heard her mam's voice somewhere behind her in the throng spilling into the inn.

It had been a lovely surprise, Vera bringing her mam with her today. And even though her mam looked white and peaky, and Vera had said she'd been having a mustard poultice on her chest each morning and inhaling eucalyptus oil for the cough that was with her night and day, she seemed happier than Josie had ever seen her. Which wasn't surprising in the circumstances. The relief of not having Bart around had been evident in her mother's eyes when they had hugged each other earlier, and her mam had said how good Vera and Horace were to her.

Her thoughts roamed on as she pushed the twins down on to a long bench at the side of the room and warned them to sit still, before raising her hand in greeting to Vera and her mam and the others who had entered the inn in a small group. She couldn't wait to look for a new job; she would do so as soon as she had seen the doctor on Monday. She hadn't paid Vera back for the clothes yet, and she owed Betty two weeks' board, and now there was her mother to think about too. She couldn't let Vera look after her mam for nothing. But how on earth was she going to do it all? Jobs were scarce, certainly for bit lasses – unless she went into service. Perhaps she'd have to do that, even though she hated the thought of it. She'd rather try Haggie Brothers at South Shore than go into service. They included lots of women and lasses among their hundreds of employees in rope- and wire-making, but Betty had been aghast when Josie had mentioned trying there. Haggie's Angels, as they were known locally, were notorious for their ripe language. However, Josie was sure she'd heard as bad in the pubs in the East End, and the thought of service – of having to bend the knee and bob the head to all and sundry – seemed worse than even Prudence and the laundry.

The thought of Barney's sister brought Josie's eyes across the room to where Prudence was standing with Pearl's parents – for all the world like royalty – and in the moment or two before Vera and Betty and all the others reached Josie's corner, Prudence turned her head and looked straight at her. It was an icy cold look, nasty; a look which spoke volumes all by itself. However, Josie had been expecting nothing less and she found herself returning the glare as she lifted her chin, hotly aware that Prudence had no jurisdiction over her now her days at the laundry were past. And it was Prudence who looked away first; sweeping her head round in a haughty gesture which didn't sit well with her small dumpy figure and nondescript appearance.

The large room at the back of the inn, originally a supper room but now used for general purposes, had been decorated for the bridal meal, and once everyone had walked through and seated themselves, the meal commenced amid much laughter and conversation. It was generally agreed Stanley and Marjorie had done their daughter proud. Chops, kidneys, poached eggs, welsh rarebits, mealy potatoes baked in their jackets, rabbit pie, faggots, pig's pudding, mussels and whelks . . . The mountain of food was enormous, and the jugs of beer on the tables were replenished as soon as they were emptied, along with those of lemonade for the bairns and teetotallers, although of the abstainers there was barely a handful.

As the afternoon progressed and the beer flowed, the laughing and shouting grew louder. Once the three fiddlers and the melodeon player had arrived, the tables were cleared and pulled back and the dancing began, Barney and his new wife taking the floor first and then other couples following their lead. Some of the older people who didn't want to dance, like Vera and her mam and Barney's parents, had wandered back into the first room where a roaring fire was blazing in the blackleaded range at one side of the long shiny wooden bar. Marjorie Harper and a woman who looked to be her sister were asking who wanted a cup of tea, and although Josie didn't want to remain in this room she did so. It was preferable to seeing Barney and Pearl wrapped in each other's arms. For some reason the sight was paining her.

She talked to her mother and Vera; kept Betty's brood under control; made sure Gertie was in a warm seat by the fire – her sister having been up all night with earache had been dosed with a diluted mixture of belladonna by Betty, and was sitting with a warm flannel pressed to the affected part – and generally made herself useful. She didn't, however, offer to help in the kitchen with the washing up, having seen Prudence ensconced in there with Pearl's mother and some other women, when she'd been on her way to the privy. In all the time she'd been staying with Betty, to her knowledge Prudence had never once washed any dishes, and yet she had been up to her elbows in suds for Pearl's mother.

Later that evening the tables were pushed into place again and a supper of sausages and mash with baked onions and turnips was served. Josie only nibbled at her portion; she was tired and could feel every one of the bruises she'd received a couple of weeks earlier, added to which her head was aching.

'Ee, lass, I canna remember when I've enjoyed meself so much.' Her mother's voice was soft at the side of her. 'An' the bairn looks better, don't you think?' she added, nodding across the table at Gertie who was busy tucking into her sausages and mash, the earache apparently having vanished.

Josie opened her mouth to agree but the words were never voiced. Her mother was overtaken by a paroxysm of coughing that seemed to go on and on, and when it had finished and she removed her handkerchief from her lips, the cloth was stained bright red in places.

'*Mam!*'

'It's nothin', me bairn, nothin'.' Shirley had tried to secrete the handkerchief away before Josie had seen it, and now she stuffed it quickly into her pocket, adding, 'I've had a bit of phlegm on me chest, that's all, but it's movin' now. I'll be as right as rain come next week. An' I live the life of Lady Muck at Vera's; aye, I do that. Won't let me lift a finger, bless her, so don't you go worryin' your head about a bit cough, now then. You've more than enough on your plate. Where you thinkin' of tryin' for work, hinny?'

Only partially reassured, Josie told her mother about Haggie Brothers, mentioning Betty's objection in a low undertone. Her mother raised worldly eyebrows. 'Well, lass, all I can say is that I've heard what you call bad language an' it's bin like "God bless you" at heart, an' other times them as wouldn't soil their lips with a "damnation" can make your flesh creep with a "good mornin' "'.'

Josie nodded. She knew exactly what her mother meant. Prudence was mealy-mouthed in the extreme.

It was a full hour later when Josie, focused on taking Freda to the privy before the little girl wet herself for the umpteenth time that day, bumped into Prudence just as she stepped into the pub yard. The moon was high, its white light gleaming on the frost-covered cobbles, and over the gabled windows of the pub translucent icicles had formed, tapering to sharp frozen points. It was a bitterly cold night, but as Josie looked into Prudence's narrowed gaze, the temperature dropped even further.

Josie was conscious of the muted din from within the pub, Freda hopping from foot to foot at the side of her and the sound of a tram clanking along outside the yard somewhere on Barrack Road, but for now she was taken up with the resentment staring out of the muddy green eyes in front of her. Prudence made a small inarticulate sound low in her throat before she hissed, 'You! Acting as though butter wouldn't melt in your mouth all day!'

Josie's eyes grew larger for a second as she gazed back into the angry face, and then she pulled herself together and said crisply, 'Freda needs the privy. Excuse me.' For a moment she thought Prudence was going to continue to block her way, but then the older girl moved aside, her eyes not leaving Josie's face for a moment, and Josie hurried the squirming Freda into the dark dank little box across the yard.

She wasn't surprised to see Prudence waiting for her when she and Freda emerged, and after urging the little girl to go and find her mother she opened the back door for her before turning to face Prudence again. 'What do you want?' she asked calmly and steadily.

Josie could tell her manner had both astonished and disconcerted the young woman in front of her. Barney's sister had probably expected her to shy away from any confrontation, but now Prudence no longer dwelt at the house in Spring Garden Lane and Josie had finished with the laundry for good, she saw no reason to try to humour the other girl.

For her part Prudence was experiencing acute irritation at the sound of Josie's voice. She'd noticed this before, Josie's ability to control and modulate her voice, and it had never rankled so much as now. This was just a young lass of twelve or thirteen and from what she'd heard, Josie had never had the benefit of much of an education. How *dared* she act as though she was somebody?

The two girls stared at each other for a moment, and then Prudence's voice was bitter when she said, 'You think you've got them all in the palm of your hand, don't you? All that fuss because your da came to take you home which is where you should be in the first place. If you'd just agreed to go quietly back with him that would've been an end to the matter but no, not you. Madam Burns has to go and upset everybody. And now Barney's fallen out with me and it's all your fault.'

Josie looked into the plain fat face and wondered if Prudence was really so deluded that she didn't know what she had done. But then what did Prudence know of the likes of Patrick Duffy and his kind? She'd been brought up in a decent family surrounded by good honest folk. Prudence might spout on about social reform and all the other things she had a bee in her bonnet about but really, Josie reflected, she'd lived in clover all her life compared to some of the poor wretches in Sunderland's East End.

'My da didn't come to take me home, Prudence,' Josie said coolly, her voice holding the barest quiver. 'Don't you even understand that? He's not like your da, he doesn't care about me or any of us. He would have done the same to Gertie as he did to my other sisters, and he's angry with me because I stopped him. His only intention in coming to Newcastle and bringing that other man with him was to harm us.'

'Huh!' Prudence glared into the beautiful face in front of her, her thin nostrils flaring. 'So says you. Well, I don't believe you, see? You might have got Aunt Vera to swallow your story along with the rest of them, but not me. No da would do what you said yours had done to his own bairns. If your sisters went down that road they likely decided to do it themselves.'

'That's not true.' Josie knew Betty had told her step-children the full facts relating to Josie and Gertie's sudden arrival on their doorstep. Prudence was seeing only what she wanted to see, likely as much to assuage her secret guilt at how things had turned out as anything. And she must be missing Barney more than a little.

And then any faint stirrings of sympathy went flying out of the window when Prudence took a step towards her and hissed, 'It *is* true! Your sisters are scum, you're scum, the whole lot of you. And your mam is an' all. Sponging off Aunt Vera now, isn't she?'

Josie fought to gain control of herself. She wanted to smack the other girl's face and shout at her that her mam was the best person in the world, but somehow she knew that was exactly what Prudence expected her to do. And then Barney's sister would have won. Well, she wouldn't give Prudence the satisfaction of seeing how much her spiteful words had hurt her. 'What a truly stupid person you are, Prudence,' she said shakily, and then – quite unwittingly and only because she'd been searching for something to say so Prudence wouldn't have the last word

– Josie hit upon the secret fear which had been eating away at the other girl for months. 'My mam is staying with Vera because Vera wants her,' she said emphatically. 'They're friends, real friends – but you can't understand that, can you? The only people who have ever bothered with you are Barney and Pearl, and now they're married they won't want you tagging along any more.'

She had turned on her heel and opened the door to the pub before Prudence could respond, banging it behind her as she marched through into the small narrow hall which led to the supper room.

Prudence stood quite still where Josie had left her, the angry colour in her cheeks draining away and leaving her sallow skin an even more unattractive colour. She didn't know she was twisting her hands together, over and over, until the rubbing of her skin became painful, and then she forced herself to stop, staring up into the breathtakingly cold sky for a full minute without moving. And then she turned, very deliberately, and looked towards the pub door. She had everything, Josie Burns. There wasn't a man alive who wouldn't want her when she was a bit older; even now they were drawn to her like bees round a honey pot. Look at her da, fussing over her like an old woman, and Barney was the same. She had thought Barney was her friend as well as her brother, but since that little chit had come into the house he had changed. The hot thoughts bit into her mind like drops of acid but she fought the inclination to cry, drawing great draughts of the icy air deep into her lungs as she listened to the sounds of merriment from within the building.

What would that chit say, what would any of them say, if they knew that the only thing she had ever wanted from when she'd been a small bairn was to be married and have bairns of her own? Laugh their heads off, most likely. The only little lass among four lads, you'd have thought her da would have made something of her, wouldn't you? But he never had. No, he never had. In fact, he had always acted as though he didn't like her, even before Betty came on the scene. But she'd known by then she was as plain as a pikestaff. Bairns were cruel and school could be a lonely, frightening place when no one wanted to be your partner for the walk round the playground before prayers in the morning. Porker Prudence, one of the more imaginative wits had called her in her first week of school, and the rest of them had taken it up immediately, thinking it a great joke, and she'd been Porker until the day she left.

Her eyes were burningly dry now, the subtle torture of those far-off days very real again. Pearl had come to the school six months after she'd first started when her mam and da had bought the pub at the end of their street, and perhaps because everyone else had got their own particular pal by then, Pearl hadn't rebuffed Prudence's tentative overtures of friendship. And of course the lads had always made much of Pearl; she'd been a pretty little lassie even at five years of age. And so she had had her friend at last; someone to whisper and giggle and play with, and with Barney to talk to, she shouldn't have had to continue to fight against the loneliness which constantly assailed her, should she? But she had. All her life she had. And now the only two people to show her friendship were married, which made everything different. Josie's parting shot burned in her mind and it was another minute or two before Prudence went into the house.

If Prudence had but known it, the confrontation had upset Josie as much as herself. Once Josie was back inside the warmth of the pub she realised she needed a few minutes to compose herself before she returned to her seat with the others.

Everyone seemed to be having a wonderful time. Josie glanced around the room at the flushed faces and wondered why she was feeling so low. It wasn't because of the altercation with Prudence, nasty though that had been. She had been feeling like this all day. It had started as a gradual thing, when she'd first woken up, and then intensified as the day had progressed. Strange, really, how another person's excitement and joy could make you feel just the opposite, but that's how it had been since she had first seen Barney at breakfast that morning.

He had been sitting in old but clean clothes – his wedding suit and polished boots hanging in splendid isolation in the scullery with a starched darned sheet draped over them – and he had smiled at her as she'd come into the kitchen. 'Last meal of freedom.' His smile had widened as he'd spoken.

'You don't seem as if you mind,' she'd answered lightly.

'Too late now if he does.' Betty had bustled her way from the oven with a steaming dish of baked buttered herrings and a round of stottie cake cooked fresh that morning, and to the twins' oohs of delight she'd said, 'Special weddin' meal in honour of your brother, all right? I don't expect we'll be eatin' very early what with the service an' all.'

Barney had hummed his way through his breakfast and, having risen to go upstairs, had ruffled Josie's hair as he'd passed, saying, 'Now don't forget, you're not to be a stranger to our door, you an' Gertie.' Josie had smiled but said nothing, and he'd continued on his way humming 'Blaydon Races', which coincidentally was the song the fiddlers were playing at the moment. One of Barney's friends was singing very loudly and rather tunelessly in the middle of the room, finishing to a round of enthusiastic clapping. Thus encouraged he went on to perform 'Champagne Charlie' with an imaginary cane and eyeglass, and then 'The Daring Young Man on the Flying Trapeze', before making way for a small child with golden ringlets. After she had finished reciting a short but heartrending poem about a sailor lost at sea and his last thoughts of his wife and family before he sank under the waves, again concluding to a round of loud applause, the cry went up for more turns.

. 'Come on now, don't be shy!' As fresh jugs of foaming beer were brought in, Stanley's voice was hearty. 'It's a grand night for a bit carry on, eh, Marj?' He accompanied the last words with a nod and a wink at his spouse, and the icy look his good lady wife sent his way sobered him up quicker than a bucketful of cold water, much to the amusement of most of the men present.

Whether it was the fact that something of an awkward pause in the merriment had occurred, or because Josie was still smarting from the exchange with Prudence, or because she wanted to sing for her mother and bring a smile to her face, or simply that she had missed her singing more than she'd realised up to that moment, Josie wasn't sure. But somehow she found herself squeezing past one of the tables into the middle of the room and looking shyly at Barney's new father-in-law as she said, 'I can sing a song, Mr Harper.'

'Is that so, lass?' Stanley Harper recognised the slim lassie in front of him as the one who had supposedly caused all the trouble at Prudence's house, but she looked a bonny little thing to him. And he didn't want the evening to finish like a damp squib. 'Well, you just go straight ahead then, eh? What are you goin' to sing?'

Josie turned to the fiddlers who were taking the opportunity to drain their tankards. 'Do you know "Masks and Faces"?' she asked. The song about a virtuous maiden which Jenny Hill had made popular years before was one of her favourites and had always gone down well in Sunderland. Josie was quite unaware that part of the appeal was her own fresh innocence and beauty which made the song all the more poignant.

As the fiddlers struck up the first few bars, Prudence's caustic words about her mother were burning in Josie's head. Calling her mam a sponger and saying that they were all scum! Josie's small chin raised itself higher. Well, they might not have a lot of money but she would make sure she paid Vera and Betty every single penny due to them, oh aye, she would. And she'd show Prudence the night! She'd sing like she'd never sung before. Her da might be no better than he should be, but that wasn't her fault or her mam's, and her mam couldn't help being poorly all the time either. Prudence was horrible, she was.

Her head was so full that she missed her cue to sing, and as the fiddlers began again and Josie's cheeks reddened, she happened to catch sight of Prudence who was now standing leaning against the wall on the far side of the room. The other girl was smirking nastily, and nothing could have sent the adrenalin pumping more. She'd show her, she would.

And she did.

Barney was sitting with his new wife on one side and his in-laws on the other when Josie began to sing, and as the room went quiet – much the same as it had that night five years ago in the Mariners' Arms on Custom House Quay – he found he was holding his breath. He couldn't believe that the voice pouring forth out of the small frame was from the young lass he'd got to know so well lately. In one of their late-night talks she'd mentioned she'd sung in a few of the pubs in Sunderland, but this . . . This wasn't just singing, this was . . . His mind struggled to find words to match his emotion and failed. He glanced dazedly about the room for a second and saw the same wonder on other faces. She'd captured them all and was holding them entranced. *What a voice!*

'By, lad.' His father-in-law leaned across, his voice reflecting his surprise. 'She's a show-stopper, all right. You know she'd got a voice on her?'

Barney shook his head. 'No, not till now.'

'Look at our Ernest, he was near nodding off a minute ago.'

Barney glanced across the room to where Stanley's brother was sitting, and saw the small man, who managed Ginnett's Amphitheatre in Northumberland Road, straining forward in his seat, his eyes riveted on the small figure in the middle of the room.

'Don't be surprised if he wants to book her in for a few nights,' Stanley continued. 'He was saying just the other day they need a bit of new blood, and he'd pay well. Gets some canny acts, does old Ernest, and many a one has gone on to make a name for themselves.'

'Book her in?' Barney was talking to Stanley but his eyes were fixed on Josie. 'She's just a little lassie.'

'Thirteen in January according to your Betty,' Stanley answered. 'She won't be a bairn much longer.'

Barney drew in a long, deep breath. There was a vague feeling in the pit of his stomach that he couldn't place, similar to the sensation he'd had at school when he knew he'd missed something vital in one of the examinations old Walton used to love to set them. His brow wrinkled in bewilderment. But nothing was wrong, this was his wedding day, for crying out loud, and it had been a grand day. Grand.

Nevertheless, when Pearl stirred at the side of him and her voice came, tight and scratchy, saying, 'Forward little piece, isn't she! I can see what Prudence means now,' his own was uncharacteristically harsh as he replied, 'Prudence doesn't know what she's talking about,' and not at all as one would expect an ardent groom to address his radiant bride on their wedding day.

Barney was instantly contrite, turning quickly to face Pearl and taking her smooth hands in his as he said quietly, 'I'm the luckiest man alive. You know that, don't you? There's not one here today who wouldn't step into my shoes, given half a chance.'

'Oh, you.' Mollified, Pearl smiled sweetly.

'How much longer do we have to stay?' Barney murmured. 'I want to have you all to myself.'

'Silly.' Pearl extracted her hands from his, stretching out the left one in order to admire the rose-gold wedding band nestling next to the garnet and pearl engagement ring. 'We've got years and years together.'

She was quite aware of what Barney had meant, however, and felt a moment's sharp irritation that he had to bring *that* up now, at their wedding feast when she was having such a lovely time. All through their courtship Barney had wanted to fondle and touch her; men were such *base* creatures. Her mam had told her she had to set the tone regarding the physical side of married life right from the start, and she intended to. She wasn't quite sure exactly what was involved, but her mother had said it wasn't pleasant but had to be endured – within moderation, that was.

That being the case, she was in no rush for this special day to be over. She'd looked forward to it for so long:

wearing her beautiful dress and veil and looking like a princess; walking down the aisle and hearing everyone gasp in admiration; all their friends and family coming back here and making a fuss of her, and all the lovely presents for her dear little house which she'd got just the way she wanted it . . .

And she was going to sort Barney out. She wasn't going to have him working in the concrete factory much longer, not when Uncle Ernest had already made it plain he'd take him on. She didn't want a fellow who came home each night covered in dirt and filth and messed everything up, and everyone knew the music halls were where the money was. If they were successful, that was, and her Uncle Ernest's theatre was *very* successful. Barney could dress smartly when he liked and he looked good in a suit. Pearl slanted a glance at her new husband under her eyelashes. Yes, she'd make something of Barney all right, now he was out of that dreadful hole of a place in Spring Garden Lane. She had never once visited there without a mental shudder at the lack of cleanliness, and if she had her way they would cut the contact completely, especially now Prudence lived elsewhere.

Pearl's light opaque eyes travelled round the room until they rested briefly on Prudence's ample frame. Poor Prudence. There was no real sympathy in the thought, rather an underlying satisfaction as her gaze took in the squat body and unattractive face. She would never marry, of course, not looking like that. Pearl glanced down at her own slim tight figure in the clouds of satin. But unmarried women were always useful to have in a family. Someone you could call on at a moment's notice and know they would always be willing to help, whatever the chore. When the bairns came she could envisage Prudence living with them at some point, especially if everything went according to plan and Barney went up in the world. She'd like to be the kind of wife who had people round for dinner and that sort of thing, and Prudence could be . . . well, not exactly a servant, of course. Pearl paused reflectively. But someone who saw to the children and dealt with the mundane. Of course that wouldn't happen for years yet, but as her mother always said, it didn't hurt to plan for the future.

The sound of uproarious applause jolted Pearl out of her thoughts and brought her gaze on Josie, who was now blushing and smiling in the centre of the room. Pearl glanced round and saw that every eye was on the small figure; even her father was shouting for another song.

She bit her lip with vexation. This was *her* day, not that of this troublemaker who'd been thrust upon them. Personally she didn't know what the fuss was about. Anyone could open their mouth and sing a song, for goodness' sake. She slanted a glance at Barney, and saw he was clapping as hard as the rest, and although Pearl had brushed his attention away just a minute or so before and had wanted him to leave her alone, now, perversely, she felt extremely hard done by. Barney had neglected her enough for this chit!

'I want to dance again.' She stood up as she spoke, her voice high and sharp as she flicked at the table in front of her. 'Da, tell them to move these tables back so we can dance.'

'Aye, aye all right, lass. In a minute.'

'*Now.*'

Josie had to work her way through a crowd of folk who all wanted to say how well she had sung before she could reach her mother and Vera, who were now sitting on a long bench against the wall, their table having been one of the first to be taken away.

There was a small man sitting on the other side of Vera but Josie didn't pay him any attention as her mother said, immediately she saw her, 'Ee, hinny, that were grand, right grand. Brought to mind some of the sing-songs we had at home when your da was out. You remember, lass?'

'Aye, I remember, Mam.' Josie smiled at her mother's pleasure. She'd stand and sing all day long if it brought that look to her mam's face.

'An' now . . .' Shirley's voice was suddenly pensive, 'scattered here, there an' everywhere, the lot o' us. Mind, I'm not complainin', lass. Never had it so good as at Vera's. But me mind goes to the lads at times; whether your da is lookin' after 'em right.'

'Jimmy will take care of himself *and* Hubert, you know that, Mam. If anyone can handle Da, Jimmy can.' She didn't add that the reason for this was because her brother understood the way her father's mind worked, being so like him.

'Aye, you're right there, me bairn. By, you are. An' I dare say in a month or two the lot of 'em will turn up like bad pennies. Mind, your da'll get a gliff then, 'cos I'm not budgin' from Vera's.'

'Josie,' Vera cut in before Shirley could say any more, 'this is Mr Harper, an' he wants a word with you, lass. He's somethin' important to say.'

Josie smiled and said, 'How do you do?' to Mr Harper, but her mind was mainly on her mother's last words, along with the two figures on the dance-floor. The fiddlers had just begun to play a lively tune and Pearl had swept on to the floor with her new husband, smiling and nodding at everyone as they clapped the bridal pair.

'It's like this, lass.' Ernest Harper was not a man who wasted words. 'I'm looking for a fill-in for a couple of nights at Ginnett's, you know? Northumberland Road? I had a canny musical clown with a violin but he upped an' skedaddled south last week.'

'He did?' Josie didn't have a clue what Mr Harper was talking about.

'Aye. Now I've got a nice comedian who plays the bagpipes an' banjo an' a one-string fiddle an' goodness knows what, an' he has been doing extra an' standing in, but old Joey had got a right canny voice, an' that's what's needed. They like a tune, you see, an' I've only one other singer at present, although I've wizards an' ventriloquists an' acrobats coming out of me ears.'

In spite of herself Josie's eyes were drawn to the little man's ears which were long and pointed and stuck straight out at the side of his head. And then she took hold of herself, and said a little breathlessly, 'I don't quite understand. Are you offering me a chance to sing at your theatre, Mr Harper?'

'Just for a night or two, to see how it works,' Ernest Harper said quickly. He didn't want to commit himself too far – sometimes they got onstage and dried up worse than old Finley's backside; you never could tell. But – and here he nodded reflectively – he felt in his water this one was going to come up trumps. She'd had 'em in the palm of her hand when she'd sung just now; if she could do the same at the theatre . . . He felt the stir of excitement – the same feeling he'd had once or twice in the past when he'd come across an act that had something extra. 'But if you suit us an' we suit you . . .'

Josie stared at him, her head spinning. There was nothing she would like more than to accept this little man's offer; it was the sort of chance she'd been dreaming about for years, but since her mind had cleared over the last few days and she had learned that her father had skedaddled with the lads, the weight of her mother's welfare had settled even heavier on her shoulders. She needed to find work, steady regular work, and pay Betty and Vera what she owed them before she did anything else, and that would take months when you considered the ongoing debt of their board and lodging. The bill for the doctor hadn't been cheap either, she knew that, and she couldn't let Frank and Betty cover it. What's more, her mam couldn't stay with Vera for ever . . .

Her racing thoughts were cut short as Vera spoke again, saying, 'Obviously with the lass bein' so young her mam'll have a say in this. Can you give us a minute to talk it over?'

'Oh aye, aye. Aye, of course.' Ernest hid his disquiet at the thought that this particular prize might slip away from him, but what he said was, 'Mind, the best of 'em started young on the halls – mostly bairns, the lot of 'em. Look, I'll say a trial of seven nights, all right? An' we'll say two bob a night – that's more than I'd start many a one off, I tell you straight. You have a think with your mam, lass, an' I'll see you afore I go.' He bobbed his head at them all and moved away.

Had he said two shillings a night? Josie had bargained with too many shopkeepers and the like in her young life to let her amazement at what she considered a huge amount of money show, but two shillings a night! That was fourteen shillings for just singing seven evenings, and she still had the days free. The laundry had paid three shillings and tenpence for five and a half days of backbreaking work, and she knew she'd been lucky to get that. In some of the factories and shops hereabouts, bit lasses of her age were paid no more than two and sixpence a week on account of their age and sex, whilst being expected to do the same day's work as women three times their age. And a collier like Frank only earned double what Mr Harper had just offered her! Had she heard right?

'Fourteen shillings, Josie.' Vera's voice was hushed, and Shirley sat with her mouth agape staring at her amazing offspring. 'An' that's just for starters, lass. You've got to give it a go. Now look, don't worry about your mam. Me an' Shirl've already decided she's not leavin' whatever your da says when he turns up. I'm clearin' me front room an' your mam's havin' that, an' there'll be room for the lads if needs be.'

'Oh, Vera.' Josie reached over her mother and took Vera's hand. 'Not your lovely front room,' she protested. 'You don't have to, really. I'll sort something.'

'You can't say anythin' your mam hasn't said already, hinny, but me mind's made up. My Horace has never liked me front room anyway – says he don't dare breathe in it.' Vera grinned wryly. 'An' you're settled here now; our Bett says she don't know how she managed with the bairns an' mendin' an' all afore you come. Little godsend, she says you are. Gertie's doin' fine, too, aren't you, lass?' The little girl had just sidled up to them and this last was said bracingly; Gertie still didn't like her new school.

Josie looked into the rough square northern face in front of her but found she couldn't speak for the emotion filling her throat. She saw now why Vera had got Mr Harper to leave them for a while; her friend had known she was teetering on the brink of refusing his offer and the reasons for her hesitation. The love in Vera's eyes was shining out at her, and it was in answer to that that Josie said, 'I . . . I could give it a go for a week, couldn't I? I've lost nothing that way. And if it doesn't work out I can look for something else.'

'Aye, lass, you could.'

But she would make it work. As Josie looked at their

faces – her mam's, Vera's and Gertie's – they were all expressing different emotions. Her mam's expression was one of incredulity and a certain amount of bewilderment, Vera's, one of fierce pride and encouragement; and Gertie was simply trying to work out what was going on and what she had missed. As Josie stared at the three people she loved best in all the world, she knew she would make it work whatever it cost. This was her chance; this was what she had dreamed of ever since she had first started singing in the pubs as a wee bairn – to earn her living singing. True, in those days she had never set her sights further than the pubs and supper rooms, but why couldn't she aspire higher?

She could learn what to do – how to sing properly, to walk, what clothes to wear and everything – she wasn't stupid, but unless she put her toe in the water she'd never get started, would she? This was her chance, it was. Everything seemed to have conspired to bring her to this moment; even the nasty run-ins with her da and Patrick Duffy. She felt a moment's chill but shrugged the spectres aside; she wouldn't let her da and that other evil man ruin this moment.

She said the words out loud: 'I'll do it.' And then louder: 'I'll do it, I will.'

Shirley hadn't taken her eyes from Josie, and now she said very quietly, 'Lass, are you sure? I mean, a music hall? Some of them actress types an' singers are no better than they should be.'

Josie looked steadily at her mother. It was strange, but in this moment she felt years older than the woman who had given birth to her. Her mother had allowed her to go into some of the worst pubs in Sunderland from when she was little more than knee high in order to scratch them a decent going-on, and her father had brought men like

Patrick Duffy into their home and moreover started her brothers on a life of crime as soon as they were off the breast, and now her mother was questioning the morals of the performers in the music halls?

For a second she wanted to laugh, and then the well of pity which always accompanied her dealings with her mother made itself felt. She didn't understand her mam at times, and she would never comprehend how she could have stood by and let Ada and then Dora go down that road, but she was her mam and she loved her. 'I'm going to give it a go, Mam, and see what happens because I'd regret it the rest of my life if I didn't.'

'Well, if you're sure, hinny.'

'Aye, I am sure.'

And so it was settled.

Part 2
Ambition
1900

Chapter Seven

Josie smiled and curtsied as she stood listening to the tumultuous applause spilling over the gold radiance of the footlights, and not for the first time she reflected that the music hall was an enchanted place to its patrons. People just wanted to enter a warm world of magic and romance where their troubles were forgotten for a few hours, and who could blame them? She even managed to escape from the real world herself when she was onstage – or at least she usually did, she corrected herself in the next moment as the heavy velvet curtain swung across the stage and she heard the dapper Sidney Potts – in his role of chairman – begin his exposition to introduce the next act.

Josie moved gracefully into the wings of the theatre as the Amazing Lamphorcini Brothers passed her. They were a troupe of five Italian brothers who presented a skilful juggling and acrobatic knockabout comedy routine, including grotesque gymnastics and outrageous innuendo. The youngest of the brothers, a cheeky seventeen year old, winked at her as he caught her eye, and Josie smiled back at him absently.

She was so glad she was finishing at Hartlepool tonight. She needed to get back to Sunderland and see how her mam was. This wretched influenza. All that stuff they had written in the newspapers at the beginning of the year about inventions and suchlike, and yet no one knew how to fight the illness which was sweeping the country and ravaging its occupants. It had already taken old Maud and Enoch Tollett before Christmas.

The new century had been ushered in on the heels of a decade which many had glowingly described as one of unparalleled achievements. The spectacular discovery by the German physicist Wilhelm Roentgen of some kind of ray streaming out of gas-filled bottles when he passed electricity through them (which he'd called X-rays simply because X was the standard symbol for anything scientists didn't understand) had been hailed as miraculous.

Residents of Coney Island in America were the first folk to try a novelty ride called an escalator; a miracle drug – aspirin – which contained properties to reduce fevers and pain and came in the form of easy-to-take tablets was now available, and most exciting of all – and the hardest for Josie to comprehend – was the birth of radio communications which had been pioneered in Britain at about the same time as she had first set foot on a stage.

When Guglielmo Marconi was granted a patent which met with Royal approval and Queen Victoria herself communicated wirelessly from Osborne House with the Prince of Wales on board the Royal Yacht, the newspapers had been full of it, along with the news that Lord Kelvin had sent the first ever telegram by wireless.

Which was how it should be, Britain's inhabitants had declared patriotically. Didn't one in four of the world's population look to Britain as their ruler? The Empire was the greatest power on earth, and there was no doubt in anyone's mind that Britain ruled far-flung lands as well as the waves and that this would always be so.

However, as the influenza epidemic which had taken hold in December grew worse, there was less thought about the glory of the Empire and more about who was going to be the next to die in all the towns and cities of Britain. Fifty people a day were dying in London alone, and the illness which had been regarded as something of a fashionable malady when it had first occurred several years before, was now inspiring widespread panic and alarm. Gravediggers were working day and night all over the country, and due to a shortage of nurses and closure of some hospital wards, the situation was getting worse daily.

As with the dreaded typhoid and cholera, the influenza seemed to hit the old, infirm and very young most severely, and this was on Josie's mind as she walked down the thirty or so stone steps leading from the stage to the dressing rooms.

The room designated for the female performers was long and low, with whitewashed walls and one window. Gas jets gave feeble illumination, but overall it was dark and hot and smelly, two ventilators releasing draughts of unpleasant air. Apart from several wooden forms to sit on and a large wardrobe, the room was empty. An ancient stone sink stood in a corner. The dresser, a blowsy old woman with a permanent dewdrop at the end of her nose, used the sink solely for the purpose of keeping her grey hen – a large narrow-necked stone jar holding a vast quantity of beer – cool, and consequently there was always a pool of water skimming the floor where she'd had to remove it for a few minutes for performers to wash either before or after applying their stage make-up.

Since entering the brassy, rumbustious world of the music hall, Josie had appeared at numerous venues, from halls which were little more than the song and supper rooms which constituted the origins of the music halls, to theatres which had been purpose-built. Certain music halls, she had found, had personalities of their own, but by and large they were all much of a pattern. However, she'd never travelled further afield than some thirty or forty miles from Sunderland, simply because she always felt she must be within easy travelling distance of home, should she be needed. Josie knew her mother was ill, very ill, and wanted to be able to reach her within a couple of hours, should it be necessary.

The fact that this had severely restricted her choice of venues and undoubtedly held her career back had caused Josie some regret but no real dilemma. During the last four years she had been approached by numerous agents, most of whom had made extravagant promises that they would take her to top billing if she was prepared to put herself in their hands, but knowing this would mean travelling all over the country and undoubtedly working the London halls, she had refused them all.

And so, with Gertie by her side, she had done a few weeks here and a few weeks there all over the north-east, comforting herself with the knowledge that she was getting plenty of valuable experience and a good basic understanding of how things operated. Josie knew she was fortunate never to have been without work since she'd first started. Most weeks she would appear at two or occasionally three halls a night in the area in which she was working, earning a certain amount at each per week which added up to her final wage.

She could now command a fee of thirty shillings a week or more at any one hall, but her expenses were considerable. Board and lodging for herself and Gertie, carriages to whisk her from one venue to another several times a night, her costumes and make-up all took their toll, and she sent home regular payments to Vera for taking care of her mother, along with extra funds to cover her mother's doctors' bills and medication. Although Gertie was her dresser, in some of the halls the management would insist that the artistes contributed to the wage of the resident dresser, whether they availed themselves of her assistance or not, like this present one.

Gertie was waiting for her when she opened the door to the dressing room and as ever, amid all the chaos and bustle, her sister had contrived to secure a small corner where Josie's clothes were folded neatly and securely and her hat box and other possessions were in place. 'Here.' Gertie handed her a mug of hot, sweet tea. 'Drink this afore you do anything else, lass.'

Josie took the tea gratefully, remarking, as she did most nights, 'I don't know what I'd do without you, Gertie.'

From the moment Josie had put her hair up that first night she had stepped on to Ginnett's Amphitheatre's stage four years ago and received a hearty encore, she had no longer felt like a young girl, but a young woman. Sure enough, within the following eighteen months her figure had filled out, she had grown another few inches and now – at seventeen years of age – she had turned into a composed and very lovely young woman. Gertie, on the other hand, had barely changed at all, and at fifteen was still tiny. However, what she lacked in inches she had gained in confidence, and although her health was never particularly robust, Gertie had developed into a force to be reckoned with, Josie reflected fondly, as she gazed into the plain little face smiling at her.

'You tired, lass?' Gertie asked her and then, shaking her head at herself, she said, ''Course you're tired, hark at me! Dashing about like a blue-arsed fly seven days a week, it's no wonder. I wish you'd take a break for a few days.'

'I can't refuse bookings if they're there, lass. You know that.'

'Aye, but they'll always be there for you; folk know a good thing when they see it. There's another of them agent types been asking about you, by the way; old Aggie just told me. He was here earlier, apparently. I tell you, lass, if you let one of 'em look after you, you'd be making a mint in a little while. You're too good to kill yourself haring from one flea-pit to another.'

The sisters had had this same conversation a hundred times, and now Josie answered as she always did, 'There's Mam.'

Aye, there was Mam. Gertie's voice was brisk now as she said, 'Sit yourself down an' let's get that hat off.' Josie's stage clothes were elaborate and on the gaudy side, and not at all what she would wear outside. As Gertie moved behind her sister, carefully extracting the hat pins and lifting the concoction of lace and feathers off the golden-brown hair, the younger girl was frowning.

She'd been in this business nearly as long as Josie, having started travelling round with her sister as soon as she had finished at school, and one thing she knew was that you needed an agent. The music hall was a world within the world; it had its own managers, agents, scouts, touts, newspapers, slang, fashions, and no one – no one – got anywhere without an agent; they didn't even take you seriously for a start. Josie could be earning three, four times what she was on now, even playing the same halls if she had an agent behind her, but no – there was Mam.

'Stop frowning,' Josie said suddenly.

'How do you know I'm frowning?' Gertie asked, quickly straightening her face.

Josie swung round on the bench and stared up at her sister. 'I can feel it,' she said softly. 'And I'm not daft, lass. I know we need an agent but I'll get one when I'm ready. You know how bad Mam is; she . . . she could go any time.'

'We've been thinking that for the last two or three years,'

Gertie retorted, and then added quickly, 'Oh I'm sorry, lass, I don't mean that nasty, but it's true. Sometimes folk hold on for years an' years in Mam's state, an' you're missing opportunity after opportunity.'

This was where Gertie normally said she wasn't getting any younger, Josie thought, as she rose from the bench and, with Gertie's help, stripped off the satin and brocade dress she had been wearing. She knew her sister meant well, but they were poles apart in their thinking on this. Perhaps it was because their mam had always been ailing and Josie, herself, had been more like Gertie's mother – protecting her, watching out for her and generally mothering her – but Gertie didn't seem to have any deep feeling for Shirley. Or for anyone else for that matter, apart from her big sister.

'Bloomin' 'ell!' The dressing-room door opened and in came a big blonde woman who was billed as a classical and exotic dancer; swathed in veils of crepe de chine, her feet were bare beneath her diaphanous costume. Everyone turned and glanced her way. Lily went under the name of Madame de Vonte, but she was a Newcastle lass born and bred, and something of a card. 'You heard that new 'un who's supposed to imitate the sound of a harp? Harp my backside! You know what old Sidney said on the quiet?' Lily struck a pose and imitated the la-di-da voice of the chairman as she said, '"That woman has grossly libelled the instrument if you ask me."' And as everyone fell about laughing, she added, 'He did, he did! I nearly died. An' Madam had just finished warbling her first song and that lot in the gallery were shouting and heckling when some bright spark in the stalls shouted, "Knock it off! Give the poor cow a chance!" An' you know what she said? "Thank you, kind sir. It's good to know there's *one* gentleman in the audience."'

Pandemonium reigned for a few moments, and Josie,

wiping the tears of laughter from her eyes as she continued dressing, thought, Oh, I'm going to miss Lily when I'm back home. I've never laughed so much as these last twelve weeks and it's better than a tonic. It had even put Gertie in a good mood; the young girl was chattering quite happily as the two sisters stepped into the greasy street ten minutes later, where, through the steadily falling rain, loomed the carriage they'd ordered to transport them back to their lodgings some streets away.

'Miss Burns?'

Josie nearly jumped out of her skin as a figure materialised seemingly out of the brickwork at the side of them, and she knew Gertie had reacted the same when her sister's voice came in a sharp snap, saying, 'An' who wants to know?'

'I startled you. Do forgive me.'

It was a cultured voice, deep and pleasing to the ear, and as Josie stared at the big tall man clothed in a top hat and a long grey cloak which almost covered him from head to foot, she managed to answer quite naturally, 'It's quite all right, but I'm sorry, we have to go. The rain . . .'

'Dastardly weather,' he agreed immediately, adding, 'Please let me introduce myself, Miss Burns. Oliver Hogarth, at your service.' He bowed, raising his head as he said, 'I do need to talk to you, Miss Burns. May I perhaps ride with you and your lovely chaperone?'

There had been irony in the perfunctory bow and enquiring glance, and something mocking in the way he had proclaimed himself. Josie looked into a dark, handsome face in which the eyes were slightly hooded and excessively bagged, with bright irises, and now her voice had reverted to stilted correctness when she said, 'I don't think so, Mr Hogarth. Good night.'

She had crossed the wet pavement and climbed into the

carriage, Gertie just behind her, before the man had time to collect himself, and as Gertie called to the driver to move on, they could just see Mr Hogarth stroll out of the shadows and into the light of a street-lamp, before the horse was clip-clopping them away.

'Cheek.' Gertie's voice was a little bemused. 'Fancied his chances, didn't he?'

Josie nodded. 'He did an' all.'

'Did you see his face when you said "I don't think so"? His mouth sort of fell open a bit, like this.' Gertie dropped her mouth into an exaggerated gape and the two began to giggle.

'Oliver Hogarth.' Josie's voice was thoughtful once they had sobered up. 'I've heard that name before but I can't remember where. If Lily gets back before we're in bed, I'll ask her.'

Lily was staying in the same boarding house as the sisters, and, having been in the music-hall business since she was a toddler featuring in her parents' high-wire act as a human balancing pole, was the fount of all knowledge.

Mrs Bainsby's terraced boarding house in the less salubrious part of Hartlepool always smelt of cabbage and faggots when one stepped into the dark brown hall, but the lady herself had a heart of gold and moreover understood her guests who mostly consisted of visiting music-hall performers. The rooms were clean and cheap – two attributes which Josie had found rarely went together – and unlike some landladies, Mrs Bainsby didn't lock the door after a certain hour and refuse to open it again until morning. Indeed, the landlady seemed to relish the more wild goings-on of some of her guests, like Lily, for example, and was always hovering around with cocoa and seed cake whatever time her lodgers got home. Josie suspected that she and Gertie were something of a disappointment to the good lady, although Lily's escapades more than made up for their unexciting behaviour.

Lily hadn't returned by the time she and Gertie snuggled into their narrow iron beds, wearing several layers of clothing beneath the thin grey blankets, but Josie hadn't really expected her to. The middle-aged blonde had several men friends among whom she divided her favours and was often out all night, returning in the early hours heavy-eyed and tousle-haired, whereupon she would sleep the rest of the day away until it was time to get ready for the theatre.

It was all the more surreal, therefore, when in the pitch blackness of the night, Josie was brought out of a deep, thick sleep to a hand shaking her shoulder and Lily's voice hissing, 'Josie? Josie, lass. For cryin' out loud, wake up! *Josie!*'

'Wha . . . what?' Josie could smell Lily had got a load on her, she stank of whisky. 'What's the matter?'

'I need to talk to you. Wake up, lass. It's important.'

The fact that Lily wasn't slurring her words told Josie the other woman wasn't as drunk as she had thought at first, and now, pulling herself up out of the warmth of the bed, she groped her way over to the battered chest of drawers on the other side of the room and felt for the candlestick and box of matches at the side of it. After lighting the candle she carried it over to the bed, sliding her legs back under the covers as her frozen toes searched for warmth. She looked at Lily in the flickering light and whispered, 'What's the matter and how did you get in this room? I locked the door, didn't I?'

Lily flapped her hand impatiently. 'I've been picking locks since I was a bairn,' she said matter-of-factly. 'Look, I had to speak to you before you went tomorrow morning, an' you know what I'm like once I get me head down. The roof could cave in an' I'd sleep through it.

It's Oliver, Oliver Hogarth. He said he spoke to you tonight.'

'Oliver Hogarth?' Gertie was awake now. 'Do you know him, Lily?'

'In a manner of speaking.' Lily didn't say here that normally the likes of Oliver Hogarth wouldn't be seen dead consorting with a tuppenny act like hers, and that she had nearly passed out with shock when she'd found him waiting for her outside the female dressing room earlier. She'd known as soon as he opened his mouth that he was after Josie, but it wasn't often she was wined and dined by such as Oliver and she'd made the most of the experience. She smiled inwardly. By, she had. She'd heard he liked the women and drink and he'd proved her right the night. But even after he'd had his way he'd been a gentleman – which was more than you could say for some. Couldn't get rid of you quick enough after, some of 'em.

'Do you know who he is, Josie?' Lily asked now, her voice low. 'One of the best agents in the business, that's who. He lives in London but often travels about here an' there, an' one of his touts told him about you – well, more than one actually – so he thought he'd come up and take a look for himself. He wants to talk to you about him becoming your agent.'

Lily couldn't keep a thread of envy out of her voice at this point. She'd have given her eye-teeth for Oliver Hogarth to be after her.

'You know how things are,' Josie shrugged. 'I don't want an agent at the moment.' Lily knew all about Shirley's poor health and the hold the north-east had on Josie for the immediate future.

'Don't talk soft, lass. We're not talking about any old agent here! This is Oliver Hogarth. He's got some of the best on his books an' he's loaded, lass. Absolutely stinking with money. Look, I promised him I'd get you to talk to him before you leave, an' he said he'd come and take you to lunch, Gertie an' all. All right? And let's face it, lass, you're not exactly dashing off anywhere particular in the morning, are you! Oh, I know you want to spend a bit of time with your mam, but I mean – Sunderland. Now if it was the Theatre Royal in Drury Lane, or the Gaiety in Manchester, I'd be up at the crack of dawn meself.'

'There's nothing wrong with Sunderland.'

'No, no, I give you that, lass, an' you've got work which is more than some can say, but you've got something that'll take you beyond the provinces if you let it. That's what I'm saying.'

'I intend to get somewhere one day, Lily,' Josie said quietly and levelly, 'but not at the cost of going against my conscience or my heart. And if that sounds silly to you I can't help it,' she added a trifle aggressively. 'Speaking of Sunderland, Henry Irving made his stage debut at the Royal Lyceum, you know, and he still speaks fondly of it to this day, according to the newspapers. Now if Sunderland is good enough for the greatest actor of our age, it's good enough for me.'

'All right, all right.' Lily was laughing now. 'By, you can be a fiery little thing when you want, can't you! I don't want to stop you visiting your precious Sunderland, lass. All I'm asking is that you hear what Oliver has to say first. He's on for a nice meal you know, and he goes to all the right places. Likes to be seen to be seen, does Oliver Hogarth, if you know what I mean. He was telling me how the Prince of Wales enjoys meeting performers and hearing them sing; has his own private parties, apparently, *and* he's generous – jewelled tie-pins and snuff boxes and all sorts. Oh aye. Oliver's been there and seen it. You could do a lot worse than having him speak for you. Mind, one look into

152

them big peepers of yours and he might want to do more than just speak for you. Bit of a ladies' man, is our Oliver, but nice with it. Reckon he could charm the drawers off the old Queen herself if he had a mind!'

'Oh, Lily.'

'Don't oh, Lily me! Flippin' 'ell, any other lass I know'd be falling on me neck crying in gratitude, I tell you. You're one on your own, Josie Burns. Oliver Hogarth – and she sends him away with a flea in his ear!' There was no animosity in Lily's tone; in truth she had thoroughly enjoyed Oliver's story of what had happened when he'd tried to approach Josie. Some of those agents at the top had more power than the Queen herself within the business, and fancied themselves rotten. It had undoubtedly been an unusual experience for Oliver Hogarth to find himself put in his place by a bit lass. 'Anyway, you'll talk to him tomorrow then? You can still catch the train home later.'

'You could at least hear what he has to say, Josie. That wouldn't matter, would it?' Gertie added her two-pennyworth from her bed.

Josie herself was remembering the strange little shiver which had sped down her spine when she'd looked into Oliver Hogarth's dark face. There was an insouciance about him that was curiously magnetic; something which drew as well as repelled. How old would he be? Forty? A little younger maybe? And tall, six foot or so. And although he was good-looking it was his manner which formed most of his dark attraction; the self-possession and cool authority had been entirely natural, as had the blatant cynicism which had carved deep lines into his tanned skin. He wasn't a bit like Barney.

The last thought brought her stiffening, and she said abruptly, 'It's the middle of the night and we're all going to look like death in the morning at this rate. If I say I'll see him, can we all go to sleep, please?'

Lily grinned into the face she privately thought was one of the most beautiful she had ever seen. Those great eyes of Josie's were killers, and if Oliver Hogarth could see her now with her hair all spread out on her shoulders . . . 'He'll be here at midday.' Lily slid off the foot of Josie's bed, holding out her hand for the candlestick, which she carried over to the chest of drawers before extinguishing the flame with her thumb and forefinger. And then her voice came in the darkness, saying, 'And dress up a bit, for goodness' sake, lass. Even if you're going to refuse him it's better to leave 'em panting!'

There was a saucy laugh, which found an echo from Gertie's bed, and then Lily was gone, leaving Josie herself grinning in the blackness. She was a card, Lily, and no mistake. Nothing ever seemed to get her down, and what she didn't know about life and men wasn't worth knowing.

'Josie, what if—'

'Gertie, we're not discussing this any more now. We'll talk in the morning. We both need our beauty sleep.'

'Aye, all right.' Gertie knew better than to argue when that note was in her sister's voice.

However, long after Gertie's steady breathing indicated she was asleep, Josie lay wide-eyed in the stillness. She usually kept her mind from thinking about Barney, having found from experience that she suffered for it. And tonight was no exception. She twisted restlessly in the narrow bed, the ancient, flock-filled mattress lumpy and hard beneath her limbs.

Since she and Gertie had left Betty's for good, some nine months after she had first appeared at Ginnett's and just after Gertie had finished her schooling, her contact with the family had been spasmodic, depending on her current work venue. Those nine months when she'd continued to live with Frank and Betty had seen a change in Barney that she knew had alarmed his stepmother and father, because Betty wasn't one for keeping her anxieties to herself. He had been subdued on the occasions he popped in to see them all, even taciturn, and he hadn't repeated any of the invitations he'd made before the marriage for them all to visit his wife and himself. And Pearl never accompanied him.

Josie had left Newcastle to work first in Gateshead for a season, and then travelled some sixteen miles or so down country in Durham, before moving backwards and forwards to other theatres scattered all over the north-east, and during that time she hadn't seen Barney above once or twice. The encounters had been strange – Barney had almost seemed like someone else – and uncomfortable, but it was the last time she had been at Betty's, just over six months ago, that she had been actually shocked at the change in the tall, laughing, bright-eyed lad of old. She'd heard from Vera that Betty thought the marriage had run into real problems. Knowing Betty's conviction that a happy marriage was one in which the wife presented the husband with a baby every twelve months, Josie had found herself wondering if Betty's verdict was based largely on the fact that as yet, Pearl and Barney were childless.

Of course, there could be innumerable explanations for Barney having appeared to have aged ten years, along with the brooding expression his countenance had assumed whenever he wasn't forcing himself to act bouncy and cheerful. Betty might speculate that things had gone from bad to worse since Barney had begun to work for Pearl's uncle at Ginnett's, but Josie couldn't see that herself. She'd found Ernest Harper to be a nice little man and he'd been well respected by his own staff and performers alike. She couldn't see Barney finding it difficult to get along with Ernest. And Barney and Pearl had been able to move from St James Street into the prosperous suburb of Jesmond which was almost exclusively occupied by handsome dwelling houses – Pearl must have liked that. Betty said their large gracious home in Windsor Terrace was big enough to house ten families, let alone one bit lass and lad, the one time she and Frank had been invited there just after the couple had moved in.

Whatever, Barney's marriage was not her concern. Josie repeated this vehemently in her mind as she'd done many times before when her thoughts wandered into forbidden territory. Whatever went on between husband and wife was the couple's business and theirs alone, but oh, those cosy nights in front of the kitchen range in Betty's house so long ago seemed to belong to another lifetime and different people now. And Barney had looked so sombre, so bleak the last time she'd seen him . . .

Enough. Enough, enough, enough. She sighed irritably. She was going home tomorrow and come Monday she was starting at the Avenue Theatre and the Palace. She'd have a word with Vera and see if they could get her mam in to see a show one night if she was up to it. She could arrange for her mam and Vera and Horace to have a box all to themselves; her mam'd be tickled pink at that.

And Oliver Hogarth? Her heart beat a little faster and she put a hand to her chest. She didn't know what she thought about him, except that if he knew what she was really like under the paint and flamboyant clothes she had worn onstage, he wouldn't be interested in her in *that* way as Lily had intimated. He was a roué and used to experienced, worldly women. His eyes had told her so. But there was something about him . . .

Well, she would see him tomorrow – she really couldn't

do anything else now – and she'd make it plain where she stood. And that would be the end of that, at least for the time being.

She turned over in the bed again, the movement sharp, and asked herself why bad men were always so much more attractive than the other sort.

Chapter Eight

Despite her promise to Lily, Josie did not meet Oliver Hogarth for lunch the next day; at eleven o'clock she and Gertie were on a train to Sunderland after an early-morning visit from Horace to say her mother was very ill and asking for her.

She left messages for both Lily and Oliver Hogarth with a clucking Mrs Bainsby whilst Horace transported their trunk and portmanteau out to the carriage he had waiting, but they were succinct in the extreme. All Josie wanted to do was to get home.

She had thought, when Mrs Bainsby had first tapped on the bedroom door to say that there was a gentleman downstairs with news about her family, that at last there had been some sort of contact from her father and brothers. Since the night she had been attacked in Newcastle, her father — and two days later Jimmy and Hubert — seemed to have vanished into thin air. Patrick Duffy had turned up some weeks after the incident and had claimed no knowledge at all of the affair when the police questioned him. The last time he'd seen Bart Burns, Duffy stated, had been at least a week before the alleged episode with his daughter, and then Bart had been talking about signing on with a ship leaving for foreign parts. Some trouble concerning gambling debts, so he'd heard. But of course he'd be only too happy to keep his ear to the ground and let the authorities know if he heard anything.

The absence of her husband had been a great relief to Shirley but not so the loss of her lads, and although some months later the doctor had confirmed her cough was due to the consumption and that a stay in a sanatorium would benefit her greatly, she had refused to move from Vera's house. The lads would know to look for her there when they came home, she'd insisted, and no one, not even Josie, had managed to persuade her differently. And now the influenza had curtailed even the short amount of time she'd had left to her, and there could be no doubt her demise was imminent.

There was a bitter north wind blowing when Horace and the two girls alighted from the train in Sunderland's Central Station, and the January air was redolent with the unmistakable smell of snow as a horse and cab carried its three occupants and the girls' luggage to Northumberland Place.

Vera's front room had been turned into a very pleasant bedroom, and Josie never stepped into her mother's little sanctuary without deep relief and gratitude flooding her. Vera's sacrifice had made the last four years possible.

A single bed had been placed at one side of the room under the window, so that Shirley could see passers-by through the lace curtains, and next to this a small table held her medicines and a flowering potted plant. The horsehair suite and the glass-fronted cabinet had gone but Vera had kept the piano which Horace now played most days; two large, resplendent rocking chairs with voluptuous cushions meant Vera and Horace were comfortable when they kept Shirley company each evening before they retired to bed. Evenings which, according to Vera, they all enjoyed immensely and which were filled with laughter.

There were no smiling faces today, however.

Vera had opened the door to them, which indicated she had been waiting at the window in Shirley's room, and she embraced both girls silently in the hall before opening the front-room door and standing aside for them to enter.

Shirley's skeletal frame barely made a bump under the eiderdown – which like everything else in the room was bright and clean – and her lined skin had taken on a pallor that had the reflection of death about it. Bronchopneumonia, the doctor had declared – inflammation of the lungs arising in the bronchi due to the side effects of the influenza which Shirley had been battling with for some time. According to Horace, she'd had some sort of seizure and coughed up basin after basin of phlegm and blood twenty-four hours since, but after the doctor had allowed free rein with the laudanum this coma-like calm had prevailed, and the bouts of coughing had become infrequent.

Her mother's head was sunk into the pillow, her eyes closed, and as Vera followed them into the room, saying quietly, 'The doctor's just left an' he don't think she'll regain consciousness,' Josie thought her mother had already gone, so still was the shape beneath the covers.

And then there was a deep shuddering breath and Shirley's eyes opened, focusing slowly on the two girls at the side of the bed. Josie was crying, 'Oh, Mam, oh, Mam,' deep inside, but she forced herself to speak gently and without tears as she said, 'We're here, Mam, and we love you. Everything's going to be all right. You just rest now.'

'Me . . . me bairns.'

One of the parchment-like hands lying on the eiderdown tried to reach out, and as Josie quickly enfolded her mother's fingers with her two hands, she said, 'It's all right, Mam, it's all right. We're here.'

Gertie made a small sound in her throat at the side of Josie and as Josie turned to look at her sister, she saw Gertie's face was awash with tears, and was conscious of thinking, She does love Mam after all.

'Here, come away out of it, hinny, an' have a sup tea for a minute,' Vera said. 'You don't want to upset your mam, now do you?'

As the two of them, along with a silent Horace, disappeared through to the kitchen, Josie was left alone with her mother, and now she knelt down by the bed without loosening her grip on her mother's hand, saying quietly, 'I'm here, Mam, and I'm not going to go anywhere until you're better. All right? I'm staying with you.'

'Lass . . .'

'Don't try to talk, Mam.' She couldn't bear it – she couldn't bear for her mam to die, she thought wildly, desperately controlling the grief that had the tears welling against the back of her eyes. Her mam had had such a miserable life, and it was only in the last few years she'd had anything approaching happiness, and then only with accompanying ill-health and pain. Her mam was forty-four or forty-five, she couldn't remember exactly, but she looked decades older. Vera had said her mam had been pretty once; prettiest lass in the street and with all the lads after her, so why, *why* had she chosen her da out of them all? He'd never been any use to her and his last act, that of taking the lads away with him wherever he'd gone, had been pure spite. And greed. Doubtless he was living off them somewhere or other.

And then, almost as though her mother had followed her train of thought, Shirley murmured, 'All . . . all broken up. Jimmy an' Hubert, you an' Gertie an' then . . . Ada an' Dora. All broken up,' before her voice faded away.

162

'Only for now, Mam. I'll find them all, I promise, and we'll be together again. All right?'

She had only spoken thus to bring her mother some comfort, not because she believed it, so now, when Shirley's hand in her daughter's moved and the bony fingers gripped the younger flesh with a strength that was surprising considering her condition, Josie was taken aback. 'The lads,' her mother said. 'They're somewhere near, lass. I feel it in me bones, always have. They're . . here.'

'Here?' This was wishful thinking on her mam's part.

'Aye. I never felt it with me lasses – they've gone.' Shirley took another deep, shuddering breath that sounded so painful Josie found herself wincing. 'But you'll find 'em all, some . . . day.'

When Josie felt the grip of her mother's fingers slacken she realised she had fallen into the deathly slumber again, and so she sat quietly, her hands still holding her mother's.

She didn't move, not through the long afternoon and evening and not even when Gertie went to bed in Vera's spare room, Ruby the lodger having long since moved out. She had told her mother she was going to stay with her and she was; she explained this to Vera when that good lady, heartsore and weary, tried to prise Josie away from the unconscious woman lying so still in the bed.

During her vigil, Josie found herself thinking about all sorts of things, painful on the whole but with a few happy moments mixed in among the dark memories. Like the time her mam had made her and Gertie a small rag doll each the first Christmas after she had started the singing. It had been the only real Christmas present she'd ever had – before that, Christmas Day had been just like any other day. She and Gertie had been ecstatic. They had played with their 'babies' every spare moment until their father, some months later, whilst drunk and angry with her mam about something or other, had thrown them on the fire.

It was after a visit to the privy in the early hours that Josie noticed a change in her mother. It followed a bout of coughing when Josie thought her mother was going to speak again, although she hadn't. Now Shirley was only drawing breath seemingly every minute or so; the break between her long-drawn gasps unending.

Vera joined her at three o'clock in the morning and sat quietly beside her after making a cup of tea, which they both drank without speaking. Josie was glad of its warmth because the control she had been keeping on herself had seemed to freeze her limbs as well as her insides. She dare not let the tears fall, not now, not when her mam might open her eyes again and need her, but the hard tight lump in her chest was unbearable.

And then, just as the dawn was breaking, the hand in hers moved. She saw her mother's eyes flicker, as though she was trying to open them, and then the grey lips parted and her mam's voice, a whisper, a breath, said, 'Josie . . .'

And she answered, bending near, 'I'm here, Mam, and I love you. I love you all the world,' before she kissed her.

And then her mother's hand went limp, the last breath was expelled softly and slowly, and she had gone. As quietly and as peacefully as that. Josie put her arms round the frail, workworn body and gathered her mam to her, hugging her as though she would never let her go and quite unaware of the tears pouring down her face as the pain in her heart imploded. Never again would she see her mam's eyes light up when she popped her head round the door and said she was home; never again would she see that look of joy and pride on her mam's face when she sang to her, or hear her soft, 'Oh, go on with you, lass,' when she told her mam how dear she was.

She knew her mam had loved her; whatever else, her mam had loved her more than she had loved anyone else, and for a moment her loss was more than Josie could bear.

'Lass, leave that. I've told you we'll see to it later. You're all done in.'

'It's all right, Vera. I'd rather do it now, really.'

Vera stared at Josie, and she had to admit she was at a loss. First the lass had insisted on laying out her mother herself, which wasn't a pleasant task and certainly not one for a young lassie to Vera's mind, and then she had stripped the bed once her mam was clean and laid out on the wooden trestle Horace had brought into the front room, and had proceeded to scrub at the stained bedding in the wash tub until her hands were raw.

Vera remained standing at the door to the wash-house for a minute longer, her eyes on the young girl wringing the bedding through the wooden rollers of the iron mangle, and then she sighed deeply before saying, 'I'll make a sup tea, hinny.'

'Aye, thanks.'

'An' you're havin' a bite, lass, whether you want it or not.'

Josie made no reply to this, and after standing a moment more Vera made her way back into the kitchen from the yard. The lass had taken it hard, not like the other one. Oh, Gertie might have wept and wailed a bit at first, but it was surface emotion nevertheless. She was a funny little thing, was Gertie.

'She's insistin' she'll finish it afore she comes in.' Vera walked across to the range as she spoke to Gertie who was sitting at the kitchen table, lifting the big black kettle and pushing it deep into the glowing embers before reaching for the brown teapot on the shelf at the side of the range. 'She's half frozen out there; she'll be bad next, you mark me words. I'll make some girdle scones to go with the tea, eh? Nothin' like a hot buttered girdle scone, is there?'

'I'll help.' Gertie sprang to her feet, glad of something to do. She knew Josie and Vera were all upset – their eyes had been so red and puffy when she'd come downstairs this morning that they'd hardly been able to see out of them – but she just couldn't feel the same way they did, no matter how she tried. She was sorry her mam had gone, of course, and she'd had a gliff when she'd first seen her the day before, but . . . . She wrinkled her nose as she tried to sort out her feelings. Her mam had always been sickly, not like a proper mother somehow, and it wasn't as if they hadn't known she was middling . . .

'Here, hinny, sift the flour an' everythin' together.' Vera's voice was brisk as she measured the currants, half a teaspoon of salt, a level teaspoonful of cream of tartar and a half a level teaspoonful of bicarbonate of soda into the plain flour in the mixing bowl, before walking across to the cold slab in the pantry and bringing out the lard and milk. Gertie stared after Vera's bustling figure. Her mother's old friend was trying to act normally but she was the same as Josie really; forcing herself to keep active to hide her feelings. Did they think she was awful?

Vera smiled at her as she tipped the fat into the big bowl, and as Gertie began to rub in the lard and mix it to a soft dough with the flour and milk, Vera said, 'There's a good lass. You'll make a canny wife for some lucky lad, Gertie.'

Gertie smiled back into the kind, rough-textured face. If she had spoken her true feelings on the matter, she would have told Vera that marriage was the last thing she envisaged for the future. She might not be particularly bright

– certainly her last year at school had been a nightmare she wouldn't inflict on her worst enemy – but over the last three or four years she had come to realise she had talents of other kinds. Practical talents. However, her whole body shrank inwardly at the thought of employing those abilities in the role of a wife. She had seen what marriage meant; subjugation, misery, enslavement. She would never willingly give the control of her life and well-being over to a man unless she could be absolutely sure he wouldn't turn out like her da. No, she was more than happy in her capacity as Josie's dresser and companion. Josie's star was going to be a brilliant one, and she could assist its rise. And no one deserved success more than Josie.

'That's grand, lass. Now, roll it out to about a quarter of an inch thick an' cut it into rounds, an' we'll have 'em cookin' on that girdle afore you can say Jack Robinson. A good girdle cake, nicely browned, is hard to beat. You go an' call your sister, eh? Tell her to take the weight off.'

Gertie nodded at Vera. Power. Power and prestige; that's what got you anywhere in this life, and she didn't need to be top of the class to know that. And what was at the root of power and prestige? Money, that's what. She'd heard the talk in the dressing rooms; she reckoned she knew more than Josie as to what the big stars earned. Marie Kendall was earning £100 a week three years ago, and even the middle-of-the-road performers were getting anything from £10 to £30 a week in London. And Josie was better than middle of the road. By, she was that. When she sang she could make them laugh or cry or turn somersaults . . .

Gertie finished cutting the last of the scones and brushed her hands on her skirt. Would Josie be vexed if she knew she'd left Vera's address with Mrs Bainsby in case the agent feller should ask? And then she gave herself a mental shake of the head. Why ask the road you know? Josie'd go stark staring barmy. But it was done now. And she wasn't sorry. If he was keen enough, he'd follow them here to Sunderland, and if he wasn't, well, in spite of what Lily had said there must be other agents with as many connections as this Oliver bloke. And now their mam was gone, Josie was free to work further afield.

'I'll get Josie then.' She spoke to Vera's back; Vera being busy turning the first batch of scones on the hot girdle.

'Aye, you do that, lass, an' I'll pour us all a sup tea. I don't know about you but me tongue's hangin' out.'

Vera's voice was suspiciously thick and Gertie suspected she was crying again. It was going to be a long few days till the funeral. Horace had had a word with the parson on his way to work that morning, and the parson had been straight round before Josie had even finished laying their mam out. 'Course, the fact that Josie had told Horace to say they wanted a funeral with all the trimmings might have something to do with his promptness. Waste of good money, she called it. You were either going straight to heaven or the other place from what she could make out, and neither venue took any notice of what sort of send-off you had on this mortal plain. Still, she wouldn't alter Josie's mind on this, same as she wouldn't on anything else. Josie thought with her heart more than her head but she had a mind of her own, and that mind was formidable when it was put to anything.

She thought again of the hastily scribbled address she'd left with their old landlady, and found herself biting hard on her lip as she opened the back door and walked across the small yard to the wash-house. By, if Oliver Hogarth followed them here she'd get it in the neck from her sister. Gertie wasn't sure if she wanted the agent to persist or not now.

Chapter Nine

Owing to the opening of London's Hippodrome Theatre in Charing Cross Road on 15 January 1900, it was over ten days before Oliver Hogarth made his way north again. He had been a member of a party which included lords and ladies of the highest rank, and an invitation to a house-party the following weekend after the prestigious opening – which had included none other than the Prince of Wales himself – had meant a further delay before he could legitimately leave London.

He had also had other, less welcome matters to attend to; matters which he had procrastinated about long enough, but which had proved to be every bit as unpleasant as he'd expected. Damn it, women were the very devil. Oliver stared out of the window of the train, scowling at the snowy vista outside the luxurious first-class carriage.

He would have thought Stella had quite enough to occupy her without kicking up about his departure from her life, or to be more precise, her bed. Since she had married Stratton she'd acquired all the social privileges she'd ever wanted, and the man was clearly besotted with his beautiful wife. Seven large trunks she'd brought on that last weekend, and he had noticed half-a-dozen changes of clothing on the first day alone. With Godfrey Stratton being a member of the Prince of Wales's inner circle, Stella now dined out or entertained every night, and last year alone the Strattons had spent a short time in Paris, several weeks in Biarritz, and several more cruising in the Mediterranean before returning to London at the beginning of May for the Season. Then there had been the move to Ascot in June for the races, their stay with the Duke of Richmond for the racing at Goodwood in July and then the regatta at Cowes. A month's cure at Marienbad; Balmoral for the grouse and deer throughout October, and then the whirl of Christmas parties at which the entertaining had been more relentless than ever. Why the hell did she think she needed *him*?

He closed his eyes, leaning back against the thickly upholstered seat and letting his breath escape in a long slow sigh. That scene she'd created, it had been wearying. But then he had to confess that for some long time now he had become weary of the lady herself. Stella had been a novelty when he'd first got involved with her some five years ago, he admitted it, but the attraction of having a cultured, charming mistress with the right family history, who behaved like the worst bawdy whore he'd ever had in private, had soured on him this last year. Perhaps even the last two. Her passions had become like her rages, exhausting and distasteful. He didn't like displays of jealousy, in a man or a woman, and Stella was jealous to the core.

Still it was done now. He understood Godfrey had business in Madrid and that Stella was going with him. When she returned in a few weeks' time, he hoped she would be calmer. Whatever, the affair was finished.

He stretched his long legs, settled himself more comfortably in the seat, and put his ex-mistress out of his mind with a ruthlessness that was typical of the man himself. Born of aristocratic parentage but to a father who had gambled away a vast country estate before killing himself and his wife in a yachting accident, Oliver Hogarth had found himself penniless and homeless at the tender age of twenty. The benefits of a first-class education and influential friends had proved invaluable however, and Oliver had found he was adept at making full use of both. He also discovered a leaning towards anything theatrical, and a natural flair for knowing what the common – and not so common – man liked. By the age of twenty five he was well on the way to making his own fortune, and by the age of thirty had secured some of the biggest stars on the music-hall stage in his own net.

However, the trait which had ruined the father was in the son, and although Oliver was a more proficient and skilful gambler than the late Squire Hogarth, he also had a weakness for the fairer sex – which had proved just as expensive a vice as the gambling. Nevertheless, Oliver was able to indulge in a lavish way of life that had made him, at the age of thirty-eight, a wealthy, attractive but deeply cynical man.

So what was it, he asked himself now, straightening in his seat and calling one of the waiters to bring him a double brandy, what was it that had captured him about this young girl, this Josie Burns? True, she was beautiful, and had a presence to go with the exceptional voice, but then so did half the artistes in the music hall. She appeared intelligent enough on brief acquaintance, and not too forward. The promiscuous ones were entertaining enough, but he avoided taking them on his books, knowing such women created difficulties at some stage.

The brandy came and he swallowed half the glass immediately. If he told anyone he was chasing off up the country again after some chit of a girl who had refused him once before, they wouldn't believe it. He wasn't sure if he believed it himself. She might have talent but it was raw at the moment; she needed moulding and shaping if she were to compete with the likes of Marie Lloyd, Marie Kendall, Vesta Tilley and the rest of them. But the potential was there.

His guts contracted as the same excitement he'd felt on that night in Hartlepool gripped him once again. It'd been a long time since he'd felt like this, and even longer since he'd considered taking on the task of grooming an artiste himself. He had others he could call on for that. But this time . . . this time he just might indulge himself. A picture of a young sweet face and wide, startled, heavily lashed brown eyes flashed before him and he swallowed the rest of the brandy, his mouth curving slightly in a wry smile. Yes, he just might make an exception for Josie Burns.

It was snowing again when the train pulled into Sunderland Central, and as Oliver alighted and glanced about him, he sighed irritably. Damn gloomy place. How he hated visiting the provinces! It was only just after two in the afternoon and already the lantern oil lamps, placed strategically every few yards along the platforms, were burning of necessity.

He had only brought a small portmanteau with him for his planned overnight stay, and after declining the assistance of a porter he strode out of the station before hailing a horse-drawn cab. After asking the driver to recommend a good place to stay, he dropped off the small travelling bag at the hotel in Fawcett Street, then told the man to take him to Northumberland Place, at which point he settled back in his seat and contemplated the forthcoming meeting with the young woman called Josie Burns.

'It always comes in threes. Didn't I say to you just t'other night it always comes in threes, lass, after Horace had that fall? But I didn't expect this. By, I didn't. How's Betty takin' it, lad?'

'Bad.' The monosyllable carried a wealth of feeling.

Vera nodded slowly. 'First Shirley, then Horace nearly breakin' his neck, an' now your da. What we've done to deserve this packet I don't know. An' you say Reg an' Neville'll be off for a few weeks?'

This was directed to the man sitting next to Barney at the kitchen table. 'Aye.' Amos, Barney's elder brother, was very like Barney in appearance, or had been a few years ago. Now his face – although clean and scrubbed – carried the unmistakable stamp of the pit. His brow and nose were marked with small blue indentations from the coal he worked, and his eyes were rheumy and pink-rimmed. 'Reg's arm is broken an' our Neville copped it on his legs. Right mess, the left 'un is, but Nev's not sayin' much. After what happened to me da, it's nowt.'

Vera nodded again, glancing at Josie who was sitting at the side of her. In Josie's face she saw reflected her own shock and distress.

A fall of the roof at the coal face had taken two miners' lives – Frank being one of them – and injured six more. Not an uncommon occurrence in the precarious labyrinth of low tunnels where hundreds of men worked six days out of every seven, hemmed in below millions of tons of rock, slate and coal, but nevertheless, devastating to the families concerned. Labouring long, exhausting hours in the darkness, often soaked to the skin or crouched hewing narrow seams, it wasn't always possible to swiftly obey the warning that the tell-tale creaks and groans in the roof gave to the colliers. Explosions, foul air and accidents involving the props and equipment took a heavy toll, and suffocation and poisoning were among the swifter deaths the mine could inflict.

Vera spoke to Amos again as she said, 'Was . . . was it quick?'

'Aye, lass, it were. If nowt else, that's summat to thank God for.'

Thank God? Barney shifted restlessly in his seat. He wouldn't be thanking Amos's God for any of this, by, he wouldn't, but he didn't doubt for a minute that his brother had meant exactly what he'd said. Reg and Neville played in the colliery's brass band in their spare time, but Amos's bent was in quite a different direction. Right from a young lad he'd had religion, had Amos, Barney reflected silently. The rest of them had played the wag from Sunday school when they'd had the chance, but not Amos. He'd met his wife through the church and she was as bad as him; he still did a bit of lay preaching on the odd Sunday according to their da. *Da.* Oh Da, Da, Da . . .

He forced his mind away from the mental image of his da's broken, twisted body which had been in his head ever since he had heard about the accident at the pit, and returned to the issue of Amos's God as his brother talked on to Vera. Maybe there was something in this religion thing after all, he thought bitterly; of his da and three brothers, Amos was the only one who had emerged from the pit whole and unhurt. Mind, he'd heard Amos preach once, and his brother had said something which had stuck with him somehow. 'The sun shines on the righteous *and* the unrighteous,' that's what he'd preached, and Amos had maintained God had no favourites.

He'd pulled Amos's leg after, about the sun bit. 'Not much sun on you most days, man,' he'd said. And Amos had looked at him with the Robson green eyes, and answered, 'There's nowt else but the pit round here for most of us, lad, an' I thank God I've got work, good honest work, an' with a bunch of right good mates an' all. There's worse things than bein' underground, an' worse worries than whether the props'll hold.'

He hadn't been down into the bowels of hell then, being in his last year at school, but within the year he had known he couldn't agree with Amos. Nothing, *nothing* was as bad as that netherworld. The panic and fear he'd felt as he'd descended in the cage on the first day he'd gone down, and the physical reaction of his body, had made him feel as though he was dying. He'd stood it nigh on a week, passing out three times in the process, until the day when – according to his da because he couldn't remember anything for a full twenty-four hours – he'd not come round. They'd got him up top and called the quack, and Dr Winter had diagnosed claustrophobia. An abnormal fear of confined places, the good doctor had told his da. But his da had only heard the word 'fear', nothing else. From that day on, Frank had never looked at him without the shame and disappointment showing in his face.

Whisht. Barney shut his eyes for a second, angry with himself for thinking the way he was. None of that mattered and now was not the time to think about it. He'd come to terms with how his da saw him years ago. It was being here within sight and sound of Josie that had him thinking this way, because at the back of his mind he'd wondered for years now how *she* saw him. Did she think he was a coward, a weakling for not mastering his fear and following his da and brothers down the pit? She hadn't seemed to, when he'd first confided in her before he was married, but she'd been nowt but a bairn then and bairns accepted things adults questioned. She must know he got the job at Ginnett's through Pearl's family. Did she despise him for that as well?

He glanced across the room and at the same moment Josie turned her head slightly and met his gaze, her eyes sympathetic at the tragedy which had befallen the family. Their gaze held for a moment before she looked away, but it was the expression on her face which stayed with him as he half listened to the others talking. Josie and Gertie had stayed with his family probably a year in all, but Pearl had known the Robsons since she was a little bairn, and had been made welcome in his da's home for that long. As a child she'd fairly lived in their house, having tea with them all, tagging along with Prudence when he and his brothers let the two lasses join the lads; she'd even called Betty and his da Aunty and Uncle for a time. And yet she'd had a job to say she was sorry about his da. Aye, she had. And it hadn't rung true when she had managed to force the words out. And yet Josie had looked as though she was heartsore for them all.

By, he'd been a fool to ask for Pearl. Why hadn't he seen what she was really like afore they were wed? But he had thought he knew her, that was the thing. In fact he'd have bet his life he knew her inside out, but it just showed. Aye, it showed all right. Living with someone was a darn sight different to Sunday tea at her parents' house or visiting in the evening and sitting on the sofa with her parents fluttering in and out. Even when they'd joined the other courting couples for the ritual walk round the park when it was fine, or tea at one of the tea houses in town when it was wet, it had all been artificial. Aye, that was the word. Artificial.

He'd looked at Pearl and he'd seen the pretty, petite, smiling lass she'd wanted him to see, but beneath the sweet face and childish manner had been a cast-iron selfish woman who was a replica of her mother. And now, when she acted girlish and skittish in front of other people it had the effect of making him feel sick.

He hadn't thought she'd like the intimate side of marriage; women didn't, did they, but he'd told himself if he was gentle and patient to start with she'd come round eventually. Come round! The thought was bitter. But it wasn't even that she made him feel like some sort of depraved debauché if he so much as touched her; he might have been able to cope with the lack of physical love if everything else was all right. No, it was the cold-blooded alienation from his family she'd set out to achieve from day one; the nagging from morning to night and the fierce, even obsessional desire she had to climb socially. She consulted with her mother about everything before she talked to him; she insisted on seeing to the finances and gave him pocket money like a bairn – or she had done until this last year when he'd suddenly realised he was daft, mental to put up with it. He'd put his foot down then with the result that they'd had a bitter exchange of words and he had moved into one of the spare bedrooms.

Strangely, in a funny sort of a way, it had been a relief to physically remove himself from her. Ever since they had been married she had insisted he eat his main meal of the day at a café near his place of work, refusing, as she put it, to slave over a hot stove just for the two of them. His evening meal would invariably be cold meat and cheese, even the bread was shop bought, and very often she was out when he got home. At her mother's. The only time they really ate together was when she invited friends round for what she liked to call dinner-parties. Her friends, not his. So all in all, the physical removal of himself from the faint possibility of any bodily contact had just been the final nail in the coffin of their relationship.

He often wondered these days how many other couples lived separate lives once the front door was shut and they were alone. More than he'd ever dreamed of before he was wed, he'd bet. He knew now he'd been a young lad still wet behind the ears when he'd got married – gormless and as naive as they come with regard to women. But then unless you went with a lass who'd got a bit of a name for herself – and who'd want to be seen out with a girl like that? – there was no other option.

'. . . if that's all right, Barney?'

The sound of his name jerked him out of the black morass of his thoughts and he spoke quietly, saying, 'I'm sorry, Vera?'

'I asked if it's all right if I come back with you an' Amos today? Horace is on the mend after that fall on the ice, he went back to work the day, an' the lassies'll see to his meals. I'd like to see our Bett through the funeral if nowt else.'

'Of course it's all right, we expected nothing else. It's one of the reasons I accompanied Amos when he said he was coming, me having the use of Pearl's uncle's carriage. It'll make it easier with whatever luggage you want to bring with you. Your place is with your sister at a time like this and I know Betty is longing to see you.'

'Aye, I'd like to see her through the worst,' Vera repeated somewhat dazedly. By, for this to happen now. She'd been wondering about looking for work now Shirley was gone, but had decided to stay her hand until Josie had finished at the Avenue and the Palace so she could see a bit of the lass while she was here. They had said they'd have her back at the corn mill, and after the last few years of looking to Shirley's every need, she would go stark staring barmy if she sat on her backside all day. She had given up her job at the mill within a few months of her old friend moving in, recognising there was going to be a period of intensive nursing involved, and she'd been glad to do it. Mind, with what Josie had insisted on sending she'd been better off than working.

The last thought prompted her to rise, saying, 'I'll just go an' pull me things together then. You lads help yourself to a bit more gingerbread an' jam roll, now then, else I'll think I'm losin' me touch. Josie, come with me, lass, an' I'll fill you in as to what wants doin' while I'm gone.'

However, once the two women were in Vera's bedroom, Vera said softly, in what could be termed a conspiratorial whisper, 'Look, lass, I don't know how long I'll be with our Bett or what's goin' to happen about the house an' everythin'. I can't see Bett managin' the rent an' all on her own with her lot to feed an' clothe.'

Josie nodded. There had been three more additions to the family in the last four years – two boys and a girl – and with the twins only ten years old, things looked bad.

'It'll take a while to sort out what's what, but I'm goin' to stay until things are settled one way or t'other, an' then I might be bringin' the whole lot of 'em back here from where I'm lookin', it bein' a tied house an' all. Anyway, we'll cross that bridge later, hinny, but afore I go I want to give you this.'

Vera had been rummaging in the blanket box tucked away in a corner of the room while she spoke, and now she pulled out a small cloth bag which she thrust at Josie.

'What . . .' The bag was heavy, and Josie stared in amazement at the notes and coins it contained. 'Vera, what's this? Where has all this come from?'

'You, lass.' Vera smiled at her. She hadn't intended to give Josie her money in these circumstances, she'd had it planned quite differently, but needs must. 'I told you in the beginnin' me an' Horace didn't want to make owt on havin' your mam, but you wouldn't have it. So I thought if it made you feel better I'd take the money you sent an' put it away until . . .' Vera paused; she'd almost said, 'until your mam was gone' '. . . until the situation was different. There's nearly sixty pounds there, mounted up over the last years, an' that's with us havin' the money for your mam's medicines an' the doctor, an' a bit besides, enough to carry on like when I was workin' at the mill. But we don't want this extra, hinny, we really don't. If we can't help each other out as we walk this road it's a poor do. An' Horace sees it same as me, afore you ask. We never had no bairns of our own an' we both see you as ours. I know there's bin times when you've gone without to send your mam's money, an' only the thought of this day has helped me sleep nights.'

Josie was beyond words. She stood quite still, the bag held in her hands, and stared open-mouthed into the smiling face of this woman she loved so much. Not as a mother, although that was part of the feeling she had for Vera, but it was wider than that. Vera was mother, friend, confidante, ally, advocate – oh, a million and one things, and all of them precious.

'Vera, I can't. I can't.'

'Aye, you can, if you want to please me, lass.'

'But it's too much.'

'It's yours, lass. I'm only givin' you back what's yours, what I've been holdin' for you if you care to look at it like that. It's four years' hard graft an' you know it.'

What had she ever done to deserve being loved like this? Josie's eyes were large and dark with the force of her feelings. 'Vera, I don't know what I'd do without you, and I don't mean because of this,' she added, flicking her head at the money. 'I do love you.'

'Go on with you.' Vera flapped her hand, evidently embarrassed. Josie was always ready to put her thoughts into words in a way no one else would dream of doing. They might think it but they wouldn't say it. You just didn't. But then the theatre was like that, she supposed. Them sort of people were different, people with a gift.

And her lass had a gift, all right. 'Put it away with your things an' let's hear no more about it.'

'Vera, you'll never know what this means, and I appreciate it from the depths of my heart,' Josie said, causing the older woman to blink rapidly and shake her head, 'and I agree with you it's a poor do if we can't help each other out. So with that in mind I want you to take this to Betty.'

'Bett? Oh no, no, lass.'

'Please. You know how things are. She won't get much from the colliery and the union will only help out so much, and it will be at least another three or four years until the twins can work full-time, even if they get something after school and on a Saturday in the meantime. She could buy one of those three-roomed cottages on the West Side with this if she puts it with the bit she'll likely get from the colliery.' Josie was warming to her theme. 'I'm sure Barney and the others will try and help out a bit as best they can, but things are going to be tight for all of them with Reg and Neville off.' She had been there herself in the old days; you missed one week's rent and then another, and before you knew it the debt was huge. Oh yes, she could remember times when her da had drunk or gambled away every last penny they'd had, and the soul-destroying visits to the pawnshop with anything that wasn't nailed down would stay with her for ever.

The last thought created a sense of urgency flavoured with deep compassion, and she said, 'Vera, you know what this would mean to Betty, and her with nine bairns. And it's not really mine anyway, it's yours. It is, it's yours.'

'Oh, lass.' A quiver passed over Vera's face and she looked down at her feet bewilderedly. They were killing her the day; her ankles overflowing the tops of her heavy black shoes. And then she caught herself sharply. What did her feet matter, for crying out loud! She raised her eyes again, but she had only said, 'This isn't right,' before Josie interrupted her, her voice eager.

'It is, Vera. It is right, and you know it at heart. What would Gertie and me have done if you hadn't taken us to Betty's that day? And she welcomed us with open arms, her and Frank. I owe them more than I can ever repay.'

'But what will *you* do, hinny?' Vera was finding it hard to take in the turn-around. 'You need new stage costumes, shoes an' hats an' all – Gertie was saying. An'—'

'What's that compared to Betty's need?'

The truth was unarguable, but Vera had one last try. 'But I wanted *you* to have it.'

'And I've taken it, and now I'm giving it to you to give to Betty,' Josie said softly. She couldn't say she didn't want the money; it would sound like the height of ingratitude and she didn't mean it like that, but the truth of the matter was that she *didn't* want it. It was Vera's first and foremost, but her mam's too in a funny sort of way. It might be a small fortune but no, she didn't want it.

'Aye, well, I know you when you make up your mind about somethin'.' Vera sighed. 'An' I can't say I won't look forward to seein' Bett's face when I give her it. By, you're a one.' Her face was comical. 'I dunno whether to smack your backside or hug you, lass, an' that's a fact.'

'I'm too big for the first so it'd better be the second, Vera.'

The two men hadn't touched the gingerbread or jam roll when Josie and Vera came downstairs, and it didn't seem as if they had been conversing either. Each was sitting with their hands on their knees, and they seemed awkward and ill at ease.

For Amos's part, his mind was on his wife who was due any minute with their fourth child. She'd been near hysterical ever since the siren had sounded at the pit, and he was worried about her. As the eldest brother and head of the family, it had been his duty to come and see his stepmother's sister, but he wanted to get back to Newcastle as soon as he could.

Barney, on the other hand, was not thinking about his wife and had no wish to pre-empt the return journey. His earlier reflections had led him on to thinking about the first time he had paid a visit to Ginnett's to see Josie performing. It had been Josie's last week there and he had been married nearly nine months by then; it was Pearl who had forced the issue of the visit. He would have gone to see Josie earlier, but Pearl had been driving him mad with her demands that he leave the concrete factory and work for her uncle, and it had put him off visiting the theatre before. He had been of a mind in those days that he wanted to succeed or fail in his job of his own accord and not have one handed him on a plate by his in-laws. Now, in view of the enormity of the disaster that was his marriage, working for Ernest seemed neither here nor there. However, eventually he had given in and they'd gone along. He could remember every minute of that night.

There had been the usual bairns doing a bit of clog dancing; a female impersonator who had ranged from falsetto to robust tenor; a burlesque actress turned dancer; a xylophonist-cum-comedian; a troupe of clowns and a wizard dressed as a Chinese Mandarin who'd juggled silver balls, keeping a hypnotising stream of them weaving through the air, but the real spell-binder of the evening had been a young slim lass with golden-brown hair and enormous dark eyes. Josie had been wearing an old stage dress that one of the other female performers had kindly given her; she'd cut it down and added a few ribbons and a bit of lace too, she'd confided later. By, she had looked bonny. And then she had sung, much like she'd done at his wedding do, and suddenly he had known . . . But it was too late. Months and months too late.

Maybe he had been stupid to suggest they all go out to dinner afterwards to celebrate Josie being offered a spell at a theatre in Gateshead at double what she was getting at Ginnett's, but Pearl had been all for it at the time. Or had seemed to be. They had enjoyed a slap-up dinner at a classy hotel in Newcastle, and he'd felt he had come alive for the first time in months. He couldn't remember what they'd talked about, only that the time had sped by and when he and Pearl had dropped Josie off at Frank and Betty's, he'd been unable to believe it was after midnight. Contrary to the way she had chattered all evening, Pearl had maintained a stony silence until they were home and he had paid the driver of the horse and carriage. And then all hell had broken loose.

Pearl had accused him of all sorts of things concerning Josie, and when he had reminded her that Josie was not yet fourteen and that in spite of her air of maturity and the fact that she had been working in the theatre for a good few months she was still very young, it hadn't made any difference. Perhaps he hadn't been convincing enough. Or perhaps the knowledge that had exploded on his consciousness earlier that evening, the knowledge that fate had played one of her nasty tricks in not telling him to wait for two or three years, had been all too evident? Whatever, Pearl had been beside herself.

The things she had thrown at him had caused him to remind her that in nine months of marriage – *nine months* – they had only made love three times, and that included the fiasco of their wedding night when she had sobbed and cried before he'd so much as laid a finger on her. He was sick and tired of treading on eggshells all the time in case he offended her finer sensibilities. She wanted a provider, a male eunuch, who would give her the respectability of being a wife with her own home but who would obey without demur, giving in to all her whims and fancies and effectively subjugating himself on every front. She'd barely bothered to deny it. That had been the beginning of the end.

'Right, lads, we'd better be makin' tracks.' Vera's voice was overbright, and as if realising this she turned to Josie, her tone more subdued as she said, 'Explain to Gertie won't you, lass, that I couldn't wait to say goodbye?' Gertie was at the Winter Garden in Bishopwearmouth with an old friend. The conservatory at the rear of the museum and library building which was an idyll of tropical plants and flowers was a regular meeting-place for folk. The invitation had been extended to both Josie and Gertie but although Josie had encouraged Gertie to accept, she'd declined herself, preferring to stay with Vera who seemed a little lost since Shirley's passing.

The men were standing now, and as Amos pulled his cap on to his head he nodded at Josie, saying, 'So long, lass,' before turning to Vera and taking her travelling bag as he added, 'Here, let's get this into the carriage, shall we?'

'By, hinny.' Vera gathered Josie into her embrace in an unusual show of affection and the two women hugged silently for some moments.

'Doubtless Horace will be up at the weekend, Vera, when I explain. Give Betty my love, and if there's anything I can do . . .'

'Anythin' you can do? Oh, Josie.' Vera's eyes were full. 'It'll make all the difference, lass. All the difference.' And on this enigmatic note – as far as Barney and Amos were concerned – Vera pressed Amos before her, saying, 'Come on then, lad, let's be off.'

'Goodbye, Josie.' Barney was within an arm's length of her, and his face was grim.

The feeling that always rose in her when she saw him brought its tight control to her face and voice, but there was only friendliness in her eyes when Josie said, 'Goodbye, Barney. I'm so very sorry about your da. He was a grand man.'

'Aye. He was an' all.'

He still stood looking at her after he had spoken, and something in his gaze brought Josie's heart jerking in her chest, even as she warned herself, Don't be daft. You're imagining it. Barney's a married man, and whatever the situation between him and Pearl he wouldn't think about you in *that* way. And Pearl's bonny, right bonny.

'How . . . how long do you think you'll be staying? I mean . . . at the Avenue and Palace. How long are you contracted for?' By, he was making a right mess of this, stuttering and stammering. Barney took a hold of himself as he added, 'You know Ernest'd be keen to have you back at Ginnett's any time you fancy a stint in Newcastle. And likely he could offer more than two shillings a night, eh?'

The last had been said jokingly in an effort to lighten the atmosphere, and Josie responded with a smile as she said, 'I know, I know, two and thruppence, no doubt!'

'Josie . . .' Barney stopped. And then he said again, 'Josie.' And then he just looked deep into her eyes.

She stared at him, her eyes wide and her stomach churning. No, no, it couldn't be . . . could it? And then the moment was broken as Vera spoke from the doorway. 'Josie? Josie, lass.' Her voice was slightly uncertain. 'There's a man here, a gentleman. He says he's spoken to you before.'

Josie wrenched her gaze from Barney's and it was only

in that moment that she became aware that for a little while she had been blind and deaf to anything but the tall young man in front of her, and also that Vera was looking at them very strangely.

'A gentleman?' Her voice sounded dazed even to herself.

'Good afternoon, Miss Burns.' Oliver Hogarth was standing just inside the doorway. 'I must apologise for presuming to call without an appointment but I had some business in these parts with an old friend in the profession who has links with the Palace, and he happened to mention your name and where you were residing. We never had a chance to continue our conversation in Hartlepool, did we, and so I thought that, as I was passing . . .'

Oliver Hogarth here. *Here.* And now, with Barney. Convention necessitated her responding, 'Good afternoon, Mr Hogarth. Come in, won't you,' but Josie was flustered and it showed. 'This is my friend, Mrs Briggs,' she added, as Oliver stepped into Vera's large kitchen, 'and this is her . . .' here Josie's mind couldn't work out exactly what Barney was in relation to Vera, and so she continued quickly, 'this is Mr Robson. He . . . he called with some bad news, I'm afraid.'

'Oh, I am sorry.' Oliver had turned to look directly at Vera, and now said quietly, 'If I have called at a difficult time, Mrs Briggs, please accept my apologies. I will take my leave at once.'

Vera looked at the tall commanding figure in front of her, her eyes taking in the quality of his greatcoat and hat, and the overall odour of wealth, but it was more what she had glimpsed in the few seconds when she had caught Josie and Barney unawares that made her say, and warmly, 'Not at all, Mr Hogarth, not at all. Do come an' have a seat, you look frozen. Josie, lass, put the kettle on.

I'll tell Amos to come an' sit himself down for a minute or two.'

Oh, Vera. Short of being downright rude there was nothing Josie could do but smile and do as she was bid, but she had seen Barney's eyes narrow and darken as he had surveyed the big man in the doorway, and she suspected Oliver Hogarth had too.

However, it was clear Vera didn't intend to leave her alone with this unknown entity – something Josie would have been thankful for in other circumstances – and as she busied herself making a fresh pot of tea and listened to the others making small talk, it became apparent that everyone was being careful not to speak out of turn. At least, that's how it was at first.

Interest was politely expressed when Oliver mentioned his occupation but when he didn't elaborate on the reason for his visit, Vera jumped into the brief silence, first explaining about Josie's recent loss before going on to disclose what had brought Barney and Amos to Sunderland.

Oliver nodded slowly. He had friends among mine owners; most of them the kind who never set foot outside London and controlled their fortunes with managers and overseers, but he didn't think this was the time to mention such connections. The last time he had had a conversation with one such friend, the man had been seething about the liberties the unions were trying to take; he had countered by sacking the miners he'd heard were the ringleaders and throwing them out of their cottages. 'Warning to the rest of the rabble,' was how he had put it, if Oliver remembered correctly. 'They can rot, them and their families with them. They'll be begging me for the privilege to work before I'm finished.'

'I understand five thousand miners are on strike in

Austria?' Oliver now said carefully, deciding caution was
the best policy. He didn't want to get on the wrong side
of Josie's friends at this stage, if indeed these two men
were her friends? Certainly the younger one, the one who
had been eying him somewhat aggressively ever since
he'd set foot in this miserable room, seemed hostile for
some reason.

'Oh aye?' Amos was acutely uncomfortable. This acquaintance of Josie's was a toff, you only had to look at him
to know that, and when he opened his gob his accent
confirmed he'd never got his hands dirty with real work.
'Dunno nowt about that. All I know is that this country owes
where it is now to the miners, but you wouldn't think so,
the way it treats us. The Durham Miners Association was
formed nigh on thirty years ago, but all the unions are still
fightin' for decent livin' wages an' safety underground,
same as then, an' nowt's improved. 'Course, you don't have
the lasses an' bairns underground now, but the conditions
are the same. Mebbe it's the same in Austria an' that's
why they're out?'

Oliver cleared his throat. If he had spoken the truth he
would have had to admit he shared Lyndon's view of
the average miner. From what he could tell from the
troubles reported in the newspapers, they were underground peasants, most of them ignorant and coarse with
none of the sensibilities that differentiated noble man from
lowly beast.

Perhaps something of this feeling came through in his
face, because Barney now entered the conversation and his
voice was belligerent. 'Can't be worse than here anyway,
Amos. In most pit villages you can't call a miner's wage his
wage at all; it's merely a juggling of payments and fines by
the coal company. The weighman makes sure he keeps in
with the owner by downgrading or rejecting as much stuff

as he can; didn't Da say he could remember his own da coming home with less than he started with because of the weighman's fines? And what hope of a fair hearing in the courts when only the employer is entitled to give evidence and not the employee? Magistrates are landowners which means they're employers anyway, so it's pretty short shrift for a pitman when his summons is heard.'

'Aye, well, we're not here the day to discuss the whys an' wherefores of all that,' Vera said briskly. 'Here, have a cup of tea, Mr Hogarth, an' a piece of me gingerbread.'

Oliver didn't want a cup of tea or a slice of gingerbread. Although he was looking at the older woman he was seeing a slim figure in a pale blue dress with the most beautiful head of golden-brown hair. Josie had looked charming on the stage, and their brief encounter that night in Hartlepool when he'd waited for her had told him she was a beauty, but it had been dark then and she had hurried away before he'd had a chance to look at her properly. Now, without any stage make-up or artifice, he could see that the cream-coloured skin was perfect, without blemish, and her eyes were the largest, the most arresting he had ever seen. But he must be careful not to stare or display undue interest; he didn't want to frighten her. This thought was a new one to Oliver; the sort of women he usually consorted with were not the kind to be nervous of a man's attentions. But this was different. *She* was different. Like a diamond set amongst the damn coal they'd been discussing.

'Thank you, Mrs Briggs. This is most kind of you.' He turned his charm on the older woman, sensing he needed a foothold here.

'My pleasure, Mr Hogarth.' Vera was rising to the occasion, and although she was burning with curiosity as to the reason for his visit, she didn't betray the merest flicker as she said, 'How long are you stayin' in these parts?'

'I return to London tomorrow.' At least, that had been his original idea. Now he wasn't so sure.

Vera nodded. He was one of these agent types and not a poor one either, and he'd sought her lass out. And at just the right time. She agreed with Gertie on the quiet over this; Josie needed to spread her wings.

'I had been hoping . . .' Oliver allowed himself a moment's hesitation, having decided on the strategy he was going to employ. 'But this is clearly a difficult time.' He turned his head, looking straight at Josie now who had just seated herself at the kitchen table. 'I had been hoping to discuss a business proposition with you, Miss Burns. Perhaps over dinner? And of course your family are most welcome to join us,' he added with a winsome smile at Vera. He wasn't dealing with a brash young thing here and poor as they obviously were, he sensed the proprieties would be expected to be upheld. Indeed, the working class were fiercer on that sort of thing than the middle and upper classes, from what he could make out. Certainly with regard to their women. Well, he'd play the game. He turned back to Josie, and the wide, heavily lashed eyes were waiting for him, causing his pulse to leap. Oh yes, he would play the game.

Strangely, the whirl Josie's mind had been in – first due to the shock of Barney's unspoken declaration and then Oliver Hogarth's sudden appearance – had cleared in the last moments. She knew why Oliver was here, of course; Lily had been explicit on that – he wanted to become her agent. And Barney? She didn't know what he wanted, she only knew she needed to get as far away from him as possible. He was married. To Pearl. He shouldn't have looked at her like that, he shouldn't. The beating of her heart was loud in her ears. It was wrong, and this feeling she had for him was wrong – this secret, guilty feeling that had been with her since the night he had rescued her from her da and Patrick Duffy, and which had grown relentlessly in the following years despite all her efforts to destroy it.

She knew Barney's eyes were hard on her face when she smiled at Oliver, and said quietly, her voice level and low, 'My sister and I – you met her that night outside the theatre? – would be pleased to have dinner with you, Mr Hogarth. My . . . my situation has changed considerably since we last met due to my mother's passing. Until now I have always felt restricted to working in the north-east.'

'I see.' Oliver forced himself to show no sign of the surge of excitement that made him want to grin from ear to ear. 'I am, of course, sorry to hear of your loss, but there is no doubt the London stage would benefit from your presence, Miss Burns.'

Smarmy blighter. Barney's teeth were clenched, his jaw rigid. The London stage. So that was the carrot he was dangling under her nose, was it? And he had business in these parts, did he? Business be damned. The only business Hogarth was interested in was Josie. He swallowed deeply, his voice brusque as he said, 'This old friend you're up to see, wonder if I know him?'

'You?' There was no animosity in Oliver's tone, merely surprise that a miner's son should think they might have a common acquaintance.

'Aye. I'm in the business – under-manager at Ginnett's in Newcastle,' Barney said, before Josie, her face straight now and her tone cool, said, 'I think Mr Hogarth's business here is his own affair, don't you?' and before Barney could reply one way or the other, added, 'Another cup of tea, Mr Hogarth?'

'No, thank you.' Oliver smiled as he spoke, even as his mind was saying, So that's it. He wants her. This great lout of a man wants her. Does she want him? He is good-looking enough and young. Nearer her age . . . He rose to his feet somewhat abruptly, saying, 'I must apologise again for delaying you, Mrs Briggs, but the tea was most welcome. Thank you for your kindness.'

'Oh, it's nowt, lad.' Vera had been thrown off-balance by the tense atmosphere in her kitchen as her reply indicated, and she hastily added, her face flushed, 'It was very nice to meet you,' in a primmer tone.

When, in the next moment, the front door opened and Gertie's voice called, 'There's a carriage outside! What's goin' on?' the interruption came as a relief to more than Vera. 'Oh!' Gertie stopped at the doorway, her eyes taking in the assembled company and widening at the sight of Oliver.

'Hello, lass.' Vera bustled forward, quickly explaining the reason for Barney and Amos's presence before she added, 'An' this is Mr Hogarth up from London.'

'We have met briefly,' Oliver said smoothly, nodding at Gertie before he added, speaking specifically to the small girl in the doorway, 'I was visiting a colleague, Miss Burns, who happened to mention your sister's name. A fortuitous coincidence after our meeting in Hartlepool.'

He wasn't going to give her away. Gertie smiled at Oliver, her eyes bright, and if he had but known it, he'd won a friend. 'It's nice to see you again,' she said circumspectly.

'You'll be seeing me a little later, too. Your sister has accepted an invitation to dinner on behalf of you both.'

She had? Gertie regarded him steadily as her smile widened. London, here we come. There was nothing to stop them now, and she had the feeling Oliver Hogarth was a man who would let nothing stand in his way when he wanted something. And his presence here today proved he wanted Josie.

Certainly she, for one, wouldn't be sorry to leave Sunderland. Several times lately, starting at her mam's funeral, she'd had a funny prickly feeling on the back of her neck and found herself looking around her, and today it had been stronger than ever. She'd actually found her heart pounding as she'd walked home along Borough Road, and by the time she'd got to Church Street East she'd thought twice about taking the path at the back of the church which was a bit more lonely. Likely she was being daft. As she listened to Oliver arranging to meet them after Josie's last evening performance, Gertie shivered. Aye, likely she was, but she'd pack her bags this very minute if she could, and that was the truth.

It was late when Barney eventually let himself into the imposing hall of the house in Windsor Terrace, and he stood for a moment just looking around him as though he was a stranger in the place. But that was how he felt at heart about this house. Pearl had spent a lot of thought and time on furnishing the downstairs of the house and their bedroom – her bedroom now – but the other three bedrooms had been empty until he had moved into one of them, and then all he had required was a bed and a wardrobe. Four bedrooms for the two of them when whole families lived in one room! Why had he agreed to move from St James Street? And then he answered himself bitterly. Why ask the road you know? He had still hoped then, deep in the heart of him, that somehow he and Pearl could learn to live together. She'd insisted this house was her dream house, that she'd never ask him for another thing if they could move here, and a tiny part of him which had longed for peace – just peace, nothing else – had thought it might make her happy. And for a time she had seemed more contented. But it hadn't lasted and it certainly hadn't made her softer towards him.

There was Betty back in Spring Garden Lane, consumed with grief over his da to the point where it had been painful to look into her face, and yet other couples, like him and Pearl most likely, would continue down the years and into old age together but in a state of semi-hostility. Life was damn ironic. Barney felt the tidal wave of grief for his da which had been threatening to overwhelm him all day sweep in with renewed intensity, and he fought it frantically. He couldn't give way now, not until he was in his bed and there was no chance of Pearl surprising him. Somehow he'd rather walk barefoot through burning coals for the rest of his days than let Pearl see him cry.

And then, as though the thought of her had conjured her up, his wife stepped into the hall from the sitting room. Pearl looked poised and calm as she stared at him for a moment, but Barney saw the tightness of her mouth and the faint flush staining the creamy skin of her neck and he knew she was het up about something. 'I thought I heard the door.' Her voice was clipped and cold. 'Did you really have to take so long? It's gone eleven.'

'I'm aware of the time.' He had long since given up trying to pacify her when she was in one of her moods.

So that was the tack he was going to take, was it? Pearl's light blue eyes were icy cold. She'd had to cancel a dinner-party she'd been looking forward to for weeks just because Barney had insisted on accompanying his brother to Betty's sister's house. And it hadn't really been necessary. Amos could have used the train or hired a carriage himself. Pearl chose to ignore that either option would have stretched Amos's limited income to the limit. Barney must think she was stupid if he didn't realise she knew the reason he'd gone to Vera's: it had been to see

Josie. She had warned him, when she'd refused to go to Josie's mother's funeral with him, that if he went she'd make his life hell. And he had merely answered that he would have to care about her for that to be a reality, but as it was she could do whatever she liked, and he was going to Shirley's funeral with or without her. And gone he had.

Pearl drew her small tight body upwards. 'So, you've finished with your gallivanting for one evening?' she said testily. 'Now you've managed to ruin the evening for me. Had a nice cosy chat with her, did you?'

'Her?' For a moment Barney thought Pearl meant Vera before the penny dropped, and then his voice was loud when he said, 'What's the matter with you, woman? I went to tell Vera me da had been killed. Me *da*, Pearl! Doesn't that mean anything to you?'

Pearl glared at him, and then she knew she'd gone too far when she said, 'No, it doesn't, if you want the truth.'

He'd hang for her before he was finished. It took Barney a full thirty seconds before he could master the hot fury her words had caused, and in that time he dared not move. He knew he wouldn't be responsible for what he might do to her, should she say or do anything. She was fond of the caustic one-liners, Pearl, and she delivered them with venom, but more often than not Prudence was round here of an evening and so he tended to direct most of his conversation at his sister before he retired, often before Prudence went home. It was ironic, when you thought about it, the number of times he had thanked God for Prudence's presence at the house in the evenings, and not just as a buffer between him and his wife either. Prudence talked sense and she kept up with the political and social events in a way Pearl was incapable of.

But Prudence wasn't here tonight and he had to go carefully. He had never yet raised his hand to a woman but he'd come damn near the night. One more word out of her, one more disdainful glance from those soulless clear eyes of hers when she talked about his da . . .

But Pearl had seen what was in her husband's eyes and she remained as still as he was, and she still stood there for some moments more after Barney had turned on his heel and left the room.

Chapter Ten

Sitting in front of the long dressing-room mirror at the Palace Theatre as Gertie arranged her hair in elaborate curls and waves on top of her head, Josie could hardly believe the two of them were off to London the next day.

It didn't seem as though five weeks had passed since she had promised Oliver Hogarth she would join him in the capital once her contracts here were finished. The time had just flown by.

Of course, there had been Frank's funeral. That had been harrowing for more than one reason. All the family had been there apart from Pearl, and when Josie had looked across and seen Barney standing all alone at the graveside, his face torn by grief, she'd remembered what he'd confided all those years ago during one of their long chats. His da had been disappointed in him, he'd said, adding that if there was any way he could have managed to work underground he would have done it – just for Frank's sake. 'Me da felt he lost face with some of the other blokes.' Barney's eyes had been fixed on the glowing coals in the range but the pain in his voice had told her what he was thinking. 'And he's never been the same with me since. He don't mean to be different, I know that, but somehow that makes it worse.'

She'd reached out and taken his hand at the time, giving it a comforting squeeze because words seemed inadequate, and at the funeral, when she'd watched him standing stiff and rigid as he had tried to hold on to his control, she'd walked across and done the same thing. In that moment she hadn't cared about what anyone else thought – if they had thought anything at all; she had just known Barney was hurting, and badly, and she hadn't been able to stand by and do nothing.

He had gripped her hand as though it was a lifeline but although his jaw had contracted he'd said nothing, continuing to stare straight ahead as the gravediggers had heaped dirt into the gaping hole in the ground into which the coffin had been lowered a minute or two earlier.

Later, at Betty's little home where family and friends had gathered, Josie saw Prudence walk across to Barney who was standing looking out of the window into the small back yard. The girl had put her hand on his sleeve and said something, her face earnest, and whatever it was, it had seemed to bring a measure of comfort to his face. Three months after Josie had left Newcastle, Betty had told her Prudence had eaten humble pie as far as her brother was concerned and asked his forgiveness for her part in the attack at the house; somewhat reluctantly on Barney's part apparently, the two had begun speaking again. Betty had commented that this had been a means to an end as far as Prudence was concerned; she reckoned her stepdaughter's prime concern had been to make things easier for her and Pearl to continue their friendship as before, but Josie wasn't so sure. If Prudence had genuine love and respect for anyone it was her brother, she felt, and the withdrawal of his companionship must have been a bitter blow to the girl. She didn't like Prudence – she would never be able to like her – but in her better moments she did feel sorry for Barney's sister, and she had no wish for a family feud to continue because of her.

Nevertheless, Josie had been well aware of the cold glances in her direction from that quarter at Betty's house, although as she had been busy helping Vera in the kitchen most of the time she hadn't let Prudence's antagonism trouble her. It had been late evening when folk were beginning to take their leave and Josie had just emerged from the children's bedroom after getting the little ones off to sleep, when Prudence cornered her at the top of the stairs. Josie knew immediately that the encounter was not going to be pleasant.

'You didn't have to come here today, you know – you're not family.' Prudence's voice had been low but her sallow cheeks had been flushed with the force of the emotion within.

Josie had raised her chin unconsciously, but her tone was non-confrontational when she said, 'I know I'm not family, but I'm Vera's friend and Betty's too. More to the point, I thought a lot of your da and I wanted to show my respects.'

Prudence looked into the beautiful face in front of her, at the creamy skin, the great dark eyes, now wary and guarded, and her eyes travelled to the rich golden-brown hair that was a crown to the beauty beneath. As she stared at Josie she realised for the first time that part of her dislike was because the other girl took her loveliness totally for granted, was unaware of it, even. And it wasn't only her physical appearance. Even Pearl, who had come to loathe Josie as much as Prudence did, had said that her voice was remarkable.

The thought of her friend who was not her friend, and who was making her brother wretchedly unhappy, caused the old guilt feelings to rise. Prudence knew she should have warned Barney before he was wed that Pearl was not all she'd seemed to him. Her feelings caused her to say, and bitingly, 'Your respects! Don't make me laugh. You're here to tell us all how well you're doing, little Miss High and Mighty! Nothing but an upstart you are, girl, and however much you get on and however much you earn you can't get away from your beginnings.'

'What makes you think I want to get away from my beginnings, Prudence?' Josie answered her, purposely misunderstanding the context. 'My beginnings are linked with Gertie and my mam and Vera, so why would I want to get away from them?'

'You know what I mean.'

'If you mean I want to succeed in life, surely you're all for that?' Josie challenged swiftly. 'I can remember you saying years ago that things must change, that women have as much right as men to rise in the world and that they should be paid for the job they do, not a subsistence wage based on their gender. *And* you used to argue that the unions had to fight for each individual member regardless of their age or social standing or gender. Didn't you? *Didn't you!*'

It would be true to say here that if thoughts could kill, Josie would not have lived to see another dawn. Prudence stared at her, desperately searching for an answer that would put this thorn in her flesh in her place, but she was still speechless when Josie turned away from her and made her way downstairs to the others.

Shameless, she was, Josie Burns. Prudence continued looking after her after Josie had gone down the stairs. Her type always had an answer for everything. She'd smarmed her way in at home, Prudence thought bitterly, had her da and Barney eating out of her hand and even now she was still setting her cap at Barney. Thought no one had noticed, no doubt, but she'd seen Josie make up to him at the graveside. At the *graveside*, of all places! And then to go and talk about showing respect for her da. She was a baggage and an upstart, always had been and always would be, and all her fine talk wouldn't alter that! Prudence's thin lips twisted with rage, and then she stamped back downstairs. Not for a second did she allow any particle of her mind to suggest that Josie had been absolutely right in all that she had said.

Betty had moved back to Sunderland a week after the funeral, but it was Amos and one of the other brothers who had moved her, so Josie hadn't seen Barney again. Betty was now established in a small terraced property in Brougham Street; due to her windfall – for which she had thanked Josie over and over again – and the small amount of money paid out on Frank's death, she had been able to purchase it outright.

Brougham Street was not too far from the corn mill where Betty and Vera had both obtained part-time shifts – Vera working mornings and Betty afternoons – with the idea that whichever sister wasn't working would take care of Betty's little brood.

It had all worked out very well, and Betty was as happy as she could be, given the tragic circumstances.

'You're on next, Josie. After the chaser-out.' One of the troupe of Oriental dancers who had just come off-stage spoke to Josie as she passed, and Josie nodded in acknowledgement.

This new invention of moving pictures which the Palace had had for two or three years now provided a useful breathing space halfway through the evening. The films shown were of short duration and usually of topical or local interest, but even though the movements were jerky and the projection machine broke down at some point every week, the patrons loved them.

Josie's eyes moved upwards to the framed page of the

Sunderland Citizen hanging above the middle of the mirror. The article had appeared two years before in August, so amusing the Palace's manager that he'd cut it out and kept it for posterity. It read:

> *The Cinematograph.* This is a most extraordinary invention, but I think the inventor(s) will be almost regretting that he ever produced it, since instead of being used for the improvement and advancement of mankind, it has hitherto been used for exhibitions of a most degrading nature. The prize-fight was bad enough, but *The Bride's First Night* and suchlike exhibitions were outrageous. A friend of mine went to both. He went especially to see the effect upon the people. The effect was so vile that he assured me he doubted whether any decent working man would ever dare to admit to his children or womenfolk that he had been there. Is there really no way to stop these things? We prohibit prize-fighting by law, we also prohibit public indecency. Have we not the power to prohibit exhibitions which are life-size and amount to the same thing? Surely these are things for the Watch Committee to watch.

The manager had written underneath the article, in great black letters, *A friend went to see* The Bride's First Night? *Who does he think he's kidding? But don't worry, my bairns – this is just a seven-day wonder, moving pictures, and no threat to the legitimate theatre.*

Josie wasn't so sure. She remembered Vera's enthusiastic commendation of the Victoria Hall's picture-show in the first week of January. The hall had presented what were proclaimed to be 'The Most Beautiful Animated Pictures' ever seen in Sunderland, 'A Triumph of

Animated Photography, 10,000 pictures of the Boer War and our Navy.' The hall had been packed every night and although Vera was not easily impressed, she had gone twice. And according to the *Sunderland Echo* in December, when the Olympia Exhibition Hall in Borough Road – a giant pleasure-drome with roundabouts, gondolas, a free menagerie and the best circus entertainment – held a special performance of Edison George's *Special War Pictures*, the large audience enjoyed themselves most heartily, joining in with the Olympian band as it played patriotic songs.

Yes, there was a place being carved out for moving pictures all right, Josie thought. It might be a novelty according to most folk, but it was a novelty that the public was taking to its heart, although she agreed with the manager that the music hall would continue. Anything else was unthinkable.

'So, our last night here then.' Gertie was looking at her sister's reflection in the mirror, and Josie nodded to the face behind her shoulder. 'Oliver must think a bit of you, lass, to insist he come up here tomorrow and escort us down to London himself.'

Josie shrugged. 'He probably does that for anyone new he signs up, Gertie. And he knows we haven't been to London before so likely he thought we'd get lost. But aye, it is nice of him.'

'Do you like him then? As a person I mean, not an agent,' Gertie asked nonchalantly.

Josie understood her sister too well to be fooled by the casual tone, but a sudden crash and thud at the far end of the dressing room announced that Sybil – a serio-comedienne who indulged strongly in doubles entendres in her patter and often downright vulgarity – had fallen off her stool again, after partaking too well of the whisky flask she kept hidden from the management's eagle eye in her bag.

Josie and several of the other girls rushed to help her up, and once they had hauled her none too light bulk back on to the seat, Josie asked Gertie to make a pot of strong black coffee. This was the third time the ageing veteran – who had married her first husband at the tender age of fifteen and was now on her fourth, and again unhappy, marriage – had been the worse for wear due to the drink. Sybil tried to mask her unhappiness in a round of gay living, and was in fact holding one of her famous parties that very night to which all of the players had been invited.

Amid a few feathers from Sybil's shocking-pink boa that were floating in the air, the girls poured coffee down her throat until it was time for Josie to go onstage, and so further conversation regarding Oliver was forgotten.

It was hard to believe now, Josie thought soberly, as she walked into the glare of the footlights a few minutes later, that the wreck of a woman in the dressing room had once been the toast of London.

It was common knowledge that Sybil had drunk champagne with princes in palaces but also eaten winkles with her old friends round street stalls, and because of that she was a favourite with everyone. In her hey-day, Albert Edward, the Prince of Wales, had asked for a private performance because Sybil was one of his favourite artistes, and she had been more than half an hour late at his apartments, due to keeping a promise she'd made to visit an old impoverished fellow performer in hospital. Everyone loved Sybil – except, perhaps, the lady herself.

The incident in the dressing room had been depressing, but like every music-hall artiste, Josie became someone else once she was onstage. She sang a somewhat flirtatious song first, dimpling at the audience as she heard appreciative chuckles from parts of the building. It was the late session, and here and there a cigar hung lazily from a smiling mouth as patrons considered each song or dance or other performance with an air of languid contentment; a hazy sense of smoke and drink and general enjoyment pervaded the theatre.

After two songs of a faintly suggestive nature, sung with wide-open eyes and a small pout, Josie knew the audience were with her. Now she moved into the very centre of the stage, a slim, graceful figure leaning forward to accentuate the refrain of the sentimental ballad she began to sing. She felt the spontaneous movement of sympathy and attention her voice and demeanour evoked, and now the patrons' sombre, intent faces threw into more brilliant relief her beseeching gestures, bathed as she was in rays of rosy-pink lights from the centre of the roof and from below in the glow of the footlights. Part of her was sorry to be leaving the place of her birth for the capital, and something of this feeling must have come across in the pathos of the song, because there was a collective sigh from the audience when she finished the last note before they broke out into tumultuous applause.

And it was only then, as she curtsied and smiled before agreeing to sing another song – more to give the girls in the dressing room extra time to sober Sybil up than anything else – that she noticed the big handsome man in one of the boxes to the left of the auditorium. *Oliver.* But she'd thought he was arriving tomorrow? And then he smiled at her, blowing her a silent kiss of approval, and she found herself blushing scarlet as she wrenched her eyes away from the magnetic blue gaze. This would never do. A man like Oliver Hogarth was used to elegant, sophisticated creatures who were conversant with the ways of the world. She had discovered a great deal about the man since her fellow artistes had realised who her new agent was. Sybil in particular had been very blunt.

Oh, she knew he had won Gertie over; her sister was transparent in that regard, much as she would have protested the issue. But Oliver Hogarth was something of a libertine and a rake according to everyone else, and after she had thought the matter over, Josie realised it was true. He had charmed Lily to get to her that night in Hartlepool, and without any conscience whatsoever. 'A bit of a ladies' man but nice with it.' That's what Lily had said. Of course, it could have all been innocent, but it had been three or four in the morning when Lily had returned . . . If Hogarth thought Josie was *that* sort of girl, he had another think coming. By, he did.

'Keep your knickers on and the elastic tight, and you'll be all right, dear.' That's what Sybil had said to her when Josie had first mentioned Oliver Hogarth. 'He's not a bad man, not like some – oh, the stories I could tell you, dearie, they'd make your hair curl – but he *is* partial to a well-turned ankle, and there's many a young gal woke up in the morning regretting the night before when Oliver's been around, if you get my meaning.'

Josie had got her meaning, and once got, was not going to forget it. So now she sang her last song, arousing nostalgic memories for more than one or two in the audience with her rendition of 'Bobbing Up and Down Like This', along with much laughter, and left the stage on a wave of cheering and clapping.

She heard the chairman, who was sitting at a table in front of the orchestra, begin his flowery speech to announce Sybil, who was waiting in the wings, and she spoke softly to the other woman as she moved past her. 'Are you all right, Sybil? Are you up to going on?'

Heavy stage make-up couldn't hide the wrinkles in the face looking back at her, but Sybil smiled widely as she whispered, 'It'll take more than a dram or two to stop me, dear, but bless you for asking. My main worry now is wetting me drawers after all that coffee.'

The young woman and the older one leaned against each other briefly, both shaking with laughter, and then as the chairman resumed his seat with melancholy dignity and banged his little auctioneer's hammer, the orchestra broke into Sybil's signature tune and she flitted lightly on to the stage, losing twenty years as she did so.

Dear Sybil. She had a heart of gold and such a warm, generous nature, and yet everyone knew her present husband had indulged his roving eye ever since they had been married. Why was it that some women seemed to have a penchant for philanderers and rotters? Josie asked herself as she hurried back to the dressing room. And then an image of Oliver's attractive face came into her mind and she bit her lip hard, just before she opened the dressing-room door and was enfolded in a wave of chatter and cheap scent and colour. And then Gertie was at her side.

'Oliver's here! He's sent you this.' Gertie handed her an exquisite corsage as she spoke, her voice bubbling. 'An' he's asked us out to dinner after the show. Look, he got me one an' all.'

She pointed to a smaller corsage that was nevertheless just as pretty, and which she had already pinned to the lapel of her serge dress.

Josie glanced down at the delicate arrangement of pale peach orchids threaded through with cream lace, and she couldn't quell the flutter of pleasure and excitement that speeded her pulse. However, her voice was quiet and steady when she said, 'I presume Billy brought these along?' Billy was the young lad who ran errands, assisted Oswald – the stagehand – and was general dogsbody and jack-of-all-trades. 'And no doubt you accepted the invitation to dinner on behalf of us both?'

Gertie turned her head and stared at her sister for a moment before saying in a slightly defensive tone, 'He's come all the way from London, lass, an' he *is* your agent, isn't he?'

Josie nodded, seating herself on the stool Gertie had kept clear for her amidst all the mayhem. 'Aye, he's my agent,' she said very softly, 'but that's all he is, Gertie. You understand? I . . . I don't want him to get any ideas.' That went for Gertie too, so it was better to nip any misunderstanding in the bud right now. 'We don't know how things are going to turn out down south and I'm going to have more than enough on my plate as it is. My work is the only thing which interests me. All right, Gertie? Is that clear?'

My work is the only thing that interests me. What stupid things we say sometimes. As the thought took form, along with another – different – man's image in her mind's eye, Josie lowered her head and fiddled with the buttons of her dress. She had had a difficult time keeping the picture of Barney all alone at the graveside out of her mind, and even now it still crept in at odd moments when she wasn't on her guard. And she could do nothing at all about her dreams.

She was glad she was going down south, she told herself savagely, whipping the hairpins out of her hair and massaging her head with the tips of her fingers, ignoring Gertie's protests at the cavalier treatment of her painstakingly arranged curls and waves. It was the best thing all round, it was. And she was grateful, so, so grateful, that no one could read anyone else's mind.

And then just for a moment that last thought was brought into question when Gertie's hand lightly touched her shoulder and patted it twice, and her sister's voice said quietly, 'Aye, it's clear, lass, it's clear.'

Josie looked at her sister's small elfin face in the mirror

and Gertie stared back at her for a moment without speaking. And then she said, with a lilt in her voice, 'So, what's it to be then? Bread and cheese all by ourselves with water to wash it down, or a slap-up meal with Oliver where you'll be fêted and adored? Difficult choice, I know.'

Oh, Gertie. In spite of herself Josie grinned back at her sister. 'I don't think bread and cheese was on the cards for tonight,' she said drily, 'but I get your point. And as you so rightly said, Oliver *has* come all the way from London.'

'Exactly.' Gertie beamed at her. 'And I wouldn't expect you to do any other than follow Sybil's advice about the elastic on your drawers, by the way.'

'Gertie!'

At that moment the dressing-room door was thrown open and Sybil herself entered on a gust of plumage and perfume. The painted face was smiling, and on catching sight of Josie, Sybil called, and loudly, 'Josie, darling, there's someone out here waiting to make your acquaintance! Come and put him out of his misery, and do feel free to bring him to my party tonight, dear. Such a nice young man and so polite. I do like politeness in a man, don't you?'

Oliver. He hadn't had the good grace to wait until she left the theatre, but had come to the very door of the dressing room. What would people think? Her mouth smiling but her eyes cold, Josie ignored the last part of Sybil's ringing proclamation which had had all the girls' heads turning interestedly towards her, and said quietly, 'Someone, Sybil? Can't you give me a clue?'

Sybil had almost reached her now but as was her wont when she had had a few, her voice was still strident when she exclaimed, 'A handsome young fellow m'lad, dearie. The sort who makes me wish I was a few years younger, I tell you. He said his name was . . .' she paused, more wrinkles joining the others as she screwed up her eyes. 'What was it? Harry . . . Horace . . . No, I have it!' She beamed at Josie triumphantly. 'Hubert. He said his name was Hubert and that you would want to speak to him when you knew he was here.'

'Hubert?' She and Gertie had spoken together, and now, as Josie's eyes met those of her sister in the mirror, she said dazedly, 'That's my brother, Sybil.'

'Darling child, aren't they all?' Sybil gave one last leer before she tottered over to her stool and crashed down on its long-suffering legs.

'Josie.' Gertie was clutching her so hard on the shoulders Josie knew she would have bruises in the morning. 'Oh, Josie.'

'It's all right. It's all right, lass.' Josie was speaking mechanically, her head whirling. She suddenly had the most inordinate desire to laugh, but she knew it was the kind of laughter that would finish up with her weeping. Hubert, here? Then Jimmy . . . And her da. All this time with no news. Her mam had been right. They *had* been here. Oh, *Mam* . . .

Josie was on her feet now, and she took Gertie's arm as she said in a low, soft hiss, 'Be careful what you say if it is Hubert out there. Remember how things were the last time we saw Da and the lads. It's not so much Jimmy and Hubert, but I wouldn't trust Da an inch.' This wasn't quite true. She didn't trust Jimmy any more than she did her father, but now was not the time to go into that.

'Josie, I've felt . . .' Gertie paused, giving a small embarrassed laugh. 'I've felt someone was watching us since we've been back. It started at Mam's funeral so it could be them, couldn't it?'

'If it is, I shall want to know why the lads didn't go and see Mam at least once, to put her mind at rest that they were all right,' Josie said grimly. 'And that's just the start of it. Where have they been all this time?' She had been pulling her hair into a ponytail as she spoke, and she now twisted it into a low chignon at the back of her head and secured it with a few pins. 'Come on.' She took Gertie's arm and they walked towards the dressing-room door. 'Let me do the talking, lass,' Josie warned, 'especially if Da and our Jimmy are anywhere near.' She hadn't forgotten the fate her father had intended for his youngest daughter, nor his brutality that night in Newcastle. Whatever this meeting was meant to accomplish, it would be for her father's benefit, that was for sure.

For a moment, after they had opened the door and stepped into the passageway outside, Josie knew a feeling of relief mixed with disappointment. The youth standing with his back to them was far too tall for little Hubert. Her youngest brother had always been undersized and skinny, and although the last five years were bound to have wrought some change, he would now still only be twelve.

And then the lad turned, and a voice in her head said, *It is him.* And in spite of all she had said to Gertie just moments before, Josie found herself springing forward and taking him in her arms. 'Hubert!' she cried. 'Hubert, I can't believe it!' And then Gertie joined them and the three of them were hugging and laughing and crying all at the same time.

It was Hubert who pulled away first, wiping his wet face with the back of his hand as he said, 'I had to come but I've got to be quick. You must listen to me, both of you, but you can't let on I've been here. He'll kill me if he finds out.'

'Da?'

'Da? No, not Da.'

He was as tall as she was, Josie was thinking. And good-looking. 'Who then?' she asked, baffled.

'Patrick Duffy. You remember him? He took me an' Jimmy in when Da cleared off. He said there'd been some trouble, that you'd put the polis on to Da, an' on to me an' Jimmy an' all, 'cos of the thievin', you know? So he took us in, looked after us, like.'

She just bet he had. Josie stared at her brother, and when Gertie said, 'That's not true! Hubert, it isn't true,' she didn't say anything for a moment.

'Is it, Josie?' Hubert's voice was tremulous. 'Patrick said you made Da skedaddle, that he signed on a ship leavin' for Norway or somewhere foreign. He said Mam was part of it, too; that the pair of you had shopped us.'

'Patrick Duffy and Da came to Vera's sister Betty's house in Newcastle and attacked me a couple of weeks after we'd left home.' The words were slow and painful, and Josie looked hard into her brother's blue eyes as she spoke. Hubert's eyes weren't the cold icy blue of her father's eyes and Jimmy's, but warmer, with an almost violet tinge. 'They wanted to put Gertie on the game, probably me too, but Barney – Betty's stepson – came home and there was a fight. I only told the police about that, Hubert, I didn't mention you or Jimmy, and Mam had no part in anything.'

'Do you swear that, Josie? On Mam's grave?' Suddenly the small lad was very evident inside the lanky youth.

'Aye, I do, but you must have thought Duffy was lying, else you wouldn't be here now,' Josie said very quietly.

Hubert nodded, and then grinned. 'Still the same old Josie, sharp as a knife. But you're right. Mind, Jimmy thinks the sun shines out of Patrick's backside, an' I have to say he don't knock us about like Da did, an' he always gives us our fair whack. He's bin good to us, lass. Credit where credit's due.'

Josie made no comment. Whatever Patrick Duffy had done he would have done it for his own gain, she had no doubt about that, and she didn't like to think what the tall, fresh-faced young lad in front of her was involved in. Duffy would taint everything and everyone he came into contact with, he was that type of man. 'Mam's last words were about you and Jimmy,' she said suddenly, reaching out and grasping her brother's arm. 'She loved you, Hubert, she did, and she wanted us all to be together again. Look, I'm going to London the morrow with Gertie – you and Jimmy could come with us.'

'What?'

'I mean it. You could make a fresh start – I'd help you. You don't have to stay here with Duffy. He's rotten, Hubert, through and through. You must see that?'

She watched her brother's face straighten, and his jaws champed for a moment or two before he said, 'I told you, Patrick's bin good to us. In his own way he's bin right good when no one else cared a penny farthin'. Da cleared off and Mam – well, she might not have shopped us but she wasn't o'er bothered about me an' Jimmy, about any of us.'

'That's not true, lad. That's Jimmy talking.'

'An' you an' Gertie were in clover an' out of it all. Patrick took us in 'cos he was Da's friend an' there was no one else. Anyway,' he paused, rubbing his hand hard across his mouth, 'him an' Jimmy are as thick as thieves like I said, an' Jimmy wouldn't go anywhere.'

And what Jimmy said and did, Hubert lived by. By making sure of the elder brother, Patrick Duffy had known he had the younger too. Oh, she hated that man. She really hated him. Josie looked into Hubert's troubled face and tried one more time. 'Won't you at least talk to Jimmy about it and see what he thinks? He might like the chance to leave here and try his hand in London. Please, Hubert?'

The lad turned his gaze from her and stared at the floor, and his voice was very low as he said, 'You don't understand, lass. Jimmy believes every word Patrick says, an' he thinks you were the cause of Da leavin' us an' all the trouble. He don't know I've come to see you, but I had to. They're plannin' to . . .' He stopped, raising his head but still not looking Josie directly in the face as he said, 'Patrick knows people, people who'd do anythin' for a few bob. He's got a finger in every pie there is; nowt happens here without him knowin' about it. He knows you're goin' tomorrow.'

Josie merely stared at him, but it was Gertie who said shakily, 'What are you saying, lad?'

'It'll be tonight, later, when you go back to Vera's. He's already got blokes watchin' an' he's told 'em however long it takes they wait till the time's right. If you're walkin', all to the good; if you're in a carriage or with someone they see to them an' all if they have to – whatever's necessary, Patrick said. But he wants you an' Gertie alive an' kickin'.'

'And you're saying Jimmy knows about this?' Josie blinked her eyes as her vision blurred with shock. 'He's part of it?'

'He's goin' to be the one who steps out an' stops you afore you open the door. He'll make out he's friendly like, that he wants to talk to you about Mam dyin', that he's only just heard.'

'But . . . but you can't just kidnap people,' Gertie stammered. 'Duffy must know he wouldn't get away with it. When me an' Josie didn't come home Vera'd contact the authorities an' there'd be a stink.'

Hubert looked at her, and for all his tender years his

gaze was pitying. 'He'd get away with it. I've seen—'
And then he stopped abruptly. He wasn't here to shop
anyone or to frighten his sisters any more than he had to.
But they *were* his sisters, his own flesh and blood. He just
couldn't understand their Jimmy over Josie. Jimmy hated
her every bit as much as Patrick did, perhaps even more
so, and in this – as in more than one or two things lately
– his brother gave him the willies. He remembered how
Jimmy's face had changed when he'd pointed out they
only had Patrick's word that she'd blown the whistle on
them all. By, fair mental Jimmy'd gone. He'd agreed with
Jimmy and Patrick before, that no contact with their mam
and Josie was best, but once they'd started talking about all
this . . . The thieving and such was part of life and he was
good at it, he knew he was, but lately there'd been things
that had fair turned his stomach.

He forced his mind away from the mental picture of
Jimmy's boot driving again and again into a man's face
until it was an unrecognisable bloody pulp, and all the
while his brother and Patrick and Patrick's henchmen
laughing like a bunch of loonies, and now he repeated,
'He'd get away with it. He's got away with a lot worse.'
And he felt the twitch in the side of his jaw that worked
his eye and made his mouth rise up at the corner flare
into life for a moment before he scrubbed at his face with
his hand.

Josie closed her eyes for a moment. There was something in the back of her mind nagging at her. 'Have you
heard from Da at all in the last few years? Has he been
in touch with Duffy?'

'No. No, I told you. Da told Patrick he was signin'
on a ship. That's one of the reasons Jimmy feels like
he does. He thought a bit of Da. Don't ask me why,
'cos as far as I remember all Da did was knock the

hell out of us, but anyway,' Hubert shrugged, 'there it is.'

'Don't go back tonight, Hubert.' Josie put out her hands and gripped those of her brother. *Her da had been scared of the water.* She remembered that now. Why hadn't she remembered before? But then she'd only been a wee bairn of five or six that warm summer's night down at the dockside when she'd been begging outside one of the waterfront pubs as usual. Her da and one of his cronies had passed quite close by but she'd melted into the shadows before he'd seen her; his usual greeting on such occasions being a skelp of the lug along with a command to get her backside home, as though he hadn't ordered her out begging just hours before. The other man had been trying to persuade her da to do something, she couldn't recall his words or what it had all been about now, but she did remember her da saying, 'Never. Never, man, an' I don't care if it's easy pickin's. You'll not get me on a boat, even one in dock, for love or money. I like me feet on solid ground an' there's an end to it.' *Her da had said that.*

'I'll be all right. No one knows I'm here.' Hubert had let his hands remain in hers but his voice was determined.

'Hubert, Da would never have gone off without a word to anyone, and I don't believe boarding a ship would enter his mind. He didn't like the water, he was frightened of it.'

'What's that got to do with anythin'?'

'Well, Duffy said Da told him he was signing on a ship.'

'You'd just put the law on 'em both. Likely he thought he might go down the line an' it was the lesser of two evils.'

'He wouldn't. I just know he wouldn't.'

'Josie?' Gertie put a hand on her sister's elbow.

'Don't you see?' Josie swung from one puzzled face to

the other. 'Patrick Duffy bought a whole host of alibis for the night he and Da came for me and Gertie, and with Da out of the way there was no one who could prove he'd been in Newcastle. It was my word, that of a twelve-year-old bairn, against a dozen or more folk.'

'Oh come on, what're you sayin'?' Hubert shook his head, his tone openly scornful.

'Da was the key, don't you see? The police would accept I know my own da, but someone accompanying him could be more doubtful. And Duffy got hurt that night, burned on his legs and maybe his hands. He would have been mad. You know his temper, Hubert. He's got a nasty streak.'

Nasty streak? Hubert thought of some of the things he had witnessed in the last few years. Nasty streak described a normal man and the little Irishman wasn't normal. And those first weeks with Patrick – he *had* had something wrong with his hands. He hadn't been able to do much, and he'd been constantly swearing and cursing. 'You're sayin' . . . ?'

'I'm not sure what I'm saying, but if Duffy did away with Da . . .' Josie's eyes moved from Hubert's face to Gertie's white one. 'He could have. He's capable of it, isn't he?'

This last question was directed at Hubert, and now the young lad nodded dazedly. 'Aye. Aye, he's capable of it all right, but his own mate? An' why take on me an' Jimmy?'

'Guilty conscience?' No, that wasn't right, Josie thought. Duffy was without conscience. Oh, she didn't know all the ins and outs but the more she thought about this, the more certain she was that Duffy knew more than he was letting on about her father's disappearance. They had always been so sure her da and the lads were together somewhere, and if her da had been alive, that's what would have happened.

She looked at Hubert and saw his eyes were fixed on her. 'You're wrong, Josie. You have to be.' He swallowed, and then made an impatient movement with his hand as he added, 'An' that's by the by for the minute anyways. I came to put you on your guard. What are you goin' to do?'

She stared at him, and it was a few seconds before she said, 'If it's me and Gertie they're waiting for, we obviously can't go back to Vera's tonight. My . . . my agent was going to take us out to dinner later on so I'll have to explain the situation to him.' And at Hubert's involuntary movement of protest, Josie added, 'He's not from these parts, Hubert, and he won't say a word to anyone if I ask him not to, so there's no harm in him knowing. Gertie and I will have to book into a hotel or something. Oliver will help with that, and then we'll go back in daylight to Vera's. They aren't going to wait for us for ever, are they?'

'I shouldn't think so but they're scared of Patrick – even Jimmy is, though he'd never admit it. Do you have to go back there at all?'

'I don't suppose so.' Josie's lips pursed in thought. 'I could send a message to Vera to pack our things and bring them to us. A note or something.'

'Be careful what you say.' There was fear in Hubert's voice. 'Don't mention me or anything like that. If it fell into Patrick's hands . . .'

'Oh, Hubert.' Josie forgot about her own situation as she read the panic in his eyes. 'If you're so scared of him, why won't you come with us? You could, right now. You don't have to go back to wherever you live. You could be free of Duffy for good.'

'Jimmy—'

'Jimmy's chosen his own road,' Josie cut in, her voice harsh. 'And you know it. But you're different. You're not like them.'

'It's not just Jimmy.'

'Then what?'

He wished he could unburden himself, really unburden himself to Josie, but he couldn't. The thing was, no one ever walked away from Patrick, and on the rare occasion someone had been stupid enough to try they'd been found floating face down in the docks sooner or later, mostly sooner. A sudden rush of terror gripped him, and his voice trembled as he said, 'Nothin', nothin', I just can't, that's all. Look, I've told you now an' I've got to go, all right? I . . . I'm glad you didn't shop me an' Jimmy, Josie. I didn't think you'd do that somehow.'

Josie said again, 'Oh, Hubert,' but now in a voice strangled with tears, and the three of them were hugging again, Gertie openly crying, when Michelle Bousquet appeared in the passageway with her ladies from their *Living Statue* act. The ladies in the tableaux appeared to be almost nude, their bodies heavily covered in lacquer, and always caused a stir with the audience and more than a little collar adjusting and clearing of throats with the male fraternity, so now the effect of these well-proportioned, nubile creatures on Hubert was immobilising. He became transfixed, watching them pass with stunned eyes and an open mouth, and then blushed furiously when Michelle herself – a buxom, sleek-haired Parisian – turned and winked at him before she closed the dressing-room door and they were left alone again.

'You see what you're missing by not throwing your lot in with Josie?' Gertie said wickedly, smiling up through her tears at this 'baby' brother who was a good eight or nine inches taller than her.

'They . . . they were . . .' Hubert's voice failed him.

'They weren't, actually.' Josie was grinning now, she couldn't help it. 'Although it looked like it.' And then her face straightened as she said, 'Promise me one thing. Promise me you'll think about what I've said, about you coming to London and staying with me and Gertie. We're leaving with Oliver Hogarth, my agent, from Central Station at two tomorrow. If you want to come, be there. That's all you have to do. I'll sort everything, I promise. I hate the thought of you going back to . . . all that.'

The boy hung his head for a moment, then muttered, 'It's no good. You don't understand.'

'Promise me you'll think about it.'

'Aye, aye all right, I promise.'

He was already backing away from them as he spoke, and the answer had been too quick – they all knew it. What could she do? What could she say that she hadn't already said? All this time and now he was going to vanish again, but knowing Hubert and Jimmy were with Duffy, and that no one had seen hide nor hair of her da since that time in Newcastle had made everything a hundred times worse. *He was only twelve.* Twelve! But a streetwise, sharp, old twelve over whom she had no jurisdiction.

'Hubert!'

Her cry went into empty air. He had already disappeared.

Chapter Eleven

'And you suspect this man, this Patrick Duffy fellow, is responsible for your father's disappearance?'

Oliver had been sitting looking at her for the last moments in stupefied silence, so Josie was quite glad he had found his voice at last. She suspected their dinner conversation was not quite along the lines he had expected or desired.

They were seated, along with Gertie, at a very pleasant table in the Bridge Hotel situated in High Street West. The coaching inn had been converted from the eighteenth-century Sunderland residence of the Lambton family and was known for its good food and respectability. Oliver enjoyed the former and felt he needed to emphasise his acquaintance with the latter where his new protégée was concerned. He was well aware of his reputation, and normally it didn't worry him a jot, but he didn't want Josie thinking . . . What didn't he want her thinking? He'd asked himself this several times whilst he'd waited for her to emerge from the stage door of the theatre earlier. That he wanted her in his bed? That he desired far more from her than a mere working relationship? Both were true. But he fancied – no, he *knew* – that he had to proceed carefully with this particular damsel. She wasn't like the rest. Most of his set would doubtless laugh their heads off if they knew how he was thinking – Oliver Hogarth, the world's greatest cynic with regard to affairs of the heart. But nevertheless . . .

'I'm sure Patrick Duffy knows more than he is saying.' And then Josie drew in a deep breath before adding, 'In fact I'm convinced he did away with our father for reasons of his own, but unfortunately there is no proof. That's the truth of it.' She stared at him, her face almost defiant, and Oliver stared back at her in quiet amazement.

It wasn't often he underestimated anyone – man or woman – but in the last hour as he had listened to Josie's story over what had turned out to be an excellent meal, he'd had to admit to himself that that was exactly what he'd done regarding this particular female. She was strong, she had character and a mind of her own, and the air of innocence which sat so well with her fresh beauty and undoubted talent was not the kind of which naivety formed the base. He had had several mistresses in his time, but not one of them had affected him like this young woman who had, by her own admission, been born in the gutter and had started her singing career as a street urchin.

He cleared his throat twice before he said quietly, 'That being the case, what do you wish me to do? From what you have told me, it would put your brother at risk if the authorities were informed of this plan to snatch both of you' – he included Gertie in the sweep of his head – 'but it goes against the grain for the man to assume he can behave however he feels so inclined.'

It might go against the grain for a man like Oliver Hogarth, born with a silver spoon in his mouth, to do nothing against an adversary he considered socially and morally beneath him, but then Oliver hadn't started life in the East End of Sunderland in a two-roomed hovel frequented by rats and cockroaches and disease. Josie's thoughts were not bitter, merely rational. Oliver had no idea of the power a man like Patrick Duffy wielded within his own community, nor of the protection that power gave him. Patrick was feared and loathed, but the respect brought about by blind terror ensured that whilst those about him might go down the line, Patrick wouldn't.

'No one would speak against Patrick Duffy,' she explained, 'they just wouldn't. My father was a hard man and people were frightened of him, but he was scared stiff of Duffy. If you met him you'd understand why.'

'After what you have told me, if I met him I would make sure only one of us was left breathing.' And as Oliver saw her eyes widen, a slight smile touched the corners of his lips. 'I might have had something of a sheltered upbringing, Miss Burns, but the last twenty odd years in the big bad world have ensured I am neither callow nor easily intimidated. I hold the opinion that certain men are like rabid dogs. The kindest thing for them and the individuals around them is to put them out of their misery.'

Now it was Josie's turn to realise she had underestimated the man sitting watching her so calmly. She knew Oliver must be intelligent and intuitive to have reached the position he now held, but she'd had him down as one step removed from the idle rich; a womaniser, a gay blood, one of those aristocratic types with gold-knobbed canes and gold toothpicks who lived in a world where everything ran smoothly and harmoniously. But she'd misjudged him. The piercing quality to his eyes and the set of his mouth told her he hadn't been joking in his remarks about Patrick. She saw Gertie shift uneasily on her seat and knew her sister had recognised it too.

'I can understand how you feel but I have to think of my brother first and foremost. We're leaving here tomorrow but he might choose to stay, and then there's Vera and Horace . . .' Her voice dwindled away, but then

Oliver was disabused of the notion the pause was due to feminine feebleness when she raised her head and looked him straight in the eyes as she said, 'But if it wasn't for the safety of my loved ones I'd be only too pleased for you to meet Patrick Duffy, Mr Hogarth. I have a feeling you would deal with him exactly as he deserves.'

And it was at that moment that Oliver Hogarth first became acquainted with the onslaught of an emotion he had previously thought to be an illusion; a sentimental indulgence embraced by poets and other romantics he privately scorned. Namely, love.

Josie left Sunderland in the week in which the Grand Theatre in Islington, London, was totally destroyed by fire, and – a more momentous event to those outside the theatre fraternity – it was the same week in which the trade unions created the Labour Party.

Keir Hardie's words on that emotional occasion – 'It has come. Poor little child of danger, nursling of the storm. May it be blessed' – could have applied equally to the heartsore Sunderland lass who stepped on to King's Cross Station one grey winter's afternoon. And, as had been the case with the delegates leaving the Memorial Hall in Farringdon Street to face the future, it was raining.

Hubert hadn't come. It had been the only thing Josie and Gertie could think of on the train-ride down to the capital, although Vera's tearful farewell on the platform at Sunderland Central – surrounded by Betty's numerous offspring who had all been darting off in different directions which had necessitated Vera, Josie, Gertie and a very irritated Oliver Hogarth retrieving little people at frequent intervals – had taken the edge off their bitter disappointment at the time.

The night before, everything in Josie had balked at

226

the thought of not returning to Northumberland Place to explain the circumstances personally to Vera, although she had accepted the wisdom of actually sleeping elsewhere. The more Gertie and Oliver had tried to persuade her not to return, the more determined she had become as the evening had progressed. 'He's a nasty little bully of a man, Patrick Duffy, and he would just love to think he'd frightened us away,' Josie had said vehemently at the coffee and brandy stage of the meal.

'Him with the sense to run away, lives to fight another day.' Gertie's voice had held no humour although her words had made Oliver's mouth twitch. 'An' frankly, lass, he'd love it far more if he got his hands on you, so think on.'

'I'm not intending for him or anyone else to get their hands on me,' Josie said firmly. 'And I'm certainly not suggesting that we're foolish enough to go back without adequate force.'

'But if we tell the police, Patrick an' Jimmy will know that Hubert—'

'I'm not suggesting the police either.' It was indignant. She wasn't stupid, for goodness' sake! 'You know Sybil's party tonight? Well, everyone's going to be there, aren't they?'

'So?'

'So we round up a good few of them and go back to Vera's in a crowd. They can wait outside while you and I nip in. We needn't tell the others the full story, just make it clear that we're being bothered by a couple of unsavoury characters, that's all, and once at Vera's we can pack our things and tell her what's what. Perhaps Vera and Horace would like to come back with us to the party after? Sybil won't mind. The more the merrier as far as she's concerned. It'd do Vera good too. She's been a bit down in the mouth over Frank and everything; an evening out would set her up.' Josie was blowed if she was going to creep away from Sunderland like a little whipped puppy because of that man.

That was true. Gertie stared at her sister and was aware of Oliver doing the same. She glanced at him out of the corner of her eye and read admiration in his face, although his voice expressed none of this sentiment when he said, 'You're putting yourself in harm's way for no good reason except to demonstrate this Duffy fellow cannot intimidate you.'

'That's good enough reason for me.' Josie's face had set determinedly. She *wasn't* frightened of Patrick Duffy; she wouldn't *let* herself be.

'And I don't suppose there is anything I can say to dissuade you from this course of action?'

'No.'

'Even though this protest will be something the fellow is unaware of, considering he doesn't know you're privy to his plans tonight?'

'*I'm* aware of my protest.'

Oliver sighed deeply. 'I will make no comment. Suffice to say I have never understood how a woman's mind works and that I insist on being at your side at all times tonight.'

Josie considered for a moment, then replied, 'All right, but nothing will happen, I can assure you of that.'

She was right. Oliver was on tenterhooks the whole time he, and a large crowd of revellers, milled around on the pavement outside Vera's house, but he had seen no one other than their party. The would-be assailants had been primed to look out for two young women, not a carousing band of merrymakers which featured, amongst others, Signor Bianchi, The Famous Weightlifter from Italy, and

Rumbo Austin, Juggler Extraordinaire; the latter used to be a blacksmith before he had entered the music hall and was built like a tram. The criminal element of Sunderland knew when the odds were stacked against them, and were well versed in becoming invisible when necessary.

With Sybil's warm agreement, Vera and Horace found themselves whisked back to the party – Signor Bianchi carrying the girls' trunk and other luggage as though it weighed nothing – with the result that Vera had the time of her life, and Horace had so far forgotten himself as to allow Sybil to teach him the Cakewalk, an American dance which was all the rage in theatrical circles.

'Come along, my dear.' Oliver now took Josie's arm as the porter he had commandeered wheeled their luggage out of the station on a large wooden handcart. 'And please, don't distress yourself further about your youngest brother. You said all you could. You gave him the opportunity to escape the life he is leading and that's all you could do.'

Josie looked at him, holding his gaze for a moment before saying sadly, 'But it wasn't enough, was it, Oliver?' It had become Oliver and Josie halfway through the previous evening when the agent had reached across the table and asked her permission to address her and Gertie by their Christian names. Josie wasn't to know it was the first time he had ever thus petitioned the female of his choice.

He shook his head slowly, including Gertie in his glance as he said, 'He has free will, as do we all, and this gift from the Almighty can be used for good or ill. Life is a series of choices for everyone.'

Josie removed her arm from his hand with an impatient movement. 'He's frightened, Oliver. Scared out of his wits, and frankly he has every reason to be so. And I don't think Hubert has ever had this free will you speak of. First my father controlled him and now Duffy has an even tighter hold.'

He stared at her, aware of the porter waiting some distance away and of the bustle all about them. She was right. And he must have sounded patronising in the extreme. 'I'm sorry, forgive me,' he said quickly. 'You're absolutely right, of course. Maybe there will be an opportunity in the future for you to help him. He contacted you once, he may do so again.'

'He needs to break free of Jimmy.' Gertie entered the conversation somewhat abruptly. 'An' he won't do that until he's a mite older an' can see things for what they are. Jimmy's like our da – no good to man nor beast.'

They stood in an embarrassed silence for a moment or two before Oliver said, his voice loud and over-hearty, 'What are we doing standing here! The porter has the valises and trunk, so let us make haste and find a carriage, and once everything is on board I shall instruct the driver to take us by way of Buckingham Palace and the Tower of London before the light fades. Tomorrow I shall take you both on a tour of some of the music halls, small and great. In London you can see more clearly than anywhere else the three popular elements that have gone to make up the present music hall.' He was leading them out of the station as he spoke.

'The three popular elements?' Josie queried.

'The pleasure garden with its saloon theatre, the song and supper rooms, and the catch and glee clubs and harmonic meetings in tavern concerts,' Oliver said jovially. 'The sort of West End boltholes immortalised by William Makepeace Thackeray and his set. Those were the days, my dear. Singers hired at a pound a week and all the free drink they could consume! Gargantuan suppers enjoyed by all the young bloods at one in the morning and no ladies allowed. This went on until the late 1860s. Oh, some of the old-timers can tell a tale or two about those days, believe me. Of course, when the ladies *were* admitted, to boxes with latticework screens in front, it stopped some of the more . . . exuberant excesses of the supper rooms and clubs, but that's when more far-sighted individuals began to build the gilded palaces in which you play now.'

He smiled at Josie as they paused at the entrance to the station and watched the porter load their luggage on to a waiting horse-drawn carriage. Then Oliver hurried the two girls over to the open door, helping them up into the upholstered depths before he tipped the porter handsomely.

Gilded palaces? Josie smiled to herself. Perhaps some of the northern halls could be termed such, like the Empire in Newcastle which was magnificently ornate from the pits right up to the gallery which was almost square in comparison to the conventional shape of the circle below. She had enjoyed her season at the Empire; its beautifully moulded plasterwork exquisitely painted in rich lush colours and everything of the very best. But some of the smaller halls in the north held no more than four or five hundred patrons at best; their dingy, somewhat faded interiors only enlivened by the players themselves.

As Oliver slid into the carriage he took the seat opposite Josie and Gertie, and it was clear he had warmed to his theme as he said, 'Music halls have become palaces of variety, especially those here in the capital. This is the place to be, all right.'

He was leaning forward as he spoke, the heavy grey greatcoat he was wearing and his top hat making him seem even bigger in the close confines of the carriage. He exuded strength and vitality; his dark, handsome face alight, and a clean and faintly pleasant smell coming from him. Josie felt the little shiver she had experienced once or twice before when he had been close, and it disconcerted her.

She felt herself blushing, but Oliver didn't appear to notice, continuing, 'The halls in London are the resort of wealth, fashion and influence, where can be seen the most prominent and distinguished representatives of art, literature and law, together with city financiers, lights of the sporting world and a liberal sprinkling of the social elite. To that end, my dear, we must see about . . . increasing your wardrobe.'

The brief hesitation wasn't lost on either of the two girls and they both knew exactly what Oliver was getting at. It wasn't so much increasing her wardrobe that was needed, but a complete overhaul. The capital had embraced new fashions for the new century, upholding the notion that women's dress should reflect their growing freedom at work and play. The more severe corsets and stuffy bustles were being consigned to the dustbin, whilst hemlines had crept up above the ankle. There was even talk that modern woman should abandon her skirts in favour of the knickerbocker, and keen cyclists had already raised eyebrows by doing that very thing.

'I have taken the liberty of contacting a good friend of mine, a Mrs Irving, who is well versed in ladies' fashions,' Oliver said easily. 'She will accompany you to the big shops and take pleasure from doing so. You can safely put yourself in her hands, and perhaps Gertie would also like to take this opportunity to increase her ensemble?'

He smiled at Gertie who beamed back. Wouldn't she just! By, they'd landed on their feet with Oliver all right. And if she wasn't mistaken Josie was beginning to like him, just a little. Which could only bode well. If nothing else it would take her mind off the other one; anyway, Josie could do better than the likes of Barney Robson, even if he had been free. Which he wasn't. All things considered, she hadn't been sorry to leave Sunderland.

'But . . .' Josie hesitated. What on earth was all this going to cost?

And then, as though Oliver had read her mind, he said, 'This is what is called an investment, my dear. I intend to launch you straight to the top, but you need certain things to be right. Another friend of mine, Mr Golding, will take you for singing lessons and deportment every afternoon, and in the evenings we will sit and converse, the three of us.'

'Converse?'

'On literature, the arts, social etiquette . . . It is my hope that you will soon be moving in circles which will require you to be familiar with the conventional rules of social behaviour – if you should be introduced to the Prince of Wales, for example, after some performance or perhaps a private soirée.'

It was pouring with rain outside the carriage and already the grey twilight was banishing what was left of the afternoon, but Josie was unaware of anything but Oliver's smiling face and the gasp of surprise from Gertie at the side of her. Oliver was informing her, gently but nevertheless firmly, that she had a lot to learn. Well, she'd known that, hadn't she? But this talk of the Prince of Wales took it to another dimension. She liked Oliver – in fact, the more she saw of him the more she liked him which was a relief in the circumstances – it would have been awful if she had been unable to get on with her own agent – but somehow she felt she needed to assert herself. Even make a stand.

She wanted to succeed in her chosen profession. The desire that had been with her ever since she had first stepped on to a stage four years ago burned all the stronger for being curbed so long due to her mother's ill health, and she appreciated Oliver's experience, but . . .

She wouldn't be taken over, mind and soul. That was it.

She breathed deeply before she said, her voice quiet and clear-sounding, 'I shall be pleased to receive instruction, of course, but I'd like to think that even now I wouldn't shame myself or you, Oliver, my agent.'

After a moment's pause in which her emphasis on his function in her life had been received and noted, Oliver said, 'Absolutely, my dear. Absolutely.' And wisely left it at that.

Was Oliver acquainted with the Prince of Wales? He'd spoken of meeting the Prince quite naturally and Lily had said something along the same lines that night in Hartlepool. Certainly the press had made much of the Prince of Wales's unconventional behaviour and somewhat dubious associates in the past, dubbing him the Prince of Pleasure among other things, Josie thought soberly. It was common knowledge he was an ardent follower of fashion, as well as being the leader of society and the prime influence on upper-class conduct. Twice the papers had reported the Prince's involvement in unsavoury court cases, one involving adultery and the other gambling, and it was said he lived his life in a whirl of amusements. He'd been booed and hissed on some of his public appearances, and Josie could remember Frank speaking scathingly of the heir to the throne whilst being a fierce supporter of Queen Victoria.

Josie pretended to be interested in the misty view outside the carriage but her heart was pounding and the blood rushing in her ears. She was out of her league here, oh, she was. How on earth was she going to compare with the likes of Marie Lloyd and Vesta Tilley and the rest? And if – *if* – she did meet the Prince of Wales . . . She swallowed hard. It seemed impossible, certainly, but the world of theatre had a way of bringing low-born and high-born together in a way nothing else could.

And then she took hold of herself, responding naturally enough to Gertie's enthusing about the grand buildings and fine carriages even as that inner voice said, *Don't be daft, girl, you can do it.* The aristocracy, all those fine ladies and gentlemen, even the Prince himself, were just men and women beneath all their wealth and extravagance. True, half of them didn't know they were born and she dare say they'd faint at the sight of a cockroach or a rat in the street, let alone their sumptuous mansions, but they still had two legs and two arms same as her, and they had to visit the privy whether they were dressed in silk or rags.

The rain had dwindled to a drizzle when the carriage pulled up outside Oliver's large townhouse in St James's, one of the more fashionable parts of London. He had insisted that Josie and Gertie dine with him before he took them to the small hotel in Brompton where they were to reside for the time being.

As Josie looked at the house through the carriage window the door opened and a uniformed maid stood in the entrance holding a large umbrella, which she pushed up as she ran down the steps and across the cobbled pavement to the carriage. Oliver climbed down first, saying, 'Thank you, Roberts,' but without glancing at the girl, and as he helped Josie, and then Gertie down from the carriage, the little maid held the umbrella over them whilst getting wet herself.

Josie wanted to protest, and as she met Gertie's eyes and her sister raised her eyebrows she knew Gertie was feeling the same, but out of consideration for Oliver in front of his staff she held her tongue and they proceeded into the house.

From the outside the large, double-fronted, three-storey

property did not look particularly impressive, but once in the hall Josie realised this was a very big house and moreover, beautifully decorated and furnished. Another maid took their coats, hats and gloves, and probably due to the exquisitely worked, crimson carpet which ran in a strip down the hall, and the magnificent staircase in deep mahogany, Josie suddenly became aware that her dress was not new and that the colour – a pale dove grey – seemed rather dull. There was an upholstered couch with two small tables either side of it, and several fine paintings on the dark brown walls, but Josie had no time to notice anything further before a small, bustling, sharp-eyed housekeeper appeared. She was dressed in black alpaca like the maids but unlike them had no white cap or apron, and Oliver greeted her warmly, saying, 'Ah, Mrs Wilde. We have arrived, as you can see. We will have tea in the drawing room.'

'Yes, sir. I trust you had a good journey, sir?'

'Adequate.'

This was said over Oliver's shoulder as he drew Josie and Gertie towards a door down the hall to their left, and again, as Josie stepped into the room she met Gertie's eyes and saw reflected the same sense of awe she was experiencing. There was a roaring log fire set in a deep marble fireplace at the end of the room and even situated where they were, just within the room, the heat struck them. The drapes at the two sets of windows, the carpet, the upholstery of the couches and chairs scattered here and there were all in a rich peacock blue, with the walls panelled and the ceiling light brown. It was luxurious and opulent and yet at the same time very masculine. Josie didn't know if she liked it or not but it was undoubtedly beautiful.

'Come and sit down and warm yourselves.' There was a

couch placed at an angle to the fire, and as he gestured in its direction Josie and Gertie walked the length of the room and seated themselves, Oliver taking a fine Queen Anne chair with cabriole legs and drawing it close to them.

'This is very striking. You have a lovely home.' Josie glanced at a gleaming walnut-veneered occasional table enhanced by herringbone inlays as she spoke, and wondered how many families in Sunderland's East End it would feed, before mentally shaking herself. This was Oliver's home and he had the right to furnish it as he pleased. Why was she thinking like this?

'Thank you.' He had picked up a trace of something in her voice and he couldn't quite place what it was. But she didn't seem overly impressed, unlike her sister who was unashamedly gaping. Had he expected to impress her? Oliver looked into himself and had to admit the answer was that he had *hoped* to impress her. This did not sit comfortably, and his voice was somewhat tight when he said, 'We will just have tea and refreshments and then perhaps you would both like to see round the house and garden? The garden is not large, the rear of it having been cobbled over for the carriage and stable.'

What she would *like* would be to go straight to the hotel and have a quiet meal before going to bed where she could think over all that had happened and marshal her whirling thoughts, but she couldn't very well say so when he'd put himself out to such an extent and been so kind.

Josie forced all reluctance from her voice as she said, 'Thank you, that would be lovely.'

'Or perhaps you would prefer to rest quietly here? It was a tiring journey.'

She smiled at him now, a twinkle in her eye as she said, 'We're quite tough you know, Gertie and I. It would take more than a train journey to tire us,' melting all stiffness from his voice as he answered, 'Is that so? Good, good. I have a boy who comes every morning for a few hours to see to the two cobs, but they are always ready for visitors, being gentle-tempered creatures. We will find a titbit or two to take to them.'

She bobbed her head in reply, and as he smiled at her he wondered how this slip of a girl could manage to make his emotions see-saw so violently. He didn't understand it – he really did not understand it, but suddenly all he could think about was her. How on earth had he managed thus far without her?

Chapter Twelve

The next few weeks were a period of great personal adjustment for Josie and, to a lesser extent, Gertie too. Each day the two girls left their little hotel in Brompton after breakfast and rarely returned before late evening, often dining with Oliver at his own residence before he took them home in his carriage. The hotel was basically one step up from the bed and breakfast establishments Josie and Gertie had been used to in the past, but the proprietress was known to Oliver – Josie was to find that her agent had contacts in all walks of life – and she looked after the two girls very well.

The days were spent in a whirl of dress fittings, singing lessons, elocution and deportment instruction and other coaching Oliver deemed important, and the evenings – once the carriage had returned the two girls to Oliver's house – in reading and talking with Oliver himself. These were the times Josie enjoyed the most. Slowly and skilfully, Oliver was opening up her mind, acquainting her with the works of Shelley, the sisters Brontë and Robert Louis Stevenson among others, as well as encouraging her to become familiar with the social characteristics of the age. He did not discuss politics, however; such things were a man's province and only men could understand the finer points of internal and foreign affairs.

Every evening, the *Illustrated London News*, a weekly newspaper which had started life early in Queen Victoria's reign, was brought out and its contents discussed at great length, and Oliver found himself frequently surprised at how quickly Josie grasped new ideas and concepts.

From her friendly, relaxed manner towards him, Oliver was well aware that as yet Josie had no idea that he was treating her any differently from the other clients and protégées on his books, and for the moment he was content to let matters take their course. Partly, he had to admit when he examined his feelings, because he was in something of a spin and it was disconcerting to say the least. Josie was not of his class, that was one thing, and not even from good stock such as clergymen or something similar. His own father might have been a wastrel and a gambler, but his ancestry had been impeccable, and his mother's people had had connections with some of the highest nobility in the land. Of course, Josie's background wouldn't have mattered a jot if he had been going to take her as his mistress, and by the time he had finished coaching her she would be able to hold her own in any company, but . . . Oliver sighed deeply and gnawed at his lower lip for a moment in a way he did countless times a day when reflecting on the problem. He knew Josie well enough by now to know she wouldn't countenance such a proposal. She had the working-class conviction that such women were bad, and although this irked him he knew he would not be able to change the tenet imbibed since babyhood.

Another thing that was causing him some personal discomfort was the discovery of an emotion hitherto unknown, jealousy. He had been pleased once they were on the train to the capital, and seeing Josie and her sister installed in the premises run by an acquaintance of his had given him some satisfaction, but it wasn't until Josie had been in London a month and an old friend had called unexpectedly one evening that Oliver had faced the fact that he wanted to be pre-eminent in her regard.

He had resented the way she had sparkled under his friend's compliments, and after Milton had left and he had taken Josie and Gertie back to their hotel, he had returned home and sat in the drawing room in front of the fire with a bottle of whisky until dawn, by which time the bottle was empty and he had come to terms with a trait of possessiveness in his nature he hadn't known existed. It had been as much distancing her from that big, ignorant lout who purportedly had something to do with Ginnett's in Newcastle, as removing her from danger, which had prompted the relief he'd felt once the train had pulled out of Sunderland Central. And the fact that it was a proprietress and not a proprietor had influenced his choice of accommodation for the girl too. Which made him . . . What? Someone he wasn't sure he knew, he acknowledged in a haze of whisky. Which was . . . His fuddled mind searched for the right word. Disturbing. That was it, disturbing.

He was going to have to do some serious thinking in the next little while, damn it, and to cap it all, according to Milton, Stella was back and already asking questions about 'the little chit' – Stella's terminology, not his, Milton had been at pains to explain – that Oliver was apparently tied up with at the moment. All he needed was for Stella to throw one of her screaming tantrums. Not that she had any right to do so, none at all, he assured himself silently, but then when had that stopped her in the past? What's more, Josie was a good ten years younger than Stella, something Milton had pointed out before he had left. And when Oliver had asked him what the hell that had to do with anything, Milton merely shook his head, almost pityingly, before adding, 'Women, my dear fellow, set great store by such things.'

And so the days and weeks had passed. As March 1900 had gone out like a lamb, April came in on the gust of the incredible news that the Prince of Wales had survived an assassination attempt! A sixteen-year-old anarchist had fired two shots at him from point-blank range on a Brussels railway station. Brussels had been a centre of opposition to the British role in the Boer War for some time, and Jean-Baptiste Sipido told police he wanted to kill the Prince who had had so many men killed in South Africa.

'Particularly ironic, don't you think,' Oliver had commented to Josie when they had read the report in the *Illustrated London News*, 'when Queen Victoria refuses the Prince access to most serious affairs of state and treats him as a child, rather than a grown man of fifty-eight years of age?'

'Does she?' Josie had heard the rumours, of course. Everyone was aware that the relationship between the old Queen and her son was not a happy one. 'That must be frustrating for him but then he doesn't seem to mind *too* much.'

He did not answer her for a moment, and his voice had changed when he said softly, 'He endures what he has to endure for the present with a view to the prize at the end of his trial.'

Josie looked at him in surprise. They were sitting in Oliver's magnificent drawing room, she, Gertie and Oliver, and in a few moments one of the maids would come and inform them that dinner was ready and light the lamps, but for the moment the room was bathed in a soft twilight.

Josie was sitting with Gertie on a fine chaise-longue set at an angle to the full-length windows as she read items out loud from the newspaper for discussion, but Oliver was some way across the room and in shadow and she couldn't see his face clearly. But he had sounded . . . odd. As though his thoughts were not really on the Prince of Wales at all. And then he disabused her of this notion when he said, his voice brisk once more, 'The Prince pursues pleasure as an antidote to boredom, my dear, and does so with characteristic enthusiasm and determination. He is a man of enormous drive but in the opinion of most sympathetic ministers and diplomats, is given little opportunity by the Queen to exercise his energies responsibly.'

'So you are saying he puts a face on it? Makes the best of the tough end of the old mare?'

It was Gertie who spoke now, and at the same moment as the maid knocked and entered the room Oliver rose to his feet, his voice amused as he answered, 'That sums it up very well, Gertie.'

They had proceeded through to the dining room for dinner then – another area of schooling; the first time Josie had dined with Oliver she thought she had never seen so many knives and forks and spoons for one place setting, not to mention glasses and crockery and so on. According to Oliver, however, favourites of the music hall were often invited to weekend house-parties to sing and entertain, and it was imperative she become familiar with the intricacies of such dining. These dinners often comprised at least ten or eleven courses, Oliver had informed her gravely, showing her the menu of a dinner given by a friend of his in honour of Lord Rosebery:

Caviar Anchois

Tortue Claire

Saumon, Sauce Médoc   *Filet de Sole à l'Adelphi*

Poulet Reine Demidoff   *Asperge en Branches
                                        au Beurre*

Quartier d'Agneau

Filet de Boeuf Hollandais

Granit au Kummel

Canard Sauvage   *Bécasses*   *Russian Salad*

*Pouding Imperial Macedoine aux Fruits Meringue
                                        à la Crème*

Pouding Glace à la Chantilly

Desserts

And, of course, it would be all to the good if Josie could become familiar with some of the French terms. Josie said she would try.

However, she discovered she wasn't very fond of such dishes as pheasant stuffed with snipe or woodcock, with the latter in its turn stuffed with truffles, and the whole covered with some rich sauce. Nor could she understand how a house-party could consume what Oliver termed a 'simple' breakfast consisting of fruit, oatmeal porridge, kidney omelette, baked eggs, fried cod, grilled ham, potted

244

game, veal cake, stewed prunes and cream, scones, rolls, toast, bread, butter, marmalade, jam and preserves, tea, coffee, cream, milk, and then be ready for a good lunch, followed by a hearty tea, then dinner and later, supper. 'How on earth,' she'd asked an amused Oliver, 'do they find time to do anything other than eat and drink?'

'Oh, they manage quite well,' he had replied, and then, as his mind threw up recollections of some of the house-parties he had attended when Stella was present, and of the unashamed cuckoldry which was considered part and parcel of such events, he'd changed the subject.

By May, when the English papers were humming with the news of Lillie Langtry's triumph in Washington – she had taken the American city by storm with her portrayal of a dissolute courtesan in *The Degenerates* – Oliver had decided Josie would have her first stage appearance in London at one of the better variety houses which were scattered all over the capital. As in most halls, he informed her, the shows were twice-nightly, which would mean she could still continue with her singing and elocution lessons during the day if she so wished.

Josie hadn't needed to think about her reply. Claudette Belloc was an excellent teacher and already Josie had found that her range and technique had improved immensely; moreover, she liked the little Frenchwoman who was forthright and brusque and suffered fools badly. But developing and advancing her voice and polishing her pronunciation and articulation was not her only motive for tying up her daytime hours. Since she had come to London, and in spite of having Gertie with her, she had become increasingly homesick for Sunderland and worried about Hubert, and – probably due to the distance between them – hungry for any snippet of news about Barney in a way she had never been whilst still residing in the north-east. She needed to keep every minute of the day and night occupied, she admitted to herself. She mustn't think, that was the answer; at least only about the present and what she was doing on a day-to-day level.

It didn't help that Vera could barely read or write either; her friend's letters were written in an enormous round childish hand and consisted, at the most, of four or five lines of painfully laborious script, holding nothing of the warm, vigorous woman she knew. She missed Vera more than she would have thought possible, and although there had been times in the past when she had been unable to get home for a month or more, she had always known she was within a carriage ride should the situation call for it. Now, in this alien world where no one spoke with a warm northern burr and where she'd felt enclosed in a strange, isolated bubble the last couple of months, she had secretly cried herself to sleep more than once. Which was stupid, daft, for a grown woman of seventeen years of age who had been charting her own destiny for five years or more, she chided herself vehemently. But she couldn't help it. It would be better when she was working. She was longing, *aching* to throw herself into her work again. Nothing compared to stepping out on to a stage and singing and entertaining an appreciative crowd. She'd missed that too.

And so she prepared for her debut on the London stage with dedication and enthusiasm and very little nervousness. This was something she understood, something she was good at. The rest of it – the niceties of middle- and upper-class conduct, the formalities of social etiquette and the hundred and one pitfalls it contained for the unwary – was not so enjoyable. But necessary. Oliver said so. And he was an experienced and respected agent who had been in the business longer than she had been alive, as well as being a gentleman by birth, so he should know. She could trust Oliver . . . couldn't she? But she wished, she did so wish Vera was here.

Vera herself, three hundred or so miles away in Sunderland, was in something of a quandary as she stared into her sister's worried face. And when Betty said again, 'What am I goin' to do, lass? I can't abandon her; Frank wouldn't expect that,' she had to restrain herself from saying harshly, 'I'm not so sure about that. Didn't you tell me he all but threw her out after the do with Josie?' Instead she joined her hands together on the kitchen table, and leaning forward, said quietly, 'You know very well that you can't swing a cat in this place for bairns, an' with the two rooms upstairs packed to overflowin' and you sleeping downstairs as it is there's not an inch of ground to put another bed. You've got enough on your plate bein' mam an' da to your own lot, Bett. An' she's a nasty bit of work, don't forget that. Havin' the accident, bad as it is an' I don't say the poor lass isn't sufferin', won't change her basic nature.'

'Aye, I know that. I'm expectin' nowt in that line.'

'An' you say Barney can't have her? I thought him and Prudence were all right again, and she's good pals with Pearl.'

'Oh aye, Barney and Prudence get on well enough, but since Pearl's bin took bad with this disease of the blood or whatever, she can't do nowt but lie in bed most days. Her mam's round there every hour the good Lord sends accordin' to Barney, worried sick Pearl's mam an' da are. It's drivin' Barney mad, especially 'cos he's not sure how bad Pearl really is but that's another story. Anyway, Prudence can't go there.'

Vera nodded slowly. By, talk about it never rains but it pours. Years Barney's sister had worked at that laundry and never so much as the whisper of an accident, and then the girl had to go and get her hands caught in a calender. According to Betty, Prudence had been trying to untangle a sheet that had got caught and instead she'd got her hands entwined and they were dragged on to the hot steel bed and crushed by the rollers. The hospital had been good but she couldn't stay there for ever, and they'd made it clear she wouldn't be able to do much at first when she came out and would need a bit of looking after.

'What about the other brothers? Can't one of them put her up for a time?'

Betty shook her head wearily. 'Neville's still off work with his legs an' Reg's not bin long gone back as you know. They're all havin' a right time of it an' their wives are doin' all sorts to try an' make ends meet. An' with Amos's last bairn bein' – well, not quite right . . .' Here Betty's voice dropped almost to a whisper; for the shame and shock of that happening was still reverberating round the family months later, and hadn't been made any easier by Amos's wife's parents insisting there had never been anything *like that* on their side, and it must be down to Amos. 'You can't expect them to take Prudence on, can you? It wouldn't be fair, lass.'

'It's fairer than expectin' you to do it. When all's said an' done, you aren't even related to Prudence, Bett. Not really. An' she's bin a thorn in your side ever since you met Frank.'

'Aye, I know, but still . . .' Betty's voice trailed away as Vera stared at her anxiously. Her sister had been doing so well since Frank had gone but the woman was still heartsore and had lost much of her usual chirpiness. Prudence would be the proverbial nail in the coffin. 'No one else will have her – none of 'em can stand her.'

Vera took a deep breath and prayed Horace would understand when she told him. 'We'll have her at our place, lass,' she offered. 'All right? There's the spare room next to ours an' she'll be comfortable enough until she can go back to Newcastle again.'

'Oh Vera, I couldn't let you do that. She'd drive you round the bend, lass. Horace an' all.'

'Be that as it may.'

'No, no, it's not fair. You have the bairns afternoons as it is, lass, an' I appreciate it more'n words could say.'

Vera straightened up, before stretching and settling back in her seat with a sigh. 'You've said yourself the others can't or won't have her, an' you're not prepared to let her take her chance as best she can.' Personally Vera was of the opinion that Prudence's type never sunk; they remained above water even if it meant staying afloat on the shoulders of those they were drowning. 'True she wouldn't be me first choice for a lodger, Bett, but there it is. Have they said how long they think it'll be afore she's fit to work again?'

'They're not sure. Months at least,' Betty said unhappily. 'But this isn't your problem.'

Vera stared across at her sister's plump, worried face, and she said softly, 'Aye, it is. Same as if the positions were reversed, it'd be yours.' And she wouldn't have minded having Prudence, in spite of the fact she'd got no time for Betty's stepdaughter, except that it'd be bound to make things awkward with Josie if the lass came up for a visit. Still, she wasn't about to do that for the time being, not with how things were in London, and however much she wanted to see her lass's dear face she was glad Josie was out of harm's way. With hindsight it was clear that it'd been a mistake for Josie to come back and play the halls in Sunderland. It had brought her to Patrick Duffy's notice again and he wouldn't have liked being thwarted a second time. By, there were some evil so-an'-sos in the world, but that man took the biscuit, he did straight.

And then she was brought back to the matter in question by her sister saying, a broken note in her voice, 'I dunno what I'd do without you, lass, an' that's a fact.'

Neither of them was the demonstrative type but now Vera rose swiftly and walked round the heavy old kitchen table which took up most of the floorspace in the small room, and they put their arms round each other and remained quiet for a time, until Vera said, 'That's decided then. When she comes out I'll have her – if she wants to come here, that is. She might want to stay in Newcastle with friends we don't know about, of course.'

Betty had sat up straighter as her sister had moved back to her seat. 'The chance of Prudence havin' any friends other than Pearl is about as likely as the rent man sayin' God bless you,' she said stolidly, pulling the worn shawl crossed over her enormous sagging breasts more tightly in to her skirt, before she added, her head cocked to one side, 'They're a mite too quiet up there for my likin', lass. I bet the little devils are diggin' the plaster out of the walls again an' eatin' it.' And she disappeared out of the room to check on her brood in the bedroom upstairs with a swiftness that belied her bulk.

Vera sat in the warmth of the cluttered, untidy kitchen, her mind only half concentrating on the hullabaloo above her head which indicated Betty had been right about the plaster and her bairns, who were supposed to be getting ready for bed. She glanced across at the youngest Robson – a little girl of six months old – lying in the battered crib to one side of the range, but without really seeing her tiny niece.

All this with Pearl; what was it about? Was the lass really ill or just making on? Certainly her collapse, two days after Josie had gone to London, had been genuine enough, and the resulting investigations in the infirmary had thrown up this blood problem which the doctors seemed able to do little about. Something to do with the blood not functioning properly, Barney had told Betty, but he couldn't really be more specific because the doctors weren't saying much beyond Pearl had to rest and eat nourishing food. But she'd seemed to get worse lately, not better. Barney was in two minds about it all, but then perhaps that wasn't surprising with things being so bad between him and Pearl. She had played the invalid on and off since they'd been married to avoid her wifely duties, Barney had told Betty in a moment of bitter frustration. Supposedly ailing one moment, and the next gadding about shopping with her mother or whatever. Betty had said he'd spoken as though he was at the end of his tether.

The thought brought anxiety flooding into her chest in a sick wave. She remembered the afternoon they had heard about Frank's death and she had seen the way Josie and Barney were looking at each other in her kitchen. No, no, she wouldn't believe it. Her lass was a good girl. Josie would never . . . Vera shut her eyes tight for a moment. Thank God Josie was down in London and Barney was up here; likely their paths wouldn't cross in years. She was working herself up over nowt. She had more than enough to cope with here; she didn't need to go out looking for more trouble.

Vera reached for the big brown teapot in the middle of the table and poured herself a cup of lukewarm tea which she drank straight down.

Aye, she was imagining things sure enough, but all the same she wouldn't mention Pearl being middling to Josie. There was no need for the lass to be told, and it was better Josie concentrated on her new life down south where she was safe. Duffy wouldn't bother her down there for one thing, and this other, this . . . figment of her imagination, would die a natural death if it wasn't fed. Pray God.

Chapter Thirteen

He'd get it in the neck from Jimmy when he got back. Hubert hunched his shoulders at the thought, skimming a flat pebble across the water as he did so. He had walked the six miles from the East End to Seaham Harbour earlier in the day – something he occasionally did when the urge to escape his lot became overwhelming – but hadn't stayed long at the harbour itself, walking back up the coast past Seaham and towards Hole Rock where he'd found a quiet spot away from it all.

Normally, even on his worst days, he enjoyed the bustle and noise coming from the docks and outer harbour; the timber yards, iron and brass foundry and Bottle Works all adding to the vibrant life of the place. He usually spent some time watching the massive cranes in the dry harbour at the side of the South Dock, and walked down to the Bottle Makers Arms for a bowlful of thick mutton soup before he made his way back home. The last two years though, since the rebuilding and enlargement of the South Dock had begun, he hadn't felt the same about the harbour, or maybe it was just that he was growing older?

These days he was aware of the chaotic, slummy development stretching from the back of North Terrace in a way he hadn't been when he'd first walked this way with Jimmy as a little lad of five or six, and again the ropery, foundry, gasworks, chemical works and the like which hugged the coast south of the docks hadn't really registered on him. Probably because he'd been used to the pall of thick, noxious smoke and polluted air in the East End.

He tilted his head in the dying sunlight of the cool May evening, drawing the cold fresh air redolent with the scent of grasses and faint tang of the sea deep into his lungs.

Jimmy would be back from collecting the dues by now. Who would he have taken with him when he'd realised his brother had skedaddled? Albert maybe, and perhaps Harry. Both of them were big brawny numskulls who liked nothing better than beating the living daylights out of some poor soul, or scaring women and bairns witless. By, it was a filthy job, collecting what people owed Patrick. It made a rent man's job appear sweet in comparison. At least the worst they threatened was getting the bums in when folk couldn't pay. And why, *why* would people be so daft as to borrow money from Patrick anyway? Everyone knew his reputation. Still, if it was a question of Patrick or the workhouse, some of them chose the little Irishman although they usually lived to regret it. Once Patrick had a foot in, you were his, body and soul.

Hubert shivered, although he wasn't cold. Jimmy knew he hated collection days, which Patrick varied each week in order to gain the element of surprise on the debtors. There were always three of them on the job; one, himself usually, to knock on the door and ask for the dues while the two others stood in the background looking menacing. Together they would march down the streets, putting on a grim expression and looking mean. Many a time the way cleared before them like magic, bairns hightailing it to warn their das that the lickspittles, as Patrick's hirelings were nicknamed, were coming.

Some of the streets weren't so bad, and where a man was in work there'd invariably be something paid off; folk would pay Patrick and keep the rent man waiting any day. But round where he'd been born – Long Bank and the quays and the rabbit warren of streets stretching east from the river – it was bad. Wretched dwellings with barely any furniture; stinking, filthy bairns with faces covered in scabs and hardly a stitch of clothing. By, he hated going there and watching Jimmy and the others throwing their weight about. Last week had been one of the worst times; he'd had to get mortalious that night to blot out that room and its occupants in Blue Anchor Yard.

They'd climbed the stairs carefully, mindful of their creaking and rocking and the great holes in the skirting boards where rats lurked, and when Jimmy had struck a match to guide their way, lice had been crawling in their hundreds on the rotten walls. The family they'd been calling on had been on the top floor in a cell-like room which held eleven; the meagre amount of coal they'd had was kept in a cupboard and the rain was coming through the roof and soaking the foul-smelling flock mattress on the floor which was bedding for the whole lot of them. Pitiful it'd been, right pitiful, and still Jimmy and Albert had theatened and bullied the sick father whose body had been racked by St Vitus's Dance, until the bairns had been screaming in fear and the mother had promised she'd have something for them the next week. And they all knew how she'd get it; she'd go and sell herself down at the dockside. It was all she could do because everything else had failed.

Then there'd been Maling's Rigg. The gloomy dank passage they'd entered had led to a room even worse than the other one but there they had drawn a blank. The father had committed suicide two days before and his widow and their six children had been taken to the workhouse just an hour before they'd got there.

He'd go stark staring mad, he would, if he had to continue with the dues. He couldn't do it any more, and he didn't understand Jimmy over this. How could he act the way he did with folk who could've been them not so many years back, before Josie lifted them out of the pit they had been in? He sometimes even thought Jimmy *enjoyed* what he was doing; swaggering about as though he was Lord Muck.

Hubert wiped the back of his hand across his brow which was damp with perspiration. It was getting these days so he didn't know where Patrick Duffy left off and his brother began, and certainly Jimmy relished being known as Patrick's favoured protégé. It made Hubert feel physically sick every time he heard Patrick refer to Jimmy as 'son', and it was happening more and more in the last couple of years. He sometimes thought Jimmy had forgotten he *wasn't* Patrick's own flesh and blood. By, to be connected by blood with Duffy . . . Hubert's upper lip rose as though he was smelling something unclean.

How long could he go on like this, playing along with it all? But then he didn't really have an option, did he, not unless he was prepared to be six foot under. Even Jimmy wouldn't be able to protect him if Patrick decided he was for the jump. Would his brother stand up for him if it meant going against the man who had taken them in all those years ago when their da had gone missing? Hubert frowned to himself; a lone gull circling overhead in the clear blue sky causing his eyes to raise as it cried its lonely call. A couple of years ago he would have known the answer to that but now he wasn't so sure. Jimmy had changed, hardened, or perhaps his brother had always been as callous as he was now, and Hubert hadn't appreciated the fact until he'd met Josie again. Certainly since that night when he had been reunited with his sisters, he had begun to question everything more.

Hubert let his eyes roam the vast expanse of blue water in front of him for a moment, before walking away from the tiny frothy waves lapping the beach and throwing himself down at a point where wiry coarse grass dotted with hundreds of tiny resilient wild flowers met the sand.

He had listened to their Jimmy and Patrick jaw about Josie until he'd begun to believe she was this cold, brazen hussy they'd portrayed. This had been one of the reasons he had gone to see her that night. He'd needed to see for himself whether the memory he had of his elder sister – as a slight, fiercely protective little figure with melting brown eyes and a smiling mouth – was right or wrong. In spite of what Patrick had said, he'd found it nigh on impossible to believe that the Josie he remembered would have betrayed her brothers to the law. Not their da, oh no, he could have expected that all right, but him and Jimmy? She'd mopped their tears and wiped their backsides from when they were little babbies, and once she'd started the singing she'd fought their da all the way to clean up their home and make sure there was always food on the table and a fire in the range. They hadn't had much, but the little they'd had had come from Josie sure enough.

And she'd looked the same. Hubert rolled over on to his stomach, watching a large black ant as it struggled through the grass with some prize or other held above its head. Aye, she had. Older and more beautiful maybe, she was a woman now and there was no mistaking that, but the old Josie had been shining out of her eyes when she'd realised it was him. She'd been right pleased to see him. A small smile touched the corner of his mouth. And he'd known then, even before he'd asked her, that she was incapable of doing what Patrick had said. Now if

Patrick had lied about Josie, it was fair guns he'd done the same about their mam selling them down the river. Which meant . . . The ant reached the tiny opening to its nest and disappeared underground, and Hubert sat up suddenly, taking off his cap and raking back his floppy brown hair before replacing the cap on his head. It meant Patrick could well be lying when he said their da had skedaddled on a ship. Josie seemed sure about it anyway.

He continued sitting until the twilight turned the blue sky pearly grey and he knew he couldn't delay his return any more. He rose slowly to his feet and began walking reluctantly along the coastal path which led to Marstack and then Salterfen Rocks, and the ragged outskirts of Bishopwearmouth.

He would have to tackle Jimmy about all this one day, about their da and Patrick and his sisters. The thought made him bite his bottom lip. One day – but not yet. He didn't consciously think, I'll have to wait until I'm a bit older and bigger, until I can make a plan of escape and get out if I have to, but merely reiterated in his mind, as the sky turned to rivers of brilliant pink and mauve and scarlet, Aye, I'll wait a bit, that's what I'll do, but one day, one day I'll put it to Jimmy and to hell with the consequences – and Patrick Duffy.

The two individuals who had been featuring so highly in Hubert's troubled thoughts were at that moment making their way across the strip of town moor at the back of the orphan asylum and the Trafalgar Square almshouses. They were heading towards Prospect Row and Jimmy was saying, 'He's a good lad, Pat, you know that, but when all's said an' done he's only twelve.'

'He's thirteen in a couple of weeks, besides which you

were collectin' at his age an' makin' a good job of it an' all.'

'Aye, I know, but we're all different, man.'

Patrick eyed the big strapping youth at the side of him who looked far older than his fifteen years. 'I let him get away with murder 'cos I know you think a bit of him, you know that, don't you?' he said, his voice terse. 'But it don't look good, Jimmy, not to the rest of 'em.'

'The rest of 'em don't blow their noses unless they ask permission of you, and *you* know *that*. Besides, if any of 'em have got anythin' to say they can say it to me an' I'll soon put 'em straight.'

Patrick again glanced at Bart's son, and his thin mouth twisted in a smile showing black rotting teeth. Aye, he would an' all. He was nimble on his feet, was Jimmy, and handy with a knife, and he didn't fight by the Queensberry rules, neither. Even a couple of years ago, before Jimmy had put on that spurt of growth and filled out, he'd seen him take down a man double his size. He could be a nasty bit of work and people knew it and were afeared of him. His da had been big but Bart had been all wind and water; Jimmy wasn't like that. The thought carried an element of pride, as though Patrick had had something to do with the lad's character – which, indeed, he considered he had.

When Patrick had taken Jimmy and Hubert under his wing he'd had several reasons for doing so. There had been an element of revenge; he'd liked the idea of securing what had been Bart's after the time, money and pain the other man had cost him, but also he had recognised that Bart's lads were good little pickpockets and with the right training could become accomplished thieves. He'd also gained some satisfaction from breaking up the

Burns family further, especially when he knew having the lads working for him would net him a profit, and the story he'd told had gained credence by the law and others assuming Bart had seconded his boys and the three of them had skedaddled. But overall, and linking all the other reasons together, was the fact that he had always had a soft spot for Jimmy. He'd seen himself in the lad and he had liked that, and Jimmy had proved to be everything he had hoped for. Unlike the other one.

As they moved into Prospect Row and then, taking short cuts, made their way through the streets and narrow side lanes towards North Moor Street they walked in silence, but just before they reached the slipway near the offices and the Commissioners' Stairs at the far end of the quays, Patrick said, 'You'll have to talk to him, Jimmy. He's takin' advantage of me good nature.'

'Good nature?' Jimmy grinned at the small man alongside of him, his voice holding a warm teasing note which spoke of ease and friendship. 'Good nature, is it? Where you bin hidin' it all these years then?'

Patrick grinned back. 'Less of your lip, son.'

They had turned down the narrow path off North Moor Street which led directly to the slipway now, and as a shadow emerged from the side of the offices the smiles slid off both faces and two pairs of eyes narrowed into cold calculating slits.

'Ready an' waitin', eh, Percy?' Patrick said flatly. 'I like that.'

'Whey aye, man. You know me.'

The man who had spoken resembled nothing so much as a small gorilla. His pug face and thick, dark, spiky hair were definitely ape-like, but it was his heavily barrelled chest, long arms, short thick legs and perpetually hunched shoulders that encouraged the feeling one should offer a banana. He didn't seem to have wrists or ankles; the arms grew straight out of his hands and his legs straight out of his feet, and he had no waist at all.

'Sure I know you, Percy,' answered Patrick, his voice low and without expression. 'An' you know me. Bairns we were together, me an' Percy' – this last was said as an aside to Jimmy but without Patrick's head moving, his eyes intent on the bulky figure in front of them – 'an' our mams were right good pals, isn't that so, Percy? Like family they were, Percy's mam an' mine.'

Jimmy said nothing, and after a few seconds had crawled by, Percy, his voice less cheerful now, said, 'What did you want to see me about then? Harry didn't say.'

'No, well he wouldn't, would he, seein' as how I told him not to.'

Percy's gaze flicked to Jimmy's blank countenance and then back to the small Irishman, and now the nostrils in his flattened nose flared briefly, before he said, 'Is owt wrong?'

'Is owt wrong?' Patrick echoed the words, savouring them before he nudged Jimmy and said again, 'Is owt wrong? What say you, son?'

'I'd say somethin' was wrong, Pat.'

Percy's lower jaw moved from one side to the other. 'Patrick, for cryin' out loud, man, what's the matter?'

Patrick's eyes became fixed on the man in front of him and whatever Percy read in the little Irishman's expression caused him to bluster, 'Man, what's wrong? Tell me, Patrick. You know me—'

'You've already said that.' It was sharp and tight and silenced the other man. 'You've got a big mouth, Percy. Anyone ever told you that afore? An' strange as it may seem, I don't like me private business bein' spread over half of Sunderland. That little arrangement we had concerning the items that tend to fall off the boats from Sweden? I thought it was atween the two of us!'

'It is, I swear it is.'

'Then how come you were heard blabbin' the odds in the Queen's Head in Long Row a couple of nights back? An' afore you deny it, I've checked. You've bin workin' on that dockside for nigh on thirty years; you're trusted, the bosses like you, so how come all that goes out of the window an' you play the big feller, eh? Who were you tryin' to impress? A few bit bar proppers!'

'Patrick . . .' Percy gulped deep in his throat, shaking his head and then gulping hard again before he said, 'I . . . I'd had a few jars, man. I wasn't meself. Look, no one cottoned on. It hasn't got back to anyone who matters.'

'It got back to me, Percy.'

'*Patrick.* Please, Patrick . . . Look, I swear it won't happen agen, man. I'd had a row with the missus; I was drownin' me sorrows, you know how it is. I'd never . . . Please, man.'

'Aye, aye, all right.' Patrick held up his hands, palms facing the terrified man in front of him, and now his voice was understanding, warm even, as he said, 'That's all I wanted to hear, Percy. That it won't happen agen.'

'I swear it. On me bairns' heads, I swear it.' Percy was gabbling now, relief bringing the sweat shining on his forehead. 'I mean, we was bairns together, weren't we. An' like you said, your mam an' mine were as thick as thieves.'

'That they were. Well, you'd best get yerself home an' the less said the better, eh?'

'Aye, aye, man, an' thanks, thanks Patrick. There's . . . there's a boat due in the morrow as you know. Same arrangement as afore then, is it?'

'Don't see why not.'

Patrick turned as he spoke, Jimmy with him, and as he said over his shoulder, 'Missus all right, Percy?' the other man came up behind them, intending to follow them out of the small patch of ground beside the slipway. It was then Patrick and Jimmy turned as one, the knives in their hands flashing for one chilling moment before they were buried up to the hilt in Percy's chest.

Percy made a vain grab at Patrick as he went down on to his knees but he was already gasping his last, and within seconds he was stretched out on the cold cobbles and the silence of the night enclosed them again. Patrick stared down at the body for a second, kicking it with his hobnail boot. There was no response. 'Aye, well now you've convinced me it won't happen again, Percy,' he said conversationally as though the other man could still hear him.

'Are we leavin' him here?'

Patrick glanced about him for a moment. 'We'll send him down the slipway into the water. He'll be found soon enough an' it'll send a warnin' to any of the others with slack mouths.'

'Aye.' Jimmy nodded. He fully agreed that Patrick had needed to make an example of Percy. One mistake was one too many in this game, and you couldn't afford to be soft. Any sign of weakness and they'd all be taking liberties. Everyone knew Percy had stepped out of line and they'd all been watching to see what Patrick would do, especially since Percy and the little Irishman did go back a long way.

Patrick bent down, wiping the blade of his knife on Percy's moleskin trousers before slipping it back in his inside jacket pocket, and Jimmy followed suit. They disposed of the body with equal equanimity, and it was as they stepped into North Moor Street that Patrick said, as though they had been discussing the matter seconds before, 'Your sister'll be back one day, son, sure as eggs are eggs, if not to play the halls then to see that old biddy in Northumberland Place she seems to think so much of. An' when she comes we'll be waitin', you an' I. She's made a monkey of me three times; she won't do it again. I owe her an' you do an' all, for your da an' her rattin' on you an' the lad. She'd have seen you all go down the line if she'd had her way, the lyin' little upstart.'

Jimmy turned his head on his shoulder and looked sideways at Patrick as they walked on, and his voice was quiet but of a quality that pleased the other man when he said, 'Oh, I've no doubt I'll see me day with her, Pat. No doubt at all. She aimed to ruin the lot of us an' all the time actin' like Lady Muck. There's enough of the lads primed now to let us know when she comes back an' we've surprise on our side. But for that load of whores an' dolts she had with her the last time she'd be pushin' up the daisies by now.'

'Or doin' time in one of Doug's secure whorehouses,' Patrick put in slyly. 'I tell you, man, they don't last long in them places, not with the perverts Doug caters for, but the lassies' lives are hell while they're still breathin'. If we're goin' to do her in, that'd be poetic justice to my mind, considerin' all them singers an' actresses an' the like are on the game in one way or another, 'cept they dress it up to appear different.'

Jimmy stared at Patrick for a moment. Murder was one thing, but Doug's locked and guarded brothels which catered – as Doug himself put it – for a special type of customer were something else. And then, as Patrick said, 'Remember your da, son, an' how she turned your own mother agin you an' Hubert, an' broke up the family,' he nodded slowly. He'd think about what they were going to do with Josie once they had her but, by all the gods, get her they would. They'd heard this singing lark had taken her down south but like Patrick had said, she'd be back, and not just because of Vera neither. Josie was a northerner at heart; the north was in her blood, her bones, and eventually she'd return to her roots. To her ain folk. And when she did, this particular member of her ain folk would be waiting.

Chapter Fourteen

'Ee, lass, you're as white as a sheet. Put a bit more rouge on, for goodness' sake.'

Gertie's voice was brisk and meant to be reassuring, but to Josie, sitting weak-kneed and trembling on her stool in the dressing room, it was further confirmation that she didn't look the part.

'She's fine.' Gertie received a dig in the ribs which made her gasp as the young woman sitting on the next stool to Josie's physically objected to Gertie's well-meant advice. 'Any more rouge and she'll glow like a beetroot once she's onstage and enjoying herself. And you will enjoy yourself, lovey, believe me. All right?'

'Thanks, Nellie.' Josie smiled at the colourful figure who had auburn hair piled high on her head, the colour of which definitely came out of a bottle. The two girls had only met a couple of days previously when Josie had visited the large theatre in Ealing to familiarise herself with its layout and size, and to have a series of rehearsals before her début on the London stage. She hadn't been too nervous then, and it had been lovely to meet Nellie and discover she was the daughter of an old music-hall friend of Lily's. In fact, Nellie strongly reminded Josie of Lily; they had the same happy-go-lucky nature and outrageous sense of humour, and – unfortunately – the same penchant for falling for handsome rogues.

However, Josie wasn't thinking about Nellie's torrid love-life at the moment; her mind was on her forthcoming appearance which was now only minutes away. Oliver had assured her that this theatre was nowhere near as grand as the Theatre Royal in Drury Lane or Covent Garden, both of which held four and a half thousand happy theatregoers at a sitting, but nevertheless its décor and size had proved to be overwhelming. In her mind's eye she was picturing the magnificent salon reached from the street by a flight of fine curved stone steps, and the air of elegance, comfort and convenience it contained. On every side immense gorgeous plate-glass mirrors reflected surrounding objects and the massive crystal-drop chandeliers suspended from the ceiling. Against the walls on either side were comfortable stuffed seats of superior quality, in front of which were small marble-topped tables. From end to end, rows of similar tables were fixed at convenient distances from each other with as many chairs as would seat some one and a half thousand loungers.

The mirrored wall at the back of the stage itself reflected the carved, gold-painted cupids and swans which decorated tall pillars at various intervals and again made the hall itself appear far larger than it actually was. Bars were situated through a section of open arches at the rear of the auditorium but divided by a promenade from the main salon. Altogether it was gracious and undoubtedly beautiful, and the thought of it at the moment was scaring Josie to death.

'Look, lovey, them out there are just the same as the audiences in the north where you've worked,' Nellie said now, adjusting her generous bust within her low-cut, lurid green satin frock as she spoke. 'They just want to enjoy themselves, that's all. I've had a peek, and we've got a load of the crutch and toothpick brigade in tonight, and you'll go down just dandy with them with your hair and figure.'

'The crutch an' toothpick brigade?' Gertie queried at the back of them.

'You know, the swells, the Beau Brummells, the smart man-about-town type,' Nellie said, grinning. 'Them with their eyeglasses and gold toothpicks and jewellery. You can always recognise them a mile off with their gold-knobbed crutch sticks and tight trousers and immaculate hair and dress, but they're good customers and don't heckle on the whole, unlike some. You know that song Nellie Farren sang about 'em? She took the mickey good and proper but they didn't seem to mind, even the bit about how they got their trousers on and whether they hurt much!'

There was general laughter from the other girls around them who were listening to Nellie too, and one of the old hands called out, her manner ribald, 'And I bet you've helped take a few pairs down in your time, eh, Nellie?'

Nellie wasn't in the least offended; she loved being the centre of attention, and now she returned with a lascivious wink, 'Would I ever do that, Violet? I'm a good girl, I am, not like the majority these days. All they think about is where to buy their next frock and who to take it off for.'

'How many new frocks have you had recently then, Nellie?' another wit called.

'One or two, Dot. One or two.'

Josie was still smiling when the little stagehand, who couldn't have been a day over eleven years old and who blithely ignored scantily dressed females like a veteran, popped his blond head round the corner of the dressing room, calling, 'Miss Josie Burns? You're on in three minutes. And Nellie Wood, you're after her.'

'We know, we know.' Nellie slipped her arm through

that of Josie as Josie rose to her feet, her face even whiter. 'Come on, gal, I'll walk along with you.'

Josie turned to Gertie and Gertie smiled encouragingly, saying, 'Break a leg, lass. Break a leg.'

'Last time I played a house with Lily she did just that,' Nellie said as the two girls left the dressing room arm in arm.

'Did what?' Despite her nerves Josie's interest was caught and held as Nellie had intended it should be. Like many children of music-hall performers, Nellie had trodden the boards since she was knee high, and she'd always found distraction was the best remedy in situations like these. She had a hundred and one anecdotes to fit the bill.

'Broke her leg,' Nellie giggled. 'One of the girls at that time had this admirer who used to send bottles of champagne and chocolates and roses to the theatre every night. Dead keen he was. Anyway, after the show one night we all got tipsy on his champagne and started messing about onstage singing, and Cicely – that was the girl – said she'd give the latest box of chocolates to the one who could reach the highest note. Well, you know Lily – she couldn't resist that sort of challenge and she was making rapid progress, she was really, before she got carried away and slipped off the stage and broke her leg. We all made a stretcher with our hands and carried her to the infirmary like that; caused a stir when we went in all dolled up in our stage costumes, I can tell you. Anyway, Lily got the chocolates and when Cicely's admirer got to hear about it he sent a case of champagne to the infirmary for Lily, so we had another party on the day she came out. She's a card, old Lily.'

Nellie had timed her little exposition to end just as they reached the wings, and now, as the light-fingered magician who specialised in stage pickpocket routines sent his victim for that night back down in the audience amid much applause, the heavy, richly embroidered curtains swung closed and they heard the chairman holding forth once the piano had stopped.

Josie felt Nellie squeeze her arm encouragingly. She had to go and take her place on the stage now. Unlike Nellie, who was a ribald singer and a forthright, if not definitely vulgar type of comedienne, Josie's strength was in her exceptional voice. This was shown to advantage with the more poignant, emotionally stirring songs she favoured; the slightly risqué ones in her repertoire going down best when sung tongue in cheek with a demure, winsome presentation. Oliver had publicised her début accordingly and – Josie had to admit – spared no expense to promote this stage performance. Lithographers had provided 'personal' posters which Oliver had had displayed all over town, along with pamphlets, insidiously circulated with the view to providing nine-tenths of the newspaper notices he hoped for the next day. There was much more one could do a little later, he had assured her, such as issuing invitations to a private performance for persons of high rank, personalised song sheets, song collections advertised in the newspapers and music shops, and appearances at social events and so on, but that would come once she had been noticed in the capital. Which wouldn't take long, not if he had anything to do with it. But for now, her début night, she would be best displayed standing in a ray of silver limelight from the centre of the roof, and from below in the misty gold radiance of the footlights. To that end her dress was an ethereal floating cloud of silver silk chiffon, and the fresh white rosebuds in her golden-brown curls added to the picture of radiant young womanhood.

Oliver was out there somewhere. As Josie forced her feet to walk into the centre of the stage behind the welcome protection of the velvet curtain, her stomach was doing cartwheels. What if she let him down now? Dried on stage and forgot her words? Or what if they didn't like her? What if . . . And then she caught the panic that was constricting her throat, taking several deep long breaths as Madame Belloc had taught her. 'We never have the agitation, little one.' She could almost hear the small Frenchwoman's firm bell-like tones. 'We are professionals, the crème de la crème, non? And so we breathe, we breathe, we breathe, and then we sing. Like the nightingale, yes? Like the nightingale, we sing.'

And she *could* sing. She could do this. Compared to some of what she'd gone through – the early years when she'd no shoes to her feet and no food in her belly; the endless nightmarish days at the laundry under Prudence's persecution; the attack on her person by Patrick Duffy and her da; and then her da and the lads disappearing; and, worst of all, her mam dying . . . compared to all that, this was nothing. That's how she had to view it.

She heard Alistair, the chairman, finish his spiel and the signature tune they had agreed on for her presentation begin to play, and she knew the curtains would swing back any moment as Edgar, the assistant stage manager, began to work the rope and pulley. They were going to like her; she would *make* them like her. They were just people, weren't they, the same as in the pubs and music halls back home. If she made it big time, it would mean more money than she'd ever dreamed of; she'd heard some of the other performers talk, she knew what the stars of the music hall earned. And she wouldn't waste a penny, not a single penny. They could find Hubert again and she'd buy them all a place to live – a place of their own where no one could come along and throw them out on to the streets. She could buy safety for herself and what was left of her family.

She just had time to glance at Nellie in the wings who smiled and gave her a vigorous thumbs-up as the curtains glided apart with a faint squeak from the machinery, and then an ocean of faces was in front of her beyond the footlights.

Josie walked gracefully forward, smiling and bobbing her head towards Alistair – a splendid figure in his white tie and tails – who banged his gavel with white gloved hands and called out her name in ringing, fruity tones as she took her position on stage. This was it. This was what she had trained for so singlemindedly in the last couple of months and worked towards for the last few years. This was her chance and she was going to grasp it with open hands. Suddenly all the nervousness was gone.

She had had an introduction line which Oliver had thought out, but now the moment had come, Josie knew she had to speak for herself; say what was in her heart. 'Thank you so much for being here today and letting me sing to you. I was nervous a moment ago but now, looking at you all, you don't look so bad.' A wave of appreciative laughter swept round the theatre and a few loungers sat up in their seats. 'I've always wanted to sing, even as a small child, so this is a dream come true. I'd like to start by singing "Masks and Faces", a song Jenny Hill made famous and which some of you might know, followed by "One Last Sweet Kiss".'

There was more perfunctory applause and Oliver, sitting tucked away at the side of the theatre where he could gauge the audience's reaction and hear comments, found himself straining forward in his seat, his palms damp. Damn it all but she was lovely, more than lovely. And the lighting was just right. It made her appear so fragile, elusive, but when she opened her mouth and let that magnificent voice soar . . . He breathed deeply and then, as the first notes

273

sounded, relaxed back in his seat, his eyes never leaving the silver and gold figure on the stage.

And it wasn't until some ten minutes later, when an explosion of thunderous applause rocked the theatre, that Oliver came to himself and realised that far from noticing the crowd's reaction he had been blind and deaf to anything but the slim, ethereal woman singing so effortlessly in front of him. She was exquisite. He glanced about him now, seeing entranced faces wherever he looked. And they all knew it. Hark at them – they loved her. They were calling for more in a way he hadn't heard for years. She had them in the palm of her tiny hand.

Josie was laughing and curtsying on the stage but she had to sing another song before the audience would let her go and, mindful of Oliver's instruction to leave them happy, she flirted her way through 'The Farm Boy and the Milkmaid' before waving one last time and running lightly into the wings, there to be embraced by a delighted Nellie. 'I told you, didn't I!' her friend exclaimed when she stood back a pace and looked into Josie's bright face. 'They'll want to retain you here, so mind your agent bumps up your fee.'

'Oh, Nellie.' Josie was brimming over with excitement. 'I can't believe it!'

'Believe it and enjoy it, gal.' Nellie grinned, not a trace of jealousy in her voice as she added, 'You'll go far, Josie Burns, you mark my words. Nellie Wood knows a good thing when she sees it.' And then, as Alistair finished his preamble, she grinned again, saying, 'And now for something completely different. I think after all that purity and good taste they're ready for "And Her Golden Hair was Hanging Down Her Back", don't you?'

The curtain was already swinging back and now Nellie swaggered on to the stage, the long feathers in her sparkling headband wafting about her auburn hair. Josie waited in the wings. She had heard Nellie sing this song in rehearsals, and no one got the mix of sauciness and wide-eyed appeal so right as Nellie, especially bearing in mind the naked child that appeared in the latest advertisements for Pears soap. Nellie was a natural comedian and this song was perfect for her.

Nellie turned and winked at her before she announced the title of the song which met with a roar of approval from the crowd, and then she began to sing all about the country maiden who came down to London for a trip and was enticed by the bright lights.

Nellie had everyone singing lustily in the chorus, but knowing what was coming, Josie herself was laughing so much she was quite unable to join in. Nellie was thoroughly enjoying the reaction of the audience and sang with relish the cheekiest of the verses, in which the young innocent was persuaded to pose beside a marble bath upon some marble stairs in the manner of the Pears soap advertisement, with just her golden hair hanging down her back, and with Nellie's gesturing and outrageous innuendo the audience were howling with laughter.

There was more along the same lines but knowing Gertie would be waiting for her, Josie slipped away, intending to make her way back to the dressing room.

She felt as though she was floating as she walked down the wooden steps from the stage area, and when one or two of the other artistes who had come into the wings to watch her first performance called out their congratulations, she thanked them breathlessly with sparkling eyes.

Josie had just reached the corridor leading to the bowels of the theatre, when a voice calling her name brought her turning, and then Oliver was there in front of her, his hands coming out swiftly and catching hers as he said, 'You were wonderful, magnificent, as I knew you would be.'

It was more the look on his face than what he'd said which caused Josie to blink rapidly before she answered, 'Thank you. I'm glad you're pleased.'

'Pleased?' He shook his head slightly. 'Pleased does not begin to describe what I felt out there.' He stared at her, part of him – the Hogarth part, the part which had been brought up as a gentleman, his every need catered for to the point where he had never even dressed himself before he had been so rudely cast adrift at the age of twenty – protesting that this was madness.

As his mistress, Josie would be welcomed, or perhaps the word was 'patronised', by his friends, who would even then wonder why he had replaced Stella with a mistress of less . . . lofty pedigree. But they would accept her as a mistress since most men, even the Prince of Wales himself, indulged in affairs with ladies from the world of the theatre. But although his friends would talk behind their lace cuffs and snigger a little, it would be their lady wives who would cut her apart with their tongues, should he present her as his future wife. No matter that the majority of them hopped from bed to bed with scant regard for discretion, nor that a good proportion had children fathered by the current lover rather than their husband, they mated within their class, that was the thing, and so they were still ladies. Josie had more natural dignity and poise than the lot of them put together, but they wouldn't see it like that. Or rather, they might see it, and that would make them even more cruel. *But Josie would consider nothing less than marriage.* Even to suggest anything else would mean he might lose her for good.

He loved her. He had loved her from the minute he had seen her on that stage in Hartlepool – before that, even;

he had loved her from the beginning of time without recognising who or where she was, but until he had met her his whole life had been a period of waiting. If he lost her, if he let someone else snatch the prize from under his nose . . .

'Josie?' He still had hold of her hands but now he moved a fraction closer, taking encouragement from the fact that she did not immediately pull away. 'I have to ask you something and you may well think I am being presumptuous, but I know you will give me an honest answer. Do you think you could ever bring yourself to look on me as more than an agent, as a friend? I trust you do think of me as a friend?'

She blinked again but she had begun to shiver inside, the smell of him – the fresh, clean and altogether attractive smell of him – teasing her senses as she looked up into the strong masculine face staring down at her. He wasn't Barney, but Barney had been lost to her since the day he had walked out of the small parish church in Newcastle with Pearl on his arm, she knew that. And Oliver . . . Oliver was handsome and worldly and intelligent, but more than that he was gentle and kind. At least, that was the way he had been with her. She'd heard stories of his reputation of course, from various sources, but she couldn't equate them with the sober, considerate man she knew. But he *was* of the gentry. The word was loud in her ears and spoken in a strong northern accent, like her mother or Vera might have used. Such men only wanted girls like her for one reason.

And then, as though she had spoken her doubts out loud, Oliver said quietly, 'I am twice your age, Josie, I know that, but I don't consider that a disadvantage in a marriage, and . . . and I love you. I love you more than I had ever imagined it was possible to love; in fact, meeting you has made me realise I have never loved before.'

Marriage. He was talking of marriage. That, and the brief, almost shy hesitation before he had spoken of his love caught at her heartstrings. She began to tremble. This, coming on top of her recent triumph on the stage, was almost too much.

'You haven't given me an answer as to whether you could learn to look on me in a different light.' He moved her closer to him, their joined hands resting on his chest. 'I can promise you I will spend the rest of my life making you happy if you will give me a chance?'

There was nothing of the coquette in Josie, and now one of the attributes Oliver loved most about her came to the fore when she said, with touching and embarrassed honesty, 'I . . . I think you're very attractive but I never considered . . . I mean, I didn't think you looked at me like that.'

'From the first moment we met.' It was tender, and Oliver comforted himself with the fact that he wasn't actually lying. He *had* always wanted her, loved her, it had just been the prospect of proposing marriage that had been in question. But tonight had told him that if he didn't snap her up, someone else would; she had been thrust into the glare of the public eye tonight in a big way and this was just the beginning. Gertie had told him in confidence that Josie had rebuffed any advances from the opposite sex in the past although her admirers had been manifold, but here in the capital she would be swept into a different life. No, he had to act now, stake his claim as it were. He had prevaricated long enough. And he could continue to mould and educate her far more effectively as a husband than he ever could as a mere agent. Marriage to him would be a great social and professional asset to her.

Oliver did not admit to himself here that there were definite advantages on both sides, or that, whatever his feelings for Josie – and they were ones of love and desire – it hadn't been merely her working-class background which had caused him to hold his hand until this precise moment in their relationship. It wasn't in him to acknowledge that he had waited to see how London had received her before he had staked his claim, nor that his pressing debts caused by a recent run of bad luck on the horses and in the gambling dens he frequented meant that a wife with the potential earning power of Josie Burns wasn't to be sneezed at.

'So, my dear?' His face was straight now and very serious. 'What is your answer? Will you marry me?'

She stared at him, her mind racing. She liked Oliver, she liked him very much, but could she love him as she loved Barney? Was it possible to love two men? And if it wasn't, did she care for him enough to make him happy and make a marriage work? They had so much in common with regard to their professional lives and he was funny and warm and always extremely attentive, but marriage was made up of one main ingredient that was more important than all those things. Did she want to make love with him? For him to hold her close, to kiss her? Did she like him enough to lie with him?

She lowered her eyes for a moment and then suddenly, as a new thought came to her, her brain stopped its scrambling. How would she feel if she refused him and he fell in love with someone else? Unhappy. More than unhappy, devastated. Over the last months he had become a big part of her life, had woven himself into her affections and her heart, and she hadn't fully realised it till now. And he was handsome and strong, wholesome. And she had to forget that other love – it could never be and she had always known it. But if she refused Oliver she might never meet anyone else she liked so much. No, loved. The emotion she was feeling was stronger than just liking.

She looked at him again, holding the cornflower-blue gaze for a moment and she felt his hands tighten on hers as he waited for her answer. She wanted to be loved, to be married, to have a family one day . . . 'Yes, I'll marry you, Oliver,' she said quietly, and then, as his face lit up and he picked her right up off the ground and swung her round in the narrow corridor, she gave a little squeal of surprise.

And then she was on her feet again and he drew her closer, and her heart began to pound as she realised he meant to kiss her on the lips. The pleasant smell which emanated faintly from him was stronger as, her eyes shutting of their own accord, she felt his lips on hers. His mouth was warm and firm, and the feel and smell of him was exciting little nervous shivers deep inside her. She couldn't ever remember anyone kissing her on the mouth before, not even her mother, but she liked it. She liked it very much.

The kiss only lasted for a moment or two, and Josie would never know the restraint Oliver was practising when everything in him wanted to crush her to him and cover her face with kisses. She was so sweet, intoxicating, and since he had finished with Stella and brought Josie up to London he had abstained from the pleasures of the flesh for the first time in over twenty years. It hadn't been easy. Perhaps that was why he had been gambling so heavily the last little while; he'd needed some outlet for the restlessness and frustration his self-imposed forbearance was causing in the night hours.

'Josie, you don't know how happy you have made me.' He continued to hold her close with one arm round her waist as he spoke, his other hand touching one flushed cheek in a light caress. 'I am the most fortunate man in the world. Are . . . are you going to insist on a long engagement or can we break with sober tradition and have the wedding towards the end of this year?'

She did not answer straight away; in truth she was finding the whole situation more than overwhelming and Oliver must have sensed this, because his next words were, 'But we have plenty of time to sort that out, of course, my dear. And now you must inform your sister of the happy news and perhaps the three of us can go out to dinner after your next performance and celebrate?'

She smiled at him. 'That would be lovely,' she said softly, adding, suddenly shy, 'and I'll try and be a good wife, Oliver.'

Her words seemed to please him, for his grip on her waist tightened as he pulled her towards him again, this time dropping a lingering kiss on her brow before he said quietly, 'And you think you might come to like me more than a little?'

'I do already.'

'Good.' How on earth he was going to manage not to ravish her in the coming months he didn't know, but manage he would. She would stand at the altar as pure as she was now. For once in his life he was going to do it right. She was head and shoulders above any other woman of his acquaintance, and if any of his so-called friends cocked a snook at her or allowed their lady wives free rein, he'd draw blood, damn it, whoever they were. 'Because I adore you, my beautiful angel.'

She blinked at the endearment. She couldn't ever imagine Barney saying that to a woman; his love would not take the form of affectionate utterances but express itself in the way of most northern men, in the physical commitment to providing a roof over the heads of his wife and bairns and working all hours to provide for their needs. And then she mentally shook herself, silently admonishing the waywardness of her thoughts. It didn't matter what Barney did or didn't do, for goodness' sake! This was the start of a new life and she would give it her all.

'May I kiss you again before you go and tell Gertie the glad news?'

She nodded, and this time when his lips met hers he felt a response in their softness which thrilled him but which made him warn himself, Careful, careful. Her lips told him she was as innocent as they come and he could easily frighten her. He would have to go and visit one of the establishments he knew of and get some relief, however; he had satisfied the hunger of his flesh for too long to continue abstaining. Self-denial was all very well for monks and clergymen but he wasn't made that way, and if he was to get through the engagement and remain sane he would need some assistance.

They were brought apart by Nellie's voice saying, the tone bright, 'Oh, so that's the way of it, is it?'

Oliver turned to face the girl he privately thought of as far beneath him, and his voice was cool when he said, 'Miss Burns has just done me the honour of agreeing to become my wife. *That* is the way of it.'

'Really?' Undaunted, Nellie grabbed hold of Josie and hugged her. 'You're a dark horse if ever there was one; you haven't breathed a word of this.'

'I want to tell Gertie first.' Josie returned Nellie's hug before drawing back and putting her finger to her lips in a warning gesture. 'Don't say anything before I tell her, will you?'

'Wouldn't dream of it, gal.' Nellie now moved her head, looking Oliver straight in the eye as she said, her voice as cool as his had been, 'You're a lucky blighter if ever there was one. You know that, don't you.'

Oliver stifled his annoyance, forcing a smile as he said, 'Indeed I do.'

And it wasn't until much later, just before she fell asleep in fact, that Josie recalled Nellie hadn't congratulated her on her betrothal.

Part 3
The Taste of Success
1901

Chapter Fifteen

Josie married Oliver on the first day of the New Year, a day which also saw the Commonwealth of Australia come into being on the other side of the world, but which momentous event passed unnoticed by the new Mr and Mrs Oliver Hogarth. Oliver would have liked the marriage to take place some weeks earlier but this had not proved possible, mainly because of Josie's heavy work schedule throughout November and December.

London had embraced its newest sensation with all the enthusiasm Oliver had hoped for, and when Josie had been offered a part in the pantomime at the Theatre Royal, Drury Lane, throughout the last two months of the old year, they had both known it required 100 per cent commitment and had arranged the wedding date accordingly.

Josie had enjoyed the last weeks of 1900 more than she would have thought possible. The pantomime smell of gas, oranges, human beings and dust had become as familiar as blinking, along with the great gasps of anticipation from the audience as the Demon King strutted on stage by the illumination of fizzy blue and red limes. The *oooh!* when she, as the Fairy Queen, entered on the other side in a holy circle of fizzy white lime never failed to thrill her, along with the children's goggle eyes as the Demon King sang his usual song:

Hush, hush, hush!
Here comes the bogey man,
Be on your best behaviour
For he'll catch you if he can!

At the end of the traditional and very pretty Transformation
scene, which consisted of raising one by one a series
of gauzes to reveal fairies, reclining in enormous roses
and water lilies, the children's excitement when Clown,
Pantaloon and Harlequin appeared and tossed brightly
wrapped crackers into small hands in the stalls, pit and
circle was infectious, along with their high howls of
laughter as Clown burned everyone with a red-hot poker
and stole long strings of sausages from the butcher's shop
in the following front-cloth scene.

It was sheer magic for the children, from the moment
they entered the great portico at the theatre to find small
boys dressed as pages in bright blue suits with shiny buttons
and pill box caps giving away little bottles of scent; and
nymphs, golden and sparkling, reclining gracefully on gold
brackets at the side of the stage.

Flying fairies, poised but swaying gently, filled the
air and formed an archway below which the performers
gathered, and the vivid colours, sparkling bright costumes
and general air of festivity caused many a small person to
become sick with excitement. It wasn't just the children
who were enamoured; when Josie had paid for Vera and
Horace, along with Betty and her tribe to come down for
one of the shows in the early part of December, she'd been
hard pressed to decide who enjoyed the pantomime more
– the three grown-ups or the bairns.

Seated at her husband's side in the elegant hotel in
Richmond which Oliver had chosen for their small reception, Josie glanced round her assembled family and friends.

Oliver's only living family consisted of two great-aunts somewhere or other, and he had insisted they would hold an evening reception for his friends when they returned from honeymoon. It was the sort of thing expected amongst his set, he'd said, and it was better Josie had her family and friends to herself on her special day.

Josie now smiled at Vera and Horace before her gaze moved to Amos and his wife, who were sitting quietly together with their three children. The baby had died just before Christmas, and although there were those within both sides of the family who said it was a blessing, Amos and his wife didn't see it that way. As Amos had said to Josie in a quiet moment, they had loved the child more, not less, because of its problems. Hadn't the Lord Jesus Christ come to this earth specifically for the poor and needy and afflicted, so how could they, as His servants, consider it any other than a privilege that He'd trusted a little suffering one to their care?

Josie had been amazed and humbled by their acceptance and faith, but she doubted she could have thought the same in such heartbreaking circumstances.

Reg and Neville, with their respective wives and children, were seated either side of Amos and his family, but Betty had been unable to make the wedding at the last minute due to her three youngest children going down with the measles. Barney had sent his apologies too. Pearl was very poorly, as Josie knew, he had written, and they'd decided a journey of such magnitude would tire her unduly.

Josie hadn't known, and when she questioned Vera about the nature of Pearl's illness, Vera wasn't very forthcoming. She thought she'd mentioned that Pearl had been a bit under the weather? Vera had said with a surprised note in her voice. And when Josie assured her that no, she hadn't, Vera simply shrugged and mumbled that she had no doubt Pearl would soon be well again. And that was the most Josie could get out of her old friend.

Josie had included Prudence in Vera and Horace's invitation. She'd felt she could do little else with Betty's stepdaughter living with Vera, and all the lads and their families receiving invitations, but she wasn't sorry when Prudence declined. She had no wish to see the girl again, least of all on her wedding day, although Vera had reported that Prudence was a changed person. Indeed, Josie suspected that Vera felt sorry for Betty's stepdaughter, even perhaps liked her a little, because she had made no effort to ask Prudence to leave now her hands were improved as much as they were ever going to be. Vera had even put in a good word for her at the corn mill when an inspection/checking-out post had become available, so now Prudence worked with Vera too.

She'd felt strange about that, Josie admitted to herself as she watched Vera talking to Neville's wife who was seated next to her. Abandoned almost. Which was ridiculous, quite ridiculous. Vera had her life up in Sunderland and she had to do what she thought was right in any situation. Her own life was quite different now she'd met Oliver; everything was different. *Too* different? She quelled the little niggle which had been at the back of her mind for the last day or so, angry it should rear its head on this day of all days. She was happy, very happy, and she had the most wonderful husband and friends, and Gertie. Precious Gertie.

She turned to Gertie who was sitting at the side of her and who looked charming in her deep blue bridesmaid's dress which had a matching cloak edged with white fur, and said very quietly, 'I wonder where Hubert is today? Jimmy too.'

Gertie nodded. 'And Ada an' Dora. By, they had a rough start, didn't they, and I'd have bin sent along the same road but for you, lass.'

Josie nodded but didn't pursue the conversation, conscious of Oliver on her other side. She had told him all about her childhood and her flight with Gertie to Newcastle and the reason for it, and he had been as shocked and distressed as she had expected. But she had felt it was right to tell him it all; she hadn't wanted to continue with the engagement under false pretences. After a few moments he had taken her hands in his, his face grim, and said, 'I make no judgement on your sisters, Josie. They were clearly more sinned against than sinful, but nevertheless if this were to come to light it might throw a shadow over you yourself. Do you understand this? Society is quick to condemn, my dear, and can be very cruel. I think it would be better if we do not discuss this painful subject again but consign it to the past where it belongs.'

'They are my sisters, Oliver.'

'Of course they are, but by your own admission it has been almost a decade since you saw them last. You could pass them in the street and not know them, and – forgive me, my dear – the life they have embraced is a hard one. There is no guarantee they have survived it thus far.'

She had stared at him for some ten seconds or more before saying, 'Nevertheless, I must repeat they are my sisters and the fault was not theirs. If you are asking me to admit to being ashamed of them, I cannot.'

'Oh, my dear.' His tone had changed and he had pulled her stiff body into his arms, saying softly above her head, 'Your attitude does you credit but I would have expected nothing less from you. I am the most fortunate man in the world.'

She would have said more but he had begun to kiss her

and the moment had passed, but since that day – the day after he had asked her to become his wife – they had not talked of her two elder sisters again simply because the matter had not arisen. Josie told herself Oliver had dealt with the unwelcome confidence with typical male logic and lack of emotion, and had endeavoured to see the situation from his point of view, but deep inside, barely acknowledged, had been a shred of disappointment . . .

'Happy, my darling?' Oliver's voice was soft and deep and now, as she turned to him, the look in his blue eyes made her quiver. They were to spend their wedding night in Oliver's London house before leaving for a week's honeymoon in France where one of Oliver's friends had a château. They could have spent longer abroad but Josie was beginning a new season at Covent Garden beginning the third week of January, and so regretfully they had decided a week was all they could manage. 'You look quite exquisite.' Oliver stroked her flushed face before looking down at the ivory silk dress encrusted with hundreds and hundreds of tiny crystals across the low-cut bodice, and then back upwards to her golden-brown hair under its lacy veil. 'Even the good Reverend Whear was mesmerised by your beauty. He nearly forgot his words, did you notice?'

'Oh, Oliver.' She smiled now, and he grinned back at her, suddenly very much her Oliver. Everything was going to be all right. Once this first night of marriage was over she would know what to expect and then it wouldn't be so frightening. Women the whole world over survived this thing that happened once the lights were out, and most of them loved their husbands. Look at the Queen – she had been devoted to her Albert and utterly devastated by his death, and they had had nine children. She had openly idolised him, and he her, so this . . . activity couldn't be that bad, could it?

* * *

It wasn't. A little painful perhaps on the first night and certainly somewhat embarrassing, but Oliver's gentleness and restrained passion, along with his almost reverent adoration, had even made that night enjoyable. And as the honeymoon progressed in the wonderful old château where they were waited on hand and foot by Oliver's friend's old retainers, Josie blossomed under her husband's skilful and experienced lovemaking.

They arrived home in England, tired but happy, on a very wet and windy January evening, and Gertie, who had her own quarters now in Oliver's house, had opened the door and run down the steps to greet them as though Josie had been away for a month instead of a week.

It was some time later after they had enjoyed the excellent homecoming dinner Mrs Wilde had prepared, and the maids had cleared away the dishes, and Josie and Oliver along with Gertie were sitting in front of the roaring drawing-room fire, that Josie said, 'Is anything wrong, Gertie? There is something, isn't there? What is it, lass?'

'I wasn't going to say anything tonight what with you just coming home, but . . .' Gertie hesitated. 'It's a bit of a shock but Pearl, she's gone.'

'Gone? Gone where?'

'She died, Josie. The day after you went to France.'

'She *died*?' Josie was aware of the crackling bright orange flames licking round the big log on the fire which Constance, one of the maids, had attended to some minutes before, and Oliver at the side of her saying, 'Who is Pearl?' but for a moment she was having a job taking the news in. Pearl had been young, so young and bonny; it seemed impossible that she was dead. She turned to Oliver. 'Pearl is – was – Barney's wife, Betty's stepson.'

Gertie chimed in again, with, 'I couldn't believe it

when I heard, an' apparently all them back home got a gliff an' all. No one realised she was so bad, you see.'

'How old was this Pearl?' Oliver asked quietly.

'Only twenty-four or twenty-five,' Josie said. 'We'd invited them to the wedding, if you remember, but Barney wrote to say she was ill. I never realised it was anything so serious. Vera seemed to suggest it wasn't much at all . . .' Her voice trailed away. This was awful. Pearl had had her whole life in front of her. And her mam and da would be devastated. According to Betty, they'd built their life round Pearl. And Barney – how would he be feeling? She could still hardly believe it. 'Do we know the cause of death?' she asked Gertie.

'A disease of the blood, so Vera wrote. She . . . she started bleeding at the end apparently, from everywhere, an' then she went into a coma an' within a few hours she'd gone.'

'It was in the newspapers in November last year that the blood is far more complicated than doctors had expected.' Oliver stood up and walked across to the fire, standing with his back to the flames as he continued, 'Three different blood groups have been identified by a scientist in Vienna, and he thinks this explains why different people react differently to blood transfusions among other things. Did your friend have transfusions?'

'I don't know.'

'I'm so sorry, my dear.' Oliver returned to the sofa and sat down, patting Josie's arm as he spoke. 'It is always so much worse when one hasn't lived out the three score and ten.'

Josie nodded. She hadn't liked Pearl and now she felt awful because she hadn't.

'Barney was the gentleman I met once at Vera's house, wasn't he?' Oliver said after a moment or two.

Josie nodded again. 'When you came up to Sunderland to see a friend of yours,' she agreed.

'I think we both know why I came up to Sunderland.' He smiled and she half smiled back, but she felt shaken and disturbed. 'What are the funeral arrangements?' Oliver asked Gertie.

'It's tomorrow morning, early, so there's no chance of going,' Gertie said. 'I let them all back home know that you two weren't due back till late tonight so they don't expect us.'

'Thank you.' Josie felt doubly guilty now as a sense of relief made itself known. She would have gone if there had been time but she wouldn't have known what to say to Barney, or Prudence either for that matter. Prudence had thought the world of Pearl. She'd be absolutely heartbroken . . .

'Well, lass, this took us all by surprise. I never thought that she wouldn't get better, did you?'

Prudence shook her head. She knew Vera was wondering why she wasn't more upset, and she *was* sorry Pearl had died, it was terrible, but she couldn't pretend to something she didn't feel. Not any more. Not with Vera. For years now she had squirmed at Pearl's treatment of Barney, and only she knew how awful it had been in that house. Not that she wished Pearl dead, never that, but it had happened and that was that.

As they entered the church and took their seats, Prudence glanced across to where Barney was sitting, his head bowed and his hands joined as they hung down between his knees. Pearl's parents were on one side of him and Betty on the other, but he appeared oblivious to anyone else.

'First Shirley, then Frank and now this.' Vera's voice at the side of her brought Prudence's head turning, and

Horace – on Vera's other side – nodded mournfully. 'They say it goes in threes so please God this is an end to it. What say you, lass?'

'Aye.' Prudence nodded in her turn, and then she wondered what Vera would say if she came out with the truth and told her she was the happiest she'd ever been these days.

When she had first gone to live with Vera and Horace she knew it had been on sufferance. Oh, not that anything had been said, Vera was too nice for that, but she'd known all right. And it had been difficult, the first few weeks. Her hands had still been paining her a lot then, and she'd felt . . . Oh, she couldn't have described to anyone how she'd felt in those dark days. She had prayed she wouldn't wake up when she'd laid her head on the pillow more times than she could remember, and the river had beckoned to her more than once. It would be easy, she'd thought, just to let herself fall into the river and for the waters to close over her head and end all the struggling and heartache and pain. She'd spent hours in the little room designated to her; thinking, thinking, thinking until she'd felt she was going mad. She was never going to be married, never going to have bairns or be loved, never even have any real friends. She was an oddity, a freak, that's what she was. And then, to put the tin lid on it, she'd come out in a rash all over her face and torso.

It had all come to a head that day she'd looked in the little hand mirror in her bedroom and seen the gargoyle she'd become looking back at her. At least that's how she'd felt at the time. And she'd thrown the mirror to the floor where it had smashed into a hundred pieces, and Vera had come running up and thought she'd dropped it because of her hands and told her not to worry, she'd get another one. And she had screamed at Vera that she didn't *want* another mirror! Why would anyone want to see what she saw when she looked in one? And then somehow she'd found herself in Vera's arms sobbing her heart out and once started she hadn't been able to stop. Horace had gone for the doctor when she was still crying an hour later, and he'd given her something to make her sleep. And Vera had been there when she'd woken up, and they had talked. For hours they'd talked. And everything had changed after that. She couldn't remember her mam much but she couldn't have thought more of her if she'd lived than she did Vera. That's how she felt now. And Horace was kind. Oh, he was. And easygoing. He didn't gripe about much, Horace.

'Come as somethin' of a bolt out of the blue to Barney an' all.' Vera was whispering as befitted the solemn occasion, and again Prudence nodded, whispering back, 'He'll be all right, Vera. It's terrible, but it's not as if he and Pearl were as close as you and Horace or anything, is it?'

'No, no. You're right there, lass. Aye, you are, an' I've always said God works in mysterious ways.'

'His wonders to perform,' Horace chimed in.

'What?' Now Vera turned fully to him. 'What are you on about?'

'Isn't that the next part of that verse? God works in mysterious ways His wonders to perform?'

'It might be.' Vera clearly didn't like being caught out on something she didn't know, and she sniffed before she said, 'But I would hardly call Pearl's death a wonder, Horace.'

'I wasn't sayin' that, now was I?' He leaned forward, appealing to Prudence, who was secretly amused. These two were like a double act at times but now was not the time to smile. Poor Pearl. As Horace settled back in his seat, Prudence glanced at the back of Marjorie and Stanley's heads. And her poor parents. But at least there were no little ones left motherless, that was something. And Pearl hadn't bothered to come and see her in hospital when she'd first hurt her hands – and that was before she'd got ill. Barney had come, and he'd said Pearl found hospitals upsetting but that she'd sent her love. That day, Prudence had realised that she didn't actually *want* Pearl to visit her, which had been a great surprise at the time.

Barney turned round once as the service began, his eyes searching out Prudence, and when she inclined her head at him he nodded back before facing the minister again. He was glad his sister was here. He hadn't seen much of her since she had been living with Vera, and to his surprise he had found that he missed her. She was an intelligent lass, Prudence, and they'd had some good cracks together, but moreover he didn't have to pretend with her. He knew that most people would cast him in the role of heartbroken husband, and respect for Pearl prevented him from telling the truth, but the pity and sympathy in people's faces had him wanting to stand up and shout, 'Don't none of you feel sorry for me! Feel sorry for Pearl, aye, in as much as you would for any young life cut short, but not me.'

A stifled sob from Pearl's mother at the side of him brought his head towards his mother-in-law, but she was staring rigidly ahead and did not glance at him. Barney had gleaned enough over the last years to know who he had to thank for Pearl being the way she was in the bedroom and out of it, but there was no doubt her mother had loved Pearl in her own way. Marjorie Harper had had a deeply possessive streak where her only child was concerned, and she'd projected all her warped ideas about the intimate side of marriage on to her daughter, along with the compulsive desire she had to control every aspect of her husband and her marriage. Pearl's father had never spoken of his relationship with his wife, but within weeks of being wed Barney had read what was in the other man's eyes and recognised it for what it was. How Stanley had stuck Marjorie for nigh on thirty years he didn't know.

Barney slanted his eyes at the couple beside him. Pearl's parents were sitting stiff and straight and without any part of them touching, but there was no doubt both were deeply distraught. But then again, if Pearl hadn't died he'd be in the same boat as Stanley unless he had upped and skedaddled, and what man worth his salt did that?

By, in all his wildest imaginings of how things were going to work out he'd never thought it would be like this. And he wouldn't have wished Pearl's end on anyone. Not that he'd been allowed to be with her when she died. Pearl's mother had been sleeping on a put-you-up at the side of her daughter's bed ever since Pearl's first collapse and had made sure Barney didn't contaminate her daughter with his foul presence for more than a minute or two a day. If she could have surrounded the room in barbed wire and kept him out completely, she would have. They had taken Pearl to hospital, that last forty-eight hours, but Pearl had just got distressed when he had tried to sit near her and take her hand, and so the doctors had advised him to leave her to her mother. But he had gone in to see her after it was over and her father had taken her mother home, and he had hardly been able to recognise the young, pretty lass he'd fallen in love with so many moons ago. He'd felt a sense of desolation then, standing looking down at what once had been a living, breathing human being, and memories from the past – from their courting days – had come flooding in. But those days hadn't been real; he knew that now. They had been an illusion.

The service was not a long one and after the burial in the churchyard the funeral entourage returned to Barney's house in Jesmond. Pearl's mother had wanted to see to the meal which, although consisting of various cold meats and such, was substantial, and Barney had let her, knowing Marjorie needed to be able to do something. It was as he was filling everyone's glasses that Vera spoke to him for the first time that day, her voice quiet as she said simply, 'I'm sorry, lad.'

'Aye, thanks, Vera.' Barney felt he didn't need to say any more. Vera being Betty's sister would know the marriage had not been all it should be; they were as close as bricks and mortar, those two. 'It's hit her mam and da hard.'

Vera nodded. And then she forced herself to say, as naturally as she could, 'Gertie wrote me an' said she'd explained them down in London wouldn't be able to make it, Oliver an' Josie only just gettin' home from their honeymoon late last night an' all.'

'Aye, she did.' Barney drew in a long breath. He had kept his mind from thinking about Josie, or more particularly Josie and Oliver, because he had known there was only so much he could take and he needed to get this day over.

And then Vera surprised both Barney and herself when she said what she'd promised herself she wouldn't say, certainly not on this particular day: 'She's got a new life now with how things have gone for her, her success and all. It's all different, lad. Not that she'll forget her roots and her old friends, Josie's not like that, but it wouldn't be natural if she didn't shake off the dust so to speak, would it?'

Barney raised his head and looked at Vera, and his lips

moved, but he didn't speak until he turned and looked across the packed sitting room. And then he said, his voice flat, 'It's a good turn-out. Marjorie and Stanley will take some comfort from that. Marjorie sets great store by such things.'

'Aye, well everyone to their own, lad.' Vera was feeling mightily uncomfortable and, searching her mind for something to say, she added, 'Will you keep this house up now?'

Barney shook his head. 'I'm selling it. I've been told I'll make a nice profit on it. And I'm leaving Ginnett's.'

'Oh aye? You had the offer of another job then?'

'No.'

Vera inhaled deeply and tried again. 'So you'll be doin' what? Going back to the concrete works or lookin' for something else in the theatre line maybe?'

'I don't know yet. I haven't decided. I might take off for a bit, travel around.' And then, when the silence stretched and lengthened Barney turned again, and what he read on Vera's face caused him to say, and curtly, 'It's all right, Vera. London won't be one of my calling places.'

Vera didn't protest her innocence of the unspoken accusation, she merely looked at him for a moment or two before nodding slowly, and what she said was, 'One town is very much like another in my book.'

No, one town was not very much like another, not when it had Josie in it. Barney watched Vera move away and for a moment he had it within him to hate her for the none too subtle plea to stay away from Josie. What did she think he was, anyway? Pearl barely put to rest and Josie just married; did she really think he was going to hightail it to London and plead his cause? Barney had decided to go to Glasgow, or perhaps Edinburgh. He'd make a bit out of the sale of the house, even after he'd paid the Building

Society their whack, and he owed no one nowt. He needed to get away for a time, right away. Aye, that's what he'd do. He would go to Scotland and if things turned out right he might even stay there for good.

'You all right, Barney?' Prudence was at his elbow.

He nodded. 'And you?'

'Aye.' She had hoped to have a quiet word with him today but there was as much chance of that with friends and family milling around as flying. She hadn't known quite how she was going to approach what she needed to say, it being a delicate subject, so perhaps it was better left unsaid anyway. She got on all right with Barney now and she didn't want anything to upset that.

She hadn't liked the look of the little ferret-faced individual who had spoken to her in the market a few weeks ago, but within a moment or two of him opening his mouth she had realised he had approached her for a purpose. He had known where she lived and her name and where she'd come from in Newcastle; he'd have had to ask questions and probe a bit to find that out.

She'd been tempted to tell him to be off about his business initially, especially when he had laid a claw-like hand on her coat-sleeve to detain her, but her curiosity had been stronger than her unease. He'd been careful in what he said, but it had been enough to indicate that he was aware she was the person who had tipped Bart Burns the wink all that time ago, and at that point she had to admit she'd become interested. And so she had swallowed her distaste and walked with him for a while, and although they had parted without anything of real importance being said, and without him stating the reason he'd spoken to her in the first place, she had gleaned enough to understand that the small Irishman had no more time for Josie Burns than she had. It was only when she was within sight and sound of Vera's that she'd suddenly remembered the description the police had given of the accomplice who had been with Josie's father that night at her da's, and it seemed to match the little man to a T.

She should have told Vera about the meeting straight away, of course, but she hadn't wanted to bring that whole unpleasant episode up, not with the part she'd played in it. Vera made no secret of the fact that she thought the sun shone out of Josie's backside.

Aye, perhaps all in all it was better to say nowt. She might not see the man again anyway, so what was the point in stirring up a hornet's nest, and if he wanted to settle a score with Josie that was his business.

Decision made, Prudence continued to stand at Barney's side, and she felt no sense of guilt when she put all thoughts of Josie Burns and the man who clearly intended her harm out of her mind.

Chapter Sixteen

'I'm sorry, Oliver, but just as you are a product of your upbringing, so am I.' Josie was speaking with studied calmness but the atmosphere in the drawing room was anything but tranquil. 'You were brought up in a house full of servants, you said yourself you couldn't recognise half of them, so I can understand that your attitude to Constance and Ethel and Mrs Wilde differs from mine. Why can't you offer me the same consideration?'

'Because it isn't a matter of consideration.' Oliver had been pacing the fine Persian rug in front of the blazing fire, but now he stopped in front of the chair upon which Josie was sitting and stared into her face, holding her eyes. 'They are *servants*, for crying out loud.'

'They are human beings whom we employ. I am employed by whichever theatre wants my services and you are employed' – here Josie checked herself. She had been about to say, 'And you are employed by me' – 'by your clients. It's all the same.'

'It is not all the same and you know it. Mrs Wilde and the maids are in service and they live here in my – *our* – home.'

'I'm aware of that.'

'You cannot speak to them as if they were . . . were . . .'

'Equals?' Josie put in icily.

'Yes, exactly. What do you expect our friends are going

305

to think if the servants are allowed to become familiar? These people have to be kept in their place or they won't be slow in taking liberties, I can assure you.'

'I don't think speaking to people as if they have feelings constitutes giving them a licence to run wild.'

'Josie!' His voice was a bawl.

'Don't shout at me.' She had shot up from her seat with such abruptness that Oliver was surprised into taking a step backwards, but her voice had not been loud. 'I won't be shouted at, do you hear me? Nor will I be bullied. And while we're on the subject of your friends, I have heard and seen the behaviour of some of them, both to those they consider beneath them and to each other, and it does them no credit.'

Oliver frowned angrily at her words. Yet if he had spoken the truth at this point he would have had to agree with her, and had he but known it, his concurrence would have persuaded Josie to meet him halfway and set the tone for any future compromises. Unfortunately, he would have looked on such an admission as a failing.

'My friends are not under discussion here,' he said icily, 'and not one of them has to explain their behaviour to *you*, but I will say I would have thought you to be more grateful for their ready acceptance of you as my wife.'

'Then you thought wrong.' Josie seemed to have grown in stature, so tensely did she hold herself. She was remembering the dinner-party they had attended the previous evening, a few days after their own delayed wedding reception. There had been a couple there she was sure hadn't been at the first event although Oliver had seemed to be on very friendly terms with them. A Lord and Lady Stratton. Godfrey Stratton had been quite pleasant, she supposed, in a stolid sort of way, but his wife had gone out of her way to ignore her, or that was how Josie had felt at the time. The woman's attitude had made her feel awkward and ill-at-ease all evening, especially when she visited the powder room; Stella Stratton had been there, holding court to a group of ladies, and had stopped speaking very pointedly when she had entered. Josie had been determined not to be intimidated, although her legs were shaking when she emerged from the little cubicle into the larger area filled with mirrors and several small stools to one side of the two wash basins.

She had opened her vanity bag and pretended to see to her toilette, fixing her hair and dabbing a touch of Eau de Cologne on her wrists, and all the time no one had said a word, although one or two of the ladies had sent a nervous smile and nod her way. As she left she had heard Stella speak, although the other woman's voice had been too low for her to make out the words, but the gust of high titters which had followed had sent her back into the beautifully lighted dining room with her face burning. And he dared to say he expected her to be *grateful*?

Oliver glared at her a moment more, before turning and walking across to a cabinet on the other side of the room which he opened and, after pouring himself a stiff brandy, closed. Josie was seated again and pouring herself a cup of coffee from the tray at her elbow, the manner of her thanks for which, along with her sending her best wishes to Constance's sick mother when the little maid visited her home that day on her afternoon off, had caused the altercation with Oliver.

Josie was trembling inside although there was no outward sign of her agitation, and she was thinking, Our first argument – and over something as silly as little Constance and Ethel. And yet it wasn't about the maids, not really. It was deeper than that. Stella Stratton's beautiful cold face swam into her mind and she pushed the image away as she said, her voice surprisingly steady, 'Would you care for a cup of coffee?'

She watched Oliver swallow back the brandy and set the empty glass down on the polished wood before walking across to join her. She looked up at him, not knowing what to expect, and when he reached down and drew her to her feet she went without demur. 'I do not want us to quarrel,' he said very softly, kissing her gently on the lips before enfolding her in his arms. 'Our time together is too precious to waste on cross words.'

She didn't reply to this but when he kissed her again she kissed him back. She didn't want to quarrel either, it was the last thing she wanted. She had realised a few years ago, when she had started working in the theatre and she and Gertie had become autonomous most of the time, that the equable quality of their relationship was balm to her soul. All the years of violent rows and bickering at home throughout her childhood had left their mark, and her spirit recoiled from conflict. Nevertheless, she also knew she wasn't her mother's daughter with regard to allowing herself to be subjugated or oppressed, and again, this was probably due to the same reason. She had to be true to herself, that was it first and foremost, and much as she regretted the need for confrontation she would meet it head on when it was necessary. That was the way she was, and she wasn't going to apologise for it to Oliver. He had *known* before they were married that they saw certain issues very differently; she had broached that very matter several times during their engagement and he had assured her they would work things out as and when difficulties occurred. But if he thought this working out meant she suppressed everything which made her *her* and tried to turn her into someone like Stella Stratton, he could think again.

And because the niggle which had been at the back of her

mind since the previous evening now became too strong to ignore, she reseated herself, pouring Oliver a cup of coffee and passing it to him as he took a seat opposite hers, before she said, 'That couple last night – Lord and Lady Stratton. How long have you known them?'

'How long?' He considered, his head slightly tilted. 'Some fifteen years or so; at least that's as far as Stratton himself is concerned. He's a member of the Prince's set, a very useful friend to have.' He smiled at her, but when she didn't smile back and sat looking at him, he swallowed a mouthful of coffee and added, 'Regards his wife, perhaps five or six years at most. She is a great deal younger than him, of course, but they seem happy enough.'

'How long have they been married?'

Again he said, 'How long?' as though he was having to think about it. 'Two years, I think.'

'She doesn't like me.'

'What?' He raised his eyebrows as though he thought she was talking nonsense, and his tone confirmed this when he said, 'Of course she likes you, my dear. How could she do otherwise?'

'She hardly even looked in my direction last night, let alone spoke to me.'

'No, my dear, you're imagining it. It's just that . . . Stella can be difficult to get to know. Some people are like that.'

Josie had noticed the pause before the use of the other woman's name, and now there was a sickness churning her stomach which she endeavoured not to let show in her voice as she replied, 'I don't think she ignored me because of any reticence on her part, Oliver. She simply doesn't like me.' She couldn't bring herself to tell him of the incident in the powder room somehow. 'Were . . . were they invited to our reception?'

'Yes, indeed.'

'Then why didn't they attend?'

It was a long moment before he answered and then only when he had drained the cup. 'I understand they had a previous engagement.'

She wasn't sure she believed that. In fact, she wasn't sure Godfrey Stratton had even been aware of their reception. He had looked very surprised when someone had mentioned it the night before, anyway. Had Stella meant their absence to be taken as a snub directed at Oliver's new wife? Or was she herself simply being silly? Prevarication wasn't in Josie's nature, and now she said outright, 'Do you mind me asking how well you know Stella Stratton?'

She saw Oliver's blue eyes widen just the slightest and knew she had surprised him with the directness of the question. 'She is a friend; Godfrey and his wife both.'

'And before she became his wife?'

Oliver's eyes left hers and he pulled out from his waistcoat pocket a gold watch on a thick gold chain, glancing down at it before saying, 'She was a social acquaintance, a friend, but I really can't go into the history of everyone who was at the dinner-party last night at the moment. I should have been at my club over half an hour ago.'

Josie would have said more but for Gertie choosing that moment to burst into the room. Had they heard the news that the Queen had been taken gravely ill on the Isle of Wight? Stricken with paralysis? They hadn't, and the next few minutes until Oliver left for his club were spent discussing the implications of the Queen's ill-health.

Oliver returned from lunching at his club just in time to drive Josie and Gertie to the theatre in his carriage in time for the first of her evening performances, and much later, once they were home again, he made love to her so beautifully and so tenderly all thoughts of Stella Stratton were forgotten.

The next morning Josie awoke early. She lay for some time watching Oliver as he slept beside her in the enormous double bed the master bedroom boasted, and she forced herself to face the issue which Oliver's experienced love-making had clouded the night before. This Lady Stratton, Stella, had meant something to Oliver at one time. She didn't know how she knew it with such certainty, but know it she did. And along with the knowledge was the unwelcome conviction that whereas Oliver might not care for Lord Stratton's wife any more, the lady in question certainly cared for him. But she had always known Oliver had had affairs before he met her; he hadn't tried to hide the fact that he had lived life to the full, and in a manner which had embraced many of the vices.

Aye, she'd known it in her head, she admitted, biting hard on her lower lip, but it was different when she was faced with the living reality. If she was right in what she suspected, that woman had known him intimately. She had kissed him, she had lain with him, she had caressed and touched him and he her . . . *But it was in the past.* It was, and that was the important thing. She had to believe in him; she had to trust him and believe that he had been trying to spare her feelings in keeping the truth from her, and in all honesty, what good *would* it have done to admit that Stella had been his mistress? He had never questioned her about Barney, not once, but she knew he sensed something between them. The past was the past, that's how she had to look at this or she was in very real danger of spoiling what they had in the present, and she wouldn't give that horrible woman the satisfaction.

She snuggled down beside him again, feeling his body stir as he became aware of her presence, and in the moments before he reached for her she told herself that men and women were very complex creatures, each with their own sets of values and principles. Oliver had told her he had never loved anyone before her and that there would be no one after her, and she believed him. She must have done, to have married him. And coming from such different backgrounds and cultures they were going to have problems enough without dredging up the past. She would let sleeping dogs lie in this particular regard, that was what she would do, but should Stella Stratton make the mistake of cold-shouldering her again – and more especially repeating that little tactic she had tried in the powder room – she might just find that a born and bred northern lass was tougher under the skin than m'lady had bargained for.

Queen Victoria died three days later on 22 January at her seaside home on the Isle of Wight, and the death of the 'Monarch of an Empire where the sun never sets', as she had been hailed through her sixty-four years of reign, hit the ordinary people of England hard. The Queen had travelled to more parts of Britain than her predecessors, using the steam railways which linked her rapidly growing cities, and despite her years of public withdrawal after Albert's death the people adored her. This 'grandmother of Europe' and 'mother of the Empire' was someone her common subjects could relate to; hadn't she been worried to death about her eldest son's behaviour the same as any mother the world over, and hadn't she adored her Albert to the point where she nearly went mad when he died? What's more, she was a woman who knew her duty, who maintained standards and stood for everything which had made Britain great. How, the ordinary fellow in the street wondered, would the Prince of Wales behave now he had succeeded to the throne?

Oliver, as Josie had expected knowing his leaning towards the Prince of Wales, took the publicly expressed doubts about Edward's capacity to be King – put most forcefully by *The Times* – as a personal insult.

The morning after the Queen's death they were sitting having breakfast with Gertie when he almost made the two girls jump out of their skin. *'This is an outrage!'* He threw the newspaper down on the table, his face turkey red, only to snatch it up again and thrust it at Josie as he growled, 'Read that! Just read what the damn upstarts have written.'

Josie cast a quick look at Gertie who stared back at her, her eyes bright with concealed mirth, and picked up the paper. In its leading article that day, *The Times* had commented that the new King must often have prayed 'lead us not into temptation' with a feeling akin to hopelessness, and while acknowledging that as Prince he had never failed in his duty to the throne and the nation, the newspaper continued that 'we shall not pretend that there is nothing in his long career which those who respect and admire him would wish otherwise'.

'This, on the day he makes his accession speech,' Oliver ground out furiously. 'The Queen refused to let him take on many of the royal duties which, as heir to the throne, he expected and wanted to perform, everyone knows that. And what sort of message does this send to the rest of the British Empire, eh? *Eh?* It's a disgrace. An absolute disgrace! The bounders want taking to the Tower, if you ask me. He'll be an excellent King, you mark my words.'

And even by the time of the Queen's funeral on the second day of February it looked as though Oliver was going to be proved right, something he pointed out at the breakfast-table almost every morning. 'Eight minutes, the King spoke for at the Accession Council, and without notes. Said he's fully determined to be a constitutional sovereign in the strictest sense of the word. His judgement in deciding to call himself King Edward VII rather than King Albert I has been noted and well received, I tell you. He'll make the bounders eat their words before the year's out.'

By the time King Edward opened his first Parliament two weeks later Josie was heartily sick of the subject, and more than a little irritated by her husband's excessive championing of someone she felt could well look after his own interests. Unlike one of her old friends who had recently been brought to her attention by Nellie, who was now working with her again in the current venue at Covent Garden.

Gertie had been helping Josie into her stage costume when Nellie burst into the dressing room in a whirl of cold air and melting snowflakes from the snow storm raging outside the warm confines of the fine theatre. When one of the other girls commented, 'You'd better jump to, Nellie, else you'll have old Angus on your back,' her friend had responded with uncharacteristic sharpness, calling back, 'I don't need you to tell me the time, Amy Dodds.'

'Sorry, I'm sure.'

Amy had settled back on her stool in a huff of hurt feelings and bristling taffeta, and Josie had let the buzz of conversation – which Nellie's arrival and subsequent exchange with Amy had killed – rise again before she leaned across to her friend, who was busy slapping rouge and powder on her face with unnecessary vigour, and whispered, 'You all right, lass?'

'Oh, Josie.' For a moment Josie thought Nellie was going to burst into tears, but then the other girl said shakily, 'It's poor old Lil. Blimey, gal, I had the shock of my life last night, I don't mind telling you. Me and a gentleman friend were walking past Shepherd's Bush Green just as a load of ne'er-do-wells the constable had moved out of Hyde Park ended up there, and one of the women caught my eye. It was Lily, Josie, I'm sure of it. And I reckon she recognised me because she ducked her head and hurried off.'

'But . . .' Josie sat back on her stool, staring at Nellie's face. 'Didn't you call to her? Stop her?'

'I should have.' Small white teeth nipped at Nellie's lip. 'I know I should have; I don't know why I didn't really, except I was with this bloke and we were going back to his place, and . . . Oh, I don't know. I was taken aback and they were all so dirty and some of the men were drunk. I didn't want to know her, I suppose. Only for a minute,' she added hastily. 'But by the time I'd turned round and gone back she was nowhere to be seen. I went half-mad then. Told this bloke where to go as if it was *his* fault, and searched the streets for her. Oh Josie, I feel so rotten.'

'Well, don't.' Careless of her silk and satin dress Josie hugged Nellie. 'It was the shock of seeing her like that, it's perfectly understandable. Look, we'll find her. All right? I'll have a word with Oliver and we'll find her.'

In the event her word with Oliver had yielded nothing beyond causing Josie to acknowledge that if she wanted to help Lily, she would have to do it by herself.

She'd related her conversation with Nellie word by word and her husband's reaction had disappointed her greatly. He had been amazed and nonplussed at her desire to find Lily for a start, and then ill-disposed to help in any way. 'My dear, the profession is full of individuals like Lily and you cannot help them all.'

'I don't want to help them all, just Lily,' she had objected.

'Even if you could find her, that would be very unwise.

Your star is in the ascent, hers is all but extinguished. Please, my dear, trust me on this and let's not discuss the subject again.'

She had stared at him, long and hard, before replying, 'I won't discuss Lily with you again, Oliver, but it's only fair to tell you I shall make my own enquiries as to her whereabouts, and should I find her, I shall help her.'

At this point he had sighed deeply, shaking his head. 'If you must, you must, but your enquiries will be fruitless no doubt. If, as you say, she is one of the flotsam and jetsam of which the *Illustrated London News* talked recently, she will have no fixed abode and be impossible to trace.'

'And this doesn't bother you? That these people are ill and dying and have no roof over their heads?'

'There is no need for it. There are the workhouses, aren't there?'

She had continued to stare at him for a moment before turning away. The divide between them was huge, massive – how could she have not realised it before they were married? But even as she asked the question of herself, she knew the answer. Oliver had skirted any confrontational issues during their engagement, just as he did now most of the time. It was only occasionally, when something like this incident with Lily cropped up or yet again the matter within their own home concerning Constance and Ethel, that his true feelings were expressed.

For a moment she knew a terrifying feeling of blind panic – the knowledge that she had made a catastrophic mistake. And then she cautioned herself, her mind becoming filled with a voice not unlike Vera's which said, A day at a time, lass. A day at a time. He loves you and you love him, and love covers a multitude of sins.

And so she had stiffened her back and faced the fact that this was something she had to do on her own. After consulting with Angus, the under manager at the theatre who was sixty years old and a mine of wisdom, Josie had ventured into Ealing to the premises of Turner & Webb, Private Investigators. There she'd employed Mr Webb to discover the whereabouts of a Miss Lily Atkinson. She gave him all the facts and the location where Lily had last been spotted, and told him to contact her at the theatre with any information he might unearth.

It was a cold but sunny morning when Josie and Gertie, along with Mrs Wilde and Constance and Ethel to whom Josie had given most of the day off, joined the boisterous crowds lining London's streets to see the new King open his first Parliament. There was a carnival atmosphere prevailing at the revival of pageantry and the release of the monarchy from many of the restraints Queen Victoria had put upon it; the street vendors were doing a roaring trade selling hot baked potatoes, mussels and whelks, and fragrant roasted chestnuts at tuppence a bag, along with the organ grinders and their beautifully dressed little monkeys providing a tune, and stalls galore lining the pavements selling small Union Jacks for the children and penny whistles to add to the noise.

Josie and the others managed to push their way forwards to a perfect spot on the route to Westminster, and they knew long before they saw the magnificent state coach – which had not been seen in public since the death of Prince Albert forty years before – that it was close, from the enthusiastic acclaim of the crowd. King Edward and Queen Alexandra were making the journey from Buckingham Palace to Westminster in full state splendour, and as the coach neared Josie she could see the two figures inside and their beautiful long robes edged in ermine. Despite the splash of colour provided by the coach and the soldiers' uniforms, the prevailing colour was black – in mourning for Queen Victoria – but this took nothing away from the wonder and splendour of the occasion, and the people were wild with excitement.

The sunlight lit up the fairytale coach with dazzling beauty and the blue sky overhead, so everyone was saying, was a good omen for the new King's reign.

'Oh Josie, I wouldn't have missed this for the world.' Gertie's little face was brick-red with elation, and she and Constance and Ethel – who had linked arms and were standing just in front of Mrs Wilde and Josie – couldn't keep still as the coach and fine plumed horses rolled by. 'How Oliver could prefer to look from the windows at his club rather than be here with us, I don't know. He's missing the best part.'

Josie couldn't have agreed more and although she wouldn't have said so, not even to Gertie, she had been hurt and surprised at her husband's refusal to join the rest of the household on the streets. She couldn't help thinking that if this occasion had taken place when they had still been courting, Oliver would have been at her side. And then she brushed all thoughts of her husband out of her mind, and began to shout her head off with the rest of them.

They were all hoarse by the time they wandered into Hyde Park where many informal picnics, along with organised games for the children, clowns, jugglers, street magicians, Punch and Judy shows and other forms of entertainment, were in full swing.

Josie smiled as she watched her sister, along with Constance and Ethel – like three bairns let out of school for the day, she said to herself – deciding what memento of the day they were going to buy with the two half-crowns she had slipped each of them. The scattered stalls amongst the trees were selling everything from tiny male and female dolls in full state costume and small, beautifully painted wooden coaches, to fine framed pictures of the new King and Queen. But all the time, even as she enjoyed the day in the cold February sunshine with the others, Josie was keeping half an eye open for Lily. She couldn't bear to think of the other woman scratching a living of sorts on the streets – if, indeed, it *had* been Lily Nellie had seen. But the few facts Mr Webb had gleaned thus far did point that way. According to the information he had been given, Lily had fallen down some stairs and hurt herself, 'whilst under the influence of intoxicating liquor', which had effectively finished her stage career, and after leaving the infirmary, having sold virtually all she had in the way of clothes and jewellery to meet her debts, she had disappeared. That had been over nine months ago and no one had seen hide nor hair of her since.

Oliver was waiting for them when they got home – 'With a face like a wet weekend,' Gertie whispered in an aside to her sister before she left Josie to face her husband alone and slipped off to the kitchen with the others. But instead of the lecture Josie had half expected on the foolishness of spending the whole day in the company of the servants, rather than returning home straight after the procession had finished, Oliver had merely maintained a cool and somewhat distant manner whilst Josie changed and got ready for the first of her evening performances. He drove her to the theatre as usual, escorting Gertie and herself to the dressing-room door, but then he said, 'I shall not be home until very late tonight, my dear, so please don't wait up for me.'

'Oh?' There was a question in her tone although she knew where he was going. He had cut down on his visits to the gambling houses he frequented when she had asked him to in their courting days, but he had made it plain that he couldn't give up the 'sport', as he called it, completely. It was in his blood, he had told her quietly a few days after their engagement; he came from a long line of gamblers, although his great-great-grandfather, great-grandfather and grandfather had been very successful in their pursuit of the cards and so on. Unfortunately his father had been a foolhardy and irresponsible gambler and had lost everything his ancestors had obtained. However, his father's example had served as a warning to his son, and although he liked to try his hand now and again, he could assure her his gambling was the only vice he would carry over into his married life.

Oliver had said this with a twinkle in his eye before he had pulled her into his arms and kissed her, and at the time a little dabbling at the gaming houses occasionally had seemed unimportant.

It still was unimportant, Josie assured herself now, watching her husband disappear down the corridor which led to the back door of the theatre. After all, what Oliver did with his private allowance was nothing to do with her.

As her agent, Oliver dealt with the financial side of her career and, as her husband, he did likewise with all the bills and accounts, except those directly concerning housekeeping which Josie, as mistress, settled herself with Mrs Wilde.

Josie and Oliver had agreed it was sensible they both had their own personal allowance which Oliver drew monthly from the bank, and Gertie too now had her own income which was paid to her by Oliver at the same time. Oliver had been a little vague about the amount the agency cleared each month, explaining that owing to the business he was in – one in which clients were in and out of work all the time – it could fluctuate wildly, but he had led Josie to believe it was considerable. And as she was now earning over forty pounds a week – which princely sum Oliver had assured her would rapidly rise in line with her popularity – she knew their bank balance must be extremely healthy.

Of course there were the maids' and Mrs Wilde's wages, but at £20 each a year for Constance and Ethel, and £80 for the housekeeper, these were not excessive. Oliver always went to great pains to point out that their domestics were fed and housed far better than most, but even so Josie didn't think he was overly generous. It might be true that the standard of comfort for servants was poor and that in many of the larger stately homes three or four people were crammed into tiny attic rooms, and admittedly Mrs Wilde had her own, very pleasant room at the back of the house with Constance and Ethel sharing a smaller one next to it, but knowing that both Constance and Ethel came from large poor families she still wanted to pay the girls more. To that end she had got into the habit, since becoming mistress of Oliver's home, of slipping each of the girls two large bags of groceries when they visited their families on their afternoons off once a week. She hadn't attempted to keep this a secret and she suspected Oliver was well aware of the practice, but to date he had not challenged her on it.

However, he *had* mentioned, at fairly frequent intervals, the exorbitant costs involved in running the household. The rent alone was three hundred pounds a year, he'd declared more than once, and when added to rates and taxes, their personal allowances, wine, coal and light, the servants' wages, washing, normal household bills, and garden and stable expenses, it meant they could not live extravagantly.

The last time he had spoken thus, Josie had suggested they should consider moving away from the town centre and into the suburbs. In the last decade Middlesex, Essex and Surrey had seen large population increases mainly consisting of middle-class families, according to the *Illus-trated London News*, and in an inner suburb such as Edmonton or Clapham (called the 'capital of Suburbia' by one contemporary critic) a ten-roomed house, such as they were living in now, could be rented for less than £3 a week, perhaps no more than £2.

Oliver had been horrified at the proposal, and to Josie's insistence that the suburbs brought cleaner air, more light, larger gardens and a healthier way of living, he had countered that a price couldn't be put on a fashionable address such as his. Didn't she understand that a move to one of the areas the growing class of white-collar workers inhabited would not benefit his business? Two 'his's and not one 'theirs', Josie reflected now.

'You all right, lass?'

Josie turned from the silent empty corridor to see Gertie standing in the doorway to the dressing room. 'I'm fine.' She smiled brightly. 'We had fun today, didn't we?'

'Aye, aye we did an' all.' Gertie hesitated. She wanted to ask again if Josie was all right, if she was happy, but she didn't like to. It was none of her business, after all. Gertie did not admit to herself here that it was less a matter of tact and more that she felt she might not like a truthful answer which prompted her discretion. She was well aware that she had done everything in her power to promote Oliver's course, and also that since his return from honeymoon he had begun to display . . . what exactly? A different side to his character, perhaps. One he had kept hidden through the courtship.

But he loved Josie, Gertie reassured herself silently, standing to one side for her sister to precede her into the noisy room which was a hive of half-clothed bodies, gaudy costumes, clouds of smoke from long ivory cigarette-holders and the cloying scent of Eau de Cologne. And as her husband as well as her agent, Oliver had an extra vested interest in getting Josie to the top. Top billing. Gertie frowned thoughtfully. It was the one thing everyone dreamed of in this business, whether they admitted it or not. Your own dressing room, everyone bowing and scraping . . .

And then she swung round and followed Josie, who was already sitting at her stool, into the room, closing the door behind her.

It was over six weeks before Josie received the news she had been hoping for as to Lily's whereabouts, and by then she had almost given up hope of ever finding her old friend.

However, in the first week of April, Mr Webb called at the house in Park Place one morning when Oliver was out.

He was full of apologies after Constance had shown him into the morning room where Josie was sitting with Mrs Wilde sorting out the next week's menus. 'I know you told me to contact you at the theatre, Mrs Hogarth, but the stage manager informed me you have been indisposed?'

'Only for the last two evenings, Mr Webb. A sore throat, nothing more, but the doctor advised prudence. I shall be singing again tonight.' Josie smiled at the small man in front of her. She had liked him on sight, mainly, she supposed, because he reminded her so much of Frank. He was stockier than Betty's husband had been, and slightly taller, but he had the same perfect ears for propping a cap on and the same kind eyes, and his whole face was remarkably like the late miner's. He looked very tough too, which Josie had found reassuring, and he smoked a clay pipe which, the first time Josie had met him, looked as though it was burning the end of his nose.

'You have some news for me?' she asked once he was sitting, rather uncomfortably it seemed, on the very edge of a low divan facing her chair. Mrs Wilde immediately excused herself and bustled away to arrange a tea tray.

'Indeed I have, Mrs Hogarth, indeed I have.' But then he hesitated a moment or two before he said, 'I trust you won't be distressed by what I have to say, but I'm afraid Miss Atkinson is in rather a bad way.'

'She's in hospital somewhere?' And then, even before Mr Webb spoke, Josie told herself that was a silly question. From what Nellie had seen, Lily didn't have two farthings to rub together, so the only place that would take her would be the workhouse infirmary. Josie knew that Lily would rather be six foot under than set foot in one of those places. She remembered Lily waxing lyrical more than once about her old granny and grandda who had ended up in the workhouse back in Newcastle, and the misery Lily had seen when, as a small child, she had visited them there once a month with her mother. 'Granny in the women's section, looking like a walking corpse, and Grandda crying his eyes out in the men's bit,' Lily had said soberly. 'Me ma had used to cry an' all on the way home, but with twelve of us in a two-roomed cottage and the floors seeping sewerage and the walls running with water, she couldn't have had them at home. But by, I tell you, I'd rather kill meself than go in there.'

'No, no, she's not in hospital, Mrs Hogarth.' Mr Webb cleared his throat once or twice before easing his thick neck out of its white collar. How could he explain the circumstances in which he had found this lady's friend? Mrs Hogarth was obviously a well-to-do lady; she probably had little idea of how the other half lived. 'Frankly she would be vastly better off if she was. No, she's living in a tailor's house in the East End. Apparently this man's wife took pity on your friend when she found her lying in the doorway of their house one night, but before that I understand Miss Atkinson was carrying the banner every night.'

'I beg your pardon?'

'Oh, I'm sorry. Carrying the banner describes those who are condemned to walk the streets all night,' Mr Webb said hastily. 'The poor unfortunates are quickly moved on by the police if they fall asleep in a public place so once the parks open their gates at about five in the morning they're down on the benches and asleep whatever the weather. Of course there are those who never wake up again,' Mr Webb continued quietly, 'and without exception they are in poor health due to the lives they lead, but most of them prefer it to the workhouse. Your friend, it seems, had collapsed; but for Mrs Howard taking her in she wouldn't have lasted much more than a night or two.'

Josie stared at him. 'Does she know I have been looking for her?'

'No, no, Mrs Hogarth, don't worry on that score. I was very discreet so as not to frighten her away as you instructed. However . . .' He cleared his throat again before continuing, his tone flat, 'The area is not one with which you are familiar, I'm sure, and the conditions are – Well, not to put too fine a point on it, they are foul, Mrs Hogarth.'

Josie's face was white now but she said, 'Go on, Mr Webb, and before you say any more I'd just like to explain that I'm not unaccustomed to poverty however my present circumstances seem. I was born into it as it happens so don't worry about shocking my finer sensibilities.'

Mr Webb made no comment on this but rubbed his hand hard over his mouth before saying, 'The place is a sweatshop, Mrs Hogarth. There is a three-relay system in practice – each bed being shared by three workers who have the right to occupy it for an eight-hour shift so that the bed is never empty. Any children sleep in the spaces below the beds; they cannot do as much work as the adults, you understand?'

Josie nodded. She had heard of such places, of course, but the thought of Lily being incarcerated in one was unimaginable. Not Lily, with her wicked sense of humour and bright laughing eyes.

'Those who are not occupying the beds laid round the walls of the rooms – of which the house has three plus a kitchen – are working in the centre of them. I have to tell you that the smell from dirt and bad air in such places as your friend is living in can be unbearable, and there is no through ventilation, the windows and doors always being kept closed. I am quite a robust fellow as you can see, but it'd knock me backwards, I can tell you. Now, Mrs Hogarth, do you still feel you have to go and see Miss Atkinson yourself? There is no need; I can relay anything you wish to say to her and bring her to you if need be.'

Josie had been holding her face and body with tense concentration but now she leaned back in her chair, her face softening as she said, 'Thank you, Mr Webb, and I know you mean well, but you don't know Miss Atkinson like I do. She ran away from Nellie because she felt' – she had been going to say 'ashamed', but this might sound like a slight on Lily in some way and so she changed it to – 'awkward, and if you approached her she might do the same and I can't risk that. I have to go and see her where she is, and like I said, I'm not unacquainted with tenement dwellings.'

Maybe, but there were tenements and there were tenements, Mr Webb thought grimly, and this one her friend lived in was one of the worst he'd seen for a long time. He remained still for a moment before looking down at his hands which were resting on his knees, and then he raised his head, and said, 'May I take the liberty of asking if your husband will accompany you, Mrs Hogarth?'

'No, he will not.'

'A male acquaintance perhaps? Or a male member of your staff?'

'We have a housekeeper and two maids, that is all, and I don't know anyone well enough to ask them to accompany me, Mr Webb. But I shall be quite all right. My friend, the one I told you about who saw Lily, will come with me, and my sister too.'

'I would feel happier if you let me escort you, Mrs Hogarth.'

Oh, he was a nice man; she had been right about him. There was definitely a touch of Frank about Mr Webb. Mrs Wilde bustled in with the tea tray at that point, so it was after the housekeeper had left again and she had poured Mr Webb a cup of tea and then one for herself, that Josie said, her voice warm, 'I appreciate your concern, I do really, but I think it would be best if I go with my friend and my sister, Mr Webb. I don't want to frighten Lily, or overwhelm her.'

Anyone who had existed for any length of time in that hell-hole wouldn't be frightened by him, Mr Webb thought grimly. He recalled the pale, starved-looking children he had seen, all of them only half-clothed. One boy had been unable to walk, his legs were so bandy with the rickets, and another had had running sores all over his face. And the stench . . . 'I'd caution you to reconsider, Mrs Hogarth,' Mr Webb said, his eyes moving round the gracious interior of the room he was sitting in. 'It's not an area I'd be happy for my wife to visit, let's put it like that.'

His wife hadn't been born in the East End of Sunderland with Bart Burns as a father. Josie's voice was firm as it came now, saying, 'We'll be perfectly all right, I promise you. I can more than look after myself, Mr Webb. I'll tell Nellie about it tonight and we can go tomorrow morning with my sister. There's nothing to worry about.'

After Mr Webb had finished his tea and given her the address in the East End, Josie paid him what she owed him along with a handsome bonus which brought forth more remonstrances for her to be careful. It was just as he was taking his leave and Constance had appeared to show him out that Oliver opened the front door.

Josie saw her husband's eyebrows rise and watched the blue eyes move swiftly from herself to Mr Webb, but she was unprepared for the glacial quality to Oliver's voice as he said, 'I don't believe I've had the pleasure?'

'This is Mr Webb, Oliver; he's just leaving. Mr Webb; my husband.' Her own voice was stiff, and now she accompanied Mr Webb across the hall herself, motioning for Constance to leave, and ignored Oliver who had stood to one side as she said, 'Goodbye, and thank you once again.'

'A pleasure, Mrs Hogarth.' Mr Webb's line of business made him particularly sensitive to atmosphere and he didn't delay his departure.

Once Josie had shut the door she again brushed past the silent Oliver and walked quickly into the morning room, conscious that he was close behind her and that he had shut the door after them.

'Well?' He was the first to speak. 'Are you going to tell me what that individual was doing in my house?'

She didn't take the chair she had been sitting in a few minutes earlier but remained standing, turning to face him slowly. 'Mr Webb called to say that he had discovered where Lily is living. I employed him to find her.'

'You did *what*?'

'I told you I was going to make enquiries, Oliver.'

He glared at her, his voice loud as he said, 'And you gave him leave to call here at the house? Are you mad, woman?'

And now she answered him in like voice: 'No, I'm not mad, and if you remember I've been ill for two days and unable to go to the theatre so he was unable to see me there as I'd asked.'

'I don't believe this!'

'I don't understand why. It's perfectly straightforward. I asked Mr Webb to find Lily and that is what he has done.'

His voice came rapidly but low now. 'Don't take that tone with me. What would have happened if you had had a morning caller? Mrs Pierpont-Fitzhugh for example, or Lady Walston – what then?'

'I would have excused myself and spoken to him privately in another room. He would have understood.'

'*He* would have understood? *He* would have?' Oliver ground his teeth, the sound loud in the room. 'Don't you understand how hard I've worked to make sure you are accepted?' he spat out, one arm outstretched and his pointing finger stabbing at the air. 'And it hasn't been easy, especially—' He stopped abruptly, aware he had been about to say too much and that Stella's name would be like a red rag to a bull. 'Especially when there are some who would like to exclude you,' he finished tightly. 'And you would have allowed yourself to be seen with a man like that! Not only seen, but encouraging him into the house.'

'Mr Webb is a good, honest, kind gentleman.' She couldn't believe he was reacting so violently to the other man's presence in the house, and yet, she asked herself in the next moment, why had she asked Mr Webb to contact her at the theatre if she hadn't suspected Oliver would behave in just this very way? 'And as to me being accepted by your friends, Oliver, they can please themselves. I am not ashamed of who I am or where I have come from, and if your friends – or you – are, then that is your loss.'

Her voice quivered on the last words, and immediately he was at her side, his countenance undergoing a lightning change as he gripped her hands, saying, 'Oh my dear, my dear, my love. Of course I did not mean that. How could I? You know how much I love you; how proud I am of you. It's just that I want everyone to feel the same way I do, that's all, and people are devilish quick to talk.'

People. He always excused himself by talking about these 'people', but she had never had it confirmed so clearly that he was one of them. Why hadn't she seen it before, when they were engaged? But it was different when you actually lived with someone. During their courtship he had been as much her agent as her beau, and in that capacity he dealt with people from all different levels of the social strata. And he was not an unkind man, not really, but proud. And yet this was more than pride, Josie corrected herself in the next moment. It was pretentiousness, a self-satisfied hauteur or, as Vera would term it, uppishness.

Withdrawing her hands from his she turned her back on him and walked over to the large full-length window, staring up into the rainswept grey sky before she said, still without looking at him, 'I am going to see Lily, Oliver. Mr Webb has told me she is in a dreadful state and something needs to be done. She is living in a tailor's house in the East End and the conditions are appalling.'

He hadn't followed her, and now his voice came quietly saying, 'That would be unwise, Josie. It is commendable you are concerned about her, of course, but once you start something like this it can become a burden.'

'I'm sorry but I don't see it that way.'

She turned to face him then and she saw the muscles in his cheekbones tighten, but his voice was still low when he said, 'I see. In that case may I ask exactly what you intend to do with her?'

'I don't know. I suppose it depends on Lily to a certain extent.'

There was a long pause before Oliver turned and walked to the door, and his hand was resting on the shining brass doorknob when he said, 'I hope you do not live to regret this act of charity, Josie, because it has been my experience that very often such people bite the hand which feeds them. Nevertheless, you are my wife and for your sake I will support you in anything you wish to do, short of having the woman here. Do you understand me on this? I will not have her in this house.'

And with that he opened the door and stepped into the hall, closing the door quietly behind him.

Chapter Seventeen

'This is it; we're here. Number 13, Hanging Row.'

It was ten o'clock the following morning, and the hired carriage holding Josie, Gertie and Nellie had just pulled up outside a dingy terraced house in a squalid street, one of many such which made up the overcrowded slums of London's East End.

In spite of the drizzling rain there were several ragged children, all without shoes and all filthy, sitting huddled against a house wall, and a group of slatternly-looking women having a fierce disagreement about something or other. As the three girls looked out of the carriage window one of the women grabbed another by the hair and began beating her about the face and upper body, two more joining in the fray in the moment before a big, burly man appeared from an open doorway and hauled the women, who were now kicking and screaming, into the house.

'Cat fight.' Nellie sounded very knowledgeable but she had gone a little pale.

Josie and Gertie exchanged a glance. They had grown up with similar occurrences and this area bore a marked resemblance to Sunderland's East End. Gin shops, brothels, dirt and disease – it appeared poverty worked in the same degrading way everywhere.

'Right, ladies. Ten minutes, you said?' The driver had got down from his seat behind the two horses and opened the carriage door, his stolid face betraying nothing of the curiosity he felt about his passengers. Well-to-do women, as these obviously were, didn't usually visit Hanging Row.

Josie took a deep breath and descended from the carriage with the help of the proffered hand. 'Thank you.'

'You're welcome, ma'am.'

Nellie and Gertie were less quick to alight, their faces betraying their trepidation, and once they were standing on the greasy, muck-strewn cobbles, Josie said quietly, 'You two don't have to come in with me, you know. You can wait in the carriage if you like. I shall be out with Lily in two ticks, all being well.'

'I wouldn't bank on it.' Nellie cast a glance about her, wary-eyed. 'And we're coming in with you, gal.'

'Come on then.' The driver had climbed up into his seat, his back impartial, but as Josie called up, 'If we're not out in ten minutes, would you knock on the door?' he turned his head and said quietly, 'Oh yes, m'dear, don't you worry about that. And mind you tell 'em in there you've got someone waiting outside. All right?'

Josie smiled her thanks and nodded, and then, with the other two clinging hold of her skirt like a pair of bairns, she crossed the pavement and lifted the iron knocker on the flaking door, rapping hard three times. It was opened almost immediately and a plump, pasty-faced girl of ten or eleven stood in the doorway, her sallow skin heavily afflicted with pimples. Her gaze widened at the sight of them, and before Josie had a chance to speak the girl yelled over her shoulder, 'Mum? It's not Mr Bennett's lad for the suits; it's three ladies.'

A woman's voice came clearly from within saying, 'Three ladies? What are you on about, Rachel?' and then the owner of the voice was in the doorway peering at them.

'Mrs Howard?' Josie spoke quietly but firmly although her tone was not unfriendly.

'Who wants to know?'

'Are you Mrs Howard?' Josie repeated more crisply.

The woman nodded, her long face guarded.

'My name is Mrs Hogarth. I understand you were kind enough to offer assistance to a friend of mine, Miss Atkinson? Lily Atkinson?'

Without seeming to move a muscle of her face Mrs Howard said, 'I took her in, if that's what you mean.'

'Yes, that is what I mean and it was very good of you, Mrs Howard. May I see Miss Atkinson, please?'

The woman glanced downwards for a moment, fingering her thick woollen skirt before she lifted her head and said, 'She's gone.'

'Gone?'

'That's what I said, didn't I? She's gone.'

Josie stared into the woman's brown eyes and knew Lily's benefactor was lying. 'I don't think so, Mrs Howard. I have it on good authority that Lily is here. We wish her no harm but it is imperative I speak with her right now. If there is a problem I am happy to wait until it is convenient, but I do insist on seeing her. If you are worried about our credibility you are quite at leave to call a constable, we have nothing to hide.'

The brown gaze moved to the waiting carriage and the impassive figure of the driver sitting behind the horse and then back to Josie. 'No need for that,' Mrs Howard said sourly. 'Come in if you want, it's just that I know Lily don't want to see no one.'

More like Mrs Howard didn't want to lose an unpaid worker in her sweatshop, Josie thought angrily. When she had told Nellie where Lily was, the other girl had been aghast. Apparently the area was well known for its sweatshops which took in Jewish immigrants fleeing from Europe, families that had lost their homes and only had the workhouse to look forward to, and other such unfortunates. Working all hours in the conditions Mr Webb had mentioned and then only for the dubious shelter of a roof over their heads and a starvation diet meant that most of the inhabitants of such places were ill and weak and without hope.

The smell which had been wafting out of the doorway was considerably worse once Josie stepped into the dark narrow hall, but nothing prepared the three girls for the stench of the room beyond the passageway. As Mrs Howard opened the door and stood aside Josie took a deep breath, fighting back the urge to gag, but she heard Nellie or Gertie give an involuntary retch behind her. The room was not large – eight or nine feet by ten at the most – and the ceiling was low, but every single inch of available space was taken. Several women and one man were asleep on pallets set against the walls, one woman holding a young baby against her breasts by means of a shawl, and in the centre of the floor was a large table holding lengths of material. Around this were several high stools on which sat more men and women, and they were all sewing garments. In contrast to the floor which was filthy and showing evidence of cockroaches, the table was spotless.

Although the odour of unwashed bodies and stale air was bad, Josie realised the main source of the smell was from the back yard beyond the room where the privy was situated, and she didn't like to dwell on the state of that. She fought the inclination to raise her handkerchief to her nose, conscious of the dull gaze of the occupants as her eyes searched each pale exhausted face, and then her glance took in Lily. Her old friend was sitting at the far end of the table, one fist rammed against her mouth, and if Josie hadn't known Lily was in the room she wouldn't have recognised her at first. The once big, buxom woman seemed to have shrunk and she looked terribly ill, her face gaunt and her clothes hanging off a frame which was little more than skeletal.

Josie heard Nellie's whispered, 'Lily . . . Saints alive,' and assumed, correctly as it happened, that Lily looked to be in a worse state than when Nellie had first seen her all those weeks ago. It was a moment or two before she could speak over the great hard lump filling her throat, but when her voice came it was surprisingly normal-sounding as she said, 'We've come to take you out of here, Lily. All right? Have you got anything you want to bring with you?'

'What's that?' A tall thin man with a harelip spoke and now everyone at the table was motionless as he rose to his feet. He had been working at a piece of material the same as the others, but his seat was the only one with a back to it. Josie had noticed the young girl who had first opened the door whispering something to this man as they had entered the room.

'These are friends of Lily's, Elias.' Mrs Howard sidled round Josie before she added, 'This is my husband.'

Josie inclined her head, holding the man's eyes with her own as she said, 'I've thanked your wife for taking care of our friend, Mr Howard, but there is no need for her to stay with you any longer. We weren't aware of where she was or we would have come for her before now.'

'Would you indeed?' The harelip gave his voice a slight lisp which was all at odds with the mean, bullet-hard eyes. 'Well she works for me, see? Trained her, I have, and it's cost me 'cause she's not as fast as the others, and I've given her a bed and food an' all. She's not leaving.'

'Trained me?' Lily spoke for the first time since they

had entered the room. 'The other girl died where she sat and I was all you could find, that's the truth of it.'

'See?' The man turned to his wife. 'I told you how it'd be. You do someone a good turn and they kick you in the teeth. You should've left her where she dropped. Twenty odd suits and more we've got to get to Bennett's or else we're in trouble, and here's one of me workers swanning off without as much as a by your leave.' The voice had a whine to it now. 'This is what comes of being kind and extending a helping hand.'

'A helping hand?' said Josie grimly. 'The same helping hand these other people have benefited from, I suppose?' Her head moved in a gesture which took in the miserable room and its occupants, but her eyes remained fastened on the tall thin man watching her. 'If anyone else had taken Miss Atkinson in I would have made sure they were rewarded handsomely, but from what I have seen here my friend has more than repaid anything she owed you.'

Mrs Howard had now reached her husband's side, and Josie turned away from their combined glare, staring straight at Lily as she said, in a tone which brooked no argument, 'Get your things, Lily. You're leaving here and you're not coming back.'

It was some seconds before Lily spoke, and Josie thought for an awful moment or two she was going to refuse to leave with them, but then her old friend said, her voice breaking, 'I . . . I haven't got anything 'cept my coat, lass.'

'Put it on then.' Josie was amazed at how firm her voice sounded and how cool she must seem on the outside, especially with the pitiful sight in front of her. She looked straight into Mr Howard's face again as she said, 'Something tells me you and your family don't live in this establishment.'

'What's that to do with you?'

'I'm right then.' Lily had joined them now and Josie's chin rose higher as she said, 'You'll have to answer for all this one day, Mr Howard. God won't be mocked, do you know that? There will come a day when you'll wish you'd never been born.'

She had expected some nasty retort along with a command to get out, but when the man merely continued staring at her, one hand now clutching at his shirt collar, she swung round, pushing Lily and the others in front of her as she said, 'Go out to the carriage, all of you.'

The air wasn't pleasant in the street outside, but it was fresh compared to the fetid atmosphere they'd just left.

'How did you know, lass?' Lily's fingers gripped hold of Josie's arm as the other two clambered into the carriage with no further bidding. 'About him, Howard?'

'Know?'

'He's terrified about anything to do with the hereafter. Superstitious doesn't begin to cover it. He'll look on what you said as a curse, he will, and he'll be disappearing up his own backside in there.'

'Not an attractive thought.'

And then, as Lily swayed slightly, Josie took the other woman in her arms as she said, 'Why, Lily? Why didn't you come to me or one of your other friends? You know there's plenty who would have helped you. You're ill, anyone can see that, and working in there . . .' Josie couldn't finish but hugged Lily to her.

After a few moments she held the other woman away as she said again, 'Why, Lily?'

'They . . . they aren't all like you, lass.'

Josie looked deep into the brimming eyes and said softly, 'Nellie came back looking for you that night. She was so upset when she couldn't find you. I think at first she couldn't believe it was you and by the time she realised it was, you'd gone.'

'Oh, I don't mean Nellie, not really.' Lily flapped her hand before running it over her wet face and taking several deep audible gulps. Then, her tongue loosened, she burst out, 'I've never taken charity in me life, lass. That's it at heart. Me mam an' da were the same; for right or wrong they believed in taking nowt from no one unless you'd earned it. After our mam died an' me da got middling, one of me brothers was going to take him in, but on the morning he was supposed to move our Bernie went round there an' me da had hanged himself with his own belt.'

Josie's eyes had widened but now she said urgently, 'You can't believe that was right, lass. You can't. You've more sense than that. I can understand about . . . the workhouse, but not going to live with your own kith and kin.'

'Aye, well, I've no folk left, lass.'

'You have now.' Josie hugged her again and repeated, 'You have now, all right? Let me help you. *Please*, Lily. And it's not charity, it's not. I . . . I've been a bit low recently, I'm missing home I suppose, and having you around will be wonderful. And we've always got on, haven't we?'

'But lass—'

'No buts. Not one. Look, I'm doing all right now and if the position was reversed you'd do the same for me, you know you would.'

The tears were pouring from Lily's eyes again but when Josie pushed her towards the carriage and the other two inside reached out eager hands to pull her up, Lily didn't protest.

She was at the end of her tether, Josie thought, and who could blame her? If that place in there wasn't hell on earth she didn't know what was. Those poor people, and they all looked starving. As she joined the others it was to find Nellie had her arms tight round Lily's slumped body and was saying over and over again, 'I'm sorry, I'm sorry, I'm so sorry,' and Gertie was leaning forward holding one of Lily's limp hands.

Josie looked at the three of them, taking in Lily's closed eyes and the mortification and shame that was coming off the older woman in waves and, making a quick decision, she poked her head out of the carriage window and called to the driver, 'Do you know a good pie and peas shop anywhere round here?'

'I don't right off, ma'am, but ten to one there'll be one a couple of streets away if not at the end of the road. Them and the gin shops is what keeps folks alive round here.'

'Could you drive to one, please?' Settling back in her seat again Josie said quickly, 'Do you fancy giving that man back there another gliff, Lily?'

'What?' Lily raised herself, taking the handkerchief Josie was holding out as she said again, 'What do you mean?'

'How about we get enough pies and stuff for all those people back there and take them in? For the people in the other rooms too – there *are* people in the other rooms?' And at Lily's nod, Josie continued, warming to the theme, 'We'll get milk for the baby and children, and beer for the others too, and bread and oh – masses of stuff. Yes? If we gave them money old Howard might well find a way to take it off them, but he can't stop food going in their bellies today. If nothing else they'll eat till they're full for once.'

'You an' your sister come with me an' at least you'll go home with full bellies the night.' Vera's words came back down the years and Josie realised she had never really

forgotten them, or what it had meant that night, so long ago now, when she had eaten her fill for the first time she could remember.

'Do you mean it?' Lily sat up straighter. 'There's a good few of 'em, you know,' she added through her tears.

'That doesn't matter.' Josie grinned. 'Do you fancy giving Howard and his wife one in the eye then?'

'Do I ever, lass. Do I ever.'

By the time the carriage returned to Hanging Row the four women were sitting with parcels of pies wrapped in newspapers which reached to the ceiling, or so it seemed, and the good-natured driver had cans of peas, along with several of milk, propped next to him on his seat. Josie had also bought beer, fresh loaves of warm bread, chunks of cheese and a large barrel of biscuits, and now there wasn't sight of a tear from Lily, caught up as she was in the excitement.

It was the Howards' daughter who opened the door again. This time Gertie stayed with the carriage and horse, and the driver came with Josie into the room in which the Howards were; Lily and Nellie distributing food into the other rooms. It was evident the driver had expected trouble after Josie had told him what was occurring when they were waiting outside the pie shop, but the Howards were like a pair of lambs as Josie encouraged every-one to eat and drink in the room in which Lily had worked. It might have been something to do with the bulky figure standing guard in the doorway – the driver was a big man, and imposing, and he had large hobnail boots and enormous hands – but afterwards Lily said she was sure it was more to do with what Howard himself would have seen as a visit from the witch who had cursed him.

The thanks from the inhabitants of the grim sweatshop

were heartrending, and even the driver's stoical countenance was moved with compassion, the extent of which
became apparent when, on reaching Park Place, he refused
to take the money for the fares, even when Josie tried to
press it on him.

'What a nice man.' As the four women watched the carriage depart Gertie summed up what they were all thinking.
'And he looked so tough on the outside, didn't he?'

Oliver didn't look particularly tough on the outside; he
was elegant and handsome, and with an undeniable air
about him, but not tough. Josie turned to the others, her
expression thoughtful. Would he have been touched like
the driver had been by what they'd witnessed that morning?
She didn't know, she admitted silently, and that bothered
her greatly. It also bothered her that she was going to have
to oppose Oliver with regard to the one stipulation he had
laid down about her helping Lily; namely that her old friend
would not reside under their roof. It would only be for a
short time, until Josie could find suitable accommodation,
but at the moment the other woman was ill and in need
of a doctor and that took precedence over everything. She
didn't want Lily disappearing again, and if she farmed her
off somewhere that was exactly what would happen – she
felt it in her bones. Lily needed to be with people who cared
about her even more than she needed food and medical
attention, but Oliver wouldn't see it that way.

Oliver did not see it that way. He returned home that
afternoon feeling tired and irritable, having lost a great
deal at the gaming table the night before – money he
did not have in the first place. Instead of the serene,
orderly household which had been his before he'd married,
he felt as though he had walked into a bear garden, he
flung at Josie moments before he stalked out of the

house after growling that he would have dinner at his club.

He did not drive the horse and carriage to the Gentlemen's Club in Oxford Street of which he was a member; he walked instead, and all the time his mind was worrying at his mountain of debts rather than the fact that he had left his new young wife in tears.

He had been a fool to be tempted by that game last night, he told himself wearily. He'd known it even before he'd sat down, damn it. But Stratton had made it difficult to refuse. The thought of the other man caused Oliver to walk more slowly, wondering for the first time whether Stratton knew Stella had been his mistress. It was possible. He was a wily old bird, Stratton. Oliver would have to be careful of playing against him in the future; last night he had felt something was amiss, but how could you accuse a lord of the realm and one of the Prince of Wales's confidants of cheating at cards? Moreover he'd had no proof, just a gut instinct.

It was always Stratton who referred to the weekends he and other gay bloods had enjoyed at the Hogarth estate before his father lost everything, too. He had it on good authority that Stratton himself had been one of the young bucks who had broken his father in that last card-game, and then within days his parents had been lost at sea and he'd been left with very little more than the clothes he'd stood up in. His father's gambling made his own losses of late appear small in comparison, although that five hundred last night was damned awkward.

Still, he'd been in deeper than this in the past once or twice, and hung on until Lady Luck had smiled at him again. Luck, and his undeniable talent in both cards and the profession he'd chosen, that was. He had some of the best names in the business on his books; talking of which . . . He stopped abruptly, frowning against the cold clear April sunlight as he tapped his gold-topped walking stick against one of the iron railings fronting a smart townhouse. Confound it, he hadn't told Josie he had just secured her second billing at the new Apollo in Shaftesbury Avenue. Considering it had only been open for a couple of months it reflected well on her, and at fifty pounds a week it wouldn't do future engagements any harm at all. He had been right about her, she was going to be a star.

He adjusted his hat, tapping it forward on his brow. The last thought had not given him the pleasure it would have done a few months ago. His beautiful young wife had a mind of her own and that mind seemed set against him at every turn lately. Stella had been strong-willed but in a different way; at least she had seen eye to eye with him on matters of social behaviour and etiquette, but Josie seemed determined to make them a laughing stock with this last act of turning his home into a refuge for every Tom, Dick or Harry.

He started walking again, his blood pressure rising. Didn't she realise that the associates and friendships she formed in her private life away from the stage reflected heavily on him? Philanthrophy had its place of course, and it was a mark of England being a civilised country that workhouses and such had been provided for those who needed them, but one didn't take such people into one's home. Vagrancy was next to Godlessness, and most of these people who populated the hovels in the city only had themselves to blame for their idleness. This woman, this Lily Atkinson, she was little better than a whore, from what he remembered. She had been only too willing to sport with him that night in Hartlepool. And now she was residing in his home and being fussed over by his staff and his own private physician. Damn it. *Damn it.*

'Oliver? *Oliver!*'

It was a moment or two before Oliver heard the voice attempting to attract his attention. He was jerked out of his caustic thoughts, and on glancing across to the smart carriage and pair his gaze met a pair of saucy blue eyes set in a smiling face that was undeniably lovely.

'You were far away. Is anything the matter?' Stella Stratton said lightly. She knew from experience that such an attitude was the best line to take with Oliver. He loathed confrontation or emotion of any kind, and over the course of her liaison with this man, first before her marriage and then continuing afterwards at her insistence, she had constantly tried to hide her love for him, knowing he would find it an irritation. Desire and passion were the only emotions Oliver considered real, or had done before he had met that little chit who was now his wife. *His wife.* He had known that Stella herself would have married him at the drop of a hat and he had always insisted he wasn't the marrying kind, and it was only when she had fully accepted that, that she had married Godfrey.

'The matter?' Oliver forced a smile. 'Why should anything be the matter, Stella, and does Stratton know you're out cavorting on your own without his driver?'

'Oh, don't be stuffy, darling, you know these little traps are all the rage.' Stella's languid hand took in the smart fashionable carriage and the two beautiful chestnut mares which had cost her longsuffering husband a small fortune. 'Any woman who is *anybody* drives her own carriage these days; it's such fun.'

Stella was wearing a tailored dress and coat in dove grey trimmed with silver braid, and her hat was of three different shades of grey with two curling silver feathers tilting low over her forehead. It suited her blonde hair and warm peach colouring, enhancing the blue of her eyes, and as always she had dressed very carefully, knowing her proposed ride would take her into the vicinity of St James's. Since Oliver had finished their affair she had chosen the same route every afternoon she was in town, hoping for just such a meeting as had occurred today.

She hadn't been able to believe it for days when he had cast her off. And she still hadn't accepted it. She would not accept it, she told herself now as she smiled into the eyes of the man she loved. The reason for her dismissal from his bed after five years and more became clear when she heard the rumours that he was infatuated with one of his clients. Oliver, of all people! But she had also realised that with this new development, she couldn't cause one of the scenes she had indulged in in the past when his eye had roved. She would lose him completely if she did. But she wasn't beaten yet, oh no, not by a long chalk. Oliver belonged to her; she knew him inside out and no one could satisfy him like she did, certainly not some little baggage from the music halls.

'Come and ride with me, I'll take you to wherever you're going.' She kept her voice casual and smooth, straightening the skirt of her dress as though her appearance was the only thing of concern. 'We hardly seem to see each other at all these days. Are you in hibernation since your marriage?'

He stared at her, surprised at her nonchalant tone and the fact she had mentioned his marriage. It was true their paths had crossed but rarely since he had married Josie, but he had thought it was due to Stella avoiding contact for some reason of her own. 'No, I am not in hibernation, Stella, merely busy.'

'Not too busy to ride with an old friend, surely?' Her voice held just the right note of hurt reproach and she saw him blink for a moment. 'We *are* still friends, aren't we?' she added sadly.

'Of course we are.' But Stella knew as well as he did that it would be the height of indiscretion for them to be seen riding together. It would be a statement in itself, and although Godfrey might be dull and prosaic he was not stupid. In fact, he was an extremely intelligent man. And if something like this got back to Josie . . . 'But I chose not to drive because I wanted a walk,' he continued quickly, smiling to soften the refusal.

Stella bowed her head for a moment. 'I miss you, Oliver, but I don't suppose I should say that, should I?'

'Stella—'

'I know, I know.' She interrupted him swiftly, one gloved hand raised in fluttering acquiescence. 'But I can't help it. We had some good times, didn't we?'

For a moment the memory of his past life – when his home was his own and *he* was in control of all areas of his life, including his relationship with the woman closest to him – hit Oliver with a poignancy that took him unawares. He stared at Stella and she stared back, reading the naked sentiment with its touch of pathos in his face as her heart leaped. Was Oliver finding married life too claustrophobic? Stella lowered her head again, frightened he would read the elation in her eyes. Careful, careful, she warned herself. If she was going to get him back, and she *was* going to get him back, she had to tread carefully here. Oliver could be more autocratic than Godfrey at times, and if he suspected she still loved him . . . It was strange, considering Oliver was such a quick-witted man, that he had never really understood how she felt about him. But then, did *she*? He was an obsession, she supposed, but one which was enduring. 'Anyway, I must be going if you're sure I can't persuade you to ride to your destination?'

Oh, what the hell! After that one initial outburst she had been damned good about their split, damned good, and after the way Stratton had dealt with him last night he didn't owe her husband any consideration.

And Josie? He ignored the warning voice at the back of his mind, answering it with, Stella was an old friend – hadn't she just said so herself? And if his wife hadn't defied him – yes, *defied* him – he wouldn't even be here right now. All in all he'd been dealt with abominably, and to give Stella her due she would never have presumed to act with such impropriety as Josie had done. And what was a carriage-ride, when all was said and done? They moved in the same social circle and it was going to be better for everyone, including Josie, if any awkwardness between the Strattons and themselves was overcome.

'I'm going to my club. Is that out of your way?' he asked.

'Of course not.' Stella smiled again, the feathers on her hat dipping and waving, and after just a moment's more hesitation Oliver climbed up beside her.

Part 4
Old Ties and New Beginnings
1905

Chapter Eighteen

The last four years had seen mixed fortunes for Britain's working class. Severe smallpox epidemics brought doctors calling for nationwide vaccination programmes as people died in their thousands, and when King Edward VII had an emergency operation for appendicitis, thereby delaying the massive celebrations planned for his Coronation – and which his advisers had felt would be an uplift for everyone after the ravages of the smallpox – the King treated the poor of London to dinner. Over 456,000 diners at 700 venues throughout the capital sat down to a veritable feast, hundreds of entertainers being booked for the occasion.

Josie herself sang for the crowds at Covent Garden where the big hall was bedecked with flowers and Chinese lanterns, and in Lambeth no fewer than 6,000 people were fed plum puddings cooked over a fire in a trench. Everyone agreed there would never be another day to match it.

Less than two months after his operation Edward was crowned on a bright sunny summer's day, but the following years saw much unrest for the new King at home. A state of emergency was proclaimed in Ireland; a new militant women's movement led by a Mrs Emmeline Pankhurst caused furious controversy; the miners' unions and others began to gain ground and demand basic human rights for the working man; and although the politicians claimed greater numbers of the poor were receiving relief in Britain than ever before, every winter saw thousands dying of malnutrition and cold. The working class was questioning with a vengeance the old order of things which said the rich got richer and the poor got poorer, and all over the country different factions were challenging the wealthy upper class, the employers and land owners, and not least the judicial system itself.

To those outside her immediate circle however, it appeared that Josie's four and a half years of married life had been happy ones, untouched by the prevailing unrest. At twenty-two years of age she had blossomed into one of the most beautiful women in London; her figure slim and straight but rounded in all the right places, and her eyes and hair calling forth as much acclaim from the critics as her outstanding voice.

By the end of her second year in the capital she had become a firm favourite of the London halls, easily commanding fees of approaching a hundred pounds a week. Gone were the days when she'd found herself dashing from one theatre to another and then back again several times a night, in order to support Gertie and herself and send money home to Vera for her mother. Now, more often than not, she had her own dressing room and refreshments served there after each of her two nightly performances.

She was fêted and adored and made much of by the general public, her popularity enhanced, ironically, by the very attribute which had caused an ever-widening rift between her husband and herself. Namely that of Josie's altruistic championing of the underdog.

Lily had proved to be a catalyst both in Josie's private and public life. Her predicament and the terrible circumstances in which Josie had found her friend had opened the younger woman's eyes to the fact that Lily was one of many veterans of the halls who had never advanced into anything approaching reasonable money. These performers were often in poor health from their gruelling life on the boards and more often than not had no savings or home of their own, due to the gypsy-style life of the average entertainer. In their old age a great many found themselves cast, quite literally in some cases, into the gutter, there to die in squalor and loneliness. And once Josie's eyes had been opened there was no going back.

Against Oliver's express wishes, Josie had rented a small house at the back of the Caledonian Market – where on Fridays bargain-hunters gathered in search of everything from Old Masters and rare plate, to rusty bolts and chipped china, and which on Mondays and Thursdays was used as London's cattle-market – and she had installed Lily in it. Nellie was more than happy to depart her lodgings and live with Lily; the younger woman's only stipulation being she would finish the arrangement when her work moved her out of the capital to the provinces.

By the time this happened, Josie had already heard of two more old-timers in desperate need of help through Lily herself and her contacts throughout the halls. The older woman had been told, firmly but gently by Oliver's doctor, that she would never be able to consider a strenuous working life again, but she took great delight in caring for the other two women who were much older than Lily and pathetically grateful for a roof over their heads.

The surrounding neighbourhood got used to the sight of the latest star of the music halls delivering a sack of coal or potatoes and other groceries in her carriage and pair, and street gossip being what it was, it soon got round that 'Miss Josie Burns, her that was such a hit in the West End, had a heart of pure gold under all her fine togs'. And no one said this more vehemently than Lily.

At first she had been hard-pressed to take in her miraculous – as Lily herself termed it – deliverance from the Howards in the East End. Her weak state and ill-health caused her to sleep for twenty or so hours out of every twenty-four. But after a couple of weeks her exhausted body and bruised mind had started to fight back, and within two months she was the old Lily again, mentally at least. Physically, she was now unable to push herself and for a time she found that hard to take. However, once Josie had come up with the bright idea of moving in the other two women when Nellie's decision to leave was announced, Lily felt she was doing something again.

'I've never been one for sitting on my backside, lass,' she confided to Josie the night they discussed the possibility of the others joining Lily. 'Me mam used to say idle hands made work for the devil an' I reckon she was right. And I'll like the company an' all of an evening. Nellie's a good lass, none better, but with her working every night the evenings fair dragged.'

'But you're not to do any housework or washing or anything like that, mind,' Josie warned her old friend. 'Constance or Ethel are going to pop round for a few hours each day to deal with all that, and to prepare the main evening meal. It'll be more than enough for you to keep an eye on the others and get breakfast and a bite at lunchtime, all right? We'll see how it goes, eh? If it's too much for you we'll think again.'

'Too much for me?' Lily looked at her scornfully. 'Ee, lass, if looking after two old biddies is too much for me I might as well pop me clogs right now.'

Josie had smiled but said nothing more. Lily's fighting spirit was back and that boded nothing but good for the future.

When the house Josie was renting for the women came

up for sale after a few months she bought it – once more against Oliver's advice. Eighteen months later she was able to negotiate buying the properties either side of it, and within a matter of weeks the builders she hired had converted the three into one whole. This now housed eleven women, comprising Lily – whom Josie had put in charge of the household – along with a live-in housekeeper and cook, and eight other residents.

This was all accomplished independently of Oliver who had made it crystal clear he thought she was throwing good money after bad, and wanted no part of such a financially draining undertaking. For her part Josie made it plain to her husband that she was well aware of his gambling debts, which were beginning to eat away at every single penny she earned.

With the law of the land heavily favouring the husband in any matters of finance, after consulting with Gertie, Josie decided that she would be wise to have the deeds of the new property made out in the name of Miss Gertrude Burns. At the same time she settled a regular proportion of her income to be paid directly into an account she set up in Gertie's name. Whatever happened in the future, this made Lily and the other women safe.

By the time all this was concluded, towards the end of her third year of marriage, Josie was reconciled to the fact that she had two separate lives running parallel with each other; each one so different as to be irreconcilable with the other.

Her work in the music halls; the time she spent with Lily and the other women; her appearances for charity and good causes; and her friendships with Mrs Wilde, Constance and Ethel all belonged to one life. The other, vastly less enjoyable, was bound up with being Oliver's wife, with all that embodied.

In spite of having recognised the truth Oliver had kept hidden from her during their engagement, that his gambling was every bit as excessive and out of control as his father's had been, that it was an addiction, a disease, Josie still felt commitment to their marriage. She had married Oliver thinking he was the strong one, but in reality she provided the emotional and financial backbone of their relationship, and at times it was exhausting. But there was no going back. She had taken her vows before God and man and she was Oliver's wife.

However, what had begun as the odd altercation over issues such as Lily had snowballed into cool silences from Oliver which could last hours or days when Josie did or said something with which he disagreed. Oliver had belief in his own special position as a member of the upper class that went far beyond self-centredness. Josie had grown to understand that her husband considered himself superior to most of his fellow men simply because of an accident of birth, and along with that had developed a kind of imperiousness she found staggering at times.

Oliver Hogarth should be able to do what he wanted: hadn't his ancestors consorted with nobility and ruled a vast country estate that had taken up half of Hertfordshire? Therefore his word should be law and he shouldn't be opposed. He wanted to gamble and so he gambled; it was as simple as that, and he would not apologise for it.

Josie found she had married a man who could behave like a spoilt adolescent at times, or a cool, unapproachable stranger at others, and then again – when all was well – Oliver reverted into the charming, warm, amusing man she had first fallen in love with. It was confusing and wearing, and in the midst of the long weekend parties in country houses she attended as his wife and which she hated in the main, the select musical soirées he arranged, the dinner-parties and other equally draining social activities, she fulfilled her current commitment in the theatre several nights a week. If she had been prepared to compromise her own opinions and convictions Josie knew they would have got on better, but the price for a happy marriage was too high. She cared about people, and especially those who had come from the sort of beginnings she had been born into. It was a gut instinct to do something, even if it was a drop in the ocean in the overall scheme of things, and just as Oliver would not apologise for who and what he was, neither would she.

Oliver's counsel – as her agent rather than her husband – that she should stay in the capital and concentrate on establishing her name and position as one of the leading female performers of the halls was wise, and Josie knew it, but she missed the north-east more than she would have thought possible.

She brought Vera and Horace down to London to stay several times but it wasn't the same as going home, and although she had accepted one or two engagements in the big halls in Birmingham, and the lead female part in a winter pantomime in Manchester's prestigious Theatre Royal – such an honour couldn't be refused, Oliver had insisted – that was the furthest north she'd got.

Through Vera, Josie had learned that Barney had disappeared for some twelve months after Pearl's demise before popping up in Scotland, where he'd secured a reputable position as manager of Glasgow's massive Empire Theatre in Sauchiehall Street. Doubtless Barney would settle down in Glasgow and make a new life for himself, Vera had gone on, which would be the best thing for the lad in her book. This had been said during one of Vera's visits in Josie's second year of marriage, and when Josie had made no reply but had left the room shortly afterwards, Vera and Gertie had exchanged a long look and the subject of Barney and his future hadn't been mentioned again.

It had been shortly after this visit of Vera's that Mr Webb had reported to Josie that his colleague in Sunderland had been unable to make contact with her brother, Hubert, as she'd requested. His colleague's investigations had been fruitless and he'd suspected people were being deliberately unhelpful. Mrs Hogarth had to appreciate there was only so much which could be done in this regard, and as his colleague had been trying for well over twelve months to no avail it really was time to call it a day. Her brothers were young men now with minds of their own, and not to put too fine a point on it, they had obviously decided they did not want to see their sisters again. No doubt if they changed their minds in the future, Mrs Hogarth would hear from them. If they did not . . .

Josie had thanked Mr Webb, paid both him and his colleague in Sunderland handsomely for their trouble, and had seemingly put the matter out of her mind, much to Gertie's relief. Privately, however, there wasn't a day that passed when Josie didn't dwell on thoughts of Barney and her brothers.

Gertie herself had no desire for the north-east or anyone in it, and this feeling was cemented when, much to her surprise for she had decided long ago that she would remain single all her life, the manager-cum-bookkeeper-cum-administrator of Oliver's agency showed an interest in her which she in turn reciprocated.

Anthony Taylor was a small thin man with a pleasant face and prematurely receding hair, and was some ten years older than Gertie, but the two hit it off immediately and began walking out within a few months of Josie's marriage. Anthony lived with his mother in a small but nicely furnished house in Hammersmith which was only twenty minutes' walk from Oliver's office, and Gertie was often invited to tea before she and Anthony went to a variety show or dancing, or yet again to an art gallery or promenade concert. Like quite a few of the educated middle classes, Anthony expressed an interest in writers, musicians and painters, and he opened up a new world to Gertie. That he was an academic and somewhat phlegmatic man there was no doubt, but this suited Gertie admirably, as did their staid and passionless courtship.

'I don't want to fall madly in love, I never have,' Gertie confessed candidly to Josie one day some twelve months after she had started courting Anthony. Her sister had asked her how she felt about her beau. 'In fact, I don't think I'm capable of it, to be truthful. But I like Anthony; I enjoy being with him and I respect and admire him, and he's teaching me so much. And his mam – his mother,' she corrected quickly, since Anthony had taken it upon himself to relieve Gertie of her broad northern accent, with her full co-operation, 'she's so easy to get on with.'

And so the slow and very correct courtship had continued to the present day, although Josie had no doubt that when the time was right in Anthony's opinion, he would ask her sister to marry him and Gertie would accept.

But now it was the summer of 1905, and with the Commons giving a second reading of a bill to provide London with electricity, and car owners protesting that police speed-traps to catch anyone driving faster than the legal limit of 20mph were wildly inaccurate, the capital was in the midst of a metamorphosis the like of which hadn't been seen in previous decades.

Evidence of social advancements was not clear to Josie, however, when she and Gertie and Lily entered one of the worst tenement districts of London's East End on a sunny morning towards the end of July. Josie had been notified of the plight of an old singer-cum-dancer of Spanish-Irish descent by a mysterious 'well-wisher' a few days earlier. After checking the name with Lily, the fount of all music-hall knowledge, Josie discovered that the woman in question had been a rather temperamental performer who had become mentally deranged by the loss of her second husband. The gentleman in question had expired whilst making love to his current mistress. When the said Lottie Lemoine – the husband had been a Frenchman, Lily had said darkly; never, but *never* get involved with a Frenchman – had taken to jumping down into the audience and accosting any poor man who resembled her late husband, the music halls had closed ranks against her. Although Lily's telling of the story had been hilarious, Josie had felt immensely sorry for the tragic Lottie, and had therefore decided to visit the address which had been left by word of mouth with her current theatre manager.

Gertie had been against the idea, but then as Anthony had made it plain in recent months that his opinion coincided with Oliver's on the matter of Josie's generosity to the unfortunates of the music-hall profession, Josie hadn't expected anything else. She had told Gertie, and not for the first time, that Anthony was entitled to his views but that she would prefer Gertie to keep them to herself, and that her sister did not have to accompany her to the address in the East End. After a difficult ten minutes when a few home truths were expressed by both women, Gertie had decided she would go with her as usual.

Josie would have much preferred to just go with Lily, who was a tower of strength in these sorts of situations and always seemed to know just the right words to say to defuse any difficulties, but she nevertheless accepted the extended olive branch.

The area the three women were in was well known for its gin shops which were in full feather night and day, their swinging doors never still. An itinerant band was blowing and banging on one street corner and a scruffy organ boy grinding monotonously on another, but although the fine weather was making the smells worse, Josie preferred it to the last time she'd passed this way on a similar mission. Then gas flares had been burning in the streets at midday because of the thick choking fog, and small boys with flaring torches had guided people along the streets. In an area renowned for its crime, it was reassuring today to be able to see what was ahead.

This present mission turned out to be abortive, however. Lottie had passed away two days previously, an obese matriarch swathed in a long shapeless black dress told them, the dress somehow giving the woman the aspect of a pantomime charlady. The body had already been taken away and the room cleared, but Lottie's end had been peaceful, if that proved to be any comfort?

'Thank you.' It wasn't the first time Josie had undertaken such a task and been disappointed in the last years, but there was something different about this occasion. The woman had asked them into the kitchen straight off for a start, rather than keeping them standing at the door whilst she asked their business, and both the hall and the kitchen, although devoid of any comfort being utilitarian and starkly functional, were clearly freshly whitewashed and scrupulously clean. There were none of the bad smells associated with this poor area either, and the stone-flagged floors would have passed even Vera's standard of housekeeping. 'I understand Lottie was working at the box-making factory until recently?' Josie said quietly. 'Do I owe you anything for her board and lodging, or the funeral expenses?'

'No, lass, you don't owe me nowt.'

Perhaps it was the broad northern accent, or yet again the lively brown eyes whose brightness seemed unquenched by the hardships life had undoubtedly imposed upon the woman, but Josie had a strange feeling upon her. She ignored Gertie's, 'Come on then, let's get home,' and said instead to the woman, 'You're from the north?'

'Aye.' There was a moment's hesitation, and then the woman said, her voice still low, 'From your neck of the woods. You're Josie Burns, aren't you? The lass who's made good in the halls.'

It wasn't unusual for her to be recognised, not these days, but again, something was not quite right here. Rags, poverty, disease and death were the appropriate emblems of this district, and for the woman to know who she was and to brush aside the offer of payment she had made on Lottie's behalf was not normal. Most of the poor, broken-down inhabitants of the East End were born streetwise and as cunning as a cartload of monkeys, and those from further afield who joined their pitiful ranks soon learned to make the most of every opportunity.

'I know you, don't I?' Josie stared into the plump face in front of her. The texture of the woman's voice, the key in which it was pitched was somehow familiar, and she had a small portwine birthmark on her jawbone just under her left ear. Ada had had a mark like that but it had been more vivid against a child's pale skin. She'd forgotten about it till now, but she *knew* this woman. Josie's heart began to slam against her ribcage. 'Ada? It's you, isn't it? *Isn't it?*'

The woman blinked rapidly but she didn't deny it. She did not answer straight away, and when she did speak it was just a whisper. 'Aye, aye it's me.'

Josie heard Gertie's quick intake of breath behind her but as far as she knew her sister did not move; certainly she did not speak, not even when Josie moved forward and gripped her eldest sister's arms saying, 'Oh, Ada. Ada. I can't believe it,' through the pounding of her heart and the blood rushing in her ears. 'Oh this is wonderful, incredible. But if you knew who I was and that I was here, in London, why didn't you contact me?' And then, without waiting for an answer, she hugged Ada to her.

For a moment or two Ada remained stiff in her embrace, and then Josie felt the big body relax and as her sister's arms went round her for the first time Josie could remember, Ada's voice was thick when she admitted, 'We weren't sure if you'd want to know us, lass. Me an' Dora, we're respectable now. This is our own place an' we take in lodgers – women lodgers, you know?' This last was defensive. 'Dora works at the box-making factory an' with what she earns an' the lodgers bring in, we get by. We don't . . . We're not . . .'

Josie drew away slightly in order to look into her sister's face. Ada must be a relatively young woman of twenty-seven, but she looked forty years old if a day. Compared to her two elder sisters, Josie had had it easy. 'Hear me right when I say this, lass,' she said softly, her voice dropping naturally into the broad idiom of the north. 'I don't care about anything but the fact you and Dora are our sisters.' She included Gertie in the statement although Gertie had said nothing. 'What happened wasn't your fault. Da was after sending Gertie down the same road, and he'd got the lads thieving as soon as they could walk. Him and Patrick Duffy.'

'Patrick Duffy.' Ada moved her head slowly. 'It's bin years since I heard that name. Are . . . are Mam an' Da still . . . ?' And when Josie shook her head, Ada said, 'I can't pretend to feel sorry, lass, not after what they did to me an' Dora.' And for the first time since Josie had seen her, Ada looked hard and bitter. 'I've wished 'em all in hell's flames more times than I can remember, I tell you straight.'

'Oh Ada, I'm so sorry.'

'Aye, well, there's them that'd say me an' Dora are no better than we should be, but at least we did something about getting out of what Da put us into. We knew with Duffy's contacts we had to get right away from the north, an' when we left we'd only got the train fare so for the first few years we did the only work we'd bin used to, I admit it. Then we got enough to get this place 'cos it was all but falling down, an' we got a couple of our customers to pay in kind by doing the roof an' other bits. We could easily have turned it into a bawdy house an' made a bob or two, but we wanted . . . Well, you know what we wanted I imagine, lass. We wanted to be able to hold our heads up an' look any blighter in the eye and tell 'em we were as good as them. And so we finished with the other for good.'

'You were always as good as anyone else, Ada.'

Ada stepped back a pace. 'You mean that?'

'With all my heart.'

'We don't want a handout, don't think that, lass. No, we're all right, me an' Dora. Ask nowt of no one and you won't be disappointed, that's our motto. We look after each other and to hell with the rest. But . . . but I just wanted to see you once, proper like, you an' the little 'un. I've seen the posters an' such but it's not the same. Mind, Dora knows nowt about this and to tell you the truth, Lottie didn't neither. Me an' Dora had agreed, once we'd realised it was you, to let sleeping dogs lie. You've got your life an' we've got ours, that's what we said. But for the whole time Lottie's bin lodging with us, the thought was there in the back of me mind, once I'd heard what you do for some of the old-timers. An' I was wondering about the lads an' all; they were nowt but babbies when we skedaddled. So when Lottie got real sick I thought if I didn't take me chance it'd be gone—'

Ada stopped abruptly as though she'd suddenly become aware how much she was gabbling. 'An' you?' She looked past Josie to Gertie, her face hard again. As Josie followed Ada's gaze she saw Gertie was still standing as though she was frozen, apparently immobilised by the amazing turn of events. 'What about you? You ashamed of us then? Wishin' I'd kept me big mouth shut, are you?'

Gertie's small head moved as if in a shudder and then she spoke for the first time. 'Why didn't you take us?' She hadn't planned to say it; she hadn't even known it was what she was thinking until she had said it, but once said she knew it had been there at the back of her mind since for ever. 'Why did you leave us there with him, knowing what he was like?'

'We was bairns, lass, nowt but bairns, an' we didn't even know if we could get away ourselves. You don't run away from the sort of people we run away from, not unless you want to end up in a back alley somewhere with your throat cut, that is. We knew we were goin' to have to live on the streets and do the same work for a while once we got away; how could we have two little bairns with us?'

'You should've took us.'

'I *told* you.'

Josie watched her sisters glaring at each other and inside she was praying, Please, please, God, make it all right. Please make it all right. Make them love one another.

And then Ada sat down suddenly on a straight-backed chair, which, like everything else in the room, was battered but spotlessly clean, and she gulped twice before she said,

'You're right, we should have took you. *I* should have took you. I've never regretted goin', not for a minute, but for the fact that I left the rest of you with him. But . . . you can't imagine how it was. Me an' Dora, we thought about killin' him, or ourselves, or . . . Oh, lots of things. But we was little bairns, that's all. Little bairns.'

Ada's head swayed from one side to the other following the motion of her big body and the sight was more distressing than any loud wailing or tears. The lump in Josie's throat was threatening to choke her and she reached Ada the same time as Gertie did, the two of them bending over the enormously fat figure in the chair that bore no resemblance to the little child still trapped within the adult body. How long the three of them remained entwined Josie didn't know, it was unimportant, but by the time she and Gertie straightened all their faces were wet.

'You couldn't have taken us. I know that really, I do.' Gertie sank down to her knees, holding Ada's fleshy arm in her hands. 'But it was after you'd gone he started knocking me about all the time. I used to wet me drawers just when I heard his voice . . .'

'He . . . he didn't give you two to Duffy?'

'No, no.' It was Josie who spoke, Gertie's head now resting on Ada's lap. 'I could earn more for him with my singing, and when he tried the same game as with you and Dora for Gertie, we made a run for it. Vera, one of Mam's old friends, helped us. We lodged with her sister in Newcastle for a while, and then I went on the halls.'

'And the lads?'

'Working for Duffy now.' Josie's voice had the catch of tears in it but she couldn't help it. Never, in all her wildest dreams, had she hoped to see Ada and Dora again, but in a way this had brought all her buried fears for Hubert to the surface again. She wouldn't have believed it was possible to feel such elation and such despair at the same time.

'Something tells me we could all do with a nice cup of tea.' Lily had been standing in the doorway to the kitchen but now she pushed past the three sisters and walked over to the blackleaded range, reaching for a big iron kettle and, after checking to make sure it was full, pushing it to the centre of the glowing coals. 'Nothing like a cup of tea when you don't know if you're on your arse or your elbow,' she added conversationally.

Josie saw Ada start slightly, her sister's eyes widening as Ada turned her head to look at Lily who was grinning at them all from her place in front of the open fire, and then as Lily said, 'Nice to meet you, lass, although I've never seen three sisters look more different if you don't mind me saying so,' she saw Ada's lips turn upwards.

Thank You, Lord, for Lily, Josie prayed silently. If anyone had the knack of putting everything on a level footing again, it was her old friend.

The next hour was spent at the kitchen table over two pots of tea and a plateful of teacakes and drop scones. There were several times during the course of this hour that Josie wanted to throw her arms round Ada again and hug her hard, but the more Ada talked the more Josie knew her sister wouldn't like it. Her sister's experiences at the hands of Patrick Duffy and men like him had made her extremely chary of any show of physical affection, be it from man or woman. Ada's comfort was in eating, and from the amount she packed away it was no surprise her weight had ballooned so excessively.

It was also clear, from what Ada revealed, that she rarely left the sanctuary of her four walls. She showed them the front room which she and Dora shared, and which had two narrow iron beds with bright bedspreads and two comfortable chairs among other furniture, and also the three rooms upstairs which were taken by lodgers – two women who worked alongside Dora in the box-making factory in one room, two more who worked in a draper's shop in another, and a tiny box room with just enough space for a pallet bed and chest of drawers which had been the late Lottie's quarters.

All the floorboards were devoid of even the thinnest of clippy mats, there were paper blinds at the windows and no signs of any creature comforts, but like the downstairs of the house, the walls were whitewashed and free of bugs, the floors scrubbed and swept, and an almost clinical cleanliness prevailed throughout.

In view of the fact that Ada's house was obviously her whole world, Josie was all the more touched when it emerged that her sister had visited the theatre office herself to leave the message concerning Lottie. 'Me an' Dora can't read or write, lass, an' you couldn't trust anyone round here to deliver a message right, so it was shanks's pony or nowt,' Ada said matter-of-factly as she stood at a small side table in the kitchen stripping out the cartilage and gristle from some lambs' hearts she was going to stuff for the household's evening meal. She opened out the cavities, filled them with forcemeat and skewered them closed before placing the hearts in a big oven dish, saying the while, 'If you hadn't tumbled I wasn't going to say nowt, but it's bin eating away at me, knowin' who you were an' that you and Gertie were so close. They say blood's thicker than water an' mebbe they're right at that. What say you, lass?'

'We've got to try and see the lads again.'

It was an answer in itself and Ada recognised it as such, but now she shook her head of thick brown hair, saying, 'Don't be daft,' and her voice was flat. 'They're with Duffy, you said so yourself.'

'Which is all the more reason for getting them away.' Josie turned to Gertie who was sitting next to her at the kitchen table eating her third drop scone. 'Don't you see?'

'Look, lass, I know you think you've had your own run-ins with Duffy but believe me, you don't know the half,' Ada said before Gertie could respond. 'What you said earlier about thinking he did Da in? I wouldn't be surprised; not at anything would I be surprised where that perverted, sadistic so-an'-so is concerned. His word is law in some quarters an' he knows it, aye, an' plays on it. I was barely ten when Da sold me to him . . .' Her voice trailed away and she lowered her head, leaning heavily on the small table for a moment or two. Then she stretched her neck and moved her fat chins from side to side. 'No one could imagine, lass, no one 'cept Dora 'cos she went through the same. He's not human. On me second night with him he brought some pals in . . .' Ada raised her eyes and looked straight at her sister. 'Don't think he won't know what you're about 'cos he will, and you bein' a favourite of the halls won't protect you neither.'

Josie rose from her seat, walking across to this sister with whom she had only been reunited for a couple of hours, and yet who she felt had been a part of her life for as long as she could remember. 'He destroyed our family, Ada. Him and Da,' she said quietly, her voice vibrating with the depth of her feeling. 'He hurt you and Dora more than I can imagine,' she reached out and grasped Ada's hand and Ada's fingers wound tightly round hers, 'and he did his level best to hurt me and Gertie too, and he still has the lads. Oh, I know from what Hubert said that Jimmy might be willing, but not Hubert. I know he wanted to get away; he was just too frightened to do it.'

'And with good reason, lass. With good reason.'

'I don't doubt it.'

'You won't stop her.' Gertie had joined them, and now she looked across at Lily who was watching them all with a slightly bemused expression on her face; the revelations of the last two hours had knocked even this old veteran of life for six. 'Will she, Lily?' Gertie said. 'I think it's barmy to try and find the lads, but if Josie's made up her mind . . .'

'The Archangel Gabriel himself couldn't change it, not even with a holy visitation involving most of the heavenly host,' Lily finished for her. 'But from what's been said, I agree with these two, for what it's worth. This Patrick Duffy sounds like a right nasty piece of work to me, and once you start something with his type it's never finished until it's done.'

Josie nodded. 'Just so, Lily. You've hit the nail on the head. And it was started long ago and not by me.'

'But you said earlier that this man, this bloke up in Sunderland that you hired, he couldn't find the lads.' Ada had pulled away and was adding a chopped onion, carrots and turnip to the stock in the dish. 'What makes you think he'll have any more luck now?'

'He probably wouldn't,' Josie agreed. 'But Hubert found us once before; he could do so again. You and Dora could come with us, Ada. The four of us will go. Any of the theatres would be glad to have me' – this was said without any vestige of pride but as a statement of fact – 'and I could let it be known in the *Sunderland Echo* that I'm visiting with my sisters, two of whom I've only just been reunited with. That'll draw Hubert out, I know it will.'

'Me and Dora go back? Not on your nellie. Wild horses couldn't drag me back up there, lass. No, we're all right here; we've got a nice little goin' on and I'm not spoilin' everything to jaunt up to Sunderland for a visit I don't want to make. I'm sorry, lass, but that's how it is. Dora'll say the same.'

Josie nodded. It was probably asking too much of Ada and Dora to do what she had suggested, but now she had made up her mind she wondered how she could have waited so long before going home. 'I understand, and you and Dora must do what seems best to you, but I have to try and see Hubert again, and this is the only way I can think of.'

'What about Oliver?' said Gertie flatly. Over the last hour she had been considering her brother-in-law's reaction to the news about Ada and Dora – and likewise Anthony's. This last idea of Josie's would be sure to send Oliver into a frenzy, and she knew exactly how Anthony and his mother would view their going off on some wild goose-chase to Sunderland. Oliver was already in one of his sulks because of their visit to the East End that morning, and when he was like that it made things so difficult for Anthony at the office. Anthony . . . She had glossed over much of her life before she had come down to London with Josie; he had no idea that her sisters had been prostitutes. The word reverberated in her head. She couldn't tell him, she just couldn't, and his mother would be horrified. They had always known her as the sister of a successful and wealthy music-hall star.

'Oliver?' Josie shrugged off-handedly as though she hadn't also been considering how her husband would react. 'He will probably disagree, but after four years I don't think it's too unreasonable to have a spell working up north. It need only be for a few weeks. Lots of the stars work the provinces now and again, and there are some excellent music halls in other places but London.'

Whether Oliver agreed or not she was going to stick to her guns over this. She was grateful for the way Oliver had helped to further her career, and she knew he had opened doors with his connections which would have remained closed a lot longer without him, but he'd done all right out of her success. What would Gertie say if she told her what Oliver lost in the gambling dens he frequented? She felt it disloyal to discuss such things, even with Gertie, and especially now her sister was so involved with Oliver's right-hand man at the agency. She was aware Gertie had assumed Oliver's bad temper that morning had been due to this visit, but in reality they'd fought half the night when she'd told him she was going to seek a solicitor's advice about the possibility of her earnings being paid into a new and separate bank account from their joint one.

Maybe she should have done it years ago, but she hadn't wanted that sort of marriage and she'd felt it would belittle Oliver. She didn't feel like that any more. In fact, she didn't know how she felt about a lot of things . . .

Upon discovering Ada's identity, Josie had asked the driver of the horse-drawn cab they'd travelled to the East End in to return to the house at midday, but when the cheery-faced man put in an appearance it was only Lily who left.

Dora wouldn't return to the house until just after four o'clock from her job at the box-making factory a couple of streets away, having started work at six that morning, and Josie couldn't bear to leave before she'd seen her other sister.

The driver declared himself more than happy to return for them at five o'clock – 'You're paying the fare, missus, and I always say the customer is right' – and so Josie and Gertie spent a very pleasant afternoon getting to know Ada again. Josie thought Gertie was a little subdued, but in view of the surprise which had been sprung on them she couldn't blame her youngest sister for being bowled over.

When Dora walked through the door there were more happy tears and plenty of laughter, too, Dora being what Nellie would have described as a card. Although rosily plump and somewhat matronly for her twenty-six years, Dora looked a great deal younger than Ada. Dora's disposition was inclined towards jollity and she did not seem so severely affected by her traumatic childhood as her elder sister. She was a pretty woman, unlike Ada, with a ready smile and a mass of golden-brown hair not unlike Josie's. Just before the cab driver arrived, and amid promises that she and Gertie would return soon after the weekend, which Josie was committed to spending with Oliver and his friends at the country estate of some squire or other, Josie found herself thinking that none of them resembled their parents at all.

Except Jimmy. The thought was unwelcome. Jimmy, who had been the image of their da in every way, and who had been under the tutelage of Patrick Duffy for almost ten years . . .

Chapter Nineteen

Oliver was not at home when Josie called in at Park Place, before asking the cab driver to take them straight to the Empire in Leicester Square so that she wouldn't be late for the first of the two houses that evening. She just had time to ascertain from Mrs Wilde that her husband had not been back all day, before she had to dash off. Oliver was calling for her at the theatre that night in the carriage and they were driving straight to his friend's estate in Berkshire. There would be time enough on the journey to tell him about the events of the day, and of her decision to play a theatre in Sunderland again, if only for a short season.

The Empire was a luxurious theatre with deep pile carpets and footmen in blue and gold livery, and it advertised itself as 'The Cosmopolitan Club of the World'. The manager always wore full evening dress and white kid gloves, and would pat any young blood causing trouble on the shoulder before a footman escorted the offender out of the theatre. Bernard, the manager, always concealed a piece of chalk in his right glove which left a warning mark so that, should the young man try another entrance, he was recognised and refused admittance. Bernard had been using this ploy for years and it amazed Josie that the clientèle never tumbled the ruse.

Bernard was fond of telling of the time, some eleven years before, when the London County Council insisted

377

on the foyer at the back of the circle being closed due to it being a frequent haunt of 'ladies of the night'. Regular habitués protested in a forcible manner and a small riot ensued, when barriers were torn down by dashing young fellows led by a certain Winston Churchill, now an MP, Bernard told them. Young Winston had then marched at the head of a procession round Leicester Square, which carried debris as trophies. Josie could never quite work out if Bernard was applauding the act by the young man or decrying it, and as yet no one had had the nerve to ask the imperious Bernard which it was. Nevertheless it was a good story in view of Churchill's venture into politics, and one which Bernard derived great satisfaction from telling.

She and Gertie passed Bernard on the way to the dressing rooms and as always he was charm itself to the two women. However, they had heard him put more than one rebellious performer in their place and he could be formidable. He had been a polished artiste himself years ago, with a good light baritone voice and reportedly somewhat handsome and always immaculately dressed, but when he'd been offered the chance to step out of the fickle world of the halls and into a steady job as manager, he'd taken it.

Once dressed in the silk and satin of her stage clothes and with her face freshly made-up, Josie found she was too het up to sit quietly in the dressing room with Gertie drinking tea as was their custom. The euphoria caused by the wonder of finding Ada and Dora again hadn't abated in the slightest, but all the talk of the old days they'd indulged in that afternoon had set her thinking about Barney so strongly she couldn't force him out of her mind no matter how hard she tried. She knew from experience that only regret and pain would result from giving in to this, and she needed to be strong tonight when she talked to Oliver.

'Come and watch Annabelle with me from the wings.

This dressing room is too stuffy, and you haven't seen her act all the way through yet, have you?' Josie pulled Gertie to her feet, the excitement of the day all too evident in her animation, but once outside the dressing room the cloak of decorum and sedateness expected from someone in her position settled over her. She wondered how often other people ran and skipped and danced in their minds whilst giving an outward impression of dignified composure.

Annabelle was already climbing into her large glass tank filled with water when they reached the wings of the stage, looking as pretty and graceful as ever, and her husband, Gerald, resplendent in full evening dress, had begun the first of his announcements of each feature of her performance which was accompanied by a little discourse. 'The lovely Annabelle La Belle is now opening and shutting the mouth underwater; gathering shells underwater; sewing and writing underwater; eating underwater; drinking from a bottle underwater . . .'

'This is a good bit.' Josie nudged Gertie whose gaze had wandered to the audience. 'Gerald borrows a lighted cigar from someone in the front row and gives it to Annabelle, and she smokes underwater for a minute or more before reappearing with the cigar still unextinguished. Bernard asked Gerald how they did it but he won't let on.'

'Josie.' Gertie's gaze had narrowed and she didn't look at the tank. 'Is that . . . No, it can't be, can it? Not today of all days.'

The tone of Gertie's voice rather than what she had said checked the laughing comment Josie had been about to make as Annabelle puffed away under the water with every appearance of contentment, and as her head turned and her eyes followed Gertie's, the same thought sprang into Josie's mind. It can't be. *It can't be him.* After four years or more, how could he choose this particular day to come to London?

Her heart thudding fit to burst Josie sank back against the thick velvet curtains at the side of the stage. Of course it was him. Every fibre of her being had known it the second she had laid eyes on the big handsome man in the second row of the stalls. He looked . . . well. She would not acknowledge that her mind had used the word 'wonderful' instead. Oh, what was she going to do? *What on earth was she going to do?* Barney. *Barney.*

She wanted to laugh and cry at the same time as she raised her hands to her burning cheeks. Oh, to see him again. To have him so close she could reach out and touch him. She felt faint for a moment, and it was only in that blinding second of truth that she acknowledged exactly what Barney meant to her. What he had always meant to her. She had often thought in the last years that Oliver was a man who should never have married, but now she knew that truth could be applied to her, at least concerning every other man but the one sitting in the second row of the theatre. She had fought her feelings for Barney every day since she had first laid eyes on him as a bairn of twelve, and for a moment it was a relief to admit it to herself.

And then she brought herself up very straight, and as Gertie's head turned and her sister looked at her, saying, 'It's Barney, lass. What are you going to do?' Josie answered stiffly, 'Sing. That's what I'm paid to do, after all.'

'You know what I mean.'

Yes, she knew what Gertie meant, and her sister's tone had told her Gertie didn't appreciate the facetiousness, but at the moment all she could deal with was the immediate future in terms of her performance. Barney might be here but nothing had changed. She was a married woman.

'Ladies and gentlemen, the lovely Annabelle La Belle will now adopt an attitude of prayer.'

Gerald's voice filtered through her whirling thoughts, and as Annabelle sank to her knees under the water, folding her hands with every appearance of rapt devotion while the orchestra played 'The Maiden's Prayer' and rays of crimson and green light shone into the tank indicating morning and evening prayer, Josie made every effort to pull herself together. The conjurer was on next, and then Clarence, who had toured in burlesque before turning from singing to dramatic monologues. Clarence had revived Charles Godfrey's lurid sketch *The Night Alarm* which was ridiculously melodramatic, and featured a burning building, a horse-drawn fire cart, a maiden in distress and three songs, and the audiences loved it. With any luck, he would receive his usual encores which would give Josie time to compose herself.

'Come on, Gertie.' As Annabelle hopped out of the tank and bowed herself off, Josie was already retracing her steps and Gertie had no choice but to follow her.

Would Barney try to see her in between shows? Once in the privacy of her dressing room Josie sank down on to a stool, and Gertie walked across to the small stove in one corner and began to brew up without any prompting, her little face expressing her concern. He had obviously come to this particular theatre because he knew this was where she was appearing, Josie thought, but she didn't flatter herself that he was down in the capital just to see her. No doubt he had some business here – or perhaps he was visiting someone? Again her heart began to pound. She hadn't noticed anyone with him, but then again she hadn't looked any further than his face. The thought that he might be with a lady friend was so unbearable Josie brought herself up sharp. She addressed the tight feeling in her chest which the mental picture of Barney and another woman had caused, saying silently, Don't be so stupid. He's a free man; he can have as many women as he likes and it is absolutely nothing to do with you. You've no right to have even a moment's objection.

'So . . .' Gertie considered she had been quiet long enough. 'I'll ask again. What are you going to do?'

'Nothing.' This time Josie didn't try to prevaricate. 'If Barney wants to see us no doubt he'll make that plain, and it would be nice to see an old friend, wouldn't it? But he might not have time anyway. Did . . . did you notice if anyone was with him?'

There was a definite bite to Gertie's voice when she said, 'No, I did not notice if there was anyone with him,' and Josie knew she'd offended her sister by not talking about her real feelings. But she couldn't, she just couldn't. To voice what she felt for Barney, even to hint at it or display any agitation at his presence here would be wrong. And certainly a betrayal of Oliver.

She felt she was going to cry and was forbidding herself to do so, added to which she was exhausted. But then in view of all the day had held, was that surprising? And she'd been working so hard lately; here at the theatre, at the little receptions and soirées Oliver promoted so strongly, and other musical events. Now there was another of the weekend parties in front of her which Oliver described as 'the most agreeable form of social intercourse known to man', and she herself described as boring.

She knew exactly how every hour would be spent. People would be called by their valets or a maid of the house at eight-thirty – never a minute before or a minute after – and these servants would arrive bearing in their left hand a neat brass can of shaving water for the male guest, and in their right hand a neat brass tray of tea, toast and Marie biscuits. The male guest, blinking plethoric eyes above his silk eiderdown, would munch his share of the biscuits and sip the tea, before donning his Afghan dressing-robe and slouching his way along the passage to the bathroom. His lady wife would dress with assistance from the maid, and then they would both descend the inevitable red pile staircase to breakfast. The smell of last night's port would have given way to the smell of the morning's rows of little spirit lamps. These would be gently warming rows of large silver dishes heaped high with food.

Oh, the food. Josie sighed wearily. Around the centre table prepared for perhaps twenty-five to thirty guests and bright with Malmaisons and toast racks would be another four or five smaller tables. One for the hams, tongues, galantines, cold grouse, pheasant, partridge and ptarmigan. There was *always* ptarmigan. A further table would hold fruits of different calibre, and jugs of cold water and lemonade. A third table contained porridge utensils. A fourth coffee, and pots of Indian and China tea. The latter were differentiated from each other by little ribbons of yellow (indicating China) and red (indicating Britain's magnificent Indian Empire).

Discussions on how he or she had slept were taken very seriously, and then there would be morning coffee later, luncheon, an afternoon stroll, tea served in some gallery or other, bridge, dinner, and then a little musical diversion at which Josie was always commandeered to perform. Finally, at midnight, devilled chicken would be served and people would disappear to their rooms in ones and twos.

Sometime in the day the men would have gone shooting and the ladies would gossip; similarly in the evening the men would often hang back when their women retired to bed and some serious gambling and drinking would take place. And there were some couples who did the rounds every weekend of their lives. Josie winced at the thought. Well, she'd had enough, she suddenly realised. She didn't know if it was seeing Ada and Dora in their little house and marvelling at their quiet bravery, or Barney's unexpected appearance which had brought with it memories of Betty and Frank's existence and a whole host of other recollections, or yet again that she was just heartily sick of Oliver's set, but this weekend party would be her last. She loved her work, she thoroughly enjoyed the time she spent with Lily and the other ladies in the house at the back of the Caledonian Market, but this other life was just not real. She needed to be with her own folk again, it was as simple as that.

She would make it clear to Oliver she wanted to do a tour of the north which included a good portion of time spent in Sunderland. He wouldn't like it but then that was nothing new.

And then, as Gertie silently handed her a cup of tea, Josie faced the fact that she was purposely thinking about everything but the main issue hammering at her consciousness. Barney was here. In a few minutes she would have to step on to that stage and sing and smile and flirt a little with the audience as though this was just another night. But it wasn't. It wasn't. Oh, Barney. *Barney*.

By the time Josie did step on to the stage some fifteen minutes later she was every inch the famous music-hall star, and no one was to know she was blessing the fact her corsets commanded her to keep her back straight and her shoulders from drooping.

Barney knew his eyes were devouring her and that he was shaking slightly, but he could no more have stopped his body's reaction to the sight of the woman who had been a constant torment, mentally and physically, for the last few years than he could have stopped breathing. She had been lovely four years ago but now she was exquisite, a goddess. No, no not a goddess, he corrected himself in the next moment; she was too warm and lovely to be put in the same realm as aloof and remote immortal beings.

How could he have stayed away four years? He must have been mad. He should have come before. Betty couldn't hide her feelings like Vera, and the last couple of times he'd spoken to his stepmother he had sensed she suspected all wasn't well between Josie and Oliver, although nothing had been said directly. Or was he just imagining it because he *wanted* it to be that way?

Was Josie aware he'd moved back down to Sunderland from Scotland? When he had left the highly coveted position as manager of the Empire in Glasgow for the post of manager at the Avenue Theatre in Gillbridge Avenue, he had made Betty his excuse.

His stepmother was finding it hard to cope with her brood now the lads were older, he'd explained to the owner of the Empire when he'd told him of his decision to leave. He felt it important her bairns had a man about the place some of the time – the three eldest boys in particular. The twins and Robert were working at the docks for an individual who was well known for sailing close to the wind, and any bad habits needed to be nipped in the bud right now. The man had said he understood but had expressed regret at Barney's going, a regret, he'd gone on to say, that would be echoed by his daughter. Barney had made no comment to this. Penelope was a nice lass and they had had some good times together, but as far as he was concerned she had never been under the illusion there was anything permanent in their friendship. And friendship had been all he had offered Penelope. The ones who had come and gone at the Empire and had wanted something more physical than friendship had known the score too.

Who had ruined him for any sort of meaningful relationship? Not Pearl. No. Surprisingly he hadn't found it hard to put the years of torment with his wife behind him. No, it had been the woman standing on the stage in front of him now who had effectively wrecked his life.

Oh, that wasn't fair. He felt his guts twist with self-disgust. It wasn't her fault. What was the matter with him, for crying out loud? He had become a married man within months of their meeting and she had been nowt but a child at the time, and after he had realised how he really felt he had known Josie would never have stood for a hole-in-corner type affair which would have been all he could have offered her; Pearl had considered divorce a mortal sin.

Josie had just finished singing 'Two Lovely Black Eyes', striding from side to side of the stage as she had sung and reducing the audience to howls of laughter, but now, after the applause had died down, she moved to the centre of the stage under the rays of one limelight from the centre of the roof and a spontaneous hush fell over the assembly. This was what she did best, Barney thought. The few times he had heard her sing in the past she'd held the crowd in the palm of her hand when she was still like this.

She began to sing 'The Things You Can't Buy With Gold', gazing up above the spectators as she leaned forward slightly, her body accentuating the sentimental refrain. Barney's throat tightened, and her face, lit by the silver light, began to draw him as the rest of his suroundings melted away. She had the voice of an angel. He found he was holding his breath. It was even better than he remembered. He dragged his eyes away from the slender figure on the stage for a moment and saw his fellow listeners were transfixed too. How could such a powerfully emotive voice come from such an ethereal frame? And what the hell was he doing here? She wouldn't look twice at him, whether she was unhappy in her marriage or not; the world was her oyster. He had been a fool to come, such a fool, but she hadn't seen him. He could still make his escape and she would be none the wiser.

His heart was pounding like a sledgehammer, the force of it creating a physical pain in his chest and a dryness in his throat that no amount of liquid could assuage. She was gone from him; she was gone from them all – Betty and the bairns, Vera and Horace, all of them. She had been like one of those vibrantly beautiful butterflies that fluttered to rest on dank soil before flying off to lush pasture.

He couldn't take his eyes off her face even as the truth hit home. She wasn't the little urchin bairn Betty and his da had taken in because of her hellish situation at home any more; she was a wealthy, successful, beautiful and intoxicating woman. He hadn't been thinking clearly the last few weeks since he had come back from Scotland to Sunderland; just the thought that there might have been a chance for him had addled his brain. But his mind was now clear and working normally, and it was telling him he was the biggest clot out. He hadn't moved down to Sunderland because of Betty, at least that wasn't the main reason. Why hadn't he had the gumption to admit it to himself before? He had wanted to move into the perimeter of Josie's life again, or at least be with people she cared about so there was a likelihood of seeing her. Which made him what? He didn't like to think about what it made him.

Josie had known from the moment she'd walked on to the stage that the only way she was going to get through her performance was to look no further than the footlights. If he was with someone she wouldn't be able to bear it. It was illogical and unreasonable and a hundred other things besides, but she couldn't help it. She wouldn't be able to sing a note if her worst fears were confirmed. It was as simple as that.

Amazingly she found her voice didn't reflect her turbulent emotions. Claudette Belloc had done her job well, and all the little Frenchwoman's tuition came to the fore as Josie let her voice soar into the instinctual routine of the songs she knew so well.

Amuse and relax them a little first; then a song which would tug at the heartstrings followed by an even more poignant ballad to bring the silk handkerchiefs into play. It was the first time she had sung mechanically but no one seemed to notice.

After finishing with 'After the Ball is Over', Josie curtsied again and again to the applause before she rose finally, and it was only then, as she smiled and waved to the audience before walking from the stage, that she allowed herself to glance in the direction of the seat in the second row. It was empty.

Chapter Twenty

Contrary to her original plan Josie said very little to her husband during the ride to Squire Conway's estate in Berkshire, and Oliver, still smarting under what he saw as his wife's incredible proposition that she would seek a solicitor's advice with a view to taking control of her earnings, said even less.

It wasn't the first time they had been invited to spend the weekend at this particular house, and as the carriage scrunched on to the gravel drive which was lit by many lanterns hanging from the massive oak trees bordering the drive, Josie's heart sank at the number of empty coaches it contained. A smartly dressed footman was waiting to help them dismount, and two stable-boys were hovering in the background ready to release the horses from their shafts and take them to the Squire's stables.

They descended into a large forecourt which again was lit by many lanterns as well as lights from the many windows of the huge house in front of them, and Oliver took her arm as they climbed the massive horseshoe-shaped steps to where another footman was holding open the door for them.

Steven Conway met them in the hall, two liveried servants standing behind their master ready to take the guests' coats and hats, and the blaze of lights, the buzz of voices and the sound of genteel laughter was all too familiar. A small maid dressed in black alpaca with a stiffly starched apron and cap was waiting to escort Josie to the ladies' room where she could freshen up after the journey, the Hogarths' portmanteaux and bags already having been whisked up to their room.

The name or names of each guest would be neatly written on a card slipped into a tiny brass frame on the bedroom doors, and Josie had come to realise a little night movement between the rooms of these rambling country houses was not unusual. However, it was unthinkable that appearances wouldn't be kept up and everything was done with the utmost discretion. The hostess would always arrange things for the convenience of her guests; some married couples preferred separate rooms and there was nothing at all wrong with that – gentlemen could snore so dreadfully, after all, and some ladies liked to retire earlier than their husbands and didn't appreciate being woken in the early hours after their spouse had indulged in a bout of gambling and drinking.

Then there were the recognised lovers to be considered; individuals could get very annoyed if they had gone to the same house-party only to find themselves at the other end of the building from their current amour, especially if the hostess had made the unforgivable faux pas of putting them in the same room as their husband or wife. The professional Lothario would be furious if he found himself in a room surrounded by ladies who were all accompanied by their husbands.

This question of the disposition of bedrooms always gave the current hostess cause for anxious thought; it was so necessary to be up to date with the current gossip on who was sleeping with whom. It was part of a good hostess's duty to see to such things, and an essential part of the fevered weekend activity.

Josie had come to understand these finer points of upper-class behaviour slowly. Oliver had always arranged that they share a room, and although she invariably retired long before he did, he was always careful not to wake her and to behave with consideration. She had been shocked at what she deemed to be unprincipled and dissolute conduct by educated folk who should have known better, the more so because she perceived it was considered absolutely acceptable as long as certain unspoken rules of propriety were observed. When she'd first expressed her disquiet to Oliver he had hugged her tightly, telling her she was a rare find and that he loved her all the more for her aversion to such behaviour, but he hadn't said that he agreed with her. He had always been used to this kind of social intermingling, he'd explained when she had objected to his acceptance of what she considered blatant adultery. She had to remember he had grown up with this kind of thing, and although, of course, it was different now that they were married, it wasn't a surprise to him. Most of these people had little else to do, after all.

When Josie came out of the ladies' room she had the wives of two of Oliver's old friends either side of her. Of all Oliver's friends she liked these two women best; they happened to be twin sisters who had married two brothers, and both Victoria and Winifred had taken a shine to Josie from the first time they'd met. Both sisters had what Josie had heard referred to disparagingly as 'spirit' by some of their contemporaries, and this was frequently expressed in their involvement with the growing Suffragette Movement. The fact that the King had publicly expressed his lack of sympathy with the movement, and stated that he considered it a danger to the established order of society had not deterred Victoria and Winifred an iota.

As the three of them walked through the open doors of

the drawing room from the hall, it was Victoria who gave a smothered groan and said under cover of her hand, 'Stella's holding court again. Why does that woman think she has to be seen to monopolise every male in sight?'

'Because she was spoilt from the cradle,' Winifred answered darkly. Winifred's husband was the nearest of the little cluster of men grouped round the other woman, and Stella's hand was resting on his arm. 'And she is so indiscreet. She virtually publicises each new affair. I don't know why Godfrey puts up with it.'

'Because he's besotted, my dear. Absolutely besotted.'

Josie said nothing, but she was looking at Stella and as always happened when she saw the other woman a sickness rose up in her chest. The cold beautiful face, the large round blue eyes which always took on a steely hue whenever they met hers, the perfect creamy skin with its touch of peach . . . Stella Stratton was stunning and she knew it, but it wasn't that which bothered Josie so much. It was the hostility with which the other woman always greeted her – when she did greet her, that was. Most of the time Stella went to great pains to ignore her.

They had been late arriving and within a few moments of entering the drawing room, supper was announced by one of the servants, and the requisite devilled chicken and accompanying dishes were served in the dining room.

Whether it was because Josie's senses were heightened after the events of the day involving Ada and Dora, and not least that evening when she had seen Barney again she didn't know, but as she sat down with her plate of food, Victoria and Winifred still either side of her, she noticed that Stella and Oliver had seated themselves on the opposite side of the room and their heads were close together. Oliver was smiling at first, and then after a moment or two he threw back his head and laughed out loud, and ridiculously Josie felt the impact in her stomach like a physical act of betrayal.

She forced herself to act as though she was enjoying both the food and the company, which normally would have been the case because Victoria and Winifred were sharp-witted and interesting, especially when they were relating the latest happenings within the Suffrage Movement like now, but she was painfully conscious of the pair sitting on the chaise-longue.

At half-past twelve a number of the ladies present began to retire, Josie included. Her mind had been in too much turmoil for any discussion about Ada and Dora on the carriage-ride to the Conway estate; she had felt she needed a quiet hour or so to compose her thoughts before she related the events of the day to Oliver. She walked across to her husband now, nodding unsmilingly at Stella before she concentrated her gaze on Oliver, saying quietly, 'I'm going to our room; it has been a tiring day.'

'Of course, my dear.' Oliver stood to his feet, kissing her lightly on the cheek as he added, 'You don't mind if I take a little port before I come up?'

She was so tired of the hypocrisy. Oliver was going to do what he always did; stay up until three or four in the morning gambling and drinking with his cronics, and he didn't care if she minded or not! Nevertheless she smiled and said, 'Not at all. I'll see you a little later.'

On reaching the room which had been designated for herself and Oliver, Josie turned the big ebony handle and pushed the engraved oak door open with a feeling of thankfulness. She needed to be quiet and *think*, she told herself as she walked across to the long cheval mirror to one side of the four-poster bed and stared at her reflection. These big houses were an absolute maze at the best of times, and this one had endless large guest rooms with dressing rooms attached besides the Conways' private quarters and the staff accommodation. The big drawing room, the morning room, the breakfast room, the library, the billiard room, the gentlemen's smoking room, the grand ballroom, the large dining room and small dining room . . . The list was endless. And there were people everywhere, all the time. She had got lost the first time she and Oliver had come here and it had been all of ten minutes before she had found her way.

Josie glanced at the four-poster bed with its heavy tapestry cover, and saw that one of the Conways' maids had laid out her white lawn nightdress and negligée and Oliver's linen nightshirt and velvet dressing gown. She remained standing looking at these for some moments without really knowing why, but conscious that her stomach was churning and that Stella Stratton was at the forefront of her mind for some reason. Not Ada and Dora, not even Barney, but Stella.

And then she mentally shook her mind clear, seating herself on the satin chaise-longue at the end of the bed and shutting her eyes. Why hadn't Barney tried to see her? How could he come all this way and not even try to talk to her? And then she answered this with the same argument she'd been putting forth ever since she had first seen him in the audience that evening. The only argument she would allow herself to consider. Because he was not in London because of her. No doubt he had seen her name and thought he'd take in the performance for old times' sake, but perhaps his reason for being in the capital – business, a woman – was pressing? And it might well be a woman . . .

Josie lay further back on the sofa and let out a long sigh. If it was a woman, that would be perfectly understandable, of course. Barney was a young man in the prime of life and it had been four years since Pearl had died; time enough to get over what had clearly been an unhappy marriage and for him to consider settling down with someone else. She dug one fist into the valley between her breasts where an ache was affecting her breathing, but she did not open her eyes, not even when hot burning tears ran down her cheeks in a flood.

She shouldn't be crying on the day she had found her two sisters again against all the odds in the world. This thought did nothing to check her sobs, and after a minute or two Josie turned over on to her stomach and buried her face in a cushion and let the regret and disappointment and confusion have free rein.

She hadn't been aware of falling asleep, so when she awoke, cramped and with her neck twisted in an unnatural position against the back of the sofa, it took a moment or two to realise where she was. She pulled herself upright, wincing at the pain which lanced from her neck into her head, and looked vaguely about the bedroom which was dimly lit by two amber glass-shaded lamps. The bed was empty.

What time was it? She rose to her feet, walking across to the small fireplace which had a marble surround and an elaborate basket of fresh flowers in place of a fire, and glanced at the large decorative gold clock which took up most of the mantelpiece. Nearly four o'clock. Surely Oliver would be here soon? He must have lost enough for one night by now. This thought carried with it a strong element of bitterness, and now she began to pace restlessly about the room.

She would tell him what had transpired concerning Ada and Dora as soon as he made an appearance, whether he was intoxicated or not. And then she would go on to disclose her decision to work in the north-east for a spell. She wouldn't mention her brothers. She bit hard on her lip here. It would do no good and she was already giving him enough to take in. Hubert might not contact her again anyway, and unless he did Mr Webb had made it plain she had no hope of tracing him. But he *would* contact her. He had to.

After washing her hands and face in the big china bowl with its matching jug in the adjoining dressing room, Josie smoothed her ruffled hair into the neat chignon at the back of her head and reseated herself on the chaise-longue in the bedroom.

She waited for a full half an hour before jumping to her feet. Dare she go downstairs and ask him to accompany her to their room? He wouldn't like it and normally she wouldn't dream of doing such a thing, but it *was* half-past four in the morning. This was absolutely ridiculous. The maid would be bringing tea in another four hours and she needed to talk to Oliver properly before the rigid itinerary of so-called enjoyment of the day began.

Her mind made up, and without waiting to change her rumpled evening dress for one of the day dresses she had brought with her, Josie cautiously opened the outer bedroom door and stepped on to the silent landing outside. The corridor was faintly lit by a lamp placed halfway down the passage, but it was still difficult to see clearly. Josie groped her way through the flickering shadows to the end of the landing which opened up on to a wide gallery. Some distance to her left were more stairs leading upwards to the next two floors, and to her right the ones which would take her to the ground floor, their room being on the first floor of the east wing.

She descended the stairs slowly. The ground floor looked to be in darkness but already the first signs of dawn were streaking the sky outside the two massive leaded windows either side of the front door. The shining suits of armour lining the walls of the hall at various intervals stared at her impassively as her feet click-clicked on the marble tiles, and after opening the heavy oak door of the drawing room and finding it empty, Josie moved on to the billiard room which was some distance – and a couple of winding passageways – away. Again, the room was silent and deserted.

The gentlemen's smoking room. There were small tables and chairs in there; no doubt that was where the last few night owls were still playing cards or just lying back in their chairs talking and drinking. It took Josie a minute or two to reach the smoking room which was not situated close to the billard room as one might have expected, but on the other side of the ground floor and next to the large and opulent dining room. A strong smell of brandy and cigars assailed her nose when she stood on the threshold of this room, her feet sinking into the thick piled claret carpet as she took a few steps inside. Where was Oliver? Everyone was in bed, even the staff; she should have realised it before.

Her heart was thudding fit to burst now, but as she quietly retraced her footsteps along the passageways to the main hall she was aware of another, stronger emotion coming into play. She knew where Oliver was. She should want to cry, shouldn't she? Cry and moan and shout and scream? Wasn't that what women usually did when they had been betrayed? But the white heat of her anger had burned up everything but the need to confront him and tell him she knew what he was about. And with whom. Oh yes, and with whom.

How dare he! How *dare* he do that to her with that dreadful woman. Oliver was no fool and whatever he said to the contrary he knew how much Stella disliked her. To humiliate her by consorting with Stella Stratton . . .

She was hardly aware of her feet skimming the floor as

they took her swiftly up the stairs to the first floor of the east wing. She checked the name on each little brass plate, opening the door to their own rooms and ascertaining that Oliver was not back before she transferred her search to the floors above. Oliver had told her the Conway family occupied the three upper floors of the main house, so when she couldn't find the name she wanted she made her way to the west wing.

Godfrey Stratton's name was in a corridor occupied exclusively by gentlemen involved in matters of state, and Josie's lips came back from her small white teeth in a bitter smile at their hostess's diplomacy. Not all their lady wives – those who had wives, that was – would be about intrigue and liaisons whilst the men discussed international and home politics in the privacy of the small drawing room or the morning room or whatever, but this 'thoughtful' arrangement certainly preserved the confidentiality of those who did.

It was now almost five o'clock and no doubt the staff would soon be rising, but no power on earth could have stopped Josie from following this matter through to its logical conclusion. If she had thought about it, she would have realised she hardly recognised herself as she marched along the silent landings, but then she came to the name she had been looking for. 'Lady Stratton'. *Lady.* Lady be damned. Her rage became overwhelming for a second. And then she tried the handle of the door. It was locked, but then she would have expected it to be.

She rapped on the door; loud, ringing raps which bruised her knuckles although she would be oblivious to the pain till later. It was a moment before Stella's voice, high and startled, called, 'Who is it?'

Josie did not reply to this, but when there was the sound of movement from within and then that of a man's voice, muffled but nevertheless definitely male, she knocked again, and this time she kept knocking until the door was suddenly swung open.

'What on earth—'

Stella's indignant protest was cut short as Josie pushed her aside with enough force to cause the other woman to stumble, and then Josie was standing in the room. Ridiculously, at such a moment, Josie was conscious of thinking, This is a far better room than any we have ever had here, as her gaze flashed round the enormous suite with its high, four-poster bed in front of which was virtually a small sitting room. Then all she could see was Oliver tucking his shirt into his trousers on a chaise-longue at the foot of the bed.

'Josie! How did you—? This isn't what you think. Hell! Listen to me—'

As Oliver rose from the sofa, still adjusting his clothes, the coolness in her head which had guided her thus far vanished. She was so angry she quite literally had a red mist in front of her eyes, and as Stella grabbed hold of one arm, saying, 'How dare you force your way into my private quarters!' the other woman's voice was cut short for the second time in as many minutes as Josie shook her off in much the same way an enraged bull would shake off a rat. Stella went sprawling in a confusion of long blonde hair and silk, coming to rest in an ungainly pose which bore evidence to the fact she was wearing nothing at all beneath the diaphanous nightdress.

Stella had been spoilt from the cradle, adored by indulgent parents and then a string of lovers, not to mention her doting husband, and this was the first time in her life anyone had had the temerity to handle her in such a fashion. She'd landed against a small walnut writing desk, hitting one side of her face and her hip as she did so, and now she lay in utter shock, winded and speechless.

'I don't want to listen to you, Oliver,' Josie said steadily, amazed how calm her voice sounded. 'Neither do I wish to remain in the presence of your whore, but I felt I needed to make it plain that I will be leaving for Park Place as soon as a coach can be summoned. You are more than welcome to stay on here and enjoy the . . . entertainment,' her eyes, full of dark light, flashed to Stella for a moment, 'soiled and sullied as it is.'

'Listen to me, woman!' Oliver was completely ignoring Stella stretched out on the floor. 'This isn't what you think, I promise you.'

'Spare me.' Josie's voice was sharp and cutting. 'Your whore is known to be generous with her favours to more than one gentleman on occasions like this.'

She turned, making for the door which was ajar, and it was then that Oliver made the mistake of launching himself forward to grab her arm. Josie reacted by instinct with a lightning move of her body as she avoided his hands, and Oliver stumbled and fell, his head coming into contact with the edge of the door with a resounding crack.

Stella was now shrieking like a banshee and not at all how one would expect a lady of the realm to react, but as Oliver rolled over and then began to sit up Josie did not wait to see if he was all right. She continued out of the room into the passageway beyond, where the occupants of the rooms either side of Stella's were emerging.

She was aware of startled faces staring at her but no one said a word. 'I think one of them or perhaps even both might require the services of a doctor,' she said evenly as Stella's screams diminished. 'Perhaps someone would be good enough to deal with that? Good morning.'

Josie made it to the end of the landing and beyond

without pausing, but then the shaking in her legs reached such proportions that she had to lean against the wall before she could trust herself to walk down the stairs. She felt as if all the strength was draining out of her but knew she had to make her way back to her room before this happened.

Oh Gertie, Gertie, Gertie. Josie had never needed the support of her sister so much or felt so alone. The enormous staircase and grand sweeping spaciousness of the house enhanced the feeling that she was tiny, nothing; that she was dwindling down to a mere speck. She moved swiftly through the house, the full enormity of what had happened only now really beginning to dawn on her. Oliver and Stella. Oliver and *Stella*.

The reverberations of this scandal would go on for some time; this was one liaison of Stella's to which Godfrey Stratton wouldn't be able to turn a blind eye. The thought brought no comfort. Her mind seemed numb to emotion now, the coldness of shock having taken over.

When she reached her room Josie locked the door behind her, before walking through to the adjoining dressing room and taking her portmanteau and other bags from where the maid had placed them after she'd put their clothes away. She packed her things quickly after stripping off the evening dress she was wearing and extracting a pretty day dress in light blue muslin. Once she had washed in the china bowl, shivering a little as the water from the jug felt icy cold, she dressed in the clean clothes and then spent some time doing her hair. The face staring back at her from the mirror was chalk-white, and for a moment she felt sorry for the woman in front of her as though she was looking at someone else. That frightened her. Was she going mad? No, no, of course she wasn't, she told herself in the next instant, and she wasn't going to try to break this cold detachment which had taken hold of her either. Not now, not yet. She still had to leave this house and she intended to walk out with her head held high and with dignity.

Her toilette finished, she sat down on the chaise-longue, her bags at her feet, folded her hands and assumed a straight-backed pose, not allowing herself to slump in the slightest. Once the maid brought the morning tea she would request a carriage be put at her disposal and she would leave.

However, at eight o'clock she was brought to her feet by a knock at the door and the voice of her hostess saying, 'Mrs Hogarth? This is Elizabeth Conway. May I speak with you, please?'

Josie's legs were trembling as she walked across to the door, but her face was pale and composed when she opened it to find Lady Conway, flanked either side by Victoria and Winifred. The three women were fully dressed and coiffured which gave Josie an inkling of the frantic activity which had been going on in some quarters. 'Please come in.' She stood aside for the ladies to pass her and then shut the door behind them, taking a deep silent breath before she turned round.

'Josie, I'm so sorry.' This was from Winifred as the twins reached out and grasped her hands in theirs.

'That woman is an absolute menace,' Victoria added darkly, 'but she certainly got her just deserts this time. I hope I would have had the courage to react exactly as you did in a similar situation.'

Josie had expected censure, and for a moment she had to bite hard on her inner lip to retain her composure in the face of their understanding.

Lady Conway had glanced at the bags at the foot of the chaise-longue, and now she said, her voice soft, 'Godfrey and his wife left at seven o'clock this morning and I understand they will be going abroad for a few weeks. Your husband has talked to Steven and myself and he has offered an explanation for what occurred. Would you come to our private sitting room and hear what he has to say?'

Josie looked at the gentle-faced woman in front of her. She had found her inoffensive on the one or two occasions she had talked with her, and certainly she and Steven seemed to be one of the few married couples who enjoyed each other's company, but there was no way she could comply with her hostess's request. 'I'm sorry, Lady Conway, but that is not possible. I would be obliged if one of your coachmen would take me back to town as soon as it is convenient?'

Lady Conway was vexed. She had to admit that Oliver, dear boy that he was, had been somewhat indiscreet in view of the fact he was sharing a room with his wife. Nevertheless, it would be such a shame if the girl allowed a strumpet like Stella Stratton to come between her and her husband. Added to which, and this latter consideration Elizabeth Conway acknowledged was a far less noble one – the tittle-tattle over this matter was going to be scurrilous enough as it was; it would help water it down a little if two of the chief individuals in the unfortunate affair were seen to be reconciled.

'My dear, the doctor has advised Oliver to lie quietly for some time – he has a touch of concussion and needed a few stitches in a wound to his forehead – but I know he is anxious to put his case before you without delay.'

'He has no case, Lady Conway.' Josie was now ramrod straight. There had been a touch of reproach in the other woman's voice when she had spoken of Oliver's injuries, as though Josie herself had caused them, but in Josie's mind Oliver had brought this on himself.

And it appeared Victoria was of the same mind as she

now said, a gurgle in her voice which she couldn't quite disguise, 'Let us hope a few more men of our acquaintance take note of what occurred here this weekend, and a few women too. I understand those people adjoining Stella's room will never view her in quite the same light again after the sight which met their eyes this morning!'

'Victoria, dear, that is not particularly helpful.' Lady Conway was very much aware that Steven could have done without the notoriety of this event happening under their roof, considering his standing in the world of politics. There was enough trouble at present with these wretched trade union people always asking for something more and showing scant respect for their betters, and Steven had been so upset when dear Wyndham had resigned as Chief Secretary for Ireland over the problems of creating a coherent Irish policy. What were the Irish, after all, but a country of cut-throats and peasants? Steven maintained their intelligence was like that of the miners here and the rest of the working class. Give them any sort of power and Britain would go to the dogs. It was disgraceful, really disgraceful, the way things were going, and although Victoria and Winifred were dear girls and their mother – her sister-in-law – one of the finest women to grace the English court, she did so wish they would drop all this silly nonsense concerning women having the vote. What on earth did women know about such things as politics?

Lady Conway now turned to Josie, her voice reverting to softness as she said, 'Won't you at least listen to what your husband has to say, my dear? He really does have mitigating circumstances and all is not as it seems.' Not that she believed Oliver's explanation, not a word of it, but this young thing might if Oliver put it in the right way. And after all, everyone knew that any man worth his salt had a mistress. It really wasn't the done thing to cause such a fuss as this girl had done, but of course background would always out. It had been a mistake for Oliver to take a wife without the adequate breeding, as the dear boy now knew to his cost.

'I'm sorry, Lady Conway, but I must leave at once.' Josie could sense her hostess's concern was only skin deep and she guessed the real reasons which had brought Lady Conway to her room in defence of Oliver. And in spite of her misery it was an overwhelming relief that from this day she would be finished with such hypocrisy. 'I have no wish to cause you further embarrassment, so perhaps it would be best if I left now, before breakfast?'

It was her final word, and all three women recognised it as such.

Chapter Twenty-one

By the time the Conways' carriage drew up outside the house in Park Place the hard knot in Josie's chest was melting, and it was all she could do to smile and thank the two coachmen once they had placed her luggage inside the hall. Josie spoke to her sister in the drawing room, managing to give Gertie an outline of what had transpired before she burst into tears.

She cried for a good while, not least because of the futility of it all. Whatever else, she had believed Oliver loved her, and for him to humiliate her in such a public fashion . . . because people would have known. There wasn't a happening that went on at these weekends that wasn't noticed and talked about. Oliver himself was one of the worst gossips, and he had often expressed his amazement that some folk were naive enough to imagine that their every indiscretion wasn't observed and commented on. And for him to then go and . . . And with Stella Stratton.

The release of all her pent-up emotion did her good, and when she raised her head from where it had been resting on Gertie's shoulder – her sister's arms tight round her – she said quite normally, 'Would you go and inform Mrs Wilde what has occurred and tell her I leave it to her discretion how much she tells Constance and Ethel? And then ask her to get them to pack all my things, yours too if you want to come with me. I am going to Lily's. I can't remain another day in this house.'

Gertie gazed at her without speaking for a moment or two, and then her voice was a mutter when she said, 'Do you think that's wise? To leave before you've talked to him properly?'

Although she had half expected this it still hurt. But then Gertie had always been for Oliver, Josie reminded herself, even before there had been the added inducement of her husband being Anthony's employer. How many times had she thought that if Gertie had been born with the voice and looks to attract Oliver, Gertie would have made him a far better wife than herself. Her sister would have looked at this incident practically, working out the pros and cons of confronting Oliver before she had said anything at all, and then only revealing she was aware of his liaison with another woman if she could use it to her advantage. Money and respectability, and the security they brought with them, meant a great deal to Gertie, which was one reason her sister and Anthony suited each other so well. And such thinking wasn't necessarily wrong, not in essence, and after their traumatic childhood Josie could appreciate the reasons for Gertie thinking like she did more than most, but today it still hurt.

'Like I said, you don't have to come with me,' Josie repeated quietly.

'Don't be silly, of course I'm coming with you.'

'Then could you go and talk to Mrs Wilde quickly because I have no desire to be here when Oliver comes.'

'Do you think he'll come after you?'

'I don't know. Yes, yes I think he will, but Lady Conway said—'

'What?' Gertie paused on her way to the door.

'The doctor diagnosed concussion and told him he had to rest.'

'Oh, Josie.'

Gertie left the room without saying any more, and it came to Josie that although Lady Conway and her sister were worlds apart in every way, their voices could have been identical in tone when expressing their opinion on the matter of her husband's injuries.

Not so Lily. When the hired carriage deposited Josie and Gertie and two trunks of their immediate belongings on the doorstep of the house at the back of the Caledonian Market, Lily was 100 per cent solid in her support.

Josie talked to her old friend in the very comfortable privacy of Lily's sitting room after the housekeeper had brought them through a tray of tea, and initially Lily just stared at her, open-mouthed and lost for words for once. And then she said, 'And he went arse over head and nearly brained himself? By, lass, I'd give me eye-teeth to have been there. The times I've wanted to see some blighter who'd been messing me about get his just deserts, but I never did. No, I never did. No guts to confront 'em, you see. All mouth and hair as me old mam used to say.'

'Not you, Lily.'

'Oh aye, me all right. There's them that say an' them that do, and you're a doer sure enough. So, what *are* you going to do?'

'Divorce him.'

'*Divorce him?*' It was Gertie who spoke although Lily's mouth had dropped open even further. 'He won't let you, not Oliver. Oh Josie, you can't, you can't. Just think of the repercussions for a minute. He's your manager as well as your husband and he's so influential, you know he is. Lily, talk some sense into her.' Gertie flung her hands wide in an unconsciously dramatic appeal to the other woman. 'Tell her she'll be cutting her own throat career-wise. She *needs* Oliver.'

'I think Oliver needs Josie a darn sight more than she needs him if you want my honest opinion,' Lily said quietly, ignoring the look on Gertie's face which told her Gertie did not want her honest opinion. 'And I don't mean just in a business sense either,' she continued, turning to Josie. 'He loves you, lass, everyone knows that. Oh, I agree he's not what you'd call ideal husband material but he was never going to be. That's Oliver. And I have to say he's arrogant and self-opinionated to a fault, and this latest means he probably thought he could have his cake and eat it, but with all that – he does love you.'

'Then love is not enough, not that kind of love anyway.'

'That's for you to decide, lass, one way or the other.'

'I have decided.' Josie's head, which had been bowed, raised itself and Lily saw the lovely brown eyes were dry and burning with dark emotion. 'I could forgive his gambling and drinking and all the other excesses, but not this. This is different.' And as Gertie went to speak Josie made a sharp movement with her hand as she said, 'I mean it, Gertie, and if you can't understand then you can't, but that's how I feel. This is different.'

'If it had been with anyone else but Stella Stratton, how would you have felt then?' Gertie asked flatly.

'Exactly the same.' And then Josie corrected herself, saying, 'Well, perhaps not exactly the same, but near enough to do what I am doing now.'

She stared defiantly at her sister, who nodded abruptly. 'Nothing more to be said then, is there?'

'No, Gertie, there isn't.'

* * *

Fortunately Josie only had another two weeks of her current contract left at the Empire; Oliver had been in the process of negotiating an extension for another six weeks but as yet, nothing had been signed. This meant she could leave London with impunity, and once Bernard understood she wasn't abandoning the Empire in favour of another London theatre – Drury Lane, the Gaiety and others were after her, as he knew full well – but was returning up north for a spell, he was more amenable to letting her have the Monday night off when Josie explained she had urgent personal business to attend to. He wanted to keep her sweet for when she returned to London anyway. She was a crowd puller, was Josie Burns, and unlike some of the performers he had to deal with she didn't have an odd day off here and there due to the amber liquid. So he agreed she would be 'sick' come Monday night, and Monday morning saw Josie on the train to Sunderland – alone.

Gertie did not offer to accompany her and Josie did not suggest it; in truth she was feeling more than slightly aggrieved at Gertie's attitude since she had returned from Berkshire, and for the first time in their lives a rift had opened between the sisters. Gertie had barely said two words since they had arrived at Lily's, and when her younger sister had gone with her to see Ada and Dora, and her two older sisters had mirrored Lily's reaction to the turn of events, Gertie had become even more sulky.

The newspapers were still full of the story of the tragic death of twenty-three people when one of the new electric trains in Liverpool crashed, and that, along with the Glamorgan pit disaster which took one hundred and twenty-four miners, and reports of a further outbreak of typhus in the East End of London made for depressing reading. Josie gave up the attempt after a while and slept most of the journey away, in between visiting the dining car for a very nice lunch which she only picked at. She was very tired; she and Gertie were sleeping on two shake-downs in Lily's sitting room after Josie had flatly refused to let anyone give up their beds for Gertie and herself, and these were not conducive to a good night's sleep. Not that she would have slept much anyway; her mind was constantly dissecting the scene with Oliver and Stella whether she was awake or asleep.

The train chugged into Sunderland Central Station on a blazing hot afternoon, and when Josie stepped on to the platform and looked up at the arched roof, particles of dust floating idly in the sunlight and the sound of warm northern voices all around her, she felt like a small lass again for a moment or two.

On leaving the station she checked into the Grand Hotel which was an imposing building of five storeys and ideally situated, being just a minute's walk from the railway station, and after depositing her small portmanteau in her room she left immediately for Northumberland Place. She found it strange that nothing had changed since she'd been gone. She'd married Oliver, travelled a little, risen almost to the top of her profession and entered a privileged life which held no resemblance to the one she'd known before her marriage, and yet everything here was just the same. The same old trams creaking and grinding along, the same horses and carts piled with everything from fruit and potatoes and fresh meat to sacks of coal, the same shop awnings and, inevitably, the same raggedy, barefoot urchins darting about, the latter increasing in numbers the nearer Josie got to Northumberland Place and the East End. Likewise the smell of ripe fish from the quays fronting Sunderland Harbour. But it was home, it was home. She breathed in deeply of the warm air, thick with the odour of industrial smoke and fumes from the factories and workshops, roperies, ironworks, shipyards, limekilns and other industries clustered along the Wear, which, flavoured by the smell of fish, smelt like no other place on earth to Josie.

What would all the folk scurrying about their daily business think if they knew she was actually relishing the smelly air? she asked herself with a touch of dark humour. But it didn't matter what people thought. It wouldn't have to, certainly in the immediate future. Folk would be scandalised when she divorced Oliver. She didn't know anyone, apart from the odd one or two in the profession, who had ever had a divorce. But then, when she thought about it, and she had been thinking about it a lot since Saturday morning, that was because women put up with their men doing exactly as they pleased most of the time. And that seemed to be the case whether the woman in question was a working-class lass in the north or a Lady something-or-other in London.

There'd been a piece in one of the London papers in May when the Suffrage Bill had failed, which had reported one of the MPs saying that 'men and women differed in mental equipment with women having little sense of proportion', and he'd gone on to say that giving women the vote would not be safe. And that summed up very aptly how most men saw things, Josie told herself darkly, as she turned off High Street East towards Northumberland Place. Well, her sense of proportion was working quite nicely, thank you very much, and from what she'd seen of life thus far, the mental equipment needed to juggle bringing up a family, paying the rent, putting food on the table and often working from home which was most women's lot, was far in excess of the average man's.

There were a group of barefoot bairns sitting on the dusty pavement playing 'Kitty Cat' when Josie turned into Northumberland Place, and she stood for a moment watching them hit the pointed piece of wood with numbers scratched on it. Dirty and poor as they looked, they all seemed relatively well fed, and certainly a couple of them keeping the scores knew their numbers. They were some of the lucky ones, Josie thought soberly as she walked on. She couldn't ever remember playing in the street when she was a bairn. Her da had seen to it that they were either out begging or working most of the time, and she'd had to fight him every inch of the way to get any schooling for herself and the others.

Monday being washing day, there were lines of dangling clothes and linen strung up in the back lanes and between lamp-posts in the side streets, and now the faint smell of bleach hung in the still air.

Josie took a long breath and then squared her shoulders before she knocked on the door in Northumberland Place. She knew the dropsy which had plagued Vera for years had meant her friend giving up work some months before, and she was hoping at this time of the day that Prudence would be at work. Barney's sister would have to know about the state of her marriage eventually, of course, but just at the moment she only wanted to share the news with Vera and Horace. Once she had spoken to Vera she intended to approach a couple of the theatres in the town with a view to appearing here when she'd left London. Maybe the Avenue first; it was currently Sunderland's most respected theatre and seated fifteen hundred people, and then perhaps the Palace or the Royal. She could do a couple of weeks at each, by which time she should be in a position to see the future a little more clearly.

Vera's squeal of delight on opening the door spread a little balm on Josie's sore heart, and as she was pulled into the kitchen amid a deluge of questions that had her laughing in the end, she thought again, Nothing has changed, nothing.

'Ee, lass, I can't believe it!' Vera beamed at her, shaking her head in wonderment. 'Here was I, thinkin' the only thing in front of me was the ironin', an' then you knock on me door. Talk about a sight for sore eyes. An' don't you look bonny an' all; the tongues'll be waggin' in this street an' no mistake. Everyone's tickled pink that a lass from these parts has made good in the halls. Come on, lass, get your things off an' have a sup.'

'Oh, Vera.' Josie took her friend's hands as she said, 'It's so good to be back.'

'Good to be back? You gone doolally, lass? With your lovely house an' the goin' on you've got?' This was said without a trace of resentment, Vera's face still split in a grin that went from ear to ear. 'Now sit yourself down an' take the weight off. I've got a nice bit of ham an' egg pie that's waitin' to get on the other side of somebody, an' a sly cake made not an hour since.'

Vera pushed her down on a kitchen chair before she turned to the range and busied herself with the kettle, and it was in that moment, as Josie looked down at her friend's grossly swollen legs and feet, that she thought, No, things are not the same. Vera was getting older and it showed.

The kettle settled on the fire, Vera turned round, pulling out a chair from under the table and sitting down heavily before she said, 'Well, if this isn't a treat. You up for a day or two, hinny? An' where's that man of yours, an' Gertie?'

Josie had been worried she would burst into tears as soon as she caught sight of this woman who meant more to her than her own mother ever had, but strangely, now she was here, she didn't feel like crying. In fact, if she had had to analyse her feelings, she would have admitted to exhausted relief being paramount. 'I've got something to tell you but it's just for your ears and Horace's at the moment, Vera. It's like this . . .'

Vera had always been a good listener and she didn't interrupt once, but as Josie finished her story the older woman breathed out noisily, before saying, 'The blasted fool. I've met some stupid so-an'-sos in my time but he takes the biscuit, he does straight. An' I thought more of him, lass, I did really, him bein' a gentleman an' all.'

'Oh Vera, I could tell you stories about the so-called ladies and gentlemen of our country that would make your hair curl.'

'That'd be a first, lass. Me mam used to corkscrew me hair so tight I'd be cryin' half the night with me hair bein' pulled out by the roots, but come mornin' it'd be as flat as a pancake. That's the only memory I've got of me poor mam, her tryin' to scalp me alive.'

Josie hadn't expected to laugh that day, although Vera being Vera she should have, she reflected wryly, and it did her the world of good.

'But jokin' apart, hinny, I'm heart sorry,' Vera said when they were sober again. 'He might have bin a toff but I liked him for all that.'

'So did I, Vera.' Josie hesitated for a moment before she said, 'And there's something else, something I think is wonderful but which . . . Well, I don't know how you'll feel about it. I've found Ada and Dora.'

'Found . . .' For once Vera was rendered speechless.

'Only this last week, just before the weekend, as it happens. And I suppose I didn't so much find them as they found me.' She related what had happened, and when she had finished Vera lay back in the chair and just stared at her for a full ten seconds without saying a word.

* * *

By the time Josie left the house in Northumberland Place an hour later, she was in possession of a few facts which had surprised her nearly as much as she had surprised Vera; the main cause of her disconcertment being that Barney was working and living in Sunderland. Josie didn't know how she felt about this development. Her life was complicated and awkward enough as it was, and whatever reason Barney had for leaving the theatre in London so abruptly, and whether he had a lady friend or not, it was going to make her living up here for a spell a hundred times more difficult. It shouldn't, but it would. Just Barney being around in the town, where she might bump into him at any time, would have been bad enough, but now he was the manager of a Sunderland theatre . . .

Another surprise had been the announcement by Vera that Prudence had a man friend. 'He isn't exactly the answer to every young maiden's prayer,' Vera had said with something of a grin, 'an' he's as broad as he's tall with a belly on him that'd do credit to any of the beer-swilling dockers down on the quays, but Georgie's nice enough in his way, bless him, an' he certainly keeps Prudence in line. The lass has been a different girl since she's been courtin' him an' he seems to think a bit of her. Known him for donkey's years, I have – his mam an' da worked at the corn mill afore he did an' were decent enough folk. He might be big an' lumberin' but he's a gentle giant, you know? I think he felt sorry for Prudence to start with, what with her looks an' her hands bein' bad an' all, but the pair of 'em are fair gone on each other now. An' he's a bright feller although he don't look it.'

Josie had answered quietly, 'I'm glad for her, Vera.' And she was, she reflected now as she hurried towards the Palace Theatre in High Street West; the Avenue in Gillbridge Avenue now being out of bounds with Barney being the manager there. She was really glad that Prudence had found someone to love and was loved in return, but she just couldn't imagine the dour-faced girl she had known turning to sweetness and light.

'Barney reckons Georgie's all right, which is all to the good,' Vera had told her. 'The three of 'em get goin' on somethin' like politics or the unions an' it's like a debatin' society in here, I tell you straight. Me an' Horace sit here an' we don't know if we're on foot or horseback half the time. Aye, Barney likes him.'

Oh Barney, Barney. Josie stopped on the pavement outside the Palace, the big building with its three arches a good floor or two higher than the shops adjoining either side of it. But she should be thinking of Oliver right now, shouldn't she? And she was really, he was always there in the back of her mind, and the hard ache in the middle of her chest which had first made itself known in the aftermath of seeing him sitting on Stella's chaise-longue two days ago was still grinding her innards.

She cut off the train of thought with ruthless determination. She knew from the last couple of days that it brought pictures into her mind, images of them together which made her want to curl into a little ball and hide away from the rest of the world. And she wouldn't give Stella Stratton the satisfaction. But she missed him. Weak and impossible as he'd been, she missed him. She'd thought he loved her, and she hadn't been able to help loving him back.

Enough. Her chin rose in answer to the command inside. She was going to arrange a venue, two if possible, here in Sunderland and she was going to do it all by herself without help from anyone. She had started on her own and she would continue on her own, and this time she had the feeling that even Gertie wouldn't be with her . . .

The manager at the Palace almost bit her hand off, so

quickly did he accept her offer to perform there for two weeks, and when she made a visit to the Royal Theatre in Bedford Street an hour later it was the same. Two weeks at the Palace followed by two weeks at the Royal. She nodded to herself as she stepped out of the building some time later. She would let it be known she was staying at the Grand, and then if Hubert did want to come and see her he could do so.

She didn't know if this was sensible or not, but the desire to make contact with her brothers which had swept over her that day in Ada's house was stronger than ever after everything that had happened this weekend with Oliver. Her sisters and the lads, they were *family*. Her family. And she had thanked God more than once for the tradition within the halls which discouraged a female artiste from changing her stage-name once she was married. In the early days a couple of theatre managers had tried to persuade her to select a more flamboyant surname than Burns but she hadn't felt comfortable with that, and now she was glad she had followed her instinct.

Vera had insisted Josie join them at Northumberland Place for their evening meal. This would mean meeting Prudence again, and although Josie had concurred, she wasn't looking forward to seeing Barney's sister.

She cut through the back lanes on her way home to Vera's, the narrow roads baked hard with ridges of mud and thick with bairns playing their games, and housewives gossiping over the small brick walls of their back yards before their men arrived home and demanded they be waited upon. Through one open gate she saw a young mother sitting on her back step nursing a baby at her breast while a toddler banged on an old tin lid with a wooden spoon at her feet, and the sight caused the familiar yearning to jerk inside her. This feeling had caused her to press Oliver in recent months as to when, exactly, they would start their family, but he had always come back with his stock reply of, 'When you are established enough to safely be able to take some time away from the halls.'

Well, he needn't worry about that now, need he, Josie thought bitterly as she turned into a small passageway in between some shops which linked one street to another. Oliver had never admitted it but Josie felt he was reluctant to have children interfering with his life, and that her career was just a convenient excuse to delay things. They had discussed buying a small house in preparation for starting a family too, and again he had found myriad reasons why this was not possible at any one time, without acknowledging that the main cause – that he would have to severely curtail his gambling – was the real reason for prevarication.

Emerging into the hot, busy street Josie wrinkled her nose as she passed the open doorway of a decorative plasterer's shop. It smelt like a glue factory, the heat causing the gelatine in the back of the shop to stink to high heaven. She paused outside the butcher's a few doors on. The butcher's boy was using the sausage-maker which resembled a little steam engine, and as she watched him winding the handle and the gears revolving the big wheel which pushed the meat through the nozzle, she remembered sausages were Horace's favourite treat. She bought two pounds, along with a nice bit of salted bacon, a bag of pork scratchings and a hefty piece of best beef, and then moved on to the grocer's and lastly the sweetshop.

Weighed down with her purchases she didn't notice the figure just behind her as she turned into Northumberland Place, so when a hand touched her on the shoulder she nearly jumped out of her skin. 'Oh! Oh, Prudence.' In her fright, she had nearly dropped the big parcel of meat which the butcher had tied up with string for her and now, as she adjusted her packages, she was surprised yet again when Prudence said pleasantly, 'Can I help? Let me take that for you. I thought it was you but I wasn't sure until you turned round.'

Josie's hands passed the parcel of meat to Prudence, but she was looking at the other girl's face. Prudence looked so different! And yet she was still the same physically, although . . . her hair was clean and shining, and her eyes had a different expression in them, a brightness which seemed to nullify their muddy shade and bring out the green . . . Josie became aware she was staring and said quickly, 'Thank you. I'm only up for the day but Vera has invited me to dinner and so I thought I'd get a few things by way of thanks.'

Prudence nodded. 'She'll tell you off, of course.'

'Of course.' They smiled at each other and again Josie was struck by the almost tangible happiness radiating from Barney's sister.

'I'm glad I've seen you. By yourself, that is.' Prudence swallowed before she continued, 'You've done very well for yourself and . . . and I'm glad. I mean that.'

'Thank you.' Josie didn't know what else to say.

'I wasn't very nice to you, was I?' Prudence's sallow skin had flushed with embarrassment and Josie's cheeks were also turning pink. 'In fact, I wasn't very nice to anyone in those days.'

'Look, it's all water under the bridge.'

'No, no, let me say it, Josie. I've thought about writing to you to apologise but . . .' Prudence shook her head helplessly. 'Well, I didn't. But I'm sorry for how I was.'

'You were unhappy,' Josie said gently, the other girl's humility so out of character that she felt as though she was talking to someone else.

'Aye, I was.' Prudence stretched her neck and moved

her chin from side to side before she said, 'And you were so pretty, and me da thought the sun shone out of your backside from the minute you walked through the door, Barney an' all. Pearl knew that, you know, deep in the heart of her. She knew she should never have married him once you showed up. She knew how he felt about you long before he did.'

Josie was utterly at a loss as to what to say. She wondered if Prudence was accusing her of anything, but then the other girl disabused her of that notion when she went on, 'But it weren't your fault, I know that now. Georgie – oh, he's my young man,' here Prudence's cheeks got still pinker, 'he calls a spade a spade, does Georgie, and we've talked a lot about the past. It's made me see things different.' Prudence didn't say here that all the talking had led Georgie to say that unless Prudence got herself sorted out he couldn't see a future for them. She had been hurt then, and it had been a while before she could accept that maybe Georgie had a point. He'd gone mad when she'd said to him that he was on Josie's side like everyone else, and then she'd cried and the upshot of it all had been he had taken her in his arms for the first time and kissed her . . .

'I'm glad.'

'Aye, well, I just wanted you to know.'

As they began to walk on, side by side now, Josie said, 'I'm going to do a few weeks at the Palace and the Royal soon and it would be grand to think I could call on Vera and you wouldn't mind me coming?'

'No, I wouldn't mind.' This wasn't quite true but to Prudence's credit it didn't show in her voice. She knew she would never be able to find it within herself to actually like Josie, and she didn't fancy the idea of her old enemy being around for however short a time it might be, but now she had a different life – now she had *Georgie* – she could stomach what had to be stomached. But it wasn't only Josie's presence for its own sake she didn't like the idea of; it was him, that man, Patrick Duffy. Her coming here might be dangerous.

Should she come clean and tell Josie about her conversations with the little Irishman? Looking back now she couldn't imagine why she had let Duffy talk to her in the first place. It was the one thing she hadn't confided to Georgie, but now Josie had come back perhaps she ought to warn her. Georgie would be disgusted if anything happened and it came out she'd known Duffy had it in for this woman.

She had only talked to Duffy twice more since that first time, and only then because he had appeared from seemingly nowhere when she'd been shopping and it had been difficult to get rid of him without being rude. And there was something about him, something unnerving, which had stopped her taking that tack. The man frightened her. She'd had the skitters for days afterwards each time she'd seen him.

He had always been careful not to come right out with it and say he wanted to harm Josie. He'd always referred to her as 'our mutual friend' but the tone of his voice had been enough to let Prudence know what he really meant. 'Wanting to renew the little lady's acquaintance.' 'Wanting to show the little lady in what high regard I hold her.' 'Wanting the little lady to meet some old friends of mine who have a lot to thank her for.' That had been the way Patrick Duffy had talked. And he'd only inferred what he'd inferred because he knew about her part in the attack on Josie in Newcastle.

As Prudence followed Josie into Vera's house her stomach lurched sickeningly. He had thought she would help him, and somehow that made her feel unclean, that a man like Duffy thought she would be his accomplice. When she had gone to Josie's father all those years ago she hadn't realised the type of man he really was; she hadn't believed Josie, that was the thing. But meeting Duffy, hearing him talk, she believed it all right. Oh aye, she did. And after the last time of seeing Duffy, twelve months back and more, she'd made sure she only went shopping when Vera was with her, and she'd come straight home at nights with no dilly-dallying. And then Georgie had spoken to her at work one day and asked her to go to the Olympia with him one night, and from that point on everything had changed. Or perhaps it was her that had changed.

The thing was, Georgie cared about people – really cared – and he was hot on the trade unions and social reform and everything like that, but in a *doing* way. He'd made her recall the times she and Barney had spouted on about such things to their da but with only head knowledge, not heart. At least on her side anyway.

The more she'd seen of Georgie the more she had realised the madness of what she had done all those years ago. Georgie had opened her eyes to all sorts of goings-on that happened when folk didn't have two farthings to rub together. She had helped him in the soup kitchen which had been set up at Christmas for the down and outs, and there had been little bairns come in who had been in a terrible state. She had always considered herself working class and poor with it, her da being a miner and all, but she'd learned a thing or two since she'd been courting Georgie.

She couldn't remember a Christmas as a bairn when the stockings she and the lads had hung up hadn't been full of nuts and dolly mixtures and brand new pennies, just minted, along with a toy car or a little fort for the lads and a sweetshop or shilling doll for her. But these bairns didn't know what a toy was. Starving, filthy, cold and lice-ridden, most of them had looked like little old men and women. Oh aye, she'd learned a thing or two since she had been seeing Georgie, and all that had been related about Josie's beginnings had come back to her, but this time she'd believed it.

She hadn't been able to bring herself to admit to Georgie that she'd spoken to Patrick Duffy though. Deep inside she'd been scared that Georgie might begin to look at her with different eyes, especially after everything else she'd confessed. He still might, if she let on. Georgie thought she was a decent woman and she was, she *was* a decent woman. At heart she was.

'You all right, lass?' As Vera touched Prudence on the arm, the younger woman realised she had been staring vacantly at them all. She brought the smile back to her face, nodding brightly as she said, 'Aye, I'm grand, Vera. Here, Josie's been buying up the shop I reckon,' as she handed Vera the parcel of meat.

Vera smiled back at her, obviously relieved and pleased at the lack of animosity in the air, and Prudence thought, I can't, I just can't tell them. It'll spoil everything. And there's no need, not really. Josie'll be come and gone again in a few weeks, back to her fine house and rich husband. If I say anything and I lose Georgie, what'll I have left? Nowt, that's what. And I can't lose him, I can't. Patrick Duffy's got other fish to fry now and it must be nigh on twelve months since I've seen hide or hair of him. No, least said, soonest mended.

It'd be all right. 'Course it would . . .

Chapter Twenty-two

Josie walked into the house at the back of the Caledonian Market at just after three in the afternoon the next day, and half an hour later Oliver was knocking on the door and demanding to see her.

'It's all right, Agnes.' Josie had stepped out of Lily's sitting room into the hall when she had heard Oliver remonstrating with the housekeeper who had refused him entrance. 'I'll talk to Mr Hogarth in here.'

Lily and Gertie left the room hastily at this point, and as Oliver paused in the hall to let them pass Josie saw Gertie smile at him. It was a small thing but suddenly Josie felt very angry and it steadied her racing heart and churning stomach. 'Won't you come this way?' She could have been talking to a stranger, her words cool and polite, and she saw his eyes flicker at her tone before she turned and walked back into the sitting room. Agnes cleared away their makeshift beds first thing each morning and when the alterations to the three houses had been planned, Josie had made sure Lily's sitting room was a very comfortable one and had furnished it at no small cost.

She walked across to the large ornate fireplace which had no fire in it today before she faced him again, and she saw him glancing round the room with an expression of surprise on his face. 'This is very nice.'

'Yes, it is,' she said stiffly.

'I . . . I would have come before but I was not able to leave the Conways' until early this morning on doctor's advice.' She did not reply to this, and he went on, 'Josie, you have to believe this is not as it seems.'

'Do I?'

'Yes you do, you do. I wouldn't . . . I can understand how it appeared and why you put the worst possible construction on what you saw, but there is an explanation.'

'I have no doubt about that, Oliver. You spent the night with your mistress.'

'That is not what I meant and you know it.'

'I *know* that that woman has always hated me because in her eyes I took you away from her. She's been insolent and unfriendly from the first time I met her and you have always found excuses for her. I thought it was because you felt sorry for her and perhaps just a little guilty, and I was foolish enough to think it didn't matter; that she was just a rather unpleasant and perhaps even pitiable individual. I know better now. She dared to be the way she was because you were still sharing her bed.'

Oliver gazed at her in amazement. 'Are you mad, woman?' he said loudly. 'When on earth was I ever away from you long enough to conduct an affair with anyone?'

'Most evenings,' she shot back bitterly.

'You know where I was then. Damn it all, haven't we had more altercations about my gambling than the grains of sand on the seashore?'

'It is not exactly beyond the bounds of possibility that you could manage to fit both pastimes into an evening,' she said with heavy sarcasm.

'*For crying out loud!*'

'And don't shout, not unless you wish me to terminate this conversation right now.'

'Josie, I swear to you on everything I hold sacred, I have not been conducting an affair with her! Damn it all, woman, I haven't had the time or the money or the inclination.'

Somehow she believed him suddenly about that, but it didn't make any difference to what had happened at the weekend. And she said as much. 'Be that as it may, you were in her bed this weekend and that is once too much for me. I want a divorce, Oliver.'

He was nearly as stunned as he had been when he'd hit his head on the side of the open door and it showed. He stared at her blankly and then said, 'You can't be serious.'

'Oh I am, Oliver. I am completely serious.'

It took him a split second to reach her and she had no time to evade his touch as he gripped her forearms in his hands. This close, her senses immediately registered the familiar pleasant smell which emanated from his skin and the overall bigness of him, but she made no reaction whatsoever, not even to struggle. Instead, in a small hard cold voice, she said, 'Let go of me, please.'

'Not till you listen to me, damn it. I love you. I've always loved you. The night in question I had too much to drink, I admit it. There were a group of us playing cards and some of the ladies had stayed on, just one or two.'

'Of which your whore was one.'

She heard his teeth grind before he said, 'The next thing I know, you are pounding on the door and I've got a head like a drum. But I had been lying on the chaise-longue, not the bed; my back was nearly breaking because of it. I told Steven this and he made some enquiries, and Jefferson came clean.'

Jefferson. She might have known he had something to do with this. He was a crony of Stella's and she had always disliked the tall, foppish young man who giggled behind his hand like a woman.

'Apparently it was a joke; Jefferson thought it was a joke, anyway. Most everyone had gone up to bed apart from Jefferson and one of his friends and Stella, and I'd passed out some time before in one of the easy chairs. It was suggested they carry me up to Stella's room.'

'As Jefferson hasn't got the imagination of a gnat, may I surmise the suggestion came from the female of the species? If indeed what you are telling me is the truth?'

'It is, I swear it. They carried me up' – here Oliver's voice hardened and Josie could imagine his reaction to being unknowingly handled – 'but when they got me to Stella's room and tried undressing me I came round enough to lash out at all and sundry, and so they gave it up as a bad job and left me on the chaise-longue.'

'And is that it? You expect me to believe that story?'

'Yes, I damn well do because it's what happened.' He shook her slightly. 'And don't forget the reason for my intoxication was down to you, you and your notion of separate bank accounts and the like. You would make me a laughing stock.'

'I think you have managed to do that very nicely yourself,' Josie said icily, 'and don't manhandle me, Oliver.'

'Manhandle you? You're my *wife*.'

'It's a pity you didn't remember that on Friday night.'

When she found herself almost flung down on to the sofa at the side of them she realised Oliver was at the end of his tether, even before he hung over her and ground out, 'I have told you the truth, damn it all! Why the hell would I make up a story like that – and more to the point, why would I let Jefferson spread it round, like he undoubtedly will, if it isn't the truth? There would have been some credit to being found in the bed of a beauty like Stella Stratton, but to be in one's cups and spend the night on the chaise-longue at the foot of the bed! I'll never live it down. And you, behaving like a madwoman and raising the whole house!'

'I did not behave like a madwoman,' Josie protested through lips she was desperately trying to stop trembling. 'Merely a wife who finds her husband in the bed of another woman.'

'And when I fought Jefferson and the others to stop them putting me in Stella's bed, that was because even in my drunken state I must have known she wasn't you,' Oliver said, more softly now. 'Don't you see? Jefferson said when she tried to calm me down and put her arms round me I almost sent her across the other side of the room. That was the point I was deposited on the sofa. Josie, I know our marriage is not all it should be, and I can't in all honesty say I'll ever be what the world would call a good husband, but I can say I am yours. Perhaps it was naive of me to continue a friendship of sorts with Stella, but as you so rightly sensed, I felt guilty. I make stupid decisions like that, I gamble too much and I drink too much, and I am far more suited to a selfish bachelor existence than that of a married man, but I have never betrayed you and I will never betray you.'

She stared at him. She believed him; she believed him and she loved him in a fashion, so why did she suddenly feel as if the weight of the world had been placed on her shoulders? She should be happy, shouldn't she? Happy she hadn't got to go through the horror of a divorce and the ostracism which would result from all quarters except in her chosen profession; happy he hadn't shared Stella's bed again; happy life could go on as before?

'I'm going to cut right down on the gambling, you'll see. And we can think about buying that little property and having a child. You'd like that, wouldn't you?'

He had slipped down on to the sofa beside her and now he was holding her so tightly it hurt.

'Anything you want, my angel. Anything,' he murmured as he kissed the top of her head before moving to her brow and then her lips. 'But you can't leave me. I wouldn't want to live without you. Make your own conditions but end this nonsense.'

It was some moments before she stirred, and then she said against his mouth, 'Oliver? I have something to tell you, about my sisters. The ones who ran away.' Anything, he had said. 'And about where I went today . . .'

Chapter Twenty-three

'So you're telling me she was up here herself, and you told her I managed the Avenue and she still went to the Palace and the Royal? That's what you're saying?'

'Don't take it like that, lad.'

'How else do you expect me to take it, Vera, eh? How else? What am I supposed to have done that I don't merit a "hello" or "how are you?", let alone the chance to book her for a couple of weeks? She comes straight to see you; she even spends most of the evening here with Prudence – no offence, Pru,' his sister, who was sitting at the kitchen table eating her dinner, nodded stolidly but said nothing, 'and then she's off without so much as a by your leave. She must know that a big London name gives the numbers a boost, and the fact that she's a born-and-bred Sunderland lass will bring 'em in in their droves.'

'Aye, well mebbe she didn't think of that.'

'Well, she should have.' Barney glared round the table before taking a swallow of the tea Vera had handed him some minutes before. He always had Sunday dinner with Betty and her bairns but this week, the Sunday after the Monday Josie had been to Sunderland, he had only been in his stepmother's house for a few mintues before Betty had imparted the news of Josie's flying visit. The upshot of her announcement had been Barney picking up his cap and marching straight over to Vera's. 'Aye, she should have,' he repeated when no one said anything. 'She's been in the business long enough now to know how things work. Her appearing at the Palace and the Royal'll take away business from the Avenue.'

'Perhaps she wasn't thinking about the Avenue's numbers at the box office.' Prudence went on eating steadily after making this enigmatic statement, seemingly oblivious to her brother's furious countenance.

'What does that mean?' Barney banged the pint mug of tea down on the table with enough force to cause it to slop over the side.

Prudence raised her eyes, regarding him steadily for a few moments before she said, 'She's a married woman, Barney.'

'So?' His voice was harsh and grating. 'Half the music-hall performers are married, mostly to the other half.'

'You know what I mean.'

'And if I say I don't?' But he pushed his chair back from the table, the sound rasping on the stone flags, and stood abruptly to his feet, his jaw pugnacious. 'Where was her husband when she was gallivanting about the country then? Why wasn't he with her?'

Vera shrugged. 'I didn't think it was my business to ask.'

'Look, lad, come and sit down and have a bite. There's plenty. Vera always cooks for the five thousand.' Horace was aiming to pour oil on troubled waters, but Barney shook his head, continuing to stand and glare until he said, 'When is she starting up here?'

'A week tomorrow as I understand it,' Vera said quietly.

'Huh.'

What this was meant to express, none of the three sitting at the table asked until Prudence, in true sister fashion and being unable to stand any more, said sharply, 'For goodness' sake stop acting like a whingeing bairn, Barney,' pushing her plate to the side of her. 'Where Josie works is her own business, surely.'

'I never said it wasn't.'

'It didn't sound like that from where I'm standing.'

'Then you're standing in the wrong place. Anyway, I've got to get back to Betty's, she'll be dishing up shortly.'

'Goodbye then.'

Again Prudence made it quite clear what she thought of Barney bursting in on them all, and after a look directed at his sister which spoke volumes all by itself, Barney said tightly, 'Aye, so long, I'll see myself out,' to Vera and Horace.

It wasn't until he was in the street again that the consuming rage which had gripped him on hearing of Josie's visit suddenly drained away. He stood for a moment in the hot sunshine, blinking owl fashion as though he had come out of darkness into bright light. He'd made the mother and father of a fool of himself in there, and in front of Prudence too. Oh, she might have mellowed in the last few years, especially since she'd met Georgie, but there was still enough of the old Prudence left to guarantee she wouldn't let him forget this day, by means of the odd sisterly barbed taunt.

A small group of snotty-nosed bairns were skipping at the top end of the street, and the words of their song met him as he passed them. 'When I was going to Strawberry Fair, singing, singing buttercups and daisies, I met a lady taking the air, tra-la-la. Her eyes were blue and golden her hair, and she was going to Strawberry Fair, singing, singing buttercups and daisies . . .'

One little mite, more enterprising or hungry than the rest looked up at him, her huge brown eyes with their thick lashes entreating as she said, 'Spare a penny, mister?'

He had looked at the children without really seeing them, but now, as his gaze focused on the child he saw that in spite of her hair running with lice and the filth and dirt which seemed caked on her small thin body, the face looking up at him was strikingly lovely. Josie had lived round these streets and begged round them like this little 'un. His eyes moved over the rest of the big-eyed faces, two of the little lassies having legs bowed with the rickets, and his voice was gruff when he said, 'I've no pennies but you can all come with me to the pie shop on the next corner if you want. If you're not full after your Sunday dinner, that is.'

'I'm not full.' This was from the small girl who had first spoken to him, and now there was a chorus of, 'I'm not full!' 'I'm not full, mister.' 'Nor me.'

Some Salvation Army officers were standing outside a pub opposite the pie shop, and after he'd purchased pies for each of the children and sent them on their way, one of the men spoke to him, saying, 'Suffer the little children, brother. Suffer the little children. The Good Book says what you do for the least of them will be done unto you. You'll get your reward sure enough.'

Barney nodded and walked on, his cheeks fiery now. There was only one thing he wanted but if he'd told that good soul back there what it was, amid the man's colleagues openly proclaiming their allegiance to a holy God, he doubted it would go down very well.

He didn't return to Betty's, knowing his stepmother wouldn't expect him back, the state he had been in when he'd left. He would pop in later, round tea-time, and take a few bits for the bairns, he told himself as a sop to his conscience. He was renting the downstairs of a house in Eden Street West which was close to the public baths and the Avenue Theatre, but once home he stayed in the house for no more than a few minutes before his state of mind drove him out to walk the streets. The urge to be outside in the fresh air was always on him, but it was more compelling when he was troubled about something, like now.

He walked down Long Row and on to the Durham Road, and there he continued walking, past the clay pit and Mill Farm and out towards Humbledon Hill. He had to get his head sorted about Josie once and for all. Prudence had said she was a married woman and when you looked at it, that was the final word. If she didn't want anything to do with him when she was playing in these parts, as her conduct had indicated, then he'd make sure he stayed right out of her way. No backstage visits or nipping round to Vera's when he thought she might be there, and definitely no calls at the Grand. He wouldn't go cap in hand to anyone.

Mind, with the amount of folk who would undoubtedly flock to the theatres to see one of the latest sensations of the halls, he could easily lose himself in the crowds there if he so chose. But why torture himself like that? Still, it was a thought, he told himself as he strode on in the hot summer afternoon. Aye, it was a thought.

A week later the same thought was burning in Hubert's mind. There were posters everywhere announcing Josie was playing at the Palace starting this week, and he'd nearly had a fit when the first few went up. He knew Jimmy and Patrick had seen them, not that they'd said anything to him – but then they wouldn't, would they? Jimmy wasn't daft. Oh Jimmy man, Jimmy. Hubert ran his hand across his mouth, glancing round the large room in which he was standing which smelt of oil and burning metal and fire.

It was down to Jimmy that he was learning a trade at this locksmith's rather than having been found in a back alley somewhere with a knife between his ribs. Patrick had gone fair barmy when he'd announced he wanted out that day soon after Josie had gone down south. He hadn't meant to say it then, he'd been of a mind to wait at least a couple of years, but when he'd been told he was going on the collecting regular he'd known he'd rather take what was coming from Patrick – even if it was a blade across his throat – than continue to sell his soul to the devil.

He couldn't stomach it another day, he'd yelled at them all, and when one of Patrick's henchmen had gone for him and Jimmy had cut him up and then said he'd take on anyone else who laid a finger on his brother, Jimmy had made it clear where he stood. And because of that he was still in the land of the living, Hubert thought. Oh aye, he had no doubt about that. No one had ever been allowed to leave Patrick's employ before, but because he was Jimmy's brother he'd got away with it. Jimmy had taken him to one side and asked him what he wanted to do, and when he'd mentioned this place he'd been working here within the week. It was amazing, the doors that opened through fear. 'Course, the first few weeks Mr Foster and the two other lads had been wary of him, but when he'd shown he wanted to learn and didn't mind what he did, they'd accepted him for his own sake and not through intimidation of what would happen to their wives and families if they didn't. He hadn't known that was how Jimmy had got him in here until a couple of years after, when Mr Foster had let something slip.

But he loved it here. The leather bellows blowing oil into the fire in the massive hearth at the back of the room; the wooden benches with the keys, arbor press, files, hammers, punches, dollies and the like; the small lathe and the wooden racks for storage – it was like food and drink to him. And he liked Mr Foster and Paul and Charlie, they were nice folk, decent folk.

He continued looking for the file Mr Foster wanted which had gone missing, but his heart wasn't in it this morning. He was scared to death, he didn't mind admitting, but not for himself. For Josie, for what might happen, and for Jimmy an' all. He loved his brother, he couldn't help it, even though he didn't like him, but whatever Jimmy and Patrick had in mind it wasn't like dealing with the ne'er-do-wells they usually mixed with. No one bothered about one of them floating face down in the docks – the police least of all – but Josie was somebody now. If Jimmy did anything and he got caught, he'd go down the line for it. And Josie; he couldn't stand by and see the lass hurt, but what could he do? Since he'd opted out he knew nothing of what went on any more, and Jimmy had made it plain that in spite of his protection, Hubert wouldn't live long if he talked about anything he had seen or heard in the past.

But he could go and see her perform, couldn't he? Jimmy couldn't object to that, and somehow he'd get word to her that she had to watch herself. He'd done it once before and got away with it; he could do it again. When all was said and done, he didn't know for sure Patrick was going to do anything . . .

This comforting thought was hit on the head when Hubert found his brother waiting for him in the street at the end of the day.

'Wotcher, man.' Jimmy grinned at him, his handsome face with its vivid blue eyes at odds with the man Hubert knew his brother really was. 'Fancy a jar or two afore you go back to that hole you live in?'

The day he had left Patrick's employ the little Irishman had made it plain he could lodge elsewhere, something which suited Hubert down to the ground. Jimmy had found him a place with a very nice elderly couple and their widowed daughter in a two-up two-down house in Maritime Terrace, opposite the Almshouses and just a stone's throw from Brougham Street where he worked. The house was small but it wasn't a hole at all – Mrs Turner kept it spic and span as Jimmy very well knew – but it suited his brother to refer to it as that and Hubert never argued. He also knew that although Jimmy's words might have been couched in the form of an invitation they were, in fact, an order, and so Hubert nodded.

'Aye, man, if you're buying. Reckon I've sweated a couple of pints in there the day.'

'Aye, well, whose fault is that then? You could've bin in clover with Patrick, man.'

'I'm not complaining, merely stating.'

'Aye, well I've spent the day overseein' a bit of business an' takin' me ease in the sun for most of it. I know which I prefer.'

'Everyone to their own, Jimmy.'

It was the same sort of conversation they had every time they met but it didn't rile Hubert. He knew Jimmy missed him and wanted him back at his side, and he supposed he missed Jimmy in a way, but he'd rather jump in Jarrow Slake than go back to his old life.

'So?' Once they were sitting in the pub with a pint of foaming ale in front of each of them, it was Jimmy who brought up the subject on both their minds. 'You've seen the posters then?'

'Aye.' Hubert didn't prevaricate. 'What of 'em?'

'What of 'em?' Jimmy's face screwed up at him and the faint white lines radiating from the tanned skin around his eyes formed deeper furrows. 'She's back, man, bold as brass.'

'She's here for a couple of weeks working. Singing is what she does.'

'I know what she does. I know what she did, an' all, more to the point.'

'You've only Patrick's word for that and I don't believe him – I never have. Josie wouldn't have sold us down the river and Mam wouldn't have shopped us neither, and Da would never have left without you. And on a boat. Man, he was scared of the water. He'd have gone up to Glasgow or down south, but not on a boat.'

'You seem to know a lot about it considerin' you were barely old enough to wipe your own backside.'

'Huh.' He had to be careful here. If Jimmy cottoned on he'd ever talked to Josie . . . 'We were wiping our own backsides from the day we were born in our house, and there's some things stay with you. Da was a big man, afraid of nothing and no one, so I suppose when I knew he was scared of the water it stayed with me. In the subconscious, like.'

'Aye.' Jimmy glanced down at the sawdust-covered floor. 'Well, you were still a bairn an' you know nowt about it. Patrick an' Da were as close as that' – he crossed his fingers in front of Hubert's face – 'an' if Patrick says Da was leavin' on a boat, he was leavin' on a boat.'

It was useless. His brother had a blind spot where Duffy was concerned that nothing would shift. Hubert swallowed long and deeply of his ale before he said, 'What are you going to do?'

'Do?' Jimmy looked at him and now his expression was guarded. 'You don't really want to know that, do you?'

'Jimmy—'

'Leave it, Hubert. You've made it plain where you stand on this, it was a mistake to talk to you today. Patrick said you'd react like this.'

Patrick, Patrick, Patrick. Always Patrick. 'Why did you, then?'

'Because you're me brother.'

'And she's me sister. *Our* sister.'

Jimmy glared at him, and then the anger was slowly replaced by the faintly scornful, indulgent expression Hubert recognised so well. 'You'd believe the best of the devil himself, you.'

No, no he wouldn't, because to him Patrick Duffy was the devil incarnate.

Jimmy drained the tankard and stood up. 'Be seein' ya then.'

'Jimmy, please. Please don't do anything.' Hubert had reached out and clutched his brother's arm, his voice urgent, and Jimmy glanced round the pub before bending over and speaking in a low voice as he said, 'It's out of my hands, man. It's not just me who wants a reckonin', you know that.'

'You could stop it, you know you could. Patrick listens to you.'

'Not over this, believe me. 'Sides,' Jimmy straightened and Hubert's hand fell to his side, 'I owe it to Da to get even.'

'It wasn't *her*.'

'Aye, so you say.' And now Jimmy thrust his face close again but this time his voice carried a grim warning when he said, 'Don't you poke your nose into this, Hubert. I mean it, else it won't just be Patrick you'll answer to. You understand me? An' you might be workin' for old Foster but that don't mean Patrick don't know where you are every minute of the night an' day. Who you talk to, where you go; you can't as much as blow your nose an' he don't see what colour it is.'

'Aye, well *you* understand *this*. I don't reckon the sun

442

shines out of his backside like you do, and maybe I can see things a mite clearer because of it. You chew on that awhile.'

It wasn't often Hubert talked back and Jimmy's face reflected his anger in the moment before he turned away and stalked out of the pub.

Well, that had done a lot of good. Hubert sat quietly finishing his ale but he felt anything but quiet inside. After a while he stood up and walked out into the sunshine, and it was then two small thickset men appeared either side of him. 'Hello, Hubert.' The one who spoke had a bloated stomach due to his liking for beer and a mean little face.

Hubert nodded but said nothing. He knew these two from old.

'Been havin' a drink with your brother then? That's nice. I like it when brothers get on.'

Hubert still said nothing. Whatever Patrick's lackeys had been told to say you could bet it wasn't sentimental observations about brotherly love.

'Patrick said Jimmy might be havin' a little word in your ear sometime tonight, but he wanted to make sure you understood what was what. He hasn't got Jimmy's faith in you, that's the thing, but you can understand that, lad, can't you? Patrick bein' no relation of yours.'

The man's voice had been quiet and reasonable, and Hubert's was quiet and reasonable in reply when he said, 'Docs my brother know you are threatening me?'

'Threatenin' you? By, lad, where's that come from? Threatenin' him, he says.' The man appealed to his comrade who merely continued eying Hubert up and down. 'No, lad, Jimmy don't know about this friendly little talk, an' if you've any sense you'll keep it that way, all reet? See, them as open their mouths when they oughtn't sometimes find 'em full of dock water one night, know what I mean?

Might not be next week or next month or even next year, but sure as eggs are eggs they find 'emselves fish food one dark night. An' that applies to that upstart sister of yours an' all. You stay away from her if you know what's good for you. Patrick don't want no family reunions.' The last words were ominous.

Hubert hated himself for the trembling in his stomach that was shaking his bowels to water, but his fear didn't show in his voice when he said, 'Is that it? Is that the message?'

'Aye.'

'Well, you can go back now and say you've delivered it, can't you.'

He saw the two men exchange a glance but they said no more, turning as one and disappearing into the general throng on the corner of Crowtree Road and High Street West. Hubert stood for a moment more outside the pub. He was so sick of the shadow of Patrick Duffy hanging over him. Always, *always* it was there in the background. Patrick had given him some rope for Jimmy's sake, but the little Irishman was forever hoping he'd hang himself with it. And Jimmy couldn't see it. Patrick controlled him like he controlled the rest of his seedy empire that was full of dead men's bones and rotten to the core.

He hunched his shoulders, shutting his eyes for a moment as though to blot out all the darkness in his head, and then opened them and began to make his way home.

Chapter Twenty-four

Josie opened at the Palace in the middle of August to excellent reviews and packed houses; her popularity being enhanced still more by the fact that she had brought her three sisters with her to Sunderland. It was a kind of family pilgrimage, she told the newspapers who were delighted to print such an unusual story. Her three sisters and herself, along with two brothers, were all that was left of her family as far as she knew, and it would be wonderful if her brothers would contact her now she was here. She had only recently been reunited with two of her sisters whom she hadn't seen for over ten years; if the lads got in touch as well that would be absolutely wonderful. She wasn't going to give their names for fear of embarrassing them, but they knew who they were and she just wanted them to know she was waiting for a call.

It was a great story, and when added to her beauty and magnificent voice Josie Burns was the editors' darling and newspaper sales soared.

It had been two days after she had first taken Oliver to meet Ada and Dora – and that had been the day after their reconciliation – that her two elder sisters had let her know they were coming with her to Sunderland. 'Lass, if you can treat a lady of the realm the way you did and tell 'em all what's what, I reckon the least me an' Dora can do is show the same amount of pluck.' That had been the way Ada had put it when she had told Josie she and Dora were coming, and Josie hadn't argued with her.

Oliver had swallowed hard when she had told him of her two elder sisters' decision, much the same as he had when she had told him of the reappearance of the two women in her life, but in view of recent events he made no objection, either to their presence or to the proposed trip to Sunderland. He had, however, made it clear that regrettably he would have to stay in London for at least the first two weeks due to business, and Josie hadn't objected to this. All in all he had taken her disclosure about Ada and Dora and her declaration of intent concerning the proposed trip to Sunderland very well, and she knew he was trying hard regarding his gambling too. If two weeks of her sisters and the provinces was all he could manage, then so be it.

Gertie, delighted that all was well with Josie and Oliver again, which couldn't help but reflect on Anthony and herself, was all encouragement and approval. Josie understood how her youngest sister's mind worked and could even sympathise to an extent, but Gertie's attitude during the difficult days of her estrangement from Oliver had taught her a valuable lesson. Their relationship of the past was over – it was on a different footing now – and maybe that was no bad thing, Josie reflected honestly. In the early days Gertie had immersed herself in her sister's career and life to the exclusion of everything else, and that wasn't healthy. No, it was better she had found Anthony and the apron strings had been cut. Nevertheless, Gertie's lack of support at such a crucial time had been a bitter pill to swallow.

The four women were staying at the Grand in two rooms – Ada and Dora in one, and Josie and Gertie in another – and her sisters accompanied her each night to the theatre, which made for some riotous evenings in Josie's dressing room. Ada and Dora were fascinated by the music hall and some of the eccentric characters it boasted, a couple of whom were at present playing at the Palace. Dora being a born mimic could imitate 'Lulu and Her Amazing Talking Chimpanzee' and 'Cinquevalli, The Human Billiard Table' to the point where she had the others crying with laughter.

Oliver was due to join Josie in Sunderland the afternoon of her first performance at the Royal, and after she had moved out of the room she had shared with Gertie for two weeks and into one on the floor above which would be hers and Oliver's, she sat quietly in the reception area of the hotel reading a book and awaiting his arrival. She had thoroughly enjoyed the last fortnight with her sisters; she hadn't laughed so much in years, not even when she had been working with Lily and then later Nellie, she reflected as her mind wandered from the written page. The late Samuel Butler's novel *The Way of All Flesh* was a savage exposure of the oppressions of Victorian family life which Winifred had recommended to her that fateful weekend, but it made for depressing reading in parts and she could only take it in small doses.

The four of them had been so happy but each one of them had had Hubert and Jimmy at the back of their minds, from the number of times the lads' names had cropped up. Josie knew her sisters had been anxious for her in view of the warning Hubert had given her the last time she had seen him, and she made sure the four of them were always escorted to and from the theatre in the evening, and during the day they went everywhere together on the premise that there was safety in numbers. Not that she thought Duffy would try anything after all this time if she was being truthful.

The four of them had visited Vera a few times, and as Prudence had been at work there had been no awkward moments once the initial introductions had been dealt with. Josie had seen Betty at Vera's during the middle weekend of the first two weeks, but she hadn't called in at Betty's herself in spite of receiving an open invitation. She would not allow herself to dwell on why she didn't feel able to go and see Barney's stepmother; she would just not allow her mind to ask questions linked in any way with the man who haunted her dreams night after night.

When Oliver walked through the doors of the hotel she rose immediately and went to his side, and as he kissed her and whispered, 'I've missed you so much,' she smiled her reply.

They had tea at four o'clock with Ada, Dora and Gertie, but her sisters had tactfully said they were tired and wished to stay at the hotel that evening, so Oliver escorted Josie to the Royal and they spent the time in her dressing room together. There was one tricky moment at the beginning of the evening when, after escorting Josie and Oliver to her dressing room which was filled with flowers, the manager asked if she would be prepared to stay on in Sunderland for a few more weeks after she'd finished at the Royal and play the Avenue. The same proprietor owned both theatres. Josie declined, putting forward prior commitments as her excuse, and after he'd left she sent Oliver out to the front of the theatre to buy roast potatoes from the hot potato man, who sold his wares from a funny little contraption that looked like a small steam engine to the queues outside the Royal every evening. They ate the potatoes sprinkled with salt with Josie sitting on Oliver's knee, burning their fingers in the process, and for the first time in a long while Josie felt everything was going to work out with Oliver. He was trying so hard, she thought fondly as she watched him licking his salty fingers and pretending he had enjoyed the experience.

Josie finished her second performance of the evening with two hits of a few years ago, 'Mighty Lak'a Rose' and 'Just A-wearyin' for You', and as she walked off the stage Oliver was waiting for her in the wings like he had done in the old days, and she found her heart gave a little leap at the sight of him.

They walked to the dressing room arm in arm, and once she had changed and was taking off her heavy stage make-up, Oliver came up behind her and gently kissed the nape of her neck.

She turned from their reflection in the mirror, lifting up her lips to him as she whispered, 'I love you,' and he held her for a long moment as he kissed her, before murmuring, 'And I you, my love. I, you. Am I truly forgiven?'

For answer she took his face between her hands and kissed him, something she did rarely. Normally the physical overtures were all on Oliver's side.

'I'll go and make sure the carriage is waiting.' He grinned at her as he straightened. 'Come out when you are ready, and don't worry about doing your hair again; it's going to be very rumpled before long.'

'Oh, Oliver.' She blushed as she dimpled at him, and after she had removed every trace of make-up with cold cream and washed her face, she sat looking at herself for a few seconds before she rose from the stool. Was she wicked, loving two men at the same time, or did lots of women have similar secrets they kept locked in their hearts? Her life could have been different if there had been no Pearl. She and Barney might have married if he hadn't met someone else before she was old enough, and she could be a mother by now. Her singing would have been kept for bairns' lullabies and she would never have set foot on a stage. The thought produced a funny little pang in her heart and she jumped to her feet, angry with herself for the momentary weakness after the last days of keeping her mind fully under control.

She walked quickly towards the stage door, answering the 'good nights' from other performers with ones of her own, and after Mickey, the young stagehand, opened it for her and pointed to the carriage waiting on the cobbles, she waved to the silhouette of Oliver – resplendent in top hat and tails – inside. 'Good night, Mickey.'

'Good night, Miss Burns, an' thanks for that autograph for me mam. Thinks you're the tops, she does.'

Josie was still smiling as she climbed into the cab, the horse neighing softly as it flicked its mane in the soft warm August night, and then, as it moved away even before the door was properly shut and she took in the slumped form in a corner of the carriage, she opened her mouth to scream. The man who had been wearing Oliver's hat had his hand across her mouth and nose before she'd uttered so much as a squeak, however, and as the horse paused further along the street and another dark outline climbed into the carriage, a voice said, 'I said no undue violence, Harry.'

'I only hit 'im.' The voice above Josie's head was reproachful. 'He wasn't about to sit there quietly an' let her walk into it, not even with a knife to his ribs, so I hit 'im an' put on his hat.' This was said in the tone of someone expecting praise, and when none was forthcoming, the voice said again, full of righteous indignation now, 'I only hit 'im.'

'All right, all right, you only hit him.' There was a rustling and then the voice said again, still with the irritable note paramount, 'Move your hand a fraction, for cryin' out loud.'

'Aw, Jimmy man, I'm doin' me best.'

In the second before the pad of sweet-smelling liquid was pressed over her nose, Josie knew her eyes were staring wide in the blackness. The man holding her was built like a brick wall and there was no hope of even struggling, but at that precise moment she couldn't have anyway. She was frozen with shock. Jimmy, he had said Jimmy . . . And then, as the fumes from the pad seemed to fill her head she was aware that the carriage had stopped again, and that the driver had climbed down and was saying, 'You take over the horse now, Harry. I'll sit inside,' and as she spiralled into unconsciousness the scream which said *'Patrick Duffy!'* was only in her mind.

It was gone midnight when an apologetic knock at the door woke Gertie from a deep sleep, but within minutes of speaking to the waiter who was standing in the corridor, Gertie had gone next door and raised her sisters. They were now all sitting downstairs in the night manager's office, and Ada was saying, 'We have to call the police, don't you see? If Oliver had arranged a surprise dinner like this he would never have gone off somewhere else. They must have been abducted.'

'Miss Burns, I think we are jumping to rather extreme conclusions here.' The manager was used to dealing with all sorts of eventualities and his voice was very soothing. 'True, Mr Hogarth did ask us to arrange a champagne dinner for two in their room on Mrs Hogarth's return from the theatre, and they are undeniably late, but that doesn't mean any harm has come to them.'

'What time did he arrange for this meal to start?' Ada asked forthrightly.

'Eleven o'clock, madam.'

'And it's now twenty past twelve and they're not back. I suppose he paid handsomely for it too, considering you stop serving at ten?'

'The gentleman did recompense Chef and others for the

inconvenience such a romantic gesture would involve,' the manager agreed a little stiffly.

'And you still don't think it's strange they're not back?' Ada swore, most succinctly, which startled the manager so much he almost fell off his chair. He wasn't used to hearing profanities from the mouths of ladies staying at his hotel, and certainly not the earthy ones this particular guest had employed.

'Is there anyone on whom they might have called?' he asked even more stiffly. 'Where they may have been delayed perhaps?'

'Vera?' Gertie spoke now, looking at her sisters. 'Maybe we ought to try there before we get the law involved?'

'I'll call a cab while you ladies get dressed.' The three were sitting ensconced in their dressing gowns. 'And I am sure there is nothing to worry about . . .'

'Oh no, oh no.' It was Prudence's reaction which had caused a silence to fall over the kitchen after Gertie had explained the reason for getting the household up. They were all standing looking at Barney's sister now; Josie's three sisters in their coats and hats, and Vera and Horace in their night attire, and it was Vera who said, and sharply, 'What does that mean – "oh no"? You know summat about this, lass?'

'No, not about . . . I mean . . . I didn't think . . . Oh, *Vera!*'

'That's enough of that.' As Prudence's voice approached hysteria it was Ada who stepped forward and gave the other woman a swift slap across the face. 'Tell us what you think you know – and quick.'

'I don't know anything, not really.' Prudence had sunk down on to a hardbacked chair, holding her face. 'And you've no right to hit me.'

'I'll knock you into next weekend if you don't come clean.' Ada was now every inch the streetwalker of former years who could be as hard as iron when she had to be, and Prudence must have recognised this because she began to talk, and the more she said the paler the other women's faces became, Horace's too.

Again there was a silence when Prudence finished speaking, and as everyone – apart from Prudence herself who had her face in her hands and was now sobbing loudly – turned as one to Ada, Josie's eldest sister stared back at them all before she sat down heavily on a chair which creaked in protest.

'What are we going to do?' Gertie's voice was a whimper. 'What are we going to do, Ada? I knew we shouldn't have come back. I told her, I did. But she would go on about finding the lads. She's never listened to reason—'

'Don't start on that road, Gertie.' It was Dora who spoke and her voice was as hard as Ada's had been when she'd threatened Prudence. 'Josie's in this mess because she crossed Duffy for you in the first place. She rescued you out of it, and she wanted to do the same for the lads, so don't start blaming her for that unless you want to feel the back of my hand across your mug.'

'I didn't mean—'

'Oh aye you did, you ungrateful little swine, you.'

'Shut up.' Ada's voice was flat but of a quality which brooked no argument. 'I can't think with you two going at it. One thing's for sure, we can't wait. We've got to act now. If Duffy's got her . . .' She shook her head. 'Look, me an' Dora know one or two people who might know something. We'll go and ask a few questions, all right?'

'What'll I do?' Gertie asked helplessly.

Ada glanced at her sister, her gaze softening as she saw the anxiety in Gertie's face. 'The carriage is still outside an' we won't need it where we're goin',' she said. 'It's better to go unannounced to them sort of places. Any of you know any blokes who've got a bit of brawn as well as brains an' would be willin' to help out if the worst comes to the worst?'

'Barney, my brother.' It was Prudence who spoke, her sobs having diminished to hiccups. 'He's always thought a bit of Josie. And Georgie, my young man. He'd help.'

'All right. Well, you take the carriage an' pick 'em up in case we come back an' need 'em, but don't do anythin' more until me an' Dora are back.' Ada glanced at both Gertie and Prudence as she spoke and both girls nodded obediently. Vera's face was as white as a sheet, and Ada now said to her, 'Why don't you go an' get dressed, lass, an' then put the kettle on, eh? It's going to be a long night an' a sup tea'll help.'

It was getting on for two in the morning when Ada and Dora made their way towards a certain house in Fitter's Row, a street not too far from Northumberland Place. Although the main streets were lit by dim pools of light from the street-lamps, the back lanes and alleys were as black as pitch, but this didn't worry Ada and Dora. Had it been a Friday or Saturday there might still have been some activity outside a few of the more notorious public houses, but as it was they hardly saw a soul as they hurried along Prospect Row, turning left at South Dock goods station into Thomas Street and round the back of the school into Fitter's Row.

They came to an innocuous-looking house in the hotch-potch street of tenement buildings, and Dora, who had her handkerchief to her nose to blot out the stench arising from something disgusting lying in the gutter which was made all the more ripe by the warm night, said quietly, 'By, lass, I remember this house well.'

'Aye.' Ada nodded. And the memories were all bad. But the madam of this place, Madge Hopkins, might just help them. Tough as the devil's hobnail boots, old Madge was, but Madge owed her a favour and today was collection day.

Ada took a deep breath and knocked on the door of the house, a series of long and short raps which was a code only the occupants – or prior occupants – knew. After a moment or two a window was raised and a head thrust out. 'Who is it?' It was a woman's voice.

'That you, Madge?'

There was silence for a moment, and then the voice said, 'Who's askin'?'

'It's me, Ada. You remember? Ada an' Dora Burns from a few years back? We want to talk to you, Madge.'

'Ada? I don't believe it! Ada an' Dora Burns? You two skedaddled if I remember right.'

'Aye, we went down south. Good pickin's down south.'

'What do you want?'

'Well, open the door, lass, an' I'll tell you.'

There was a moment's pause and then the window was slammed shut, and within a minute or two the front door was swinging open. 'All right, come in.' Madge peered at them both in the light from the flickering candle she was holding. 'What's so important after all these years that you have to raise the house at this time of night?'

Ada and Dora stepped into the narrow hall they remembered from their childhood. They had been made to entertain clients in the rooms upstairs from the age of ten, sometimes as many as half a dozen a night, and they had never expected to be in this house again. Ada shut off

her mind from that path and said instead, 'You remember
how I helped you out once, Madge? Eh?'

There was the sound of a door opening above them and
Madge shouted, 'Back into your rooms, the lot of you!
This is nowt to do with you,' before saying in a quieter
tone, 'Aye, I remember. What of it?'

'You said you owed me, Madge. Well, I need your
help now.'

'By, Ada, it really is you then. You an' Dora caused
a stink when you took off, you know. Duffy went fair
mental. The things he was goin' to do to you both when
he caught up with you.'

'Aye, well he didn't catch up with us,' Ada said flatly.
And then her tone changed when she said, 'I saved your
bacon that time the money was pinched an' I saw who
took it, now then. You know Duffy'd have taken the loss
out of your hide. Well, I need a favour now. Our sister'
– she included the silent Dora in the wave of her hand –
'he's took her an' we want her back. You heard owt?'

'No, I ain't, lass, but if I had it'd be more than me life's
worth to say anythin', you know that. But I haven't, I swear
it. Your sister, you say?'

'Aye.'

Madge held the candle closer to Ada's face, staring at
her for a good few moments before she said, 'Look, lass,
I don't know where Duffy'd be but I can put you on to
Hubert. He's your brother, ain't he? Him an' Jimmy? Well,
he got out of the business a while back, you know that?'
Ada shook her head. 'Aye, well he did, but Jimmy don't
let no one lay a finger on him. Thinks a bit of him,
see, an' the word is they're still close. Hubert might
know where Jimmy's livin', an' ten to one Patrick'll
be there. The lad works for the locksmith in Brougham
Street an' the locksmith lives over the shop. He'd know

where your brother lodges. That's the best I can do, lass.'

'Aye. Well thanks, Madge.'

Mr Foster wasn't overjoyed about being knocked up in the middle of the night; the Turners and their widowed daughter even less so, but by half-past three Hubert and his two sisters were approaching a three-storey house on Ettrick's Quay in the heart of the East End. Apart from a few fishing boats lying on the cobbles in front of the higgledy-piggledy row of terraced two- and three-storey houses, the quay was quiet, although within the hour it would begin to stir.

It had been a brief but highly emotional reunion between Hubert and his sisters, but he had been adamant that the three of them had to go alone to the house where he knew Jimmy was staying at present. Duffy would have his henchmen close, he'd insisted, and taking anyone else along would just end in a fight which could be dangerous. It was no use trying to break into the house; it was far better he went in alone through the front door and tried to find out where Josie was being held from Jimmy. Ada and Dora must stay out of sight and he'd come to them as soon as he could.

'I don't like it, lad.' Ada could see a hundred things wrong with the plan. 'They might turn on you.'

Hubert turned to look at them both. How could he explain that somewhere deep inside he had always known this day was going to happen? Oh, not the details of course, or that Josie would be involved like she was, but he'd always felt that Patrick Duffy would force a showdown between him and Jimmy.

Jimmy's love for his brother had always been a thorn in Duffy's side, and the older man wouldn't be content until that thorn was pulled and got rid of. Well, today might be the day or it might not, but he was tired of living in the shadows. Even living and working as he was, he was still living in the shadows because at heart he knew Patrick had the reins on him and could pull them tight at any time.

He wanted to be *free*. Free to go wherever he chose and say whatever he liked; free to make his own life and to know he could ask a lass to start courting without having to look over his shoulder all the time. A lass like Laura Foster. He knew she liked him and he liked her, more than liked her, but how could he let a nice, innocent young lassie like Laura get involved with him when Duffy was forever lurking in the background?

But after today, when he'd nailed his colours well and truly to the mast, he'd either be free or be dead. Either way he was glad. But he couldn't tell his sisters that – they'd think he was doolally. Instead he said quietly, 'Whatever they do, Ada, this is the way to do it.'

'Aren't you afeared, lad? Of goin' agen 'em, I mean?'

Hubert nodded. 'Aye, I am, but not as much as not going against them, if that makes any sense.'

Ada looked at him, holding his gaze for a moment before she said very softly, 'It makes sense to me, Hubert lad. It makes sense to me.'

'Right then.' Hubert squared his bony shoulders. 'I'll go and see what's what. If Jimmy and Patrick have brought Josie and her husband here, I'll try and let you know in some way – come to a window or something – and then you can nip and get the others and someone can go for the police. If they aren't here I'll try and find out where they are and if she's with them.'

'Watch yourself, lad.'

'I will, Ada, I will.' Hubert hugged both Ada and Dora

458

before they made themselves scarce, and after waiting a moment he walked to the flaky front door at one side of two narrow windows and knocked loudly.

Chapter Twenty-five

'*What?* How do you know Duffy's got her?'

Prudence had just roused Barney, and although her brother's eyes had been bleary a moment ago they'd just cleared like magic.

'It's a long story but he spoke to me a couple of times, Duffy – oh, ages ago now, and he means to do her harm.'

Barney raked back his ruffled hair, squinting at Prudence and Georgie on the doorstep as he said, 'He *spoke* to you? Why didn't you tell me?'

'She didn't tell anyone.' Georgie's arm had tightened protectively round Prudence's shoulders. 'She was scared we'd think less of her. Look, it's like this; Josie and Oliver didn't come back from the theatre . . .' He gave the few facts they knew quickly and clearly, including Ada and Dora's present mission, and as the full import of the situation turned Barney's face to thunder, Georgie added, 'It's too late for recriminations now, and if Prudence had said anything I doubt it would have altered a thing. Get your togs on, man, and we'll see what's happening at Vera's.'

Duffy, that little snake of a man, had got his hands on Josie. As Barney pulled on his clothes his guts were twisting and his mind was racing. He'd kill him, he'd *kill* him if he hurt a hair of her head. Dear God, dear God, do

461

something, anything. For the first time in years he found himself praying frantically. If You save her she can be with Oliver for the rest of her life, I don't care, only don't let her be hurt. He wouldn't want to live if anything happened to her. *Duffy*. Oh, God, God . . . It felt as if a knife was tearing at his innards.

Gertie was sitting in the carriage with the others when Barney joined them outside, and as he climbed in she said brokenly, 'Oh Barney, what'll we do? What'll we do?'

'Pray Ada and Dora find out where she is.' It was Georgie who answered and his voice was grim. 'In the meantime all we can do is wait to hear something.'

Wait? Barney sat down beside Gertie, twisting his hands together until it was painful. How the hell was he going to sit and do nothing? He'd go stark staring barmy. But Georgie was right, they couldn't do anything else. She could be anywhere.

'What . . . what do you think they'll do to Oliver?' Gertie murmured tremblingly. 'He wouldn't have let them take her without trying to stop them. You . . . you don't think . . .' Her voice trailed away and everyone looked at each other, but as the horse began to clip-clop through the silent streets no one said a word.

When Josie surfaced from the thick fog which had blanketed her senses, the first thing she thought was, Oh I feel sick, so sick. She felt if she so much as breathed she would vomit, and she lay absolutely still for some seconds before she opened her eyes.

To her amazement she wasn't in the big double bed she shared with Oliver in Park Place, and then after one stunned moment it all came rushing back and she jerked into a sitting position, wincing as her head protested at the sudden movement and her stomach rose up into her mouth.

It was all she could do to roll over on the narrow pallet bed she was lying on and empty the contents of her stomach on the dusty floorboards, but afterwards she felt better although by now she'd become aware of Oliver on the other side of the room lying on a similar bed. He was clearly unconscious and making a funny sort of gurgling noise in his throat, but when Josie stumbled across to him he appeared unhurt apart from the massive egg-type lump on the side of his forehead.

Apart from the two pallet beds the small room was quite empty. There was one narrow window which had thick iron bars cemented in it and no curtains, and when she tried the door it was locked. This was a cell.

Josie stood with her back against the door for a few moments as she tried to clear her mind, breathing in slowly and trying to ignore the smell of vomit.

It was a cell, and she didn't need to ask who had brought them here or why. For the last two weeks she had always had her sisters with her and had been surrounded by a crowd of people most of the time, but tonight had been different. Tonight it had been just Oliver and herself, which meant . . . Which meant Patrick Duffy and probably Jimmy too had been waiting for the right moment to snatch her.

The only light in the small room came from two flickering candles in thin metal holders either side of the windowsill and it was still dark outside, so it couldn't be many hours since they had been kidnapped. *Kidnapped.* Josie's stomach turned over again but she fought the sickness, speaking out loud to herself as she said, 'No more of that. You're not hurt and you've got your wits about you so think, girl. *Think.*' There had to be a way out of this.

She walked over to the window and pulled at each of the bars in turn, trying to see if one of them was loose but it was no use. They were rock solid and the only result was orange rust on her hands.

She still felt muzzy from whatever it was on the pad they had pressed to her nose, and the sweet sickening odour was in her nostrils. She took a handkerchief out of the pocket of her dress and blew her nose, and as the smell cleared she felt better. She would get them out of this, she *would*. Duffy wouldn't win.

There was nothing she could use to defend herself in this spartan little cell. Of course she could throw the candlestick holders at whoever opened the door next, but as they were of the cheap tin variety with thin tallow candles already half burned down, they wouldn't hurt a fly.

She walked across to Oliver again, kneeling at his side and shaking him gently as she said his name over and over. There was no response beyond the sound in the back of his throat, but she sat on the floor by his pallet bed stroking the hair back from his swollen forehead and gazing around the room.

She mustn't panic, that was the first thing. If she gave in to this feeling which had her wanting to throw herself at the door and batter it with her fists while she screamed out loud, it wouldn't do any good.

What would they do to her? And what would they do to Oliver? Oh, if he'd just wake up they could fight them together. Somehow they could try and get out.

Josie had no idea how long she sat by the side of Oliver's bed before she heard a key turning in the door. She sprang to her feet, one hand clutching her throat and the other her middle, and it was like that she faced Patrick Duffy and the two big burly men who stood just behind him.

'Hello, lass.'

Whatever she had expected it wasn't the quiet, almost friendly tone in which he addressed her, but somehow, instead of being reassuring it was more terrifying than any ranting and raving. She stared into the face of the man she had loathed all her life but she didn't speak.

'I read in them newspapers you wanted to meet up with your brothers again – is that right?'

She raised her head slightly but still said nothing.

'So I thought, why not help the little lady along? She's got involved in my affairs in the past, so why not me return the compliment, eh? Eh? What do you think about that then?'

'I think if there was any justice in the world you would have been sent down the line years ago,' Josie said shakily.

'Oh,' Patrick smiled now, 'there's justice in the world all right, but I make me own, darlin'. Yes, I make me own. Take you, for example. I've waited a long time for recompense concerning you, but finally it's come. Now, you want to meet your brothers, I understand. I can help you out with one of 'em at least.'

He motioned with his hands at the men behind him as he spoke the last words, and as Josie watched them approach she straightened her shoulders. When one of them reached out for her she flicked away his hand, saying, 'I'm quite capable of walking myself, thank you.'

The two men turned as one to look at Duffy who shrugged. 'Still got some spirit, I see. Well, I like that in a woman meself. All right, leave her be but watch her.'

'What . . . what about my husband?'

'I think he's quite comfortable where he is. Now move.'

As soon as she followed the first man out on to the landing, Josie realised she must be in the attic room of the house, and this was borne out when they went down two sets of stairs to emerge into a well-lit hall. Unlike the little attic room the rest of the house seemed to be furnished, and luxuriously too. A cord carpet covered the stairs and floors, and along with several large gilt-framed mirrors on the walls the hall boasted a couple of highly polished occasional tables. Whoever had said crime didn't pay hadn't met Duffy.

'Thought I'd be livin' in the sort of muck-heap you came from, I bet.' Duffy had noticed Josie looking about her. 'This place don't look much on the outside – don't want to attract unwelcome attention from the law now, do we? – but it's me home and I like things nice.'

Josie said nothing, and her silence seemed to infuriate him because he caught at her arm, swinging her round to face him as he said, 'There's things in this house all your fancy pals in London'd be glad to own, I can tell you, an' I bet I could buy and sell more than a few of 'em several times over.'

She stared at him disdainfully. 'My mother used to say you can't make a silk purse out of a sow's ear, and she was right.'

The slap across her face sent her ricocheting against the wall, and as one of the men sniggered, Duffy said, 'I'll silk purse you, me fine lady. Oh aye, I will at that. By the time I've finished with you you'll wish you'd never been born.' He pushed at her to start walking again, and as she followed the man in front of her they didn't turn off into any of the rooms leading from the hall but walked right to the end of it. Here a door opened into a large, stone-floored scullery; the man leading them opened another door to their left and Josie saw a row of steep stone steps leading down into a cellar which looked to be lit by several large oil lamps.

'Get down there unless you want me boot in your backside.'

She had hesitated, but now as Duffy spoke from behind

her Josie followed the man in front of her down into what turned out to be a very large room. And in front of her, standing to one side of a chair, was her da. The shock of it took her breath away but almost instantly she realised it couldn't be her father. The face was too young and the hair was fairer than her da's had been, but otherwise this person was the spitting image of Bart Burns. 'Jimmy?' she said dazedly.

'Hello, Josie.' His voice was grim and his face more so. 'It's been a long time.'

'Aye, yes it has.' She was trembling so much now that she had to grip the sides of her dress to hide the shaking of her hands. 'I . . . I've been looking for you. You and Hubert.'

'And now you've found me.' His eyes moved to the side of her face which was burning from Duffy's blow, and as his gaze went to the man at the back of her, Duffy said, 'She asked for it. Don't know when she's beat, this one, but she's goin' to learn pretty quick.'

'Why are you doing this?' Josie appealed directly to Jimmy's stony face. 'You're my *brother*!'

'It's a pity you didn't remember that years ago when you sold us all out. You'd have seen Hubert an' me go down the line, Da an' all, and because of you he had to get out so quick he couldn't even let me an' Hubert know. If it wasn't for Patrick—'

'Patrick?' Josie couldn't contain herself any longer. 'Patrick Duffy destroyed our family—'

'Shut up.'

'And I didn't sell anyone out—'

'I said shut up.' Jimmy had moved in front of her with a lightning stride, and as he now raised his hand Josie stared back at him defiantly. There was a moment's pause and then her brother stepped back a pace. 'Tie her to that chair.'

467

He gestured at one of the men who had brought her down. 'Where's her husband?'

'Upstairs.' It was Duffy who answered. 'Why? You want him down here?' And as Jimmy nodded, Duffy turned to the other man. 'Get him.'

'Jimmy, you have to listen to me,' Josie said rapidly. 'I didn't do anything. It was Da and Patrick who came for me and Gertie in Newcastle; they attacked us and then he got injured' – she nodded towards Duffy, her hands being strapped to her side on the chair – 'and they went off together. He saw Da last and—'

'You're lying.' It was flat and heavy. 'Da begged you not to take Gertie and go to Newcastle but you wouldn't listen. You wanted to make a new life for yourself and you thought the easiest way was to get rid of Da an' me an' Hubert. Mam was in your pocket, she always had been.'

'Da *begged* me?' In spite of the danger she was in she just couldn't let it pass. 'You know that's not true. Da *threatened* me. He controlled us all by threats and beatings. He sold Ada and Dora to him' – again she nodded at Duffy who was standing by with a slight smile on his face – 'and he wanted to do the same with Gertie. *That's* why I had to leave.'

'Another word and I'll gag you, I swear it.'

Oh, what could she say, how could she convince him? As the door opened and the man who had been sent to fetch Oliver entered with her husband's body draped over his shoulder, the feeling that she was in the middle of her worst nightmare was strong. She had actually dreamed of something like this happening, time and time again when she was younger, but not so much since she had married.

'What'll I do with 'im?'

Jimmy flicked his head towards a pile of old sacks in the corner and the man walked across to them, letting Oliver slide off his shoulder and land with a bump which sent clouds of dust into the air.

'He's still out for the count.' It was said with derision and Josie bit hard on her lip.

'Tie his hands and feet.' Patrick entered the proceedings again, and once Oliver was secured he said to Jimmy, 'Come on, let 'em stew a while. Doug'll be over later but you'll have a bit of time with her afore he takes her. Give it an hour or two and you might find the rats down here have made her a bit more respectful. They might wake him up an' all. Nothing like a rat or two taking a chunk out of you to bring you to your senses.'

Jimmy seemed to hesitate for a moment but then he followed the others towards the steps, and it was when he was halfway up them that a knock sounded at the front door. In a moment Jimmy had bounded up the last few stairs, the door was slammed shut and from the sound of it bolted, and Josie was left alone. She didn't have to think about what to do. She took a deep breath and began to shout and scream at the top of her voice, and it could only have been a minute or two before the door was opened again. She stared upwards, her heart pounding.

Her shouting had been mainly in the vain hope that whoever was at the door might, just might, be a policeman or someone outside Duffy's employ, but when Jimmy came down the steps again followed by Duffy and one of his henchmen, her heart sank, even before her brother said, 'Someone else to see you, Josie. Wonder how our Hubert got to know you were a guest here?' and then she saw Hubert behind the others.

'Hubert.' She breathed her younger brother's name, and he answered saying, 'Josie. Oh Josie, lass. Are you all right?'

She nodded before saying, 'They've hurt Oliver.'

'All right, all right, that's enough.' Jimmy turned to Hubert. 'So, how did you know she was here?'

As Hubert began to make some garbled explanation of how he had been waiting outside the Grand to catch a glimpse of her but she had never turned up, so then he had put two and two together, Jimmy just stood and watched him with cold unblinking eyes, his gaze only leaving Hubert's face when the other man appeared at the top of the cellar steps. 'Well?' In answer to the one word from Jimmy the man shook his head.

'Just a couple of dock dollies out there; one as big as a tram,' he said expressionlessly. 'I told 'em to skedaddle an' the big 'un gave me a bit of lip but they went.'

Jimmy nodded, turning back to Hubert as he said, 'So you were alone then,' and without waiting for his brother to answer him, 'You shouldn't have come, Hubert.'

'Aye, I should. I couldn't stand by and see me own sister disappear without doing something about it.'

'This is between me an' Jimmy an' her.' Patrick entered the conversation, his eyes cold as he glanced at Hubert. 'You'll keep your mouth shut about this little lot or else.'

'And you're going along with that?' Josie spoke directly to Jimmy. 'You'll let him hurt me and threaten Hubert and not do a thing about it? We're your *family*, Jimmy. Doesn't that count for anything?'

'Don't you put yourself alongside him.' Jimmy's voice was harsh. 'Hubert's me brother but as far as I'm concerned that's the only family I've got. You're less than the muck under me boots.'

'She's our sister, man.'

'She's nowt!'

'Let one of 'em take him upstairs.' Patrick's voice was soft as he appealed to Jimmy. 'They can keep him quiet

– not hurt him, just keep him quiet – till we're finished down here.'

Josie was straining against the ropes which held her now, the thought of being left alone with Patrick Duffy and Jimmy terrifying.

'I'm going nowhere.' Hubert had straightened his shoulders as he spoke. 'But I'll say this, man. I've stood by you up to this point but you go through with this and you're no brother of mine.'

'You'd put her before me?' Jimmy moved menacingly over to Hubert but the younger brother held his ground, his chin lifting slightly. 'After all we've been through together, you'd put that baggage afore me?'

'If that's how you want to put it, aye, I would.'

Jimmy hit Hubert with the back of his hand, not his fist, but the force of the blow still sent the slighter, younger man reeling, and as he tried to steady himself Josie shouted, 'Leave him be! You leave him! You're as bad as Da was!'

'Is that right?' Jimmy swung round, a terrible look on his face. 'So you admit you sold us all to the law then?'

'No, I didn't.' Josie was panting and struggling but she could do nothing, secured as she was. 'I swear I didn't.'

'She's lying, son.'

It was the 'son' that did it. Josie had the urge to fly at Patrick Duffy and claw and bite and kick, but tied to the chair and unable to move, her rage came out in the form of invective as she spat, 'You! *You* to call *him* son! He's not your son! A miserable piece of humanity like you is not capable of having a son.'

In her temper she must have hit what was a raw spot with the little Irishman, because he turned on her, his face contorted as he said, *'Shut up.'*

'You're scum! You've always been scum and everyone

knows it but they're too scared to say anything. The worst of your men are ten times better than you. This house and all the bits in it! Ha! They turned to filth and muck the minute you owned them because you taint everything you come into contact with, with your putrid smell.'

'*Shut up!*' It was high-pitched, almost in the form of a scream, and the sound could have come from a lunatic in the asylum.

On the fringe of her mind Josie could hear Hubert pleading, 'Don't say any more, Josie. Don't say any more,' but she went on, 'You'll burn in hell's everlasting flames for what you've done, Patrick Duffy, and there won't be a soul up here who will care when you're gone. Son! Jimmy's not your son. Me da might not have been much but he was ten times, a hundred times the man you are. Do you hear me? A hundred times the man.'

'Oh aye?' Patrick had approached Josie and it was clear he was oblivious to anything and anyone but the figure tied to the chair. His face like the devil's and his eyes seeming to stare from his head, he said, 'You think your da was better'n me, then? Eh? *Eh?* Because he sired you, you think he was better'n me, you filthy little upstart you?'

'Aye, I do. I do.' Josie was past caution, past anything but the hate consuming her for this man who had ruined her family and set out to destroy all their lives in different ways. 'At least me da was a man but you're nowt. Less than nowt.'

'A man, was he?' Duffy was crouched so close now Josie could smell nothing but his rank breath as he hissed, 'He didn't sound much like a man the night we sliced him. Squealed like a stuck pig so he did, an' you will an' all, me fine lady. Oh aye, you will an' all afore I'm finished with you.'

When Patrick was grabbed from behind and a knife

pressed against his throat under his chin he clearly didn't have the faintest idea why Jimmy was handling him in this way. His eyes popping out of his head, his voice was vacant – in the way a boxer might mumble after coming round from the knockout blow – as he said, 'Jimmy? Jimmy, man?'

'Why?' It was one word and not said loudly, but the tone was such that it caused the other two men to shuffle their feet, their expressions revealing they were stunned by the sudden change in events.

'You take one step towards us an' I'll cut his throat afore I see to you.' Jimmy had swung Patrick round in front of him as he spoke to the two henchmen. Patrick's lackeys were not chosen for their intelligence but they were bright enough to know who had the upper hand, and furthermore they were well acquainted with Jimmy's ruthlessness and knew he meant what he said. They exchanged a bewildered glance but they weren't about to argue with Jimmy's gutting knife which they'd seen in action many times before. When Jimmy motioned them into a corner of the cellar they went without demur, watching silently as, under Jimmy's instructions, Hubert untied Josie before brother and sister went across to the unconscious Oliver and between them began to haul his limp body up the cellar steps, Jimmy and Patrick following them.

'Jimmy, Jimmy man, listen to me. I had to do it. I didn't want to but I had to, you know how it is.' Patrick had been pleading softly and desperately ever since reality had dawned, but apart from keeping the knife to his throat Jimmy had ignored him.

But as they reached the top of the stairs and emerged through into the stone-floored scullery, Jimmy said quietly, 'Stepped into me da's boots and found 'em a grand fit, eh, Patrick? Took his life an' then his sons an' all? Well, you did a good job, I'll give you that. Took me for a right 'un. As Hubert's fond of saying, thought the sun shone out of your backside, me.'

He had slid the bolt on the cellar door as he spoke, locking Patrick's two men below.

Josie and Hubert were standing panting, Hubert holding Oliver's upper torso and Josie her husband's legs, and now she said, 'What are you going to do, Jimmy?'

Jimmy ignored her, looking instead at Hubert as he said, 'I should've listened to you, little 'un, but at least I can make it right for Da now. I know a nice little spot where me an' Patrick can . . . discuss exactly how me da died for as long as it takes. Then I'll disappear. I've had a bellyful of this little racket. Like she said, the smell's gone putrid. Funny, but I'd always seen meself taking over Patrick's spot one day but now I'd rather cut me own throat than touch anything with his stamp on it.'

'What'll you do?'

'Start somewhere else. I'll make sure the body isn't found' – a small whimper came from Patrick – 'and his lot'll be scratchin' their heads while they divide the plunder. I don't reckon any of 'em will object over much when they realise me an' Patrick have disappeared an' it's all theirs. Do you?'

Hubert stared into the face of the man who, in his own way, had loved and cared for him all his life. 'Will I see you again?'

'I don't think so, lad. An' that grieves me.'

'Jimmy . . .' Josie spoke again, stammering a little as she said, 'You can't . . . you can't . . . not in cold blood.'

The piercing blue eyes looked at her. 'Don't go soft on me now, lass, not after all this, an' besides,' he smiled, a cold, hard smile and the resemblance to their father was heightened, 'I've got the knife and I tell you straight, I'll take down anyone who tries to stop me. I've waited a long time to get even with the person who did for Da. Funny, but in the heart of me I think I always knew he had to be dead, even in the early days when I was always lookin' out for him everywhere I went. Da wouldn't have gone you see, not without me.'

In spite of the fact that her brother was a fully grown man who had proved himself to be every bit as dangerous and ruthless as any in the criminal fraternity, there had been something pathetic and almost childlike in the way in which he had said the last words.

'But the police would deal with him, he'd get sent down the line for sure. It doesn't have to be this way.'

Jimmy didn't even bother to reply to this last plea from Josie, but jerked his head at his brother, saying, 'Give me a minute or two an' then you can leave an' all, all right? Look after yourself, man, an' don't wait too long to start courtin' Laura or likely she'll be off with someone else, a bonny lass like that.'

Hubert's warm blue eyes widened. 'How did you know? I haven't said owt to anyone.'

'You're me brother, man. I used to wipe your nose an' your backside an' all. 'Course I knew.' And then Jimmy's voice changed as he said, 'Move out of the way an' let me pass, an' you stay put until me an' this piece of scum are away.'

'You can't let him take me.' Duffy's voice was shrill with terror. 'You can't.'

'They've no choice, Patrick. Same as you didn't give me da one, I'll be bound.'

Jimmy passed them, walking out of the scullery and to the end of the hall near the front door. He opened it and peered outside at the deserted quay before he turned, glancing once more at Hubert who had tears streaming down his face now. 'By, little 'un,' he said. And then he and Patrick Duffy were gone.

Josie and Hubert remained where they were for some moments, neither of them feeling they could move, and then they carried Oliver along the hall and out into the fresh air which was already tinged with the subtle glow of dawn on the horizon. Jimmy and Patrick had vanished.

By unspoken mutual consent they lowered Oliver to the ground and Josie sank down beside him, her legs suddenly giving way, whilst Hubert scrubbed at his wet face with his sleeve. Not a word had been spoken but they both gulped at the fresh morning air as though they had been drowning.

It could only have been a minute or two before the sound of running footsteps was heard, and Josie and Hubert both stiffened before relaxing again with relief as Barney and Georgie, hotly followed by Gertie, Prudence and the bulk of Ada and Dora came panting round the corner of the quay.

'Josie!' Barney's voice was hoarse and it didn't sound like him. 'Thank God! Are you all right?' He reached her before the others, kneeling down beside her as he took her cold hands in his warm ones. 'Have they hurt you?'

She shook her head, knowing if she tried to speak at that precise moment she would cry.

She wasn't aware she was trembling until Barney put his arm round her and said, 'It's all right, it's all right, it's over.'

Over. With her brother walking away with murder in his heart and a knife to Patrick Duffy's throat, and her husband lying on the cobbles as if he was dead? And as though Barney had read her mind, he said softly, 'Don't worry about Oliver, you're safe now and we'll get him straight to a doctor. He'll be fine.'

But he wasn't.

*　　*　　*

Oliver lingered in the infirmary for a week but never regained consciousness, and on the day of the funeral, those who cared about Josie feared for her mental health. She was blaming herself for Oliver's death, and nothing anyone said or did could convince her otherwise.

Useless to say the confrontation with Patrick Duffy would have happened one day because the little Irishman would have made sure of it; that the evil shadow of Duffy had been lifted off many lives, not least Hubert's, allowing folk to live without fear; that Josie playing the Sunderland halls one day had always been a foregone conclusion and would have happened long ago but for the fact of Oliver pressing her to stay in the capital; that what had happened was Fate. Inescapable.

Oliver was dead, and Josie seemed determined to punish herself to the maximum. The funeral was held in London and all Josie's friends and family from the north-east came down to the capital, but although she spoke politely to them all and thanked them for coming it wasn't like Josie at all. She never once looked at, or spoke directly to, Barney. He was perhaps the main barbed whip she was scourging herself with and she couldn't bear to see him in the flesh. Guilt made her voice brittle and her face tight, and the weight was dropping off her in a way that made her sisters and others desperately worried. She had betrayed Oliver. Oh, perhaps not by any physical weakness, she acknowledged bitterly, but Barney had been in her head, her mind, her heart, and now she was reaping retribution. Or rather Oliver had paid the price for her. And with his death there had opened in her a void of hopeless regret, of sorrow and of utter loneliness that no amount of calm logic and comfort from her family and friends could assuage.

Strangely, the one thing that brought her out of the abyss

to a limited extent and gave her the will to go on was the news which her sisters had feared would be the final straw to her delicate state of mind. Oliver had left debts, vast debts. Sums of a nature to be overwhelming to the average man and woman.

Josie listened to all Oliver's solicitors said, took all the papers and correspondence relating to her husband's liabilities, and wrote to each and every creditor assuring them that the debt would be honoured in full if they could but be patient.

At the end of September she walked out of the house in Park Place with little more than the clothes she stood up in and the contents of her wardrobe, and moved into the residence at the back of the Caledonian Market. At Lily's insistence, they converted the sitting room into Josie and Gertie's living quarters, and Josie threw herself into her work.

Oliver's agency had died with him, but when Anthony found another position at the end of October he asked Gertie to marry him and she immediately accepted. Josie was pleased for her sister, and when there was talk of the marriage being deferred out of respect for Oliver, she told the young couple in no uncertain terms that Oliver would not have wished it and neither did she. They must marry when it suited them to do so, she said. Time was a precious commodity and who knew what tomorrow would bring? And so Gertie and Anthony set the date for the following summer, and Gertie immediately began sewing her wedding dress in any free moments she had.

Barney wrote to Josie in November but she did not reply to his letter. He wrote again in December, a letter on the lines of the first one – kind, understanding, warm and friendly, but making it clear she was on his mind constantly. This time she replied with a cool note thanking him for his concern but making it plain she did not wish him to write a third time.

She would never go to the north again. Josie sat by the glowing range in the huge kitchen which was the focal point of the three converted houses, and glanced round at the merry faces singing carols. Lily and the rest of the women, plus Ada and Dora, had all collected for the little party Josie had thrown for Christmas Eve, and poor Mrs Wilde, who had no family of her own and didn't like her new position with a retired colonel and his wife, had come along too. Gertie was spending Christmas with Anthony and his mother.

No, she would never go home again. Josie smiled as she accepted another glass of hot mulled wine from Lily, who had had several and was singing lustily as she bustled round filling everyone's glasses and thrusting shives of Christmas cake on all and sundry. 'Get it down you, lass.' Lily bent over Josie, her eyes soft as she set a plate containing an enormous wedge of cake on Josie's lap. 'Good old northern recipe this, with a bottle of Guinness and black treacle and all sorts. None of your southern doings with a cherry and sultana a piece, and maybe a walnut if you're lucky.'

'Hey, Lily, you watch it!' Teresa, a Cockney by birth, chipped in here. 'You'd go a long way to beat my ma's Christmas cake, God rest her soul. Quarter bottle of brandy she used to use, and enough fruit, peel and nuts to feed the Coldstream Guards for a week.'

'No, no, it is the Christmas fare in my country which is best.' Maria, an old Spanish singer and dancer, spoke up, her plump cheeks glowing from the effects of the wine and the heat in the kitchen. 'And in northern Spain, where I was born, we have the hollow log known as Uncle and we place him near the fire. He is oh so noble, that log, and filled with presents and sweetmeats . . .'

More of the ladies, not to be outdone, chimed in, and Josie was content to sit and listen to these women she considered as part of her family. This house and its occupants came first, before anything, and then the slow and steady diminishing of Oliver's debts. She had estimated they would take some time to clear – maybe two years or more – and that was if she continued to earn top money. But her new agent was good; he'd make sure she was treated well. Short, balding and approaching fifty, Timothy Tattle was a staunch family man and grandfather of three, and he suited Josie down to the ground. No complications of the emotional kind with Timothy.

Josie caught Ada's eye across the room, and as her sister smiled at her and she smiled back, Josie thought, I'm lucky in a way, I am. I've got Ada and Dora in my life again and all these good friends, and my work. Aye, thank God for my work. Hubert is so happy with his Laura, and he's content working for Mr Foster. If I could just get peace of mind, just enough to let me sleep all night through without the nightmares, I'd be content. I would, I'd be content with peace of mind. But then, as Ada had said to her more than once since Oliver's death, time was a great healer. 'Look at me,' Ada had persisted when Josie shook her head in disbelief that she'd ever feel happy again. 'Times I wanted to die when I was a bairn, an' when I was a mite older an' all. But for Dora I'd have done meself in afore I reached twenty, an' Dora's said the same about me. But we're happy now, probably happier than them that've never known the valleys. How can you really appreciate the mountain tops if you've not gone through the valleys?'

Josie had said she didn't know the answer to that. She had the feeling she knew very little these days. But she did know how to sing . . .

Part 5
The New Life
1912

Chapter Twenty-six

The next seven years saw the campaign for women's suffrage waged with increasing violence, and unlike the massive unrest among the miners, the dockers, the railway workers and the rest of Britain's industry, it was not the working-class contingent who were most vehement, but those women in the middle and upper classes. These ladies had taken on the fight for their so-called sisters who lived and died in the sweatshops of the big cities, the women who worked fifteen- and sixteen-hour days in the mills and factories and shops, and in conditions not fit for animals.

Josie, encouraged by the fiercely active twins Winifred and Victoria, took an ever-increasing interest in the Movement. By March, 1912, when Sir Almroth Wright wrote a long letter to *The Times* in which he argued that militant suffragettes were sexually and intellectually embittered, Josie was as furious as the rest of her sisters in the Movement.

Mrs Winston Churchill's effective reply, also published in *The Times*, Josie considered a masterpiece. '"After reading Sir Almroth Wright's able and weighty exposition of women as he knows them, the question seems no longer to be 'Should women have votes?' but 'Ought women not to be abolished altogether?' . . . We learn from him that in their youth they are unbalanced, that from time to time they suffer from unreasonableness and hyper-sensitiveness, and that their presence is distracting and irritating to men in their daily lives and pursuits. If they take up a profession, the indelicacy of their minds makes them undesirable partners for their male colleagues. Later on in life they are subject to grave and long-continued mental disorders, and if not quite insane, many of them have to be shut up . . . Cannot science give us some assurance, or at least some ground of hope, that we are now on the eve of the greatest discovery of all – i.e. how to maintain a race of males by purely scientific means?"'

'By, lass!' Josie had just read out the letter from the newspaper to Lily, who had become bedridden over the last year and whose eyesight was failing fast. 'I wish I could pen words like that. That's telling 'em all right.'

'It's not so much that Almroth Wright wrote the letter which bothers me as the fact that the press could treat such claptrap with respect.' Josie rose from her seat at the side of Lily's bed and walked across to the open window, breathing deeply of the mild spring air, before she added, 'But it will come, Lily, the vote for women, and soon. It's happened in Finland, and if the government had the sense it was born with it'd realise women are showing themselves to be every bit as good as men. Look at Madame Curie winning a second Nobel prize this year.'

'Aye, I know, lass, I know. And I'll tell you something else; there's not a woman on this planet who can't juggle a hundred and one things at the same time, but men have this problem of only being able to do one thing at a time. What woman worth her salt isn't used to cooking and cleaning and seeing to the bairns, as well as having her man's dinner on the table for when he walks in, and all that often after a hard day's work taking in someone's washing or carding buttons or whatever to make ends meet. I tell you, lass, it's a man's world.'

Josie smiled at her old friend as she turned from the window, but she said nothing. Lily would think she was mad if she said she'd give the world to be an ordinary housewife and mother, even one who had to make a penny stretch into two, especially if she revealed who was forever in her thoughts and her dreams.

Barney had ignored her plea not to write and had written twice more before he had come down to London to see her himself. It had not been a happy meeting. She was being ridiculous, he had said, to cut off her friends and family in the north at a time when she needed them most. When she had replied that this was not the case at all, and that she would be expecting Vera and Betty, and Hubert and his young lass too, to come and see her in London now and again, Barney had said that wasn't quite what he had meant. He had not gone on to explain what he *had* meant because Josie's stiff manner had made it clear she did not wish him to.

Two more letters had arrived before he had come to the house in the Caledonian Market again, three months after the anniversary of Oliver's death. Josie had not been ready emotionally or mentally to see him, and again it had been a difficult meeting. Guilt had still been uppermost in Josie's heart, and it had made her reserved and very distant towards him. When Barney had mentioned he was thinking of taking a position in one of the London theatres, she had told him she did not think that was a good idea. He had left shortly afterwards and he had not written again for a full twelve months, by which time Vera had informed Josie that Barney had a lass, a nice Sunderland lass.

Barney's letter had stated that he understood Vera and Horace were coming to spend Christmas with Josie in her new home; she had cleared the last of Oliver's debts a few months previously and had purchased a small three-bedroomed property in a quiet part of Richmond. The house was nothing grand, but it had a pleasant rear garden and the luxury of an indoor privy being part of a new development close to Richmond Park.

Josie could have afforded a larger property but she had fallen in love with the house – and especially the garden in which the builder had had the good sense to leave several mature trees – the first time she had viewed it, and it was more than large enough for her purposes. She invited Mrs Wilde to leave the colonel and housekeep for her – something the woman accepted with alacrity – and with one bedroom spare for guests the property was ideal.

So . . . Barney's letter had gone on, he felt he ought to write and let her know that Vera's legs weren't too good and he and Horace felt it best Barney made the journey down to London with them. He had business in the capital, he'd written, which would involve a couple of visits, so he could help Horace with Vera on the return journey too. He trusted his brief presence for a minute or two on both occasions would be acceptable?

Josie's letter to Barney saying that this would be quite in order crossed in the post with one from Hubert. Jimmy had been in touch, Hubert wrote, and he could scarcely believe it but the letter had come all the way from Australia. Jimmy hadn't said exactly what he was involved in out there – here Josie had bitten on her lip and tried to dismiss from her mind the hundreds of nefarious activities the newly formed country had to offer – nor had he given his address, but he had said he was fit and well and he just wanted his brother to know that.

Jimmy had wished his brother a long and happy life and had asked to be remembered to Josie and his other sisters – Josie didn't think she believed Hubert here, but it was nice of him to say Jimmy had thought of them – and had added that Hubert had to forget the past and everything that had happened; the only thing that mattered was the present and what you made of the future. He'd finished by saying he wouldn't be writing again.

Something had changed in Josie when she had read Hubert's letter. Call it a release or a deliverance or whatever – she couldn't really put a name to it and she didn't actually try – but suddenly the weight of the remorse and guilt she had carried for two years was lifted off her shoulders, and it had been instant. For days afterwards she awoke expecting the old self-condemnation to rear its head, but it did not return, and she couldn't understand why. Oliver was still dead, Jimmy had still committed murder, but for the first time in over two years she could see that none of it was her fault. Patrick Duffy had manipulated and caused all the events which had brought her family such misery, and the eventual showdown had been inevitable from the day she had defied him and her da and taken Gertie to Newcastle.

And as to her husband, dear Oliver, *she had not betrayed him*. She hadn't been able to stop loving Barney, but she had worked at her marriage 100 per cent. She would always regret Oliver's death, and she was so glad they had been happier than perhaps they'd ever been together in those last twenty-four hours, but she had to look to the future now.

She agonised for weeks as to how she was going to put all her newfound wisdom to Barney, but in the event she needn't have bothered. He came to the door with Vera and Horace but would not even stay for any refreshments, and Vera informed her that Barney's young lady was waiting in the carriage. Harriet had never seen the sights of London before and so they had all thought it would be nice for her to accompany them.

Harriet lasted until the summer; after that a Frances was on the scene briefly, followed by Esther who hung on for almost twelve months. Josie lost track of Barney's lady friends after that, although every time she saw Vera or her friend wrote to her, Vera always included the line, *Barney wishes to be remembered to you.*

So much had changed . . . Josie sat down again and commenced reading the paper to Lily, but her heart wasn't in it. Once she'd vowed she would never visit the north again, mainly because of her feelings for Barney, but now she spent several weeks each year in Sunderland and their paths hadn't crossed once. Hubert and Laura were the proud parents of three bairns; Ada and Dora now owned a guest-house by the sea in Hartlepool with money she had settled on them once she was on her feet again – Hartlepool was far enough from Sunderland for their past not to be known but near enough for them to feel they were home – and Gertie and Anthony were now running their own agency, and very successfully too. Prudence had married her Georgie and now had twin boys, and their birth had given Vera a new lease of life, especially with Prudence and Georgie renting a house a couple of streets away from Vera. According to Horace, who wasn't totally enamoured of the situation, if Prudence wasn't in their house it was a darn good bet it was because Vera was visiting Prudence's! Everyone was sorted. Everyone.

And she . . . she had her career. Her wonderful career. And it was wonderful, oh aye, it was, but lately she had become tired of the constant travelling and different venues, and she had told Timothy so. All her family were well set up now, and if she never sang again she had enough in the bank to live comfortably for the rest of her life, and support the establishment at the back of the Caledonian Market. That was still important to her.

Timothy had been aghast at the prospect of her retiring from the halls but Josie had expected that, and in answer to what she'd do with her time she had answered that she would probably travel a little, but for pleasure rather than rushing from one venue to another.

She might do the Grand Tour of Europe for a year or two; everyone said the Mediterranean climate was wonderful, and it was well known that travel broadened the mind in a way little else could.

Josie didn't reveal her ultimate plan to her agent; that of setting up an establishment which would be a secure and safe place for mothers with young bairns. For a long time now she had thought that if her mother had had somewhere to run to when she had first understood what her husband intended for their two oldest daughters, the whole pattern for the family would have been different.

Josie felt she had cut her teeth on the dwelling place for Lily and the other elderly women; she now knew what was involved in running and maintaining a large establishment. But the other home would be different. She had no illusions that such an undertaking would be easy, and no doubt she would have to employ at least one man to provide some sort of protection against angry husbands or fathers, but her beginnings had left a deep impression on her which had been enhanced further by her involvement in the Suffrage Movement. Women had virtually no protection in the male-dominated society in which they lived from males within their own family.

Timothy had been non-committal about her plans to travel, but he had made it plain he expected Josie to continue with the project he was in the process of setting up which had already cost him a great deal of time and trouble.

Josie was to complete a tour of New York and Washington,

and she would have the honour of travelling on the maiden voyage of the *Titanic*. He would arrange for her to perform nightly on the magnificent liner, Timothy had gone on, as further publicity for the tour.

Josie knew the tickets for this voyage were like gold dust, and she rather suspected Timothy's enthusiasm for her to appear with the band was financial more than anything else. This way she would not only travel to the venue in New York in style but get paid for the privilege. However, such deals were the mark of a good agent and she had no argument with the proposal. The *Titanic*, the pride of the White Star fleet, had been launched in May the year before from the yards of Harland & Wolff in Belfast amid great publicity, and Josie, like everyone else in the country, was intrigued by the massive ship which was proclaimed to be unsinkable because of its sixteen water-tight compartments. But this would be her swan song, she told Timothy. From Washington she would probably begin her trip to Europe, and a new stage of her life would begin.

Poor Timothy . . . Josie knew she had tried his patience since he had become her agent and she was a great disappointment to the dapper little man. She simply didn't fit into the role Timothy considered suitable for such a successful and popular music-hall star. She didn't live in an enormous house or drive one of the new motor car contraptions which were becoming all the rage; in fact, she didn't even keep her own horse and carriage, and all Timothy's persuasive powers regarding more fame and fortune had failed to move her from her intended plan.

However, one aspect of it all had caused Josie great heart-searching, if only Timothy knew. The tour, followed by the trip to Europe, would mean she was away from England for many months – possibly even a year or two

– and both Vera and Lily were in poor health. She'd discussed her plans with them individually and they had both urged her to go. Vera had Horace and more especially Prudence's bairns to shower her time and attention on, and Lily was surrounded by friends in the home. 'Follow your heart, lass,' Vera had said bracingly. 'Life's too short for regrets.'

Josie agreed with the sentiment but, probably because she was still worried about her two dear friends, she told herself, night after night she had begun to dream the old nightmare again. The dark sea, the overwhelming sense of fear and panic and everyone drowning, the screams and cries as relentless waters closed over their heads . . . When she awoke, gasping and damp with perspiration, she couldn't sleep for hours. But it was just a dream, it wasn't real; not like Oliver's death and her losing Barney. And she *had* lost him, he was gone from her as surely as Oliver. If he'd been inclined to offer anything more than friendship years ago, her behaviour in the aftermath of Oliver's death had convinced him otherwise.

She'd finally come straight out with it and made it plain to Vera a couple of Christmases ago that she didn't wish to hear what Barney was doing – and with whom. Vera invariably mentioned Betty's stepson, and Josie knew she was curious as to why the two of them had 'fallen out' as Vera had put it more than once.

'There was no falling out,' Josie had insisted over Christmas dinner. 'How could there be? There was nothing to fall out over. But Barney has his own life which he obviously enjoys very much and I have mine. That is all, Vera. And I would much prefer that we didn't mention Barney and the whole scenario again. All right?'

Vera had pressed her lips together and thrust her chin into her neck but at least she hadn't related further stories from that point regarding Barney's meteoric rise in the world of business on Josie's subsequent visits. As far as Josie was concerned that was all that mattered. Not that she'd minded hearing about that side of Barney's life in actual fact – she'd been glad of every success which had come his way – but Vera never had stopped there. Invariably the current girl – all 'good Sunderland lasses' according to Vera – was brought up. If her old friend was to be believed, they were all apparently besotted with Barney; in fact, she led one to assume there was scarcely one female heart in the north which didn't beat a little faster when Barney Robson put in an appearance.

Five years ago Barney had entered into a partnership with one of the most highly respected businessmen in the town, and this man had had the vision to build a fine new theatre purely for the purpose of moving pictures which were becoming more and more popular with every year which passed.

According to Vera it had all been a great success, the building, which held a thousand patrons and had cost £4000 to build, being full to capacity every night. Consequently Barney and his partner had gone on to build two more theatres in Newcastle on the same lines, so sure were they that this 'passing fancy', as moving pictures had been labelled, was the entertainment of the future. The last Josie had heard before she had had her little talk with Vera, Barney had more projects further afield and the money was rolling in.

So, Josie thought now as the horse clip-clopped its way home, Barney had everything he wanted out of life. A different lass for every day of the week – and the prestige of being a wealthy and influential businessman. And that was fine. Just fine. If that's what he wanted, she really didn't care. Which was why her mind continued to probe at the matter right until she descended from the carriage and paid the driver what she owed him.

So intent was she on her thoughts that she didn't notice the tall, well-built man standing across the other side of the road until he called her name, and then she turned and Barney was there in front of her. But a different Barney from the last time she'd seen him five years ago. Now the powerful-looking and strikingly handsome man in front of her was familiar only by the vivid clear green eyes. He seemed taller, broader somehow, and gone was the northern cap and working-class persona. His suit looked to be of the finest tweed; his shoes of highly polished brown leather, and he was wearing his bowler hat confidently, as though he was used to the feel and fit of it.

Josie stared at him, her heart pounding so hard it constricted her breathing. For the life of her she couldn't say a word. Gone was the experienced and cosmopolitan lady who was equally at home in the most stately mansion or mean wretched hovel, and who knew exactly what to say to put those about her at their ease in both situations. The years had melted away, and Josie was back in Betty's scullery staring into the face of a handsome young man with startlingly green eyes, and she was as tongue-tied and shy as she'd been then.

'Hello, Josie.'

His voice was the same, just the same, and she had to swallow hard before she could say, 'Barney, what a surprise,' in as natural a voice as she could manage with the blood singing through her veins like a torrent. Then, as a sudden thought struck, she said quickly, 'Vera? Is everything all right at home?'

'Yes, yes. Vera's fine, as far as I know.' This was not said soothingly as one might have expected, but in a tone which carried more than a touch of impatience.

Josie watched him take a deep breath and his voice was more moderate when he said, 'Of course I should have expected you might think the worst. I'm sorry, it didn't occur to me.'

Talk. Say something. Act normal, for goodness' sake. The commands were there in her brain but she was utterly unable to obey them. She stared at him, her eyes wide, and it was with some effort that she said, 'You're . . . you're visiting London?'

It was a stupid remark in the circumstances and he made her doubly aware of this when he replied, 'Yes, Josie. As you can see, I am indeed visiting London.'

The spring weather was mild but not over-warm, but Josie felt herself beginning to perspire when, in the next instant, he reached out and took her hand, saying, 'I'm sorry. It's just that I'm nervous.'

He was nervous? This big, vigorous, commanding individual that was Barney and yet not Barney was nervous? This man who had had women galore according to Vera, and who had not tried to hide the fact? This last thought put a welcome shot of adrenalin where there had only been weakness and turmoil, and now Josie's voice was studiously polite. 'I don't quite understand.'

'Can we go inside?'

She suddenly became aware that they were standing in the street and he was still holding her hand and, her cheeks flushing still more at what she had allowed, she said quickly, 'Oh of course, I'm sorry. Yes, do come in. I'll get Mrs Wilde to serve us some tea.'

Mrs Wilde came into the hall from the kitchen as they entered by the front door, and although she might have been extremely interested in Josie's visitor she didn't betray the fact as Josie introduced her to Barney.

Barney remained silent for a moment after they had

walked into the sitting room and the door was shut behind them, Mrs Wilde scurrying away to make a tray of tea. He glanced about him, his green eyes narrowed, and Josie couldn't read anything in his face, so it surprised her when he said suddenly, 'This isn't what I expected.'

'No?' She didn't quite know how to take that and it must have showed, because he smiled slowly.

'The way you've got on, I suppose I expected . . .' He paused, considering his words. 'Something grander.'

'You are as bad as my agent.' And then she bit hard on her lip as the word brought Oliver into the room as surely as if he had materialised in front of them.

'But you do have a housekeeper.' His tone was flat, harder, and she knew he had sensed the spectre too.

'Mrs Wilde is a friend,' Josie returned steadily, 'and with the hours I work and the amount of time I spend away each year touring the provinces and so on, it's good to have someone here taking care of things.' And then she forced herself to say, and as casually as if he was an ordinary visitor, 'Won't you sit down?'

'I don't want to sit down.' It was abrupt, almost hostile.

She blinked but then her back straightened as she thought, How dare he! How dare he turn up here after all this time and act as though he has a right to behave however he likes. And if he had intended a criticism regarding her employment of a housekeeper then he could jolly well mind his own business. And it was a follow-on to this thought when she said, 'Are you visiting the capital alone or have you brought a . . . friend with you?'

She'd allowed just the merest of deliberate pauses before the word 'friend', but the tightness in her chest which always accompanied thoughts of Barney with another woman must have come over in her voice despite all her efforts to the contrary, because he said, his voice suddenly very quiet, 'My friends bother you?'

She tried to sound airy as she said, 'Bother me? Of course not.'

'Because most of them were only that – friends.'

Most of them.

'Do you still blame me?'

'Blame you?' Her brow wrinkled.

'Because he died and I'm still alive.'

'Oh, Barney.' She stared at him, utterly aghast. Had he been thinking that, all these years? 'I've never blamed you, never,' she protested quickly. 'It wasn't like that.'

'Then what was it like, Josie? You were grieving and I could understand that – contrary to what you might think I do have some finer feelings – but you were ruthless in removing me from even the perimeter of your life. And now you're planning to go across to the other side of the world without even saying goodbye.'

'But . . .' She stared at him, too taken aback to try to hide her feelings. 'I didn't think you'd care.'

'You didn't think I'd—' He was shouting, and he must have become aware of it because he stopped abruptly, walking over to her and taking her forearms in his hands whereupon he shook her slightly. 'There hasn't been a day in the last seven years when you haven't filled my mind and my heart,' he said roughly, the harsh tone of his voice belying the content of his words. 'What do you think those other women were about, if not to forget you? But it didn't work, nothing worked, how could it? You're locked into the essence of my bones, don't you know that? You're the air I breathe and the food I eat, and the last couple of years I haven't even bothered seeing anyone because there was no point.'

When Oliver had asked her to marry him he had called

her his beautiful angel and told her he adored her. She
had thought then that Barney would never pay those sorts
of compliments to a woman; that his love would express
itself in more earthy ways, but she had been wrong. She
had been wrong about all sorts of things. She had been
so lonely the last years surrounded by people all the time,
fêted, adored – it had meant nothing without this man who
had just paid her the most beautiful compliments in her life
whilst glaring at her the whole time.

'Do you understand what I am saying to you, Josie?' His
voice had changed; it was calmer, quieter. 'I'm not putting
it very well because I'm so worked up I don't know if I'm
on foot or horseback, and I know you've got your career
and your life in the theatre but I had to tell you. I had to
say how I felt or else there'd have always been a part of
me that wondered if you would have stayed in England if
I'd spoken. You looked at me once, oh years ago now.
You wouldn't remember it . . .'

'At Vera's. When you came about your da.' Her voice
was very soft.

He was perfectly still now, his eyes unblinking, and his
voice was even softer than Josie's had been when he said,
'You looked at me as though you loved me then.'

'I did – I do love you,' she whispered. 'I've always
loved you but there was Pearl, and then when you were
free . . .'

'There was Oliver.' He touched her face gently, his
voice still low. 'We didn't plan things very well, did
we?'

She shook her head, utterly unable to speak.

'And now you are going to move across the other side
of the world.' It was a statement but there was a question
in the green eyes, and she answered it with, 'I . . . I don't
have to go. I don't really want to. I was going to do a

497

tour of New York and Washington but I always intende
to come back to England.'

'You did?' His brow wrinkled. 'But Vera spoke as
you were planning to settle in America for good.'

Oh thank you, Vera. Thank you. Wise old Vera.

She opened her mouth to speak, but her voice was cu
off as he pulled her in to him, his mouth falling on her
with a passion that was beyond anything she had eve
known before. Even Oliver, with all his experience an
at the height of his lovemaking had never kissed her lik
this, and it was wonderful, intoxicating, heady . . .

'Stay with me.' His voice was husky against her mouth
'Don't go on the tour; marry me instead. And soon. Specia
licence soon. I can't wait another week or month or year.'

'Neither can I.' She heard herself murmur the words with
little dart of surprise at her forwardness but then, as his mout
closed over hers again, she let herself melt into the kiss.

Her head spinning, she returned his kisses with a hunge
that matched Barney's. Timothy wouldn't like it when sh
said she was pulling out of the tour and not going to Nev
York, but it didn't matter. Nothing mattered but this ma
holding her so tightly she could hear his heartbeat.

'Follow your heart,' Vera had said. 'Life's too short fo
regrets.' If she went to New York she would be miserable
Timothy would soon get someone else to take her place
who wouldn't want a chance like that – and with the adde
inducement of travelling on the *Titanic*? She would never le
herself be separated from Barney again, not ever. Her old lif
was behind her and the new was just beginning, and in th
new life there would be no crowds and performances an
applause, but there would be songs.

Songs in the night, songs for babies' ears, and for he
love. Songs enough to last them a lifetime.

Ragamuffin Angel

Rita Bradshaw

Orphan Connie Bell is just twelve when she enters Sunderland's grim workhouse as a laundry assistant. In time she advances to a senior position but then her dream of becoming a nurse is dashed: her mother was forced by desperate poverty to work the streets and the Bell name is tainted.

Bitterly hurt but undaunted, Connie becomes assistant housekeeper at the Grand Hotel and saves hard for her own business. There she meets Dan Stewart. There's a dark history between the Bells and the Stewarts, and Dan's mother will do anything to keep Dan and Connie apart.

As 1914 unfolds Europe is plunged into war, and the closing drama in a savage family vendetta is played out. Only when it's over will Connie know if she and the man she loves can have a future together.

'Catherine Cookson fans will enjoy discovering a new author who writes in a similar vein' *Home and Family*

'If you like gritty, rags-to-riches Northern sagas, you'll enjoy this' *Family Circle*

'What an emotional rollercoaster ride of a book! It grabs your attention from page one and does not let go until the end' *Sunderland Echo*

0 7472 6326 4

headline

The Stony Path

Rita Bradshaw

Growing up on a small, struggling farm on the outskirts of Sunderland in the early 1900s, Polly Farrow has a tough life, but she has gifts money can't buy – a joyful disposition and a loving heart that is reflected in her beautiful face. And her heart has been given to her beloved cousin, Michael, since childhood. They share a special bond, and Polly knows that one day they'll be man and wife.

But a terrible family secret is to shatter her dreams for ever. The lovers are rent apart and Polly is left to bear the responsibility of the farm and her family single-handed. Life is now a battle for survival, and Polly wonders if she will ever find true happiness, unaware that the answer to her prayers is closer than she thinks . . .

'If you like gritty, rags-to-riches Northern sagas, you'll enjoy this' *Family Circle*

'Catherine Cookson fans will enjoy discovering a new author who writes in a similar vein' *Home and Family*

'A warm-hearted tale of tough family life in the North' *Teeside Evening Gazette*

'What an emotional rollercoaster ride of a book! It grabs your attention from page one and does not let go until the end' *Sunderland Echo*

0 7472 6322 1

headline

Now you can buy any of these other bestselling
books from your bookshop or *direct
from the publisher*.

FREE P&P AND UK DELIVERY
(Overseas and Ireland £3.50 per book)

My Sister's Child	Lyn Andrews	£5.99
Liverpool Lies	Anne Baker	£5.99
The Whispering Years	Harry Bowling	£5.99
Ragamuffin Angel	Rita Bradshaw	£5.99
The Stationmaster's Daughter	Maggie Craig	£5.99
Our Kid	Billy Hopkins	£6.99
Dream a Little Dream	Joan Jonker	£5.99
For Love and Glory	Janet MacLeod Trotter	£5.99
In for a Penny	Lynda Page	£5.99
Goodnight Amy	Victor Pemberton	£5.99
My Dark-Eyed Girl	Wendy Robertson	£5.99
For the Love of a Soldier	June Tate	£5.99
Sorrows and Smiles	Dee Williams	£5.99

TO ORDER SIMPLY CALL THIS NUMBER

01235 400 414

or e-mail orders@bookpoint.co.uk

Prices and availability subject to change without notice.